THE DREAMER'S LOOM

THE DREAMER'S LOOM

In silence, the ship left anchor and headed out into deeper waters again. The flames of the funeral pyre grew smaller in the distance as Penelope watched. She shivered, wondering if the man who touched her on the pyre.

"What are you thinking?" Odysseus asked, his voice a rough whisper, softened with weariness.

"How many died?" For a moment, she couldn't face him.

"Seven. Their leader among them. Dolios found him before I did," he added, one corner of his mouth rising for a second. "The ones who lived know who they were fighting. Maybe now they will not so easily attack travelers."

"They know...you told them, and released them?" Penelope shook her head, trying to understand. "What if they call their kinsmen together for vengeance?"

"Who would justify them? Who would help them?" He sighed, closed his eyes, and leaned hard into the rudder. "Penelope, they took their lives into their hands in a wager, and lost."

"I will never understand battle, or what drives a man to cut the life from another."

"Sweet Penelope, I hope you never do."

PRAISE FOR THE DREAMER'S LOOM

"5 Stars!...A fresh look at the classic Greek legends and a compelling read in its own right. I loved this book! The characters are deftly drawn. Ms. Levigne has filled a legend with complex people, flawed, gifted and glorious in turn...In addition to having an exciting story and richly drawn characters, *The Dreamer's Loom* is full of well-chosen, historically accurate details...I knew how the story would end—most readers do—but even so, I stayed up until 2 AM to finish the book. It's that compelling...Historical fiction at its very finest. I give it my highest recommendation."

—Carrie S. Masek
Scribes World Reviews

"...Filled with research, and some surprising tidbits, The Dreamer's Loom is a great story...a finely woven tale of myths and history about a man whose courage and quick mind were rivaled by no other man. The story moves along at a steady pace, the characters exciting and appealing. I have never heard anyone tell the tales of Odysseus from his wife's point of view before...It is a fascinating story. Ms. Levigne pens an exciting romance with dangerous greedy men, jealous gods, and a love that is strong enough to weather any storm. Her multi-layered characters and fresh storyline makes *The Dreamer's Loom* hard to put down..."

—Robin Peek
The Word on Romance

"Full of Greek mythology, and a fresh telling of an old classic, *The Dreamer's Loom* is a thoroughly enjoyable read. Although it starts slowly because of the many Greek names and background history, the book soon becomes an adventurous tale of love, passion, and jealousy. If you like love stories mixed with mythology, *The Dreamer's Loom* by Michelle L. Levigne is right for you."

—Courtney Bowden
Romance Reviews Today

"4 Stars!…The story, and many of the characters, were fascinating! I was unable to stop reading and finished the story in record time! Definitely recommended!"

—Detra Fitch
Huntress Book Reviews

THE DREAMER'S LOOM

BY

MICHELLE L. LEVIGNE

AMBER QUILL PRESS, LLC
http://www.amberquill.com

THE DREAMER'S LOOM
AN AMBER QUILL PRESS BOOK

Amber Quill Press, LLC
http://www.amberquill.com

Layout and Formatting provided by: ElementalAlchemy.com

Published in the United States of America

CHAPTER 1

An owl hooted at noon, reminding Penelope of last night's dream with a suddenness and intensity that tied knots in her belly. She stumbled and caught herself before she dropped the spear she carried.

"What ails you, boy?" her grandfather, Dymis, muttered. The skeletal old man didn't turn to look at her, but continued shuffling down the dirt path that ran through the patchy forest between his run-down estate and the village of Alybas.

"A stone moved under my foot." Penelope barely heard herself as her searching gaze found the two men walking down the path toward them, coming from Alybas.

Just like in her dream last night.

She shivered and thought a swift prayer to the Goddess in all her incarnations: Athena, Aphrodite, Hera, Artemis. Even as she worked through the litany, trying to ward off the tears she had cried in her dream, Penelope knew it was no use. Dreams were never given to allow her to change the future, only to prepare her to face it with strength and calm.

"Greetings, strangers," Dymis called. He straightened from his usual hunched posture, raked his palsied hands through the white strings of his hair and tugged his wrinkled, food-stained tunic into a semblance of dignity.

He invited the two men to his home, offering the traditional hospitality as if he were still a rich man with over one hundred slaves and the barren fields beyond the forest were rich with grain, flocks, herds, and vineyards. Penelope held herself still, as poised as if she stood before her uncle, the king of Sparta, and didn't flinch when Dymis introduced her as his grandson, Dyvis.

Her Uncle Dyvis had died when he was only a boy. When Penelope came to live with her grandfather and aunt five years ago, the resemblance between her and the dead boy had prompted Dymis to see her as a boy and name her Dyvis in turn. He refused to acknowledge she was a girl.

"Greetings, Dymis and Dyvis," the taller of the two men said. He gave them a nod of respect and didn't react at all to the strangeness of the old man's words.

That meant the two strangers had stopped long enough in Alybas to hear about the harmless old madman who raised his granddaughter as if she were a boy.

"I am Kratos, and this is my fellow-servant, Anthinos. We have been sent by King Tyndareos of Sparta. Helen has at long last been rescued from King Theseus...and the princess wishes to have the company of her beloved cousin." Kratos' blue eyes met Penelope's gaze and he smiled slightly.

Helen had been rescued? Penelope kept her expression still, though her mind raced. Five years ago, Theseus had kidnapped her cousin. Tyndareos sent Penelope away to her mother's home in Alybas to protect her, though she couldn't imagine anyone wanting to kidnap her.

Helen's safe return home was good news. Or was it? Princes and kings had come to Sparta seeking to arrange a marriage when Helen was still a child. Penelope could imagine the confusion that filled the palace of Sparta now, with a flood of hopeful suitors descending to boast about their wealth, their kingdoms, and their worthiness to take Helen to wife.

Everyone wanted and loved and adored Helen. Penelope sighed as her cousin's perfect ivory and rose complexion, blue eyes and golden curls came to her mind's eye. Not that she resented Helen's beauty. She loved her cousin dearly, they two being closer in age than Penelope's older sister Iphthine, or Helen's sister Klytemaistra. But sometimes, even as a little child, Penelope had wearied of the world revolving around Helen.

"Thank Zeus, the girl is safely home," Dymis said, nodding. His jaw continued moving, as if he chewed on the news. He clapped Penelope on the back, hard enough to make her stumble forward a step. "The king will find I have trained Dyvis well, so he will honor his family. But why does he need the boy?"

"Helen is surrounded by suitors. Tyndareos needs the boy's presence to calm the disappointed princes," Kratos said after a moment. He nodded to Penelope. "Sparta needs more princesses, to give in marriage and make peace among the Achaians."

Penelope choked back a cry of protest. Kratos had just warned her of her fate.

Helen, the most beautiful woman in the world, reputed to be the daughter of Zeus, was safely home and now all the princes of all the kingdoms of Achaia wished to take her as bride. King Tyndareos feared the wrath of the disappointed suitors. Penelope could understand that. She also understood from Kratos' words that her uncle had sent for her to return to Sparta for one reason—she would be given in marriage as a peace offering, a sacrifice to soothe the anger of a disappointed prince and sway him to support Helen's husband.

"I don't want to leave Alybas," she said, looking up at her grandfather. "You need me here. Who will hunt with you and help you tally your stores and command the slaves?"

A chill ran through Penelope as those words left her lips. Most of the slaves left in her grandfather's household belonged to her. If she left Alybas, who would care for Dymis and her Aunt Bachan?

"Don't be foolish, boy!" Dymis chortled. "It's an honor to be called to serve in Sparta. You are going. No argument."

The old man softened a little as they hurried back to the household to warn her aunt and the slaves about their guests, who would follow them in another hour.

"I know it's hard. Zeus bless you for your loyalty to an old man. The world is always changing, boy. Things aren't as easy as they used to be and that's good because it makes us strong. Women can't rule like in the old days, because death is stronger. They need men to protect them. Pity your aunt, though. She's not quite right in her mind." Dymis staggered and Penelope reached out to steady the old man. "See, boy, the women in our family come from a long line of priestesses. Your grandmother would have been a priestess, but she was never consecrated. She gave me two daughters and my son, who died young. I gave one daughter to Ikarios, brother to the king of Sparta—a proud day for me, that such a powerful man would want one of my daughters. But Bachan...your aunt drove away every man who asked and now she's a lonely, bitter old virgin, filling my grandson's head with nonsense about the Goddess." He guffawed and clapped Penelope on the shoulder.

She nodded and smiled to placate the old man. Dymis thought his daughter insane. Bachan regarded her father with pity and sad amusement. The people of Alybas pitied Penelope of Sparta, living with the two strange old folks.

*   *   *

Penelope helped her aunt serve the guests, and listened as Kratos and Anthinos told Dymis about the conflicts and rumors in the rest of the Achaian-ruled world. The people of Ilion, Troy in particular, again caused trouble for merchants going through the straits of the Dardanelles. The winter had been unusually harsh for many of the island kingdoms. Such tales and gossip didn't interest her much. Not when her entire life had been turned upside down and shaken.

But other bits of news did interest her. In particular, King Agamemnon of Mycenae now had three daughters. That interested Penelope and gave her food for thought, because her cousin, Klytemaistra was Agamemnon's queen. She had been promised to another nobleman, Tantalos, but Agamemnon had been determined to have her. When gifts and bribery and cajolery hadn't worked, he had threatened the man. Klytemaistra believed Agamemnon had killed Tantalos, when the man died during a skirmish with raiders. When Tyndareos gave Klytemaistra to Agamemnon, she had vowed never to give him sons.

Penelope wondered if three daughters was her cousin's means of revenge, or she had softened toward her husband in the last six years and was as frustrated as he by the lack of an heir.

That reminded her of the reason for the visitors in the household. Tyndareos was elder brother to Penelope's dead father, Ikarios. He had sent for Penelope to use her as a peace offering and buy Helen's safety. She wondered if her uncle thought it was his only chance to get her married off. She had been referred to as the "little, dark one" all her childhood, so different from her golden sister and cousins—thin and small when they were tall and rounded and feminine even as children. Her brother, Ithios, had been especially adept at making her feel unlovely.

Penelope vowed not to feel jealousy for Helen. After all, five years had brought changes in her body. She was no longer the thin little cousin who made the others late. Penelope had grown strong, swift and taller, and Helen had always been kind to her. They had been friends. It was not Helen's fault that she was from birth the most beautiful woman in the known world.

Perhaps she should feel sorry for Helen, surrounded by dozens of warriors who wanted to own her like they owned their houses, their fields and flocks and herds. How much would her husband value Helen when she had given him a household full of children and had lost her youth and beauty and figure?

That thought occupied Penelope while she refilled the cups of wine for her grandfather's guests and brought fresh bread to set on the low table between them.

Thinking of childbearing, of enduring a man's touch and satisfying his hungers, made Penelope writhe inside. She didn't want to suffer through such indignity. Her aunt had taught her the marriage bed was meant to be enjoyed by both man and woman, but Penelope knew she never would find pleasure. Not when she went to her husband's bed and home against her will.

Klytemaistra had vowed not to give Agamemnon a son. Penelope would do the same. If she couldn't defy her uncle, if she had to return to Sparta, if she would be given away like a horse or a jewel, she could at least take some power in her life. Bachan had taught Penelope all she knew of the old ways, when women led their households and served the Goddess. There were more than a dozen ways to prevent conception, to destroy a man's lust, even to influence the gender of the child. Sitting in the shadows of her grandfather's house and listening to the visitors talk, Penelope vowed she would not be bred like a cow, even if she couldn't avoid marriage.

After Dymis and his guests had eaten, Bachan, Penelope, and the rest of the household sat down under a spreading tree behind the house to have their dinner. That was when Bachan gave the news to the slaves. After all, most of them were Penelope's property and would return to Sparta with her.

First, there was Eurynome, her nurse, who fought fiercely for Penelope to be treated as a princess even here in rough, poor Alybas. One glimpse of Penelope hunting with her grandfather, carrying a spear, ruined weeks of hard-earned respect.

After Eurynome was Dolios, the second slave assigned to Penelope at birth. The man had always been loyal, like a father to her. Aris, his wife, was a quiet, capable woman from Sikania. She could always be counted on for common sense when everyone else was frightened or furious and unable to think clearly in the middle of a crisis.

Their sons either pretended Penelope didn't exist, or they teased her when adults weren't around. She believed the four boys were jealous. They spent their days plowing and tending animals, chopping wood, sweating while she learned hunting and other lessons reserved for high-born sons.

Then there was their daughter, Melantho, two years older than Penelope. It was no secret Melantho crept away to the woods every other night to sleep with her sweethearts. No secret to anyone but Dolios and Aris.

Penelope wondered what it was like to share a man's bed. Her loathing for the marriage soon to be forced on her did not dispel her curiosity. She couldn't imagine Melantho doing anything that didn't please her—she always came back rosy-cheeked and smiling from her trysts—so there had to be some good in letting a man take his pleasure with her body. If not for fear of Melantho's scorn, Penelope would have asked the older girl for details long ago.

As expected, when she heard the news of their imminent departure, Melantho wailed, her eyes filled with tears and she jumped to her feet.

"I'm not going! Menander wants to marry me. He's saving up to buy my freedom. You can't take me away now." She dropped to her knees next to Dolios. "Please, Father, tell her—" She cast a scowl over her shoulder at Penelope. "Make her leave me behind. She doesn't need me."

"Dolios," Penelope began. Truthfully, she wouldn't mind if she never saw Melantho's face again. The older girl, rounded and lush, with golden curls and rosy cheeks, always made her feel tiny and unlovely.

"We are going, Princess." Dolios nodded to her. "We are your household. Who will protect you and serve you in the palace of Sparta? It is our duty, and the gods will punish us if we neglect it."

Melantho snarled and leaped to her feet and scurried away. Penelope didn't doubt the girl would run off to meet and cavort under the stars with a sweetheart or two. Or three. Perhaps one of them would be Menander. Perhaps she could persuade one or two of them to help her hide or run away. Penelope wished she could do the same.

Why not? That thought returned to her several times while cleaning up the house for the evening and settling down to sleep on her pallet in her aunt's small weaving room. Why couldn't she pretend to be a boy and run away? She was good with spear and sling. She could cut her hair and bind her negligible breasts and pray no one noticed the new curves to her hips and bottom. Why couldn't her body have stayed thin like a stick? Why did it have to betray her and start to blossom into womanhood this winter past? If she ran away now, she wouldn't get very far before some discerning eye saw past her disguise.

She might be even worse off than before, captured by a brute who wouldn't know she was a princess. She could be raped, beaten, sold as a slave. Dozens of dire fates awaited her.

Still, the thought of taking her freedom and the attendant risks kept her far from sleep. Finally, Penelope had to get up and leave the little weaving room and slip outside with her lap loom, to try to weave by moonlight and calm herself.

At least she wouldn't dream.

Why couldn't her dreams have warned her how to escape this fate, instead of just showing her coming trouble?

Wings fluttered, sounding close enough to be just above her head. Penelope slowly tipped her head back, expecting to look up into the huge, dark eyes of an owl. She saw nothing. A heartbeat later, an owl hooted, making her jump. She closed her eyes.

"Athena, Aphrodite, Hera, Demeter…Goddess, whichever face and name you wear, help me. I do not wish to leave. Alybas is my home, not Sparta," Penelope whispered.

"But there is nothing here for you, child," Bachan said, causing Penelope to jump again. She smiled sadly and stepped out into the night. The moonlight turned her silver-streaked black hair into a softly gleaming crown and hid her many wrinkles. "Sparta is your destiny."

"This is my home."

"This is a hiding place, nothing more. The Goddess speaks to you in dreams. You have a destiny, a duty." She skimmed one finger across the top of the small ivory loom sitting neglected in the girl's lap. "You have your own special threads to put into the cloth of time. Who can tell what damage will be done to the entire weaving if you do not put those threads in, as the Goddess decrees?"

"Who will take care of you when I am gone? There will only be the pig boy and old Bithia and Grandfather with you."

"I will not need much. There are some who still worship the Goddess in the old ways. They will watch over me." Bachan paused to smooth stray strands of fine hair off the girl's high, wide forehead and smiled. "Ah, but who can I teach the old ways to, when you are gone? That is my only regret in sending you away to your destiny and glory."

Penelope nodded, though she didn't want to ever leave Alybas, rough and isolated as it was. The old ways were still followed here; the rest of Achaia worshipped male gods, with the many faces of the Goddess subordinated to the roles of chattel and pleasure toy. Girls were discouraged from worshipping only the Goddess. When a girl became a bride, she left her mother's home instead of bringing her husband home. Fathers chose husbands and brides, and named their children. Mothers were the source of life, yet had no say in the lives they created.

"Serve the Goddess wherever you go," Bachan whispered.

"Under what name?" Penelope leaned forward, elbows on her knees, resting her chin on her folded hands.

"You must decide. The Goddess is different to each woman who serves her, I think."

The quiet changed. Penelope lifted her head and listened. She shivered and blamed the nightmares that kept her from sleep. For many nights now, she had awakened from scattered images of wars between kings who were now friends. She hated the dreams that seemed more real than the loom pressing into her lap.

"Aunt...I want to be a priestess, not marry a warrior prince. I want to stay virgin and serve the Goddess."

"What nonsense is this?" She laughed, but Penelope didn't think her aunt mocked her. "A woman's power is that of life, of serving the Goddess in creating new life and sustaining it. Men chose the illusion of power that comes with fighting, division and death. Women fight that cold pull to the land of shadows. Only women can redeem men through loving them and giving more life to the world. The old ways are gone, Penelope. That does not mean, however, that we must accept the world as men shape it. There is still much that women can and must do. We are the bearers of hope, of life. Do not deny the power residing in your body and soul. You were born for a reason, as every woman is born for a reason."

She reached out to touch the girl's cheek and they sat in silence as the gloom turned into the pearly, soft light before true dawn. Penelope heard an owl hoot, several soft, soothing notes in a row. She dared to hope the Goddess added her song of comfort to Bachan's words.

Still, it was hard.

Why had she hesitated? If she had dared to act, to snatch up food, her spear and sling, to cut her hair and slip away into the darkness, she could be halfway to the shore by now. Penelope cursed herself for a coward and vowed yet again she would take all the power she could catch in her two small hands. She would control her life, however much she could keep safe from her uncle, from her guards, from the nameless, faceless prince who would drag her into his bed.

If only she could be heartless and self-centered like Melantho, and enjoy life without fearing the punishments the Goddess exacted on those who lived for evil.

*   *   *

When she went to wake her grandfather with a cup of warmed, spiced wine to start the day, Penelope found him dead with a soft smile on his face. She comforted herself with the knowledge that he had spent his dotage happy, training his grandson. Dymis had been proud that she would go to Sparta to serve the king. Perhaps that was why he smiled when he crossed the dark river to the shadowlands.

Penelope had little enough to smile about in the days that followed.

Kratos and Anthinos hurried the household through the funeral rites. Penelope wanted to stay several days, to properly mourn Dymis. She wanted to sit in silence with his body at least until afternoon, to speak to his departing spirit and be sure he knew his family loved him. Fury made her belly burn, when the two Spartans took over and she was shoved to the side, forced to sit idle and watch her grandfather's funeral rites assembled with unseemly haste.

Kratos used Tyndareos' gold to hire mourners, who created an outcry that likely frightened away Dymis' spirit before his family could make their farewells. He paid for a lavish feast, which neither Bachan nor Penelope cared to taste. He bought expensive oils and spices to throw on the funeral pyre, and an elaborate weaving for Dymis' funeral shroud. The pyre was lit that evening, almost before the old man was decently cold.

Penelope reminded herself that Dymis had wanted her to return to Sparta. His pride in her, his joy, was the only thing that kept her from lifting the gaudily painted urn containing her grandfather's ashes and heaving it across the room. That, and the smirk of triumph on Melantho's lush lips. Penelope contained her anger because she knew it would please her slave to know she was unhappy. Melantho was the sort who enjoyed making others suffer when she had been frustrated or punished. Penelope refused to be like her.

So, to please her grandfather and to take away Melantho's bitter triumph, Penelope composed her face and kept her voice calm and pretended she didn't feel the heart-rending despair and anger that

9

consumed her whenever she thought of Sparta.

That did not mean, however, that she would stay or she would meekly accept her fate.

When the small company walked through the gates of the decrepit household the next morning, Penelope didn't look back. Her aunt had told her not to. She comforted herself with the knowledge that Bachan didn't have Dymis to worry about any longer, and she would indeed be taken care of by the villagers of Alybas. There were still some who worshipped the Goddess. Her aunt would be well.

"Goddess, show me the way," Penelope whispered, as the village vanished behind the last shallow hill. She turned her face to the horizon and the distant sea, and walked forward into her future.

*   *   *

As the black-keeled merchant ship rounded the last outcropping of rock, the wind caught at the veil covering Penelope's waist-length dark hair and tugged more strands free of her braids. She stood up from her place in the prow, which let her feel as if she guided the ship. The wind yanked harder at her veil, tugging it free of the pins holding it fast to her braids. Penelope snatched impatiently at the recalcitrant veil and twisted it through her belt. She leaned forward, laughing silently at the wind's attempts to blind her as she watched for the first sign of the docks at sandy Pylos.

It amused her how much enjoyment she found in a trip she had loathed beforehand. This trip, in fair spring weather across friendly seas, made a delightful surprise. Penelope wished she could stay on the merchant ship forever and never touch her feet to land again.

Even if she could not control her future, she would let nothing destroy her enjoyment of the present moment.

Penelope turned in her narrow perch and leaned her back against the rail. She twisted a strand of wind-loosened hair behind her ear and grimaced at the thought of what Eurynome would say to her.

"A maiden of fifteen and soon to find a husband does not run about with her hair loose like a street beggar," Penelope murmured. Her voice took on Eurynome's cracked tones. All the cousins had the trick of mimicking voices perfectly. Helen was the best of the four girls.

Penelope shook her head, vowing once again not to think about the people and duties awaiting her in the palace of Sparta. She leaned over the opposite railing and strained her eyes against the glare of light on the splashing waves. She wanted to see Pylos before the sailors did.

King Nestor had been kind to her five years before when she passed through his city. He had given her honey cakes and her ivory lap loom as a traveling present. Penelope had been delighted and awed that the well-loved king of Pylos had known how much she loved to make pictures in her weaving. The larger looms took too much time and were reserved for cloth for the household. The tiny loom, almost a toy, was perfect for the pictures she recreated from her dreams. She had dared to hug and kiss the man. He had laughed and vowed he would stand witness at her wedding feast to a great king.

Penelope hoped Nestor would be pleased with how she had grown. Maybe he would tell her another story of her father if her companions stopped long enough in Pylos, before taking horses and carts for Sparta.

And yet, for all the excitement of returning to Sparta, Penelope's heart still ached in longing for Alybas.

A shout rose from the merchant controlling the rudder at the ship's stern. Two near-naked sailors climbed the mast to lower the square sail of woven reeds, reinforced with leather.

Penelope smiled, remembering how the merchant had indulged her every question during the voyage. She had tried to stay out of his way, but still asked about the ship whenever he had a spare moment to pause and look around. The merchant who took her from Pylos five years ago had used a smaller sail of cloth. Penelope wanted to know why the difference in sails, and this merchant had explained the advantages of a reed sail, then went on to tell her little details of reading the sky and waves, the mechanics in using a rudder, why sometimes the merchant ship used both the oars and the sail, and a hundred other details.

Penelope leaned further over the railing, so she could see the white splashing diamonds of water as they hit the black keel of the ship. She wished she could follow her first plan, disguise herself as a boy and run away. Had she learned enough from the merchant and the sailors to earn a living on board a ship? That might be a pleasant life. But the sailors spent their days wearing little more than a loincloth, and how long could she pass as a boy without taking off her tunic like the others? Her body had blossomed enough to betray her, but not enough to make her desirable.

If her father were still alive, would he have let her stay in Alybas? Penelope barely remembered Ikarios. People said Ithios, her brother, resembled him only in his face. Her brother scorned their father's talent of making beauty from bits of wood and metal. She reached up and touched the pin hidden inside the neck of her dress, and knew a man who could make such beauty would have listened to his daughter's pleas, would have wanted her to be happy.

The pin, made to look like a hound strangling a hare when closed, was a gift from her father to Dymis. The old man gave it to Penelope a year ago when he thought he might be dying, and told her it would bring blessings and safety. She hoped the old man had not been raving. She needed blessings in her new life.

"Penelope." Eurynome stood below her perch. "We're coming in to land."

"I know." She turned and climbed down, balancing on the thin ledge of wood, gripping with her bare toes. Penelope smiled up at her nurse when she reached the lower deck. "Yes, I will put on my sandals now. It is time to be a proper maiden and not a sailor urchin."

"Child, what will your family think of you?" the woman said with a sigh. She smiled, wiping away the frown of worry and disapproval she wore like a badge of office.

Eurynome's light hair hid the silvering of years, but her thickening figure and the lines around her eyes betrayed her. She had been with Penelope since her mother died in childbirth and had the right to scold and correct the royal daughter.

"Please don't be cross," the girl whispered, stretching up on her tiptoes to hug the woman. "My balance is better if I go barefoot," she added with an impish smile.

"There is a different balance to maintain in Sparta," the woman said. They moved to the back of the ship, to the merchant's hold and their traveling quarters.

"I know. Aunt told me." She held herself stiff against a piercing loneliness for her aunt, left all alone.

"She will be well. Iphthine's home is near Alybas. She can send servants to Bachan or bring her to Pherai if she has need," Eurynome said.

"How do you always know what I think?" Penelope smiled. She kept her voice small and quiet, to avoid being overheard as they passed the scurrying sailors.

"Your face has grown too open. School it into care and secrecy as your aunt taught you," the woman returned.

She squeezed Penelope's shoulder as they entered the shelter of the hold. Aris and her daughter packed their possessions to disembark. Dolios and his sons helped the merchant's men unload the ship, as the price of their passage. Kratos and Anthinos would leave the ship as soon as it touched the shore, to look for their escort. Penelope didn't like either of her uncle's trusted servants. After the unseemly haste of her grandfather's funeral, they wouldn't answer her questions and spent most of their time by themselves, as if they were too important to speak with sailors, slaves, or princess.

Penelope sat on the narrow bench built against the wall of the hold and watched her servants work. It was a matter of moments to gather up the rugs, the baskets of fruit, the skin of wine, the bread and other food. She watched Melantho, envying her full curves and golden hair that glowed even when sunlight didn't touch it. She had full, red lips the village boys in Alybas had pronounced sweeter than honey cakes. Her eyes were a blue that reflected the sun, not dark pools like Penelope's, to swallow and hide her thoughts and feelings.

She wondered if Melantho had ever envied her. She knew the older girl resented returning to Sparta. Several village men had offered for her when they heard Penelope returned to Sparta. Dolios had refused, saying their duty demanded they all go.

Bachan had said often, teasing and affectionate, that Penelope asked more questions, thought more deeply than the oracles and priests. Lost now in her thoughts, Penelope didn't realize they had reached Pylos until the ship lurched, the keel touching sandy bottom. She caught at the bench to keep from toppling.

Sailor voices broke the clatter of ropes and wooden winches and the singing of wind and surf against the ship. Penelope stayed in the hold, knowing she would be underfoot during the unloading. She closed her eyes, taking in every last sensation. The splash of the plank as it hit the surf and wet sand. The clatter as another plank went down on top of it, connecting it with the shallow docks of Pylos. The piercing, strong voices of sailors hailing the newcomers. She heard snatches of news, shouted from one ship to another, or ship to shore. The wind had never smelled more alive and fresh than at that moment, when she would go inland again.

Time to return from her dreams and wishes to reality.

Once on the docks, Penelope saw the three long, cushioned carts waiting for her company, and the soldiers Kratos and Anthinos had gone to seek. She schooled her face into calm, though longing to laugh aloud. Melantho smothered a giggle behind her hand. King Tyndareos had sent a company of ten lightly armed, aging men who had seen far better days.

Their leader, a graying, stout man saluted Kratos, then bowed to

Penelope. He gave orders in a crisp, barking voice. Three men put down their spears and helped Dolios and his sons fetch Penelope's belongings.

Eurynome confronted the leader and asked him about conditions on the road, the atmosphere at the palace, and how long the journey would take. Penelope sat on a little bench in the shade of a statue to Poseidon. Searching her basket, she discovered her doll was missing.

Penelope had always been sure to put the little doll carved from olive wood back into the basket. Perhaps it was silly to be so concerned about a toy. After all, a girl of fifteen was ready to marry, with no need or time for toys. But Ikarios had made the doll with dark eyes and dark hair to look like Penelope, before he died in the boar hunt. It was a talisman, a promise for the future. She needed it, if only to hold in the dark watches of the night and dream.

She heard a snicker, and barely stopped herself from turning to look. Penelope recognized the sound of Melantho enjoying the fruits of another nasty trick. She schooled her face into calm and unclenched her hands, refusing to give her nasty slave any satisfaction.

Her doll wasn't missing, she knew now. How often had Melantho mocked her in whispers for playing with dolls when she was nearly on the threshold of her bridal chamber? The older girl had done it to punish Penelope. Hadn't she played similar nasty tricks in the past, in retribution for every imagined slight and injustice? Melantho had stolen the doll.

Where would her disgruntled slave put it? Penelope turned and looked directly at the merchant's ship. It would set sail once the new cargo had been loaded. If it left before she got someone to search the ship, she would never see her doll again.

Penelope considered accusing Melantho in front of witnesses. That would use up precious time. Eurynome or Dolios would insist Melantho go back to the ship to retrieve the doll. The girl would flirt with a sailor or two and deliberately waste time until she didn't have a chance to get on board. The ship would depart with the doll still hidden inside it.

Far easier, Penelope knew, to retrieve the doll herself. Melantho would be disappointed if she got no reaction to her nasty trick. What use was revenge if the victim showed no pain and acted as if she didn't care?

Yes, far easier to retrieve the doll herself and frustrate Melantho with her silence.

Penelope wished yet again that Dolios had left his daughter behind in Alybas. Life would be far sweeter and more peaceful without Melantho.

She went quietly back to the ship, slipping between the guards and the sailors and merchants busily moving between ships and docks. She ran up the plank to the ship, imagining she once more felt the motion of the sea. She would miss the ship. The dark-eyed vessel was a friend, the slap of the water against its prow a voice that spoke to her. It filled her dreams and made them happy. Penelope wondered if she dared hope an island prince would ask for her and take her to his home in a ship like this. Perhaps he would share his love for the sea with his bride. She had loved the journey, walking the bobbing deck, feeling the sea breezes tugging at her hair.

"Enough foolishness," Penelope whispered as she found the empty corner of the hold where she had traveled. Deep in the shadows, her carved doll waited patiently. Small enough to hide in both hands, it was golden in the sunlight, as sacred to her as the prayers she had learned to make to Aphrodite the day she entered womanhood.

The truth—Penelope faced it before she took another step from the dark, echoing hold—was that she would do well to give up her dreams and prepare for whatever the Fates decreed. Penelope was dependent on her uncle's favor and would do as Tyndareos decreed. She owed service to Tyndareos and to Sparta. There would be many disappointed men of noble bloodlines, the day Helen became a bride. Penelope would be a peace offering for an unhappy ally. She would walk with Helen and hope some powerful, influential prince would see her and want her.

Want her more than he wanted Helen? Penelope knew that was impossible.

"Like expecting a man to see a dark bowl in a dark room after gazing into the sun," she murmured as she descended the plank.

What did she have to attract a man's interest and hunger? Small breasts waiting to fill out, and the slim hips and height of a child. What man would want her before her growth finished?

She shook her head to clear it of such thoughts as she returned to solid ground. Penelope slipped between the narrow aisles of bales and baskets from the merchant ships. She hoped to return to her place before Eurynome realized she had vanished. Her nurse would scold her like a child half her age. She watched her feet, to avoid tripping as she hurried.

A shadow crossed her path, a bird shape over her head. Penelope stopped when she felt the brush of wings against her hair. She looked up and thought she saw snowy silver feathers, round eyes and the thick wings of an owl. She shivered as the bird disappeared into the glare of the sun. She caught her foot as she stepped out from behind a stack of bales and stopped to check her stubbed toe when she heard voices, two men talking.

Two sets of sandal-clad feet moved into her sight and blocked her way. Penelope followed the line of sight, up bronzed, muscular legs, to white tunics embroidered with purple and gold, and jeweled armbands on hairy, muscled arms. Golden chains and pins and purple cloaks marked both men as princes. She studied them as they talked. The larger man tried to talk the other into staying in Sparta. One had come to Pylos to check on his ship to prepare to leave. Penelope wondered which ship was his. Then the men turned and saw her.

One was of stocky build, with wide shoulders, dark red hair that burned like coals in the sun, gray eyes and a laughing face. He smiled at her, eyes sparkling with life and mischief, and she couldn't help but smile back.

The other was dark, his golden skin pale against black hair and eyes. A giant of a man, his muscles strained against his tunic. Penelope noticed food stains on his clothes. He smiled as well, but with mockery.

"Tell me, little one." The black-haired one dropped to one knee to look her in the eye. The action generated sharp dislike in her. She didn't like being reminded how small she was. "Tell me, where are you going with that toy?"

"It is a keepsake of my mistress," Penelope said.

She thought a prayer of thanks to the Goddess for the lie, and gestured beyond the bales and baskets, where she could see waving spear points and hear rising voices. Someone had noticed she had disappeared.

"Mistress?" He looked around.

"Aias, don't you listen to anything but praises for Helen?" the fiery one said. His smile included Penelope in a joke she didn't understand. "Penelope, daughter of Ikarios and sister of your friend, Ithios, is coming home to Sparta. Which you would have known if you talked to Kastor or Polydeukes more often. I heard Helen asked for her cousin to return. To relieve the boredom of our company," he added, his voice taking on a mocking drawl. He winked at Penelope and nodded toward an opening in the maze of bales and baskets around them.

16

She understood and darted away when Aias' attention left her. As she ran, she heard the giant scold the red one for letting her escape. The other just laughed.

"Your taste for tormenting and seducing servant girls is going to get you in trouble some day, my friend," he said. "Forget her."

"Where are you going now?" Aias called.

"Back to Sparta. I've decided you're right. Tyndareos' hospitality is not something to leave so easily." He laughed, his voice fading as Penelope left the men behind.

"Odysseus, my friend, you always see profit for yourself in anything." Aias laughed, his voice a harsh bellow. "I think you were kind to the servant girl so Penelope would speak kindly of you to Helen."

"Perhaps."

Then their voices faded completely and Penelope reached Eurynome. The fiery one was called Odysseus. His eyes, that moment of understanding between them, his help in escaping Aias filled her thoughts, so she barely heard her nurse scolding her for running off.

CHAPTER 2

Penelope drew her veil over her face and settled back against the railing of the cart. She couldn't find a spot on her body the bumping and bouncing hadn't bruised. Except for her short encounter with Aias and Odysseus, Penelope felt only disappointment in her journey from the moment her sandals touched ground two days before.

Her first complaint—Kratos turned aside an invitation from King Nestor to refresh themselves at his palace. Penelope had waited for a servant to come to the docks with an invitation from the aging king. She waited until they were in the carts, bouncing along the sandy road away from Pylos, before speaking. Eurynome gently scolded and said girls who wandered missed all the news. King Nestor had invited Penelope to visit, but King Tyndareos wanted his niece in Sparta as soon as possible and the ship had made landfall late. They left Pylos immediately and traveled until after sunset before making camp. They rolled out of their blankets to return to the carts at dawn's first light.

It was past nightfall now, their second day of travel, and they were still on the road. They lost hours over a wheel that had slipped off its axle. If they did not arrive soon, the king might send people looking for them.

Penelope had nearly laughed, when she overheard Anthinos mention the possibility to Dolios. Did her uncle think someone would kidnap her? The little, dark one would never be kidnapped, like Helen. No king would kill to have her, like Klytemaistra.

She shivered and hugged her cloak a little closer around her shoulders. Her face and hair felt gritty and oily, desperately in need of a long bath and perfuming. She felt burned, rough patches on her nose and cheeks where the harsh light of the plain had touched her before she used her veil.

She wondered about her uncle's specific instructions. Tyndareos ruled with wisdom and honesty. His people obeyed through adoration, not fear. Sometimes, though, they went to extremes in interpreting his wishes.

"There it is," Dolios said, touching her shoulder. Penelope pushed with her cramped legs, to stand up halfway in the cart. She caught a smear of light and the blocky shadows of buildings as the road dipped into a shallow valley and the trees slid back from the road. The man smiled at her and stepped up his pace. He had insisted on walking beside her the whole way, carrying a borrowed spear and keeping the stride and rhythm of the guards. Penelope wondered if he was glad to be home in Sparta. She had overheard Melantho complain once that Dolios loved Penelope better than his own daughter.

"Soft beds and decent baths," Penelope murmured. She scrubbed at her face with the edge of her veil, not caring that it would show stains in morning light. She had to have a clean face and neat hair to present to whoever would greet them.

Her aching back and legs, the gritty discomfort and the chill penetrating her cloak increased after seeing the lights of Sparta. Penelope held her tongue and listened to the chatter that sprang from the guards. It amused her a little that they spoke easily with Dolios, Aris, and their sons, openly flirted with Melantho, spoke to Eurynome with respect, yet feared to address her, a maiden of no threat to trained warriors. Along the way, she had tried to start a conversation with the youngest guard, a man of about twenty-six or seven who walked with a limp. He had answered her questions with mumbles, nods, or shakes of his head and never dared look her in the face.

When the road finally changed from dirt to stone paving that made the wheels rumble, Penelope bit back a cheer. Their company went the long way around, by the river, to come up through the palace grounds instead of through the city. The trees gave way to painted walls that reflected the torchlight. She knelt on the cushioned bench and tried to see around corners and over heads to catch the first glimpse of the palace proper.

She saw it first as a golden haze of light. Servants streamed out through doors carrying torches. Lystia, a cousin of Eurynome and housekeeper for Tyndareos, came down the steps last. She called orders to Aris, Dolios, and Melantho before the carts came to a complete stop.

"Well, cousin?" the woman asked, as Dolios stepped up and helped Eurynome down from the cart.

"You tell me," the nurse responded. As one person, the two women turned to look at Penelope.

Penelope held herself tall and straight. She didn't meet their eyes, but neither did she turn away. Dolios squeezed her hand as he helped her down and she bit her lip to keep from smiling thanks for his encouragement. She felt the housekeeper studying her in the torchlight. Penelope concentrated on the courtyard of the palace of Tyndareos.

The stone was still golden, the arches and pillars still sky-reaching tall. She saw the brass-bound, oaken doors, the purple and gold tapestries through the open windows, the mosaics of purple, red, blue, gold, black, and white tiles that lined the entryway floor. To her right lay the grand arch to enter the courtyard. To her left the other archway led to the stables and barracks. Behind her, the slave quarters and the archways led to the plain and the river where she and her cousins played and swam under the watchful eyes of their nurses. Nothing had changed. Penelope heaved a sigh of contentment and nodded. Satisfied and comforted by the immutability of the palace of Sparta, she turned to face the scrutiny of Lystia.

"You are a pleasant, welcome sight for old eyes, young Penelope. Welcome home." Lystia's searching, judging glance changed to a warm smile. "A bath waits and your rooms have been aired and furnished. Do you require something to eat before going to bed?"

"No, thank you." Penelope felt a tired laugh pressing against her throat. How could she have forgotten? Lystia felt every ill could be cured with good cooking. "A bath and a bed that doesn't move are all I need for now." She nodded for the housekeeper to lead the way inside. Melantho hurried to catch up, her arms full of Penelope's belongings.

*   *   *

Roses. Penelope's nose twitched as the perfume penetrated her sleep. Like pale, sweet wine, it cut through the sticky net of her dreams and helped her rise to full waking. She opened her eyes to a room full of sunlight and a haze of gold and blue perched on the side of her bed.

"Good morning and welcome home, cousin," a voice like the deeper notes of a flute said.

Penelope blinked and the haze resolved into Helen. Her eyes were as blue as a midsummer sky washed by the rain. Tiny white roses crowned her hair of gold touched with red. Two long braids hung on either side of her face, the rest a mass of curls down her back. She wore a blue dress that matched her eyes and complimented her ivory and rose skin. Penelope was pleased to note that though her bodice was tight, Helen had little more fullness under her clothes than her younger cousin.

"Helen." Penelope swallowed against the thickness in her throat. Lystia had insisted she eat bread and honey before going to bed. Her throat felt like the honey stayed to clog her voice. "I suppose I really am home."

"Of course you are. What a lovely time we'll have. I've been lonely." A teasing pout twisted Helen's perfect lips. "And soon *we* are to be married and separated. Come, get up! We must make use of the time we have!" Laughing, she tugged back on the blankets.

Penelope snatched at the blankets. It was one thing for Eurynome to pull away her covers to make her get up in the morning. For beautiful, womanly Helen to see the little, dark one without any clothes was a weakness Penelope didn't want to face. She missed the blankets and had to content herself with sitting up and letting her long hair cover her. If she hunched her shoulders, it turned into a garment hanging past her hips.

"Penelope!" Helen's voice lost its teasing. She sat on the side of the bed to hug her cousin. "You've grown up!"

"Not much," she couldn't resist saying.

"You have no mirrors in Alybas?" The older girl laughed. "How beautiful you are! You'll steal my suitors—for which I will be grateful. Good morning, Eurynome." She stood as the nurse entered the room.

Penelope swallowed her sigh and smile of relief at her nurse's entrance. She had forgotten how like a bubbling fountain Helen could be. The door to her room creaked on its leather hinges, but Helen had been talking so much, and so fast, she hadn't heard.

"I know you told me not to awaken Penelope, but she was waking already. I waited until she started to move, just like you told me." Helen swept across the room, her skirts flying behind her. She brushed a kiss on the nurse's cheek and fluttered through the door. "Hurry and dress. There is so much to do today." And she was gone.

"Like a chirping bird, all day long," Eurynome said, her smile holding a wry twist. She carried a tray with wine, bread and honey, and figs. "Come, it is true you should be up and moving. We let you sleep

21

late because of our long journey." She set the tray down on the little table next to the window.

"Helen makes me feel I am the elder." Penelope stood, tugged on a plain, beltless tunic and followed Eurynome to the table. The women's gardens sat below her window, a maze of colors and paths, bright this spring morning.

"That one needs a husband to guide her." The nurse went back to Penelope's bed and straightened the blankets as the girl ate. "If Theseus had not vanished with his idiot friend on that mysterious quest of theirs, they should have let her stay and marry him, though he was old enough to be her grandfather. He had the experience to handle her."

"You've been talking this morning," Penelope said, peeling the outer skin off her first fig.

"Indeed I have." The woman chuckled. "I suppose you want to know if I have learned anything about your two princes."

"They're not mine—I merely wish to know who I met." Penelope blamed the warmth in her face on the sun slanting through the window.

"Aias is called the Lesser—can you believe it? That is because Aias the son of Telemon was here first. He only has his prowess as a warrior to speak for him, no great bloodlines or lands to recommend him to the king. Though he carries off enough riches to take care of any well-born girl, his eating uses up those riches quickly." Eurynome chuckled again. "Odysseus is the son of Laertes, king of Ithaka. That's the leader of the cluster of islands to the west and north. We probably passed by the islands on our voyage. He's known among the suitors for his quick mind and among the servants for his gentle manners. He's a favorite here."

"Do they think he will win Helen?"

"Ithaka isn't rich enough for Tyndareos. And Menelaos, brother of Agamemnon, is here. It would be good if both brothers were tied to our southern cities by marriage." Eurynome began pulling dresses out of a chest at the end of the bed. "Come. Your uncle had new dresses made for you. We must choose which to wear when you see him."

"When?" Penelope hastily chewed on the last of the bread, licking the honey off her fingers.

"At the evening meal. He spends the morning in the megaron with the suitors, talking and testing them. Then they go to the plain with your cousins and prove how strong and skilled they are with their everlasting games, giving the king some peace to rule his land. You and Helen are both commanded to join him at the high table." Eurynome paused, giving emphasis to her next words. "It's said the king is not being difficult in deciding the best man for Helen, but he hesitates out of fear."

"Fear?" Penelope whispered the word, as if the walls would repeat the conversation to her uncle. "I've never known him to fear anything, except us being kidnapped."

"That's just it. While she is here, within his walls, Helen is safe. It took Kastor and Polydeukes four years to bring their sister home. The king is worried Helen's husband will be attacked by the disappointed suitors."

"I am home now to calm a prince and swing him to support Helen's husband and my uncle." Penelope shrugged. It was no more than she expected.

"Even Helen is not as valuable to the king as the peace and security of Sparta," Eurynome said. She shook her head, a momentary flicker of sadness making her look years older. "Come, look at these beautiful dresses. Tonight, you must look your best when your future husband first sees you."

Penelope held back the unladylike snort of disbelief she had learned from her grandfather. She doubted her chance of being noticed while in Helen's company.

"Did you notice Helen?" she said as Eurynome helped her try on the first dress, pale green with blue trimmings.

"How can anyone help but notice that one?"

"For some reason, I thought she would be...more full." Penelope gestured, accenting her hips and breasts. Eurynome eyed her as if she had never seen the girl before.

"And why should Helen—or you—want to be heavy like a woman with ten children?" She caught Penelope's chin in her hand and made the girl look her in the eye. "Is that the problem? Your shape? We spent four years too many in the northlands, I can see. Your ideas of beauty are twisted, child. Up there, all they care about is the breeding potential of their women.

"You are no peasant. You have more to offer a man than just children. Thanks to your grandfather and aunt, you can manage any estate and see past the dealings of the most thieving steward. You weave like a goddess taught you. Your singing voice is sweet enough to make a man cry for joy.

"And your mind...it's a pity you may only let the suitors stare at you. You could match wits with them in their riddles and stories."

"Match wits with the princes of Achaia?" Penelope's mind spun with delight at the idea. Then she laughed. "I would grow fumbling wits and lose my voice in a moment."

"Perhaps." The woman nodded and closed the clasps on the shoulders of the dress. "If I had known what bothered you, we could have talked sooner. If you want larger breasts and wider hips, you will have them when you've borne a child or two. Girl, listen to me and listen well. Your husband will love you at first for your body and the pleasure you give him in bed. Then he will love you for the children you bear for him. Later, when you no longer have a girl's figure and it has filled out more than you wanted—"she paused, a teasing twinkle in her eyes—"he will love you for how well you raised his children and how well you manage his home. By then, he will notice your other fine qualities and love you for them as well."

"Men are very changeable," Penelope murmured, gazing off into the distance. She didn't see the gardens and plains beyond her window, but her own tumbling thoughts.

The woman shrugged. "That is the way they are, and we women must live with it."

*   *   *

Penelope searched for a glimpse of dark red hair as she and Helen passed the half-open door of the megaron. The voices of men, raised in talk and laughter, rumbled into the very stones of the palace. It was a happy, strong, alive sound. Still, she shivered as it brought back a fragment of a dream that had frightened her often.

Men, gathered in a lesser palace, waiting for a bride who would not come to them. Death hovered in the high beams of the ceiling, but none of them could see it or feel its cold breath.

"Penelope?" Helen frowned at her, puzzled.

"Just remembering." She hurried to catch up with her cousin. When they were children, Penelope had felt they were the same age, taking care of each other. Now, she truly did feel the elder, though Helen was five years her senior.

"Remembering what?" the other wanted to know, when they and their maids had walked around two corners, taking them far from the megaron.

"The last time I saw Uncle on his throne, he summoned me to explain the fuss in the night. That you were gone and I was going to Alybas. I suppose the next time I go in there..." She refused to finish

24

the thought.

"It will be to learn who you are to marry," Helen said, a sunny smile and a bright giggle escaping her. "I'll speak to him. Perhaps we can be married at the same ceremony."

Penelope held her tongue, merely nodding and smiling. She wondered what Melantho and Helen's maid thought about the conversation. They would undoubtedly report every word when they joined the other slaves at meals.

At her grandfather's home, her slaves had been like family, keeping trusts and refusing to lower themselves to gossip with the villagers. Penelope wished for those days again. She felt defenseless and exposed.

She kept her thoughts to herself as Helen took her on a walking tour of the palace and grounds. She saw a new building to house more slaves. More ground broken for crops to the west, down near the river. The trees around the clearing where the women bathed and played had grown taller and thicker. There were more horses in Tyndareos' stables. The flowers and rose bushes had grown thicker and more numerous. Penelope almost sighed in relief when they finished the tour and walked back to the women's quarters.

Helen sent Melantho and the other girl down to the sheep pens. The shepherds had promised fresh wool, washed and dry by now, for them to card and spin that day. Penelope stepped into the women's room, wondering what had changed there while she had been away.

Wide windows hung with nearly sheer golden, pink, and azure draperies let in the sunlight from three sides. Musical instruments of all kinds hung on one wall, for the maidens to amuse themselves. Fresh rushes sprinkled with sweet, sharp smelling herbs covered the stones of the floor. Flowers were everywhere in abundance.

Yet what drew her were the two large looms sitting by the window that faced south. One held a small pattern, colorful, with the sea in the middle and an intricate border full of tiny people. The other loom held a large cloth only half begun, the warp threads hanging, waiting for a hand to finish tying the weights.

"I dreamed you sat at that loom," Helen said, stepping into the room and walking toward the southern window. "I dreamed we laughed and sang, and you taught me mastery of the loom. Was it a true dream through the gate of horn, or through the ivory gate of lies?" She stopped and turned back to face Penelope, one hand resting on the larger loom.

"A dream?" Penelope felt very young, very awkward. The sunlight surrounded Helen with gold. Even doubters would believe the princess was the daughter of Zeus at that moment. Penelope contrasted her own dark features and slimness against the ripe, golden and rose features of the princess of Sparta. "How could I teach you anything?"

"My mother knew your mother," Helen said, her own voice softening. "She said your mother was the greatest of all weavers she had ever known. Before you left, you showed skill. I merely thought that by now, your skill had grown."

"I have improved. If you like, I could have Eurynome bring out some of the weaving I did in Alybas." She stepped closer to the loom. Despite herself, Penelope's thoughts strayed to the half-begun pattern. She noted threads and colors she would like to change, and thought of how she would finish the design.

"Penelope..." Helen rested a hand on her cousin's shoulder, accenting the difference in their heights. Penelope found she did not mind. "This is your home. You do not have to prove yourself here."

"Everything has changed. And nothing has changed," she whispered. Penelope felt her face warming. How could Helen appear a mere bird of a girl, fluttering, chattering and singing as if she had not a thought in her head, and then show such insight? Was that the way of the gods and their offspring?

"I started this loom with the pattern I thought I saw you weaving," her cousin went on. "It isn't right. I wanted you to find it with the beginning work done. This is your loom, to do whatever you wish, show whatever you want."

"Mine?" Penelope's smile started small and astonished, then widened in delight. Even in her aunt's chambers, where her dreams had been indulged, she had not had a whole loom to herself. "I will make a hanging for your bridal chamber. I will weave prayers for blessing into it, that all the goddesses will smile on you."

CHAPTER 3

When the afternoon heat became heavy and the shadows grew long, Helen announced they would go to the river. Thoughts of shade and cool river water drowned the sigh of regret Penelope almost loosed. She cast one more glance at the preparations on her loom and promised herself she would finish the next morning.

The loom was finely made, every piece rubbed smooth and glossy. The warp weights nearly held the threads without need for knots. Weaving on that loom would be a joy. Watching the pattern grow would be a delight.

She gathered up her veil and slipped her sandals on. She had to hurry to follow Helen down the long, shadowed hallways to the entrance facing the river. The maids followed, carrying baskets of fruit, mending, skins of wine, anything they might need for the afternoon. Penelope heard Melantho chattering with the other maids, and she smiled, relieved. The older girl did sound happy, accepted by the other servants.

The women of the household had a clearing by the river set aside for them. The water ran shallow there, with plenty of sun-baked, smooth rocks to beat the clothes clean and lay them out to dry. Or for young bodies to stretch out and sleep in the afternoon warmth. The trees had been kept thick and wild all around it, for privacy.

"First, a bath," Helen decreed. She tugged at the beads and cords holding her hair into its braids. Laughing, she loosened her hair partway, then sat down and let a maid finish the job.

Penelope flinched, startled when another maid stepped up to attend her. She was not used to anyone touching her hair but Eurynome, and then only when she asked. There were many things, she decided, she would have to grow used to here in Sparta. Penelope almost laughed aloud at the little servant girl's surprise when she thanked her. Bachan believed that gratitude was as much a slave's due as proper food, clothing, and shelter. Penelope agreed with her, and realized now that many did not.

The river water had a bite to it, chilling like it had come straight from melting winter ice. Penelope controlled her shivers and waded in until she could kneel and let the water flow over her shoulders.

"Always braver than I!" Helen called, laughing. She stood far to the left, arms spread for balance. The water only reached her knees.

Penelope closed her eyes and turned away. It wasn't easy to stop comparing herself with Helen's perfect figure. Reminding herself that her cousin had five years of growth on her did not help. Penelope cupped her small breasts and silently prayed Aphrodite to help her grow faster. She would have peace in her future household if her husband was pleased with her body.

She scooped up a handful of sand from the river bottom to scrub her legs and arms. The exertion helped drive away some of the chill of the water, but not by much. When she waded out again, her arms wrapped around herself for warmth, she wished she had stayed submerged.

Melantho met her with a drying sheet. Penelope gave the girl a nod and mumbled thanks. She had wondered when the maid would stop letting others serve her mistress and start scurrying to do her duties.

She almost regretted letting go of the sheet, to lie on a dry sheet on the warm sand and let another maid rub her body with perfumed oil. Penelope tried to hold still in the cool wind. None of it mattered so much when she heard Helen complaining about the cold.

"Your northland people are not so soft," the maid commented, pausing to pour more oil into her hands. "You have strong, smooth muscles," the girl explained, when Penelope opened one eye to look inquiringly up at her.

"I walked with my grandfather everywhere. He has orchards, and I preferred to climb to get the fruit I wanted."

"We feared you would lose your fitness, being sent from Sparta so young."

"You're Alkippe, aren't you?" Penelope asked.

Helen had said Alkippe would be her chief maid and nurse to her children when she married. Such a position gave privilege to speak frankly and openly. Penelope was glad the maid felt those rights extended to her mistress' cousin. Eurynome could be trusted to speak even the most painful truth, but Penelope wanted someone closer to her own age to share viewpoints.

"Has my lady complained about me to you?" Alkippe asked, accenting her question with an extra deep rub. Laughter touched her voice, but it was not malicious.

"Not yet." Penelope was glad when the maid laughed with her. She knew she had found a friend and supporter.

After warming in the sun and dressing again, there were games. Races along the pebbly shore. To her delight, Penelope came in second whenever she did not win. Alkippe had been right after all. She had not grown soft and weak, but had grown stronger. She could count on one hand the races she had won or placed second in before she left Sparta.

Several of Helen's maids played the lyre or pipes. They made a game of playing songs so quick and bright that some tangled their feet when they danced. More than once, Penelope fell laughing to the sand. Some insisted on continuing the contest, trying to reach the end of the tune without falling or losing their breaths, or make the musicians lose their own breaths in laughter.

Penelope joined Helen and a few others in playing catch with a hollow wooden ball where the water lapped at their feet. They were not content simply to toss the ball around the circle, but invented contests where they had to throw over and then under. Or spin on a heel as they caught the ball. Penelope laughed as brightly as the others, glad to be in the company of maidens her own age once more.

Helen slipped on a wet stone as she stepped forward to throw the ball to Penelope. Her arm jerked and the ball went over her cousin's head and out into the river. The current caught the ball.

Penelope turned and held up her skirts in one hand, splashing through the shallows before the first shriek of disappointment left anyone's throat. She stumbled once when her foot found a hole in the riverbed, but caught herself and kept running. Up ahead, the bright gold and red ball sparkled and bobbed. The river neared a sharp bend where it went around the trees and a few high, sharp rocks. Penelope kept running.

She ran back onto shore, to reach the other side of the bend before the ball and snatch it out of the water. She dashed from sunlight to the gloom of the trees, and back out into sunlight again. Her lungs burned from the effort. The ball had been a gift from her father to Helen. She would not let it be lost.

Penelope let out a cry of triumph mixed with pain. Her ankle twisted as she spotted the ball and a stone slid under her foot. She ignored the sharp pang running up her leg and dashed to the river's edge to pluck the ball out of the water.

And the next moment lost it. The water made the painted surface slick and it slipped from her hand. Penelope spun around to chase the ball and ran into a huge, dark-haired shape that grabbed her elbows in massive, callused hands.

"Well, little one, we meet again," Aias said with a laugh. He set Penelope on her feet and smiled down at her. She smelled strong wine on his breath and he had fresh stains on his tunic. "Why so far from your mistress?"

"I am chasing the ball. It fell in the river." She gave up trying to explain and tried to step around him. He was so wide, why did they call him the Lesser? Vaguely, she had the idea it had rolled away between his legs. Penelope didn't care where the ball went as long as it was not back in the river. She gasped in frustration as Aias caught her wrist and stopped her.

"I can help you find it," he said.

"Thank you, but I can do my own hunting."

"You have spirit!" He laughed, the sound verging on a roar. "What will you give me if I help you?"

"I don't need your help." She tugged to free her wrist. Aias held her fast, like sticky clay that would suck her down into the ground.

"To help a pretty little maiden like you, I usually ask for only one kiss. One with spirit, maybe two kisses. Are you sure you don't need help?"

"I don't need help, and I don't want your kisses." She tugged harder, throwing the weight of her body into the action. Aias tightened his grip, laughing.

"Come now, pretty one. A kiss won't hurt. You might even like it."

"Let—me—go!" she snapped, accenting her words with another tug, her voice louder with each word. Aias laughed louder and tugged her closer.

"For fighting, three kisses." He reached for her other hand and Penelope twisted away from him.

"If I had my spear..." She bit back the rest of her words. Now not the time to reveal she had been raised by a madman who thought her a boy.

However, Dymis had taught her many useful things. She swung around hard with her free arm, landing her fist in the soft spot high between Aias' ribs.

He yelped like a kicked dog, his breath torn away by her direct hit. His face darkened with a scowl and he pulled her closer. Penelope brought her knee up, throwing herself back away from him. Aias saw her move and jerked away in time. She overbalanced and fell, landing on pebbles. She loosed a shout of pain and rolled away.

Before she could scramble to her feet, Aias dropped to his knees next to her. He caught her around the waist with one massive arm and drew her up against his chest, pinning her arms with her hands upraised. She couldn't move them to swing at him. He laughed. Penelope shrieked, like she had when the bear had leaped from the trees. She had managed to stab it once with her spear before Dolios arrived to kill it.

"A warrior's daughter, no doubt," Aias said, his breath short. "Don't put up such a fight. There's no dishonor. Should I ask the king for you, then? Is that what you want?"

"Let me go!" she shrieked.

"Aias!" The voice that thundered through the late afternoon warmth held a rage that made Penelope wilt inside. Aias paused, his open mouth poised above hers. Penelope leaned back, enough to free her arms to scratch. She caught his cheek, just below his temple, drawing blood.

The man roared in surprise, releasing her. Penelope fell to her knees and swung at his face and chest with both hands, wide punches, thumbs out as her grandfather had taught her. His roars changed to anger and he lunged at her.

A muscular, ruddy arm entered Penelope's field of vision and caught Aias by the front of his tunic. It tore as the newcomer yanked him sideways, flinging him down at the roots of a tree. Dark red hair caught the sharp slanting afternoon sunlight and turned gold. Gray eyes flashed in fury. Penelope fell forward onto her hands and saw the jagged scar above the man's knee, a white slash like lightning against the dark tan of his skin.

"Are you hurt?" Odysseus caught her shoulders in his hands, helping her to sit up. His touch was gentle, and she thought his hands trembled.

"No. Just furious." She swallowed hard, trying to make her voice

31

calm again.

"You fought like a Fury." A crooked smile twisted up one corner of his mouth. "Did he—" His voice caught and broke and he looked away.

"He never even got a kiss," she hastened to assure him. It was almost amusing, Penelope reflected later, how relief made Odysseus' shoulders straighten. He stood and helped her stand.

"Aias, you staggering fool," he growled as he stepped over to his fallen comrade. "I could hear her scream in the king's stables. Don't you know when a girl says no, she means *no*?"

"Now I do." The dark man pushed himself upright against the tree. "Girl, who taught you to fight like that? You could be a soldier instead of just a serving maid. A tempting one at that."

"Tempting or not, you can't take her against her will in the house of our host." Odysseus' voice began to relax. Penelope knew he looked at her again, concern in his eyes, but she couldn't bring herself to do more than steal short glimpses of him. She knew it was foolish to stay while her attacker recovered, but she couldn't move. She contented herself with watching him and keeping alert.

"So much fuss over a serving girl," Aias grumbled.

"Of all the maids who throw themselves at you... Why force yourself on the one who says no?" Odysseus sighed, loudly, and took a step away. He ran his hand through his hair and looked up at the sky as if begging strength from the gods.

Penelope wondered why she found it so amusing. All the gossip said Odysseus was never at a loss for words, so why silence now?

"Whose daughter are you, to be such a skilled fighter?" Aias grinned at her, then winced as he touched the deep scratch on his face.

"I am Penelope, daughter of Ikarios." Her smile grew wider when Aias gaped at her. "He was brother to King Tyndareos. I am Helen's cousin. And Ithios' sister," she added when the man stared, his mouth dropping open wider. She remembered Odysseus' words at Pylos. If Ithios had not changed since she went to Alybas, Penelope could well believe Aias would be his friend.

The sound of women's voices grew closer. Penelope caught a glimpse of bright dresses, heard the rattle of stones dislodged by unsure feet.

"You should go. I'll tend our fallen warrior," Odysseus said with a shrug and another sigh. His concern burned bright in his eyes.

"I'm not even bruised," she hurried to assure him. Warmth poured through her body when Odysseus smiled at her. Penelope found it hard to do, but she turned and hurried back the way she had come. She spotted the ball and snatched it up before entering the trees. Behind her, she heard the crunching of sandal-shod feet as the two men left.

"Penelope?" Helen led the group of women approaching the trees. Her eyes widened when she saw her cousin coming back through the shadows to meet them.

Penelope looked at herself. Her dress hung awry, spotted with sand and damp. Her loose braid had come apart, turning her hair into a dark tangled cloud all around her shoulders, strands sticking to her sweating face. She smiled, despite the bruises forming on her back where she had hit the stones.

"I found the ball," she said, holding it out.

"We should go back inside now," Helen said, her words slow. She caught her cousin's hand when Penelope would have walked by her. "Tell me," she commanded in a soft voice.

"Someone mistook me for a servant girl and tried to steal a kiss. I fought him off...and another man rescued me." She shrugged and smiled.

"Penelope—"

"Later." Once again, Penelope felt herself to be the elder. "When there are no spying ears or gossiping tongues."

"I'll hold you to that, cousin." Helen smiled and looped her arm through Penelope's. They walked back to rejoin the others, arm in arm.

*   *   *

Penelope was glad for the floating cloud of sheer veil across her face, her armor of jewels and cosmetics, as she followed Helen down the hall. The chatter of the servant girls about the suitors, their backgrounds, attributes and gifts to Tyndareos and Helen, had done nothing to soothe her leaping stomach and trembling hands and feet. More than two hours had gone into dressing and decorating the two royal cousins, so they could sit at the high table in the feasting hall. Penelope knew no one would recognize her now and she was glad. And worried. Memories of Aias' rage and his stupidly stunned face made her alternately want to cry and laugh. Memories of the worry and rage on Odysseus' face sent a humming sensation through her to her bones. Penelope did not know if she could look at him, meet his eyes, and present the controlled, cool exterior required of a royal daughter.

That question would soon be answered, she reflected, as she and Helen paused at the doorway to the feasting hall. The massive, bronze-bound doors were guarded by two servants, who bowed and pulled the panels apart. A wave of sensations poured from the feasting hall.

The deafening roar of scores of men talking and laughing and shouting at once. A faint undercurrent of music from lyres, pipes. and drums. The laughter of servant girls as they dodged pinches and kisses. The odors of roast meat, fresh bread, garlic, and wine. The warmth and thickness of air from many male bodies confined in one place. The sweet, thin aroma of flowers that garlanded the beams and walls of the feasting hall. Penelope took it all in with one breath. In the next, she had to fight not to step backwards, as it threatened to overwhelm her.

"Daunting, isn't it?" Helen said, her voice louder to be heard over the din. Penelope doubted Melantho or Alkippe, at their elbows, had heard. "I nearly turned and fled the first time I faced them. They will quiet soon enough."

As if they heard her speak, the men closest to the door began to quiet. The scattered clumps of tables, three or four men at each, created a maze Penelope and Helen had to navigate to reach the platform where Tyndareos, his sons and nephew sat. She had double reason now to be grateful for the shield of her veils and cosmetics. None but the man directly before her would see her features. She could handle confrontations if taken one at a time. Penelope prayed Athena to intervene that there would be no confrontations.

Quiet spread into the hall from the doorway. Penelope saw a man stand at the long table and gesture toward the door with a silver goblet. From that distance, she couldn't tell where her brother sat, or if Kastor or Polydeukes gestured for her and Helen to enter.

The men were twins, but not identical. Both had the same golden-brown hair as their dead mother Leda, the same sculptured cheekbones and broad shoulders. There the similarities stopped. Kastor was a good head taller. His beard was thicker, his eyes brown, his nose thick as if it had been punched too many times. Polydeukes had a delicacy about him that was all illusion. He could win any foot race, even in armor, and rode horses as if he were a centaur. His blue eyes, like Helen's, had a tendency to see through people. Penelope remembered that he offered her rides on his favorite horse.

"Now," Helen whispered, breaking Penelope free of her thoughts. The two cousins started through the hall to the high table, walking with measured, delicate tread, heads held high. Penelope thought she caught a glimpse of a dark red head at a table she passed, but she didn't dare slow or turn to look.

Tyndareos greeted her, announcing to the suitors that he rejoiced to have his brother's youngest daughter safe under his roof once again. Penelope concentrated on her uncle as he invoked blessings on his guests and entreated the gods to keep happy accord among them while under his roof.

Her uncle had aged in five short years. His dark hair had been thick and curly when she left. Now it looked thinner, dusted with gray. His nose, like an eagle's beak, looked sadly oversized in his thinning face. His shoulders didn't bow, but Penelope guessed the effort it took to keep them straight. A throb of pity took her heart for her uncle.

It startled her to silently calculate his age. He was fifteen years older than her father. He had married late because of the unrest in the kingdom when he took the throne of Sparta. Klytemaistra had been born to his first wife, who had died birthing the next child, a boy. Tyndareos had married Leda several years later. She had immediately given him Kastor and Polydeukes. Helen had been a surprise, born eight years later.

He is an old man, Penelope thought, and blinked away tears of pity. Perhaps it was true that Tyndareos feared to bestow Helen on the suitor of his choice.

Kastor and Polydeukes were adventurers, reveling in their youth and strength. They didn't have the experience of leadership to thwart uprisings. They would be no help.

She glanced at her cousins, and beyond them to her brother. Ithios slouched in his chair, gazing out over the crowd of suitors. His hair was a muddy yellow. He looked heavier, older. His eyes shifted restlessly over the crowd, as if he could find nothing, no friend to look at. His tunic had spots of grease and spilled wine, and that reminded her of Aias. They made fit friends, she decided.

That brought her thoughts back to her uncle. He needed a friend. Support, perhaps stronger than an army bristling with spears and swords. Penelope thought of her jewelry, the few pieces of gold and pearls. If she could, she would have sold it to send a servant to consult the prophet Teiresias for an answer. Unfortunately, Teiresias was dead. She wished she could fight off the problem for her uncle as she had fought off Aias.

CHAPTER 4

The slow, stealthy creaking of the door brought Penelope out of a dream of black-haired arms enclosing her and gray eyes that threw lightning to free her. She rubbed her eyes and sat up, smiling as she waited for Helen to creep across the cold stone floor to her bed. Her cousin looked very young in the moonlight, all her golden curls hanging loose to her waist. She wore a short tunic like a bath slave would wear, and had a blanket wrapped around her shoulders for warmth. Though it was late spring, the nights were still cool.

"Tell me all," Helen commanded with a giggle, and climbed into the bed. She perched on the end and crossed her legs.

"Aias thought I was a servant," Penelope began with a shrug. "He offered to help me find the ball if I would give him a kiss. I said I didn't want his help."

"Everyone knows he's here to enjoy Father's hospitality, not to win me, but Father doesn't dare send him away because of his friends. His two purposes in life are to win all the strength contests and kiss every pretty servant girl. Most are more than willing. Your refusal must have been a shock."

"He seemed to think I was unusually modest and said he would ask the king for me." Penelope tugged the blanket up to her shoulders against the night chill. She would have to grow used to sleeping naked again. In the northlands around Alybas, even the summer nights were too cool for that.

"So you fought him. Did you mark him?"

"Scratches, and I hit his face a few times. Grandfather taught me how to box like a boy."

"Oh, Penelope, Aias still likely doesn't know what happened!" Helen wrapped her arms around herself, shuddering with soft laughter. "You said someone rescued you?"

"Prince Odysseus. He came down on Aias like a bolt of lightning and threw him against a tree like he weighed nothing."

"He is not a tall man, and against Aias' bulk..." Helen grew somber. "He must have been furious."

"I know." A delighted shiver took her. Penelope remembered those gray eyes and the memory warmed her.

"I don't understand. Why did he think you were a servant?"

"I met them both at Pylos, when I went back to the ship to get a doll my father made." Penelope felt no shame in confessing her errand. She knew Helen would understand.

"Let me guess. Aias teased you for holding a doll."

"I told him it was a keepsake for my mistress. Odysseus distracted him and helped me escape."

"It might have been better if you had been truthful. Yet you came to no harm. You were lucky Odysseus was there. He has a reputation as one who treats everyone better than their station." Helen frowned a little. "I've also heard Odysseus prefers a fanciful story to the truth. But my brothers say you could never find a more loyal friend." She shrugged. "Sometimes, I watch the games. Odysseus wins against men taller and more visibly sure to win. He has cunning. He saves his strength and makes his opponents waste theirs."

"He was kind to me. And he was so furious with Aias."

"Penelope, guard your heart." Her cousin reached to take hold of her hand. "Don't consider a man as anything but a friend until you are in your bridal bed with him. Then it is safe to give your heart."

"Helen—" Penelope didn't know whether to laugh or be angry that her cousin would suggest such a thing. She did not want to marry anyone at all.

"I speak from experience. I don't want you hurt." Helen stared at the patterns on the blankets cast by shadows and moonlight. "When Theseus kidnapped me, I was a fool and thought it a great adventure. He took tender care of me. He was a hero, and I easily gave him my heart."

Penelope squeezed her cousin's hands, offering support for what she sensed would come.

"I was a child, enchanted that a hero wanted me. Wanted me so much he would steal me. I enjoyed lying with him. When you give your heart, a man's bed is a wonderful place."

"And?" Penelope prompted, her voice softer than a whisper, when Helen grew silent for many long moments.

"Then he went off with his friend, who also wanted a daughter of Zeus as a bride. When they vanished, he left me carrying his child. Then stories of shameful exploits came trickling in, past the watchful servants. I learned he wasn't the man I thought him. I wanted to come home."

"What of the child?"

"A boy. Dead from an early birth." Helen shook her head and sighed. "When I recovered my strength, I learned to escape my guards and send messages home through traders. My brothers came charging in with their swords flashing and there was no one to kill. They were disappointed, even though I was safe." Two tears trickled down in the moonlight. "So I warn you not to give your heart until you are wed. The dreams of a girl are illusions. I can trust my father to give me to an honorable man who will take care of me, who won't fill my head with lies and dreams. I will love him and care for his house and give him children. But I won't be as happy as I could have been, if I had not already given my heart."

"Sometimes your heart is taken," Penelope murmured. She thought of the sparks in Odysseus' gray eyes when he smiled at her. She acknowledged the wisdom of Helen's words and something inside her cried for her cousin.

"Sometimes," her cousin acknowledged. "We must resist the treachery of Aphrodite. She bestows women's hearts like prizes to the men who please her, with no thought about the hurt she brings. I still dream of a great love, a hero who will risk everything for me. My reality is the princes of Achaia feasting in my father's house, pressing him to choose a husband for me. I confess I am disappointed."

"Don't be." Penelope tried to laugh. "Listen to your own advice, Helen. It's very wise. Wait, and trust your father."

"I try." She shivered, wrapping the blanket closer around her shoulders.

"Do you want to stay here?" Penelope offered. "Like you used to when we were children?"

"Rather than risk Alkippe's wrath, if she catches me sneaking back into my room? Yes, thank you." Helen managed a weak chuckle. She crawled up the length of the bed and slid under the covers. The two cousins held each other for comfort in the stillness of the cool night.

*   *   *

"Hail the new warrior!" Kastor called from the doorway as Penelope and Helen walked from the palace to the river the next morning. He laughed at their startled expressions. "Is the tale of your battle with mighty Aias exaggerated?" he continued, and stepped out to join them.

Polydeukes and Ithios followed him from the shadows. Penelope studied her brother. She couldn't read his face. His eyes always held a spark that could be scornful laughter or mischief. She distrusted Ithios, no matter what he said or did.

"There was no battle," Helen said. She took a step forward, putting herself between Penelope and the men.

"Not according to Aias' words and the marks on his face," Polydeukes retorted. He bowed to Penelope, grinning in that way he had which made her feel important and beautiful, even as a clumsy, scrawny child. "He didn't want to talk about it at first. Especially with Odysseus sitting next to him, silent and smiling. Then he warmed to the tale. Some of the suitors say you are an Amazon, switched at birth with the daughter of Ikarios."

"I always held my sister was not mine," Ithios put in, his voice soft, the slightest smile on his lips.

"He's angry because Aias wouldn't hunt with him today," Kastor explained, giving him a disgusted look. "Whatever the tales, welcome home, little cousin."

"Not so little any longer," Helen said. "Look at her. She could take any of my suitors she wants. And I'm glad!"

"Helen the generous." He bowed to his sister. "Always willing to share the things she doesn't want."

"Oh, don't be cruel on such a beautiful morning!" She slipped one arm around Kastor's waist, then reached out for Polydeukes' hand. "Come to the river with us. You do have time to tell us news, don't you?" She led them down the path.

"She wants to know which suitors have given up now, and which prince has joined the hopeful ranks," Ithios said. He stood next to Penelope, towering over her. Helen and her brothers were already many steps away. Penelope looked up at him, remembering slaps and pinches from childhood. She remembered how she had fought Aias and her fear

39

melted away.

"Ithios, wouldn't you like to be so desirable?" Without waiting for a reply, Penelope set off after the other three.

"Be careful, Penelope." Only a few strides of his long legs let him catch up with her. "You have come to the attention of the suitors. You could very well steal some from Helen."

"I doubt that would be possible."

"Aias finds you desirable." He laughed when Penelope halted for a fraction of a second.

"If our uncle has heard the true tale of what happened, Aias would not be allowed to make his suit."

"Perhaps. But my word does carry some weight before the king. You are my sister. Aias is my friend. I could speak for him, when he asks the king."

"Do not trouble yourself." Penelope felt some tightness in her chest fade as they reached the river clearing.

"No trouble. I would enjoy giving you the husband of your choice." His grin turned nasty. "Although, the first time he spreads your legs, he might kill you in his passion. Aias is more beast than man." They emerged from the trees as he spoke.

"Stop there, cousin." Kastor stepped in front of Ithios, making him stop quickly enough to rock back on his heels. He planted his fists into his hips and glared. "Anyone can see such words hurt Penelope. You should be kinder to your own sister."

"And I forbid you to talk to Penelope unless one of us is nearby," Polydeukes added. "You tormented her when we were children. You will not continue."

"Well, little sister, you have mighty champions." Ithios tried to stare down Kastor, but soon had to look away. "I have duties this morning." He left without waiting for a reply.

"Be warned, Penelope," Kastor said. He rested a hand on her shoulder, his touch warm and comforting. "Don't let Ithios find you alone. His reputation falls in the servants' gossip."

"Has it risen?" she asked, her tone sharp with old, remembered hurt. Her brother had always delighted in tormenting those smaller and weaker than himself, while their cousins had always been the champions.

"She does have a point." Polydeukes kissed her forehead. "We are very glad to have our pretty little cousin home."

*   *   *

Penelope stood in the shadows of the doorway, watching as a suitor packed his chariot to leave. This was the fifth man to give up his suit and leave in less than ten days. Suitors gave up daily, and word had come that another young nobleman would arrive in the evening to join the ranks of the hopeful.

"It is a pity more do not see wisdom and give up," Alkippe said, joining Penelope. "Our master already speaks of preparing for winter housing for his many guests."

"The king doesn't plan on choosing a husband for Helen, then." Penelope nodded, thinking over Eurynome's words that first morning back in Sparta.

"Choosing is the easy part." The servant girl leaned against the frame of the door, her eyes on the handsome, bare-chested manservant loading his master's chariot. "There are some princes we servants would be glad never to see again. And others we would give our lives to make happy."

Penelope nodded, choosing to avoid awkward questions. She refused to admit she had come in the hopes of seeing Aias leaving. Her brother's threat sometimes echoed in her sleep, waking her in a cold sweat.

"So many have left, and the summer barely on us," Alkippe continued. "Only one has come back."

"Prince Odysseus?"

"Gossip says King Nestor talked him into returning and trying again. Everyone knows the king favors him and has already spoken with our master on his behalf."

"King Nestor favors Odysseus." Penelope smiled, glad of that bit of news.

"He insisted on loaning Odysseus his chariot when he landed in Pylos. Any other island prince, having so little experience with horses, it would have been a disaster." The servant girl shook her head, a smile twisting her lips. "Many of us wish Lord Odysseus and Ithaka were very rich, and very near. He would have Helen for wife tomorrow, if that were so."

"I heard all the servants favored him."

"Not all, but enough." Alkippe watched the suitor and his servants leave the courtyard. Her smile faded a little.

"What is it like to share a man's bed?" Penelope whispered. She felt her face warm as Alkippe stared at her, open-mouthed. Then the older girl started to laugh.

"It's true, then, and not bragging from your nurse. You truly can see things other noble ladies miss."

"I won't tell Helen, if that's what you fear."

"Thank you, Lady Penelope. Though I doubt my mistress would be angry." Alkippe shrugged. She stepped out into the courtyard, watching the departing men. Her longing showed clearly on her face. "Lying with a man is more pleasant than sleeping alone. Sometimes."

*   *   *

"Tell me, if you can," Odysseus said, standing. An expectant hush fell in ripples over the crowd of suitors spread over the plain. The only sounds were soft sighs of the night wind through the grass, and the occasional crackle of flames in the torches scattered through the gathering.

Contests of skill had ranged up and down the flat grassland since mid-afternoon. As dusk fell, the men rested by listening to the bards, singing, feasting, and telling riddles.

In her seat under the canopy with the other women, Penelope sat forward eagerly in her chair. She had heard others speak of Odysseus and his riddles, but this was the first chance she had to hear one. Others had tried to repeat some to her, but they forgot words. She felt the delivery failed from lacking Odysseus' rich, deep voice.

Next to her, Helen reached over and touched her hand with her fingertips in warning. Penelope sat back and composed her face into less eager lines, but she still listened with every particle of her being. Riddles and games of twisted words had been some of the few winter entertainments in Alybas. She wanted to test her mind against the princes of Achaia.

"It is a kingdom that touches every land, yet never marks borders. It advances constantly, yet not invading. Retreats, yet not through cowardice. It runs swiftly, but with no feet. Babbles like a doddering fool or a drunkard, but has no mouth to speak." Odysseus turned slowly, to see all the suitors sitting on the ground or standing at the fringes of the crowd around him. His gaze met Penelope's, and she thought he lingered for a moment before going on.

Some bolder suitors shouted answers immediately. Penelope listened and shook her head in scorn. How could they miss such an obvious answer? She looked at Helen, and her cousin wore a puzzled expression. Kastor and Polydeukes were the hosts that evening in their father's place. They smiled at their guests and didn't try to answer.

Ithios crossed his arms over his chest and scowled. Penelope was sure he had no idea of the answer.

Odysseus laughed, shaking his head at the answers that trickled away to nothing. Sometimes he called back a mocking response, reminding them of parts of the riddle the answer contradicted. Penelope laughed and covered her mouth to keep from shouting out the answer.

"Will the royal daughters join the game?" Odysseus asked, stepping closer to the canopy. He swept a grand bow to the cousins and their maids. His face glowed with laughter and life.

"Not I." Helen joined in with her musical laughter. "I tried once to match my wits against yours in riddles, and I will not humiliate myself again."

"And lovely Penelope?" His voice took on a husky richness that made a warmth stir in her belly. Penelope hoped no one else noticed the difference in his voice, and that her face showed none of her reaction. "There is no shame in being wrong." His grin widened again. "The greatest princes in Achaia cannot guess, after all."

"Water," Penelope said, before she lost her nerve. "Rivers and oceans touch all lands. It runs swiftly, it babbles, the tides retreat and advance."

Penelope bit her tongue to keep from saying more. She held her breath, waiting. Delight shone in Odysseus' eyes, but she still couldn't be sure. Then he bowed to her, conceding her win, and a roar of approval and more laughter rose from the men gathered all around.

"We all confess your cunning mind, Odysseus of Ithaka," a man called out of the darkness, as the uproar died. "There is no one who can match you there. Why do you stay away from the games on horseback?"

"There is a difference between reckless courage and the death-wish of a fool," Odysseus called back, stepping away from the canopy. He came face to face with his questioner, both of them lost in the deepening shadows.

"That one was born on horseback," Helen murmured, leaning closer to Penelope. "Or so he claims. Kastor says, when he is in his wine he claims his father was a centaur."

Penelope smothered a giggle behind her hand. She knew why the unseen man taunted Odysseus. After two weeks of asking questions, stealing glimpses of the suitors at their games, listening against orders at doors, she knew how the suitors stood against each other. Odysseus excelled at the games, at the riddles, the discussions of wars and strategy. Few men bested him, yet somehow he kept the respect of all. Eurynome blamed his cunning mind, always searching for an advantage. Helen's brothers said it was his gracious way of speaking with everyone. Ithios refused to speak of Odysseus unless he could find something to complain about. Penelope found that significant in itself. Some servants, those who felt comfortable enough to talk openly with her, said Odysseus was favored by Athena, who gifted him with her wisdom and would let no man harm him.

"You sit a horse well enough," the other suitor said, his voice rising through the soft murmur of male voices.

The deepening of night softened every sound on the plain around them. Servants lit more torches. Others gathered up food and extra clothes, the spears, bows and arrows and stone weights used in the games.

"Sit, yes." Odysseus' voice held a touch of laughter. Penelope thought she sensed stiffness behind the genial sound. "I can control the chariot horses well enough to go to Pylos to check on my ship, or sit astride securely enough to tour the countryside with the king's sons. The mad gallop you favor is another thing altogether."

They walked among the other men as they talked. Penelope caught a glimpse of the features of the other man as they passed between two torches, approaching the canopy. A light, short beard, body whipcord thin, his hands massive, his legs well-muscled. A rider, if she judged physical features and a man's carriage well enough. It would have been recklessness for any island man to challenge the skills of one born to horses and the plains. She agreed with Odysseus, strangely glad he knew his limits and didn't fear to admit them.

"I've seen you moving about your ship as if you had wings," the rider accused, laughing. "The same balance and control you need for sailing, you use for riding."

"I have only learned to ride since coming here to Sparta. I would be a fool to chance my new skills against experienced men. Not even to win the acclaim of lovely maidens." Odysseus paused, barely enough to be noticeable, and met Penelope's gaze.

*   *   *

Penelope saw the shadow on the courtyard paving and looked up in time to see the owl sweep over her head. She felt a chill run up her back and wondered what the omen meant. It was early morning, late for an owl to be about. Then she heard the clatter of hooves on the paving of the courtyard, racing toward her. She stepped back from the archway to avoid being trampled. Among the dust and blurred movement, she glimpsed six horses and riders, speeding away from the palace. She moved to the gates and watched them vanish in a cloud of dust. As she resumed her errand, fetching a new skein of thread for Helen, she pieced together the features she had glimpsed as the riders sped past.

Kastor and Polydeukes, of course. Where one was, the other followed, as if they were one person and not two. She knew she had seen Kastor, so his twin was the second of the six riders. She shivered, remembering whispered tales that the twins only shared one spirit between them, and if one died, so would the other. That rumor, however, didn't bother her as much as the stories that Polydeukes was also a child of Zeus.

Golden hair, a curly beard, and a blue-black cape lined with gold could only mean Menelaos. He was a good friend of the twins, according to Helen.

Penelope smiled at the thought of Menelaos. Despite her advice, Helen had given her heart to the younger brother of the king of Mycenae, or was on the verge. She talked of Menelaos constantly, except when he accompanied Kastor and Polydeukes to visit their sister.

It was almost a given that Menelaos accompanied the twins. Penelope puzzled through the features of the fourth and fifth riders but couldn't recognize their faces. She knew Ithios was not among them, and wondered if her brother had fallen from favor with their cousins yet again, or had only declined the adventure. All the men wore helmets and fire-hardened vests of leather instead of bronze armor. Round leather and bone shields had swung from their elbows. Boar hunting, perhaps? A dangerous boar bothered the neighboring villages.

It would make an interesting story and a mystery to pursue. Penelope continued going from the palace to the river clearing. Helen and the others would want to hear of this, she knew.

Penelope stopped as she entered the shade of the ring of trees. The skein of thread dropped from her hands as the features of the sixth rider came clear in her mind, like the reflection in a pool suddenly still. Red hair showed under the boars tusk helmet. The blue luck markings on the shield suddenly made sense, as she looked at them sideways in her memory. Odysseus was the sixth man. They were armed and riding away as if the Furies chased them, she thought now. Not a boar hunt, but something more important.

Penelope picked up the skein and moved on. The thread was blue, made from an expensive dye that came from Ilion, at the Straits of Dardanelles. She didn't notice the dust and specks of forest rubbish sticking to the skein. What, she wondered, had happened to send the six men racing away, armed as if for battle? She had seen other groups ride off for boar hunting. They always rode at a lazy pace, smiling. None of the six men who nearly ran her down had smiled.

A fragment of a dream came back to her. *Polydeukes shouted to the sky, tears in his eyes. And rage. Blood on the ground. A shout of treachery, that echoed in her bones even now.* Penelope shivered, then felt her face burn. She had seen Odysseus instead of Kastor, and had felt fear for him. That was ridiculous. Penelope told herself to care for no man. She didn't want to marry anyone, after all.

When she reached Helen, she found King Tyndareos had joined the group at the river's edge. Penelope slowed her pace more, though curiosity pushed her to keep moving, to hear what had happened. An inner feeling, fragments of more dreams, told her she did not want to know.

The night before, her uncle hadn't joined the feasting on the plains because a messenger had arrived with urgent news. Penelope silently scolded herself for not realizing something grave kept her uncle from his guests and the games he loved. Perhaps it was the same matter that sent her cousins, Odysseus, and Menelaos rushing away.

"I saw my cousins riding off with shields and spears," she said, when she joined Helen and Tyndareos. "Is there trouble?"

"Has anyone told you of the twin brides I had found for my sons?" the king began, watching Penelope carefully as he spoke. She fought a chill of apprehension and shook her head that no, she had not heard. "They were to come to Sparta before the end of summer. We had planned a grand wedding feast for them. And hopefully for Helen, as well." He paused, as if searching for the right words. Penelope wondered if he thought he would frighten her by mentioning her own future marriage.

"The girls' father has reneged on the agreement?" she guessed.

"That sort of trouble, we could handle," Helen said. She tried to smile, and reached for the thread Penelope carried.

"The girls had other suitors, another set of brothers," the king said after another pause. "They stole my sons' brides and have gone into hiding in Arkadia."

"And Kastor and Polydeukes have rushed off to rescue their

46

brides." Penelope nodded, understanding now. A shiver caught at her body. "I saw Menelaos and Odysseus riding with them, and two others. They are that sure of success, to take so few?"

"I sent a troop of my soldiers ahead of them last night. Seleron and Teris have volunteered to help, though I didn't think them such good friends to my sons as Odysseus and Menelaos." The king looked down at his feet a moment, his eyes hooded and full of worry. "The omens are not good for this."

"Come, Uncle." Penelope took hold of his hand, like she had done when she was a tiny child and didn't know he was a king. "We will go to the temple of Hermes, and to Apollo, and offer sacrifices and prayers for them."

"Yes, Father." Helen smiled, relief wiping away the worry that made her pale. She slipped her arm through his. "We will go and pray. It is well for us Penelope is so sensible." Her eyes were full of silent thanks.

*   *   *

That night Penelope dreamed, and knew she had dreamed that dream before. *She saw battle. She saw men leaping out from hiding. She saw blood and her cousins' faces twisted in anger and hatred. They shouted, but she couldn't hear their war cries. Their swords clashed against other swords, but there was only the silence of her dream to deafen her.*

She woke in tears and huddled shivering under her blankets. Penelope gritted her teeth, hating the feeling of being defenseless and helpless.

Her feet hit the cold tile of the floor and she reached the trunk her grandfather made before she knew what she intended. Her old hunting tunic was there, and the knife Dymis gave her. Penelope put them on and braided her hair tight against her head. She fashioned a cap out of a scrap of cloth, like herder boys wore against the dust of the day, to cover her hair. Heart pounding, she slipped out her open window and into the garden.

Moonlight turned the familiar, sheltered paths into a strange forest where deadly beasts and unfriendly nymphs and satyrs waited to pounce. Penelope gripped the knife tight in her fist and kept her mouth closed. Her breath whistled through her nose. She hated how her heart thudded at every new sound and worked to keep her pace slow and steady. She darted into the shelter of a tall bush when a movement startled her. It was only an owl flying low over the garden. Penelope wondered why the creature had not called out at her clumsy, furtive movements.

In the middle of the women's garden, she found the pool, deep black and glowing silver in the moonlight and shadows. Penelope knelt by the water and pricked her thumb with the blade of the knife.

"Goddess, please hear me. Athena, please, bring safety to my cousins. And to their companions. I fear death and betrayal," she whispered, while letting ten drops of blood fall into the dirt next to the water. At the tenth drop, Penelope plunged her hand into the pool. She waited until the cold began to numb her hand, then got up and left without looking back. She didn't dare look back, even for a sign that her prayer had been heard, the offering accepted.

CHAPTER 5

Penelope darted into the shadows of a tall, spreading bush and winced as branches dug into her back and arms. To avoid her brother, she would welcome blood and pain. Ithios approached with two men whom Penelope hoped were no suitors for Helen—threadbare clothes, scraggly beards, untrimmed hair, no ornaments of any kind. No noble or prince of Achaia would fall into such a state.

"We are all lucky Menelaos is not king of Mycenae," Ithios said. His voice sounded blurred with wine, and it was barely past noon. Penelope knew more than luck let her hear the three men before they saw her; someone protected her. "Odysseus is constantly at his elbow, telling him what to do, what to say, what to think. He would only be a toy king, and Odysseus would rule Mycenae."

"Some would find his rule better than Agamemnon's," the cleaner of his two companions offered. He dodged when Ithios swung on him, and laughed.

Penelope held her breath as the three paused. If they turned, they would see her. If either stranger attacked her, she couldn't depend on her brother for protection. He might encourage them.

"Even his friends cannot trust Odysseus. Who knows what he will do next?" Ithios hunched his shoulders, glancing around as if Odysseus would appear. "I thought we were rid of him when Aias took him to Pylos and his ridiculous ship. Whatever brought him back, it will profit him and hurt us."

"He's gone for now, and he took Helen's brothers. No one to guard her," the third man said. His voice was rough, as if made of stones. He grinned, making a suggestive swing with his hip. The other two burst out laughing.

"We're wasting a beautiful day," Ithios said. "We should spend it by the river, watching the maidens bathe."

The second man laughed, tugged a wine skin from inside his tunic and tossed it to the third. They moved down the path, spilling wine and coarse laughter as they went.

Penelope waited until their voices faded away before she left her hiding place. She looked up at the hot sun and grimaced. The women were to spend the day at the river. She had to warn Helen, to post some guards. The idea of Ithios' friends seeing her naked made Penelope feel ill.

*   *   *

The next night, and the night after, Penelope wore her boy disguise and slipped outside to explore. She couldn't lie still long enough to fall asleep.

She regained the excitement of hunting and roaming during her nighttime wandering. Penelope planned during the day where she wanted to go at night. She studied the halls and listened to the servants talking, learning who would be on duty, what passages and doors would be without guard or torch. She wandered without light sometimes, trusting to her hands and feet and ears. Her longing to run away to a life of adventure and freedom returned. Did she dare try it?

The third night, she went to the stables, wondering if she dared try to ride an older horse. There were always rumors of Amazons coming through to trade, to seek new fathers for their children, to sell weapons or buy. If she could learn to ride, perhaps she could steal a horse and reach an Amazon emissary before her uncle's men caught her.

She slipped into the stables, disconcerted to see a torch burning in a stand in the aisle between the stalls. Penelope thought the horses would need dark and quiet to rest. She slowed her steps and rested her hand on the knife at her belt. She considered the idea of someone else trying to steal her uncle's horses, then rejected it. Thieves didn't use torches any more than girls who wandered the night when they belonged in bed.

A low moan startled her. Penelope stopped, ready to turn and flee. A throaty chuckle followed, broken by a gasp and more moans. Straw rustled in a stall. Curiosity drove away her caution and Penelope crept into the next stall, pressing on the top board to lift herself up and see over.

Melantho lay under Aias, eyes closed, limbs spread, hands digging into the straw. Both were naked. Penelope watched his hips lift and fall several times before she realized what Aias did to Melantho. She thought he was in pain, his eyes clenched tight shut, until she saw his crooked smile. More low, throaty chuckles escaped the man, then his whole body shuddered. He stretched out on top of Melantho, wrapped his arms around her and pressed his face between her breasts. She brought her arms and legs up around him.

Penelope slipped out as quietly as she came. A queasy sensation began in the pit of her stomach. Helen had said if the heart was given, a man's bed was pleasurable, yet Penelope doubted Melantho found any pleasure in lying with Aias. There was something hard in her expression, satisfaction perhaps, but more like triumph. Penelope shuddered at the memory. Why did her maid let the man take his pleasure with her if she didn't enjoy it? King Tyndareos would have supported Penelope, if her maid begged protection from a man she didn't want.

*   *   *

The question still bothered her the next morning and Helen teased her for being preoccupied. Penelope searched for Melantho among the sewing women, and found her in a corner with some year-mates. Melantho wore a necklace of tiny, dull blue stones. It was new, likely a gift from Aias.

"Penelope, whatever is wrong with you this morning?" Helen exclaimed, breaking the younger girl from her thoughts. Penelope looked up, startled, realizing her cousin had addressed her several times without an answer.

"Questions," she admitted, keeping her voice low. Seeing Helen showed only concern, not mockery, Penelope dared to continue. "I saw Melantho with a man last night. She didn't seem to enjoy it. I wonder why she went to him."

"That is the way of it sometimes." She shrugged and bent back to her sewing. "The beginning of your moon flow, problems during the day. Men always find pleasure, even if they were arguing with their friends ten minutes before."

"That doesn't seem right." Penelope shook her head. Her thoughts were more on Melantho than what Helen said. Something was always wrong where Melantho was concerned. "We must lie with our husbands even when it hurts us?"

Helen laughed, drawing the attention of a few of her maids. "I know what bothers you. Have some suitors been whispering sweet words to you?" She sketched a salute to Penelope. "Dear cousin, you are welcome to all of them!"

"That's not what worries me," she retorted, feeling her face grow hot. Penelope glanced at the three maids near them, all older than Helen, all married. "It isn't right that our bodies belong to our husbands, and we have no choice in lying with them. The old ways are better."

A muffled gasp met her words. Penelope looked up quickly, searching the faces of the others. She thought she saw understanding in their eyes, despite their neutral faces. Something warmed in her, comfort that even in Sparta, some still held to the teachings of the one Goddess, even if in secret.

*   *   *

"Lady Penelope?" The voice that came from the shadows startled her, though it was soft and hesitant.

"What do you wish?" She paused and glanced up and down the darkened hallway. Penelope heard the muted voices of the women close by. She knew she could call and help would come.

"Merely to talk with you. Some say you are more closely guarded than Helen." The speaker stepped from the shadows. He shrugged, smiling, and looked down at his feet. His hands plucked nervously at the edge of his tunic.

Penelope thought he was maybe twenty-two, as golden and perfect in coloring and features as Helen. Richly dressed. Youthfully slim, not a warrior. She didn't recognize his face. He was a newcomer or very minor noble who sat in the shadows in the feasting hall.

"Shall I take a message to Helen?" Penelope considered telling this nervous young man to save his pride and time, and go home. She doubted he had made a good impression when he stood before Tyndareos.

"Oh, no—you are the one—" His face flushed red and he gulped audibly. "Will you take a token from me?" He dug into the pouch at his belt and brought out a tiny pin set with a round piece of rosy, clear stone. As he held it out, he looked her in the eyes for the first time.

His eyes were gray, staring wide and wary. Penelope felt years older than him, and pitied him.

I could never marry a man who can't look me in the eyes. Her thoughts turned to Odysseus, the myriad expressions in his gray eyes. Laughter. Rage. Confidence. She compared his wide shoulders, the scars on his arms and legs, the strength in his sleek muscles, against this stripling with only a dusting of beard on his chin.

"My uncle the king would not approve," she said, turning away. She knew if she saw disappointment or relief on his face, she would grow angry.

"He will listen to you."

"Why should he?" She turned back in curiosity. "My uncle hardly knows I am alive."

"But we thought—you flee—the king must find you a husband quickly," he stammered, his face bright red.

"Someday my uncle will find me a husband, yes, but there is no hurry. Who do I flee?"

"A man in Alybas tried to kidnap you. Someone who thought you were Helen, and would rule Sparta through you."

"No one cared who I was in Alybas. I had no suitors." Pity touched her for the young man's embarrassment. "Who told you such things?"

"Rumors." His voice dropped to a whisper. "The man has vowed death to whoever claims you as bride. The king will only give you to a strong prince who could protect you." He backed up a step, his whole body quivering. Penelope thought if she made one wrong move, he would flee. "You killed a man, defending yourself."

"I merely scratched Aias." Penelope swallowed hard to keep from laughing. Such wild stories told about her. Who would have said such things, and why?

"Please, Lady Penelope?" He held out the pin again.

"I thank you, truly, but it would not be fair to you." She bit her lip to keep from smiling. No matter the rumors, she would use them. If stories of danger kept suitors away, all the better.

"Yes, you are...right." He paled and backed away.

"Helen waits for me." She gestured down the hall to the women's chamber.

His eyes widened, his throat constricting as if he would choke. Penelope hurried away, refusing to look back. She knew she would see him wipe his face in relief. She wondered if her half-hearted suitor would add to the tales and discourage others. She prayed to the Goddess that it would be so.

*   *   *

Penelope grew tired of Helen asking every hour if anyone had heard news of Kastor and Polydeukes, so she posted a watcher at the palace gates for news. Melantho was on duty when the war party returned. She came running, out of breath, face bright, eyes shining. Her clothes were in disarray too much to blame on running. When Penelope saw Aias waiting by the gate as she and Helen hurried past, she knew the reason.

They reached the stables as the returning warriors dismounted. Almost all had bandaged arms, legs, or heads. Penelope cried out in dismay as she realized she didn't see her cousins. Both Menelaos and Odysseus turned at the sound of her voice. They supported each other when both were on the ground, like two crooked old women. Penelope couldn't look away from the dark stains on their bandages.

"Where are they?" Helen demanded. Her voice grew tight and rose several steps. "Where are my brothers?"

"Gone," Menelaos answered, when neither the other two suitors nor any soldiers spoke up in answer.

"You couldn't bring them home for their funeral rites?" She grasped his shoulder, shaking him until he grimaced in pain.

"Helen." Penelope stopped her with a hand on her shoulder. "Come away. They're injured. Let them rest."

"No!" Helen turned to Odysseus, reaching out to grab his arms next. The man closed his eyes and turned away. Penelope saw the pain in them before he did so.

"You won't help matters any. Come away. They must report to the king, first." She tugged harder on her cousin's arm, leading her for a few steps. She felt ill and bitterly amused by the relief of all the men.

"What has happened?" King Tyndareos demanded, striding into the stables. Everyone and everything quieted around him. He strode through the gathering crowd of soldiers and servants. He read something in the eyes of Odysseus and Menelaos and all color fled his face. "Helen, Penelope—go to your rooms. This business is not fitting for you."

"Father—" Helen blurted, reaching out to him.

"Go!" The king shuddered at the harshness of his voice. He turned his face from his daughter.

Penelope linked her arm through Helen's and led her cousin from the stables. Silently, they leaned on each other all the way back to the women's room. The sunshine lost its golden beauty and warmth. The shadows looked thicker, darker, colder.

Helen tottered from the doorway to the window. She curled up in the wide window seat like a child, hugging her knees against her chest, and stared unseeing out into the gardens. Penelope sat at her loom, determined to do something, anything, to control her thoughts.

Though the shadows crawled across the floor and time dragged by, she accomplished nothing. The thread sat untouched on the table next to her when Lystia came in.

"The king summons you to tend the princes' wounds," the housekeeper announced. Penelope stared, unable to understand the words. She looked over at Helen, who slowly raised her head.

"Where are my brothers?" the girl whispered, a few heavy tears glistening unshed on her lashes.

"The gods alone know. But come, my sweet ladies." Lystia's voice hovered on the edge of breaking. "Come tend to the princes and show them you are grateful for their help." Her smile was gentle and sad. She beckoned from the doorway. Like walkers in a dream, the cousins followed her.

*   *   *

Penelope was glad her grandfather had taught her to tend wounds. The smell of sweat and blood and pain, mixed with strong wine for cleansing and herbs for healing, did not turn her stomach. The room where she and Helen tended Odysseus and Menelaos was closed and small, the air thick, bitter with lamp smoke. Sounds echoed from the walls, clashing with her pulse.

Her former patients had been animals hurt in raids and she had learned patience and a strong stomach from them. She wondered if she should be grateful or amused that this time, the injured one didn't bleat and resist when she tended his wound.

Odysseus watched her, silent and unnaturally still as she washed the long, shallow gash on his upper arm. He didn't flinch when she dripped a bitter green herb mixture into the raw flesh to aid in healing. She heard him sigh, felt the brush of his breath against her hair when she rubbed oil into the wound. He relaxed and smiled gently at her when she bound the wound with clean linen.

Helen and Menelaos talked, voices muted, words mumbled, as she tended to his scalp wound. Penelope heard the other prince hiss in pain and Helen's blurted apologies, then the catch in her voice as she fought another sob. Penelope wondered if she could feel anything. She knelt to unwind the dirty, blood-crusted bandage off Odysseus' calf.

"You have tender, deft hands," he said, lifting his leg so she didn't

55

have to bend over so far. "I'm grateful you weren't given to a temple to be a healer."

"You are the first I have tended who has not been a goat or sheep or dog," she admitted, meeting his gaze for the first time. Silent laughter passed between them, then tears touched her eyes. Penelope wished she had kept silent.

"They fought bravely and would have won if not for treachery." Odysseus sat back a little further on the bench and propped his leg up. A spasm rippled through the muscle as the bandage caught, glued to the wound with ichor and blood. He never made a sound.

"Teris and Seleron have no wounds," she said, realizing that truth almost as the words left her mouth.

"I know." A chill like winter touched his voice. Odysseus cleared his throat. "Menelaos could never tell a story properly. If I tell you now, you can give the truth to Helen later?"

"When she is ready to hear." She reached for the bowl of oil, to soak the bandage so it would peel from his wound without causing pain.

"Idas and Lynceaus, the brothers who stole the twin brides, sent messengers saying they would speak truce. Teris and Seleron went with them to negotiate terms. We met at the foot of a cliff where rock falls made treacherous footing and shadows where many men could hide. Menelaos and I spoke against the place when we saw it. Teris assured us of promises of peace and trust. Kastor went first, holding his spear high to signal we had come in peace. An arrow pierced his shoulder before he could lower his arm." Odysseus' voice broke. Penelope glanced up and found his face dark with a burning anger that chilled her.

"Did those brothers escape?" she asked, keeping her voice soft. Through the hurtful pounding of her heart, she heard Helen and Menelaos talking, their voices rough, breaking. She wondered if they said anything at all. She glanced over her shoulder for the comforting presence of Lystia and Eurynome, watching at the door. Her nurse smiled encouragement to her.

"They are dead, their bodies staked out on the rocks of their treachery." His voice held a chilling satisfaction.

"And my cousins' bodies?"

"Gone." His voice held a note of question that frightened her more than his anger. Penelope had thought she would never hear uncertainty in Odysseus' voice. When she looked up, puzzlement furrowed his forehead. "Kastor lay dead at his brother's feet, the sword that killed him still in his chest. Polydeukes bled from more wounds than a man could take and live. The traitor brothers lay dead behind him. Menelaos and I drove away the warriors who attacked from behind. I heard Polydeukes shout to Zeus..." He stopped, his mouth twisting with words he couldn't speak.

"Are you fevered?" Penelope pressed a hand against his forehead. He sweated, but only a light, cool moisture. Odysseus gently moved her hand off his forehead. He held it and she couldn't tug it free. His touch—gentle, yet strong and irresistible—sent a strange trembling through her.

"Thunder roared and there was a light brighter than noonday. We were blinded, deafened. Turned into stone. When I could see again, the king's sons were gone. Not even blood remained on the ground to mark where they had fallen."

Listening to the wordless prompting of her heart, Penelope turned to look at Helen. Was it for her sake the mystery had occurred? Helen was oblivious to everything but Menelaos, listening to him stumble through his own explanations. Penelope knew Helen would spend the night with her, talking and comforting each other and trying to find some explanation to ease the sorrow. She wondered what comfort her uncle found.

*   *   *

Helen came to Penelope's room that night, trembling and distraught as expected. Penelope gave her a sleeping draught, one of many potions her aunt had taught her to make. When Helen lay sleeping soundly, not even a whimper escaping her dreams, Penelope tried in vain to sleep. Her thoughts spun through her mind. Her body longed to run far and fast. Swallowing a groan of frustration that threatened to become a shriek, Penelope slipped out of the bed. She pulled out her boy clothes and cap and bound her hair. The restlessness didn't go away when she slipped over the sill of her window.

Her hand strayed to the hilt of the knife at her waist as she reached the gate out of the women's garden. Penelope smiled bitterly at the moon, thinking thoughts of revenge. Kastor and Polydeukes had disliked Teris and Seleron. She could believe the two men would kill the twins to remove their influence.

For a moment, she thought she heard her aunt's voice. Penelope looked around, catching a movement like wings at the corner of her eye. She saw nothing, but her aunt's words stayed clear in her thoughts.

"The Goddess made women to be the source of life, not death," Penelope whispered as she turned back to the garden. She heard her aunt scold her for contemplating killing. "Men created death through treachery, so it is for men to deal with it." She shook her head, knowing she didn't quite believe her own words, and headed into the public part of the palace garden.

Her feet took her down damp stone paths, lit silver and shadowed black. Penelope let her pace increase until she almost ran with the urgency to flee her fears and pain. A low arch of stone flashed by above her as she ran. Penelope followed the path and let the sound of splashing water draw her. She stopped short on the edge of a tiny pool with a fountain, startled at the turbulence of her emotions as much as the foreign feel of the place. This had to be the king's private garden, because she had never been there before.

Heart thudding in her chest, Penelope knelt on the lip of the stone-lined pool and dipped up water to cool her face. She turned around on her knees, shifting to sit, to put her feet into the cool water. She had stubbed her toes on uneven paving stones, and they burned and ached.

"I'm glad to see others can't sleep this night," Odysseus said, appearing through the arch on the other side of the pool. He chuckled and gestured for her to stay still, when Penelope moved to get to her feet. "I've never seen you around here before, boy. Who do you serve?"

"Serve?" She swallowed hard, unable to believe her luck. Her disguise held. "I serve Lady Penelope."

"How does your mistress take her cousins' deaths?" He settled down on the bench next to the trickling fountain, his movements favoring his bandaged leg.

"She is angry."

"She is right to be angry. The king's sons were good men and skilled warriors." For a moment, despite the shadows, his eyes burned like they had that afternoon.

"There is little protection against a spear thrown by your companions," Penelope said, guessing at his anger.

Odysseys nodded sharply and smiled. A bitter, burning smile. "I wager those two spend a sleepless night watching their doors."

Penelope nodded in her turn, knowing who he meant. She let herself relax and studied Odysseus, silvered by the moonlight, and hoped the shadows hid her features enough.

"What do you think happened to the bodies?" she asked, when the night quiet flowed soothing around them again.

"Taken." He glanced up once at the stars high and softly bright above. "Polydeukes called out to Zeus...rumors say only Kastor was the son of Tyndareos."

"I didn't know." She flinched when Odysseus frowned at her. "I have been in Alybas with my lady for five years."

"I should have realized..." He nodded. "There have been rumors Zeus deceived Leda more than once."

"So when Polydeukes—when the prince called out to him, Zeus was answering his son, not just a prayer for help." Penelope nodded. It made sense. "Then the prince was immortal. That is why he didn't fall from his wounds."

"You listen where no one can see you?"

"My lady told me what you told her, Lord Odysseus," she returned quickly.

"She favors you, then?" He smiled. "Can you tell me which of us she favors as a husband?"

"I don't—" Penelope shrank back a little, hoping the shadows would hide her burning face. "They are suitors for Helen, not for her."

"Your lady is most lovely, boy. What are you called?" Odysseus stood and took a few steps toward her, frowning.

"Dyvis," she blurted, suddenly grateful for her grandfather's madness.

"Well, Dyvis, your mistress is old enough to marry and she is of royal blood. Only a fool thinks Tyndareos brought Penelope back to Sparta merely to keep Helen company. Who do you think your mistress prefers?"

"She does not want to marry."

"The old ways are gone, unfortunately, when a royal daughter could choose."

"Old ways?" Her heart stopped for nearly a breath.

"Surely they still teach the old ways in Alybas?" He sat on the rim of the pool a few paces from her. A muffled groan escaped him.

"Some," she admitted. "A few older women speak of it. Only in whispers. My lady was mocked for listening."

"They were fools to mock her. Do you hold with the old ways, Dyvis?"

For a moment she stared at him, forgetting the false name she had given him. Penelope blushed and looked away, hoping he had not seen her thoughts in her face.

"There is much truth in what the old women say. My lady is from a line of priestesses."

"I know." His voice grew thick with unspoken thoughts.

"What will happen to Sparta, with both princes dead?" she blurted to fight the strange fluttering of her heart.

"The old ways will lead. Helen's husband will be king, taking his power through her. Their child will be heir."

"If Helen has a daughter, the trouble will begin again."

"True." He closed his eyes, tilting his face up at the stars and moon, as if he could feel their light. "On Ithaka, many still follow the old ways, looking to the one Goddess before calling on Zeus and his brothers. I wish my sister lived to be queen, and leave me to explore the world."

"Sailing?" Penelope imagined him standing in the prow of his ship, looking out over sea and unnamed lands ahead.

"For the most part." Odysseus chuckled, glancing at her. "Would you like to be an explorer, Dyvis?"

"I must stay and tend to my lady." She returned his smile. "She is sorely hurt by the news today. Teris and Seleron are traitors, aren't they?"

"I believe so. But Idas and Lynceaus are dead, so there is no proof."

"It's not fair! If I could, I would kill them myself, no matter what might happen to me. Helen—she can't sleep, can't eat. She can hardly see for the tears. I can't—" She stopped with tight dread pulsing through her body. A glance at Odysseus showed him watching her with nothing but interest.

"All the king can do is send them away. Even small, rough Ithaka hasn't been disgraced by my being refused." Odysseus smiled, but it was a coldly triumphant smile.

"It isn't enough. Life for life."

"Dyvis, you are loyal and the gods will bless you for that. But you are only a boy, untrained." He stood up, a flicker of pain on his face. "Go to bed. The hour is late and you need to be strong for your mistress. No matter how brave a face she wears, no matter her strength, she hurts as much as Helen." He gestured back toward the arch she had come through.

There was nothing Penelope could do but obey. When she looked back, he stood by the pond, looking up at the stars.

*   *   *

Tyndareos held court three days later and the results were as Odysseus said. Teris and Seleron were accused, and in turn accused Menelaos and Odysseus of treachery. There was no proof to support either side. Teris and Seleron were sent away, disgraced. Tyndareos announced that the man who married Helen would become his son and rule Sparta.

When Dolios brought Penelope the news, she thanked him in a quiet voice, then went to her room and cried.

CHAPTER 6

"Come to gloat?" Ithios roared, leaping to his feet. The once-quiet clearing echoed the thunder of his voice.

Penelope rocked back on her heels and stared. She had come to the little grove by the river to be alone. Her brother was the last person she expected to see. Usually by this time of the afternoon he was asleep in his rooms, resting for the evening's feasting or games.

"Brother, what—"

"Which of you put him up to it?" He advanced on her, shoulders hunched, hands clenched into fists at his side.

"Put who—"

"I should be the next king of Sparta!"

"Our uncle has the choice and the right."

"He's so in fear of Helen he'd rather steal my right to the throne than anger her. She's no daughter of Zeus. She's a common slut that—"

Penelope slapped him, swinging with the weight of her whole body behind the blow. She had the satisfaction of seeing Ithios stumble, knocked off balance. Then the stinging burst through her hand. She thought she had cracked bones. Ithios stared, his face white where she hit him, then bright red as the blood flowed back into the flesh.

Aias laughed, startling them both. Penelope turned, her mouth dropping open. He stood to one side, leaning against a tree. She turned back to her brother, prickles of fear running up and down her back. What if he made his threats come true?

"I told you she had a strong arm." The black-haired giant's smile faded. "I'll not listen to you speak ill of Helen, either."

"You'd champion her? With no hope of bedding her?" Ithios sneered. He pressed his hand against his sore face, wincing. Anger sparkled in his eyes.

"She is the daughter of Zeus. That is enough for me."

"Then even less reason to give her Sparta! It should be mine. My uncle should have named me his heir the same day he sent Teris and Seleron away."

"You want the throne very much," Penelope said, voice quiet, disturbing thoughts running through her mind.

Ithios tried to smile and winced. "Sister, you have a duty to me. Speak to the king. He will listen to you."

"Why should he listen to me? Why does everyone think the king will listen to me?" she blurted.

"Tell him the throne is mine! I am the last male of our family left alive."

"You should go," Aias said, gesturing back the way Penelope had come. "He's gone mad with jealousy."

"Jealousy?" Ithios roared. "Jealous of what belongs to me?"

"Be careful who hears you say that." Penelope turned to go.

"Don't give me orders!" He raised his hand to hit her, but Aias stopped him with a frown.

"Advice, Ithios," she snapped.

"Why would you give me advice?"

"Teris was your friend?" Penelope waited until he nodded. "Some might accuse you of helping murder our cousins."

Ithios covered the open ground in three lunging steps. Penelope barely had time to draw a breath and duck before he knocked her to the ground. She rolled, trying to remember her grandfather's teaching. She shrieked as Ithios' foot connected with her ribs, then slammed into the side of her head.

Then Aias pulled the writhing, screaming, spitting Ithios off her.

*   *   *

King Tyndareos came to see Penelope, silently watching Helen fuss over her few cuts and her bruised ribs. He left and called Ithios before him. The next morning, Penelope learned her brother had been banished from Sparta until after she married. She nodded, thanked the servant who brought her the news, and went back to her weaving. She trembled, both angry and afraid. Finally, her uncle had acknowledged her impending marriage.

*   *   *

Penelope didn't dare leave her bed and roam for several nights. Helen leaned on her, as if Penelope were the elder and Helen a little child. It startled her to find she could give orders that contradicted Helen's, and the servants would obey. Penelope marveled at the feeling of power, the sense that she was indeed someone of authority in the palace. And the next moment, knew it for a sham. Only among the women did she rule. She devoted herself to comforting Helen and weaving the tapestry she had promised for the bridal night.

Finally, a night came when Helen didn't beg Penelope to stay with her, though she crept to Penelope's room later, when the servants slept. The next night, she didn't leave her bed. On the second night without Helen needing comfort, Penelope put on her boy clothes and slipped out the window to roam again.

She reached the fountain pool in the king's garden before she realized what she intended. What were her chances of meeting Odysseus? Penelope sat in the shadows to hide her bruises, glad the moon waned. She hoped her blush didn't show as bright hot as it felt. Three times she told herself to get up from the edge of the pool and leave, and each time she settled down again.

"Your mistress must be feeling better, if you are out walking tonight," Odysseus said when he appeared. He nodded to her and sat on the bench, with a spear's length between them. Penelope was grateful. "Did her brother hurt her badly?"

"Only a few bruises. She is...willing to pay that price, to keep him from tormenting her."

"Tormenting her how?" His voice threatened to crack, sending a streak of warmth through her.

"He threatened to give her to a husband she loathed...among other things." She shrugged, trying to appear not to care.

"Have no fear for your mistress. There are many who will guard her, if she asks." Odysseus laughed when she gaped at him. "Lady Penelope is much admired. Didn't you know?"

"No one will tell me what happens anywhere." She flinched at the frustration heavy in her voice. "I hoped you could."

"What is there to tell?" He shrugged, and she was pleased to see no stiffness in his movements. His wounds had fully healed. "Most suitors have gone away, to leave the king to mourn in peace. Many will stay away, with no harm to their pride."

"Some have not gone."

"No. Some, he asked to stay."

"Then he favors you for Helen?"

"I doubt that, Dyvis." Odysseus shook his head, grinning at her. He looked at the moon and stretched his arms as if he would reach up and touch the sky. He arched his back, stretching his tunic tight over his sleekly muscled torso, and strangely, her mouth went dry. "No, I am here because the king favors Menelaos and I am Menelaos' oath friend. Nothing more than that."

"You think Ithaka has no chance of making Helen its queen?" Penelope turned to face him.

"Menelaos is prince of Mycenae. Sparta needs good allies."

"Then war is coming?"

"With change comes turmoil. People fight to take what doesn't belong to them, or what others have wrongfully taken from them. Would you like to go to war, Dyvis?" His grin dimmed.

"I can use a spear for hunting, and a sling. Little else," she admitted. "I wanted to learn to use a bow, but Grandfather said I didn't have the strength in my shoulders."

"You do look thin." His eyes sparkled as he looked her over. Penelope tried not to flinch; if he could see her bruises, he would penetrate her disguise. "I would teach you, if you could escape your mistress each afternoon."

"Oh, I...thank you, Lord Odysseus, but I can't." Penelope thought she would be sick, her elation turned cold in a heartbeat. "My mistress needs me all day."

"You're a good lad, Dyvis. The gods bless you for your loyalty. Is Penelope better? I heard Helen still mourns and her cousin is her strength."

"She tries," she said in a near-whisper. Penelope felt her throat constrict with a hundred questions she wanted to ask and couldn't without arousing suspicions. She stood instead. "I should return to her, if she needs me. Thank you for answering."

"I often walk at night, thinking of Ithaka. You're welcome to join me with more questions."

Penelope could only nod her thanks. She hurried to the arch, pausing there with a new thought. She looked back and he still sat on the bench, watching her.

"Will you tell me about Ithaka, next time?" Her voice caught in her throat when Odysseus turned to look at her. Hunger burned on his face. "I like to learn about new places," she said, the words dragged from her, using them as a shield against feelings she couldn't understand.

"I would enjoy that. Go to bed." He watched her as she ran.

Safely back in her room and bed, Penelope shivered. She knew the expression on his face. He longed for Ithaka as she longed for Alybas and Bachan.

*   *   *

The days of mourning dragged, though Penelope welcomed the quiet. She and Helen could roam the palace wherever they wished, without fear of meeting suitors and needing escorts. The warm damp of spring turned into the crackling heat of summer. The women spent more time by the river washing clothes, mending, sewing, gossiping. Sometimes Penelope wondered if they would try to sleep along the river's edge, to escape the stifling heat of the summer nights. She knew Helen might even have suggested such a silly idea, if not for the grief that made her blue eyes gray.

The gaiety of their old times by the river did return, little by little. Serving girls giggled over sweethearts. The women raced along the river's edge and danced until they couldn't move for the fire in their legs. Penelope tried to invent riddle contests like the men enjoyed, but no maids were interested. Helen refused to play. When they couldn't remember Odysseus' riddle of the water, which they had all heard Penelope answer, she gave up in disgust.

One afternoon, when she chased a ball thrown too far, Penelope neared the woods. She took the time to snatch up a stick before entering the shadows. At the corner of her eye, she thought she caught movement.

Penelope gripped the stick tighter when her hunt took her towards that particular spot where she had met Aias. Nothing moved among the trees except herself. Not even the breeze. Penelope found the ball, and next to it were two sets of sandal prints, deep in the soft ground, almost hidden by shadows. Two men had stood there for a long time. Penelope wondered if she only imagined she had seen golden hair, and perhaps a flash of dark red. Menelaos and Odysseus were constantly together, like brothers. The idea of those two spying on the women pleased her a little. She resolved to work harder, to excel in everything.

Every few nights, she ventured from her room. Odysseus was always there in the king's garden. Sometimes he waited for her, sometimes he didn't appear until she sat alone a while. Not a single night of roaming went by that he didn't appear. Every question she asked, he answered. Penelope learned about Ithaka, its ships and rocky shores, the warriors who loved the flashing, rough sea and the battles that had been fought to hold it safe. She learned about the rich court of Mycenae and harsh, golden Agamemnon who ruled there. She learned the difference between the true and false tales that surrounded the family of Atreus, and the curses said to rest on that bloodline.

Penelope lived for those moonlit lessons about the world around her. No one, she knew, would ever talk so openly to her if they knew she wasn't a boy. She wondered what Odysseus would say if he knew the truth. Sometimes she wondered why he had not discovered it already.

*   *   *

The suitors returned, bringing bustle and feasting back to the palace. The rains returned with them, bringing relief from the heavy, hot air.

After a three-day stretch of showers that kept everyone indoors, Helen and Penelope spent the day with their maids in the garden. As night fell, the two cousins retreated to sit alone in Helen's room, planning dresses for a coming feast. Helen laughed, holding up a bright red length of cloth and declared that it matched her favorite ball perfectly for color. That was when they discovered the ball missing.

"You look in the weaving room," Penelope said, getting up, "and I'll check outside."

"Be careful," Helen said with a teasing laugh. "There might be dark-haired giants hiding in the shadows."

"If there are, you'll soon hear them running from me, shrieking in fright." Penelope laughed as she left.

She didn't find the ball in the women's gardens. Penelope retraced her steps, trying to remember exactly where she and Helen had run, playing their games. The trampled, damp grass made tracking easier. She smiled, recalling the story Odysseus told her two nights before, about the first time his father taught him to track and hunt.

Penelope didn't realize how far she wandered until she reached the arch into the king's garden. The ball *could* have rolled through the arch, she supposed. She only searched a few minutes before she found it in the deepening shadows, under the thick branches of a hedge. She had to get down on her hands and knees to reach far enough in to retrieve the toy.

"I'm not surprised," King Tyndareos said. His voice came from the other side of the hedge. Penelope stiffened, wondering why she hadn't heard him approaching. Then she heard two sets of footsteps.

"What doesn't surprise you?" A touch of laughter hung in Odysseus' voice. "That I don't seek Helen as my bride, or that I would confess it to you?"

"I may be an old man, but I am not blind or witless yet." The king sounded more alive and in better humor. "You never did look at Helen with that starvation and worship the others wear. Not even from the first day you arrived."

"I expected a different woman." Odysseus' voice came so clearly, Penelope knew they had paused in front of her, with the hedge between them. She stayed kneeling and held her breath, though her heart pounded so loudly she wondered neither man heard. "No matter what the emissaries say, trouble waits. The traders say so, and they move among the common people. I need a different kind of queen for Ithaka, if I am called away to war. A woman who can hold all the quarreling nobles and elders into unity, no matter what the gods might cast before us."

"Be that as it may…" Tyndareos sighed, loudly, wearily. "You say this to assure me I can trust you."

"If you ask me for advice, a plan to avert catastrophe for Sparta, I know it concerns Helen's marriage."

"Indeed. I should send my guests home before the fall storms strand the island princes here. Yet how can I resolve the problem that surrounds my daughter's marriage? For every prince who abides by my choice, another will attack me, kidnap Helen and kill her chosen husband out of anger."

"I've considered the problem," Odysseus admitted, his words slow. A few branches rustled in the hedge near the top and Penelope imagined him plucking at leaves. "I have a solution, but it will be costly. Very costly."

"A week of sacrifices, at every temple? I've considered it." Tyndareos laughed raggedly.

"Not that kind of cost. The solution is simple." A strange, tight chuckle escaped Odysseus. "The payment for my help is what shall cost you dearly."

"And what could that be?" Tyndareos stepped away from the hedge and the other man followed. Penelope stayed on her knees, hunched over so the men would not see her if they turned around. "Half of Sparta? I could almost grant you that with joy, if it would preserve the peace I worked so hard to make."

"More precious than that. Your niece, Penelope is my price. I want her as my wife."

"Penelope is a child." Tyndareos' voice went cold and hard.

"She was fifteen last winter. She's old enough to marry. Even if you can't see that, many do now and more will soon."

"So I should give her to poor, rough Ithaka, to spare my house another siege?" The king laughed, a bitter sound.

"You brought Penelope from Alybas to buy safety for Sparta. You would have bought another alliance with Helen, if her brothers still lived."

"I should send you away for speaking such words, but Menelaos is your friend."

Penelope bit her hand to keep from crying aloud. She heard the defeat in her uncle's voice, despite his anger.

"Let us be honest, King Tyndareos. Yes, Ithaka is small and rough, compared to Sparta or Mycenae or Pylos. But we are strong and brave and have more than enough for our needs. Penelope is the queen I need. She has been the strength of this household since your sons were taken. You say she is a child. I say Helen is the child, and Penelope is the woman grown. A woman I need. Many on Ithaka still follow the old ways. A king is judged by the queen who stands before the Goddess. I need a queen like Penelope, to hold the people's hearts." Odysseus leaned against the hedge. Penelope imagined he would push through at any moment and discover her. She knew she should flee, but couldn't move.

"You need my help," he continued after a heart-thudding moment of silence. "Without my advice, you cannot give Helen to Menelaos without fear of rebellion."

"What oracle says I will give my daughter to Menelaos?" The king's voice cracked like an old man's, wasting his strength with bravado.

"You need Mycenae. You fear Agamemnon's anger if you refuse his brother." Odysseus paused. When he spoke again, Penelope heard the smile in his voice. "More important, Helen favors Menelaos. You love your daughter. Her happiness competes with Sparta's welfare."

"What if Helen favored you, instead?" Tyndareos' voice softened. Penelope shivered, knowing he had surrendered.

"I still wouldn't ask for her. Menelaos will be a good king for Sparta and can care for Helen as she deserves. I need a strong queen. Penelope."

"She may be too strong for even you, Odysseus of Ithaka. She leads Helen by the nose and no one protests."

Penelope nearly leaped to her feet to run. Her face burned as she acknowledged her uncle might be right. She had enjoyed her power and influence too much, lately. The respect of slaves was a heady thing for a girl who knew she was nothing but a bribe to guide a warrior's hand in the king's service.

"You want to announce your decision soon," Odysseus said. "You need my plan to keep Sparta and Helen and Menelaos safe. Even if you offer me all the treasure in your palace, Penelope is still my price." His voice faded as he walked away from the hedge, further into the king's garden. Tyndareos followed.

Penelope flinched as a sob escaped her. Neither man heard, too far away and involved in the finer details of the bargain they argued. She got to her feet, still clutching the ball. She ran, never speaking to anyone until she reached her room. Eurynome was there.

"Dear child, what has happened? Did Aias—" The old nurse bit her lip to hold back the words.

Quickly, fighting the shaking in her whole body, Penelope blurted the news. "I don't want to marry anyone!" she finished, letting Eurynome cradle her close as if she were a child again.

"Especially not Odysseus of Ithaka," the woman said, her voice hard, the words sharp.

"Eurynome, the other princes favor him. He wins so many of the games…" Penelope's face warmed as she realized she defended Odysseus.

"Yes, he is admired, and he is skilled and strong and fast, but Ithaka isn't good enough for you."

Penelope barely heard as her nurse listed all the faults and lacks in Ithaka. She remembered how Odysseus' eyes gleamed when he talked about his home, the love and pride in his voice, the wonderful stories he told of hunting in the hills, building ships, sailing the crashing waves.

"I must marry the man my uncle chooses," she whispered. "I did ask Athena to give me to a prince who loved the sea."

"My dear child—surely there must be something—"

"No." Penelope was surprised to feel new tears. "I would shame my uncle by even trying to refuse."

She thought of her boy disguise, hidden away. She knew the basics of hunting and trapping and hiding. The palace would hum like a bee's hive after her uncle announced his decision. Tonight would be her chance. She had to flee now. She didn't want to marry. She didn't want to be a gift given to ensure peace. Even if the man who wanted her was Odysseus.

*   *   *

The sounds of feasting faded in the night air when Penelope slipped over the edge of her windowsill. She carried a spear, secreted under her bed weeks before in the hope of practicing under Odysseus' tutelage. Gold and silver and half a loaf of bread bounced heavily in the pouch hanging on her belt and she wore sandals. She went straight to the stables, flinching when a shadow in the moonlight resolved into an owl. Penelope stopped a few steps into the courtyard and looked around. She thought she heard the owl hoot.

Odysseus stepped into the torchlight in front of the stable door. Penelope managed to smile at him. She was only Dyvis, a boy servant, she reminded herself. Her disguise felt very thin in the bright flare of the torches. Odysseus didn't smile.

"I don't want to know where you're going, Dyvis." He rested his hand on the latch of the stable door. "Remember your mistress needs you. And runaway slaves are branded and beaten when they are caught."

"Who says I am running away?" She flinched at the thin, crackling sound of her voice.

"Your mistress has mistreated you? Threatened you? I thought not," he said, when she could only shake her head. "Your mistress is worthy of your loyalty. Stay with her, boy. She is precious to me, and she needs you."

"Yes, my lord," Penelope whispered, looking down at her feet to keep from meeting his eyes.

She knew Odysseus watched her all the journey back to her room. By the time she reached her window, she no longer cared what he saw or thought. When she turned to see where he stood, he had vanished into the night. The tears came, but whether in shame or frustration or anger, she couldn't decide.

*   *   *

The next day, a massive sacrifice took place on the plain between the palace and the river. Neither Penelope nor Helen attended. No maids went near the place. All were busy, along with Lystia, preparing for the wedding festivities.

A suite of rooms was purified and decorated for Helen and her husband. No one but Helen knew his name. She had gone to her father in private and came back smiling, refusing to even give a clue. Penelope didn't join in the teasing and begging. She was glad her cousin was happy, and glad she hadn't told Helen about the bargain. She remembered her uncle's voice, how it changed while he argued with Odysseus. She knew Tyndareos considered it an insult that Odysseus wanted to marry her, yet her uncle gave her to him all the same.

While the men were on the plain, making their sacrifices from dawn until the afternoon sun slanted into their eyes, the women kept busy with the purification rituals for a bride. The odor of burned flesh, of incense and wine spilled out in vows and offerings intruded everywhere in the palace. Penelope couldn't put it out of her thoughts, as she helped Helen through the required series of baths and perfuming. She served as her cousin's attendant for the ceremonies and it was her duty to help Helen in every step. No other hand could touch her until Helen had returned from the long afternoon of visits to the temples and goddesses, to make prayers and offerings for blessings on her marriage. Penelope fulfilled her duties and wondered who would attend her own marriage preparations. She refused to have Melantho.

Dolios was one of the first servants to return from the plain after that long day of sacrifices. He came immediately to the women's room, where Helen and Penelope and the maids sat weaving, waiting, chattering in curiosity. He waited at the door until Penelope noticed him and beckoned for him to come in. He rubbed at the stains of soot, grease, and blood on his tunic.

"Is it permitted for us to know now?" Helen asked.

"Soon the whole world will know." He gestured widely, to take in more than Sparta and the lands of the Achaians. "The suitors made sacrifices to the gods and their consorts, to the Furies and Fates, and made vows. To protect Helen and the man chosen as her husband. To bring vengeance on anyone who harms the man or tries to carry off Helen. No matter how far they might go, no matter how long it takes. All day long, the same vow, with the smoke of sacrifices everywhere." Dolios smiled. "The gods will be pleased."

"They will hold every man accountable." Helen went pale, and turned to Penelope. "How much more will they hold me accountable if anything should happen? Even if I am innocent?"

"Helen, nothing will happen. You want the man you are to marry, don't you?" Penelope hugged her cousin and gave Dolios a smile of thanks and a nod of dismissal. "With all the princes of Achaia to protect you and your honor, what could happen?"

"What could happen?" she echoed. She gave Penelope a smile and a hug in return, then freed herself. "I must prepare. Father said when the sacrifices were done, my chosen would come to see me." A slow blush began to rise in her face, and a sparkle of anticipation lit her eyes.

Watching her, Penelope wrapped her arms around herself and shivered. The marriage festivities were planned for the next day. How soon until everyone knew Odysseus had won her?

*   *   *

In Sparta, the bride and her attendants didn't join in the marriage feast. Helen and Penelope would eat together in the bridal chamber, waiting for Menelaos to come claim her. Penelope remembered the marriages she had witnessed in Alybas. The festivities had been small, but everyone shared them together, and the new husband led his bride away to their chamber accompanied by the songs of their friends.

The maids undressed Helen, anointed her with perfume and brushed her hair so it lay soft and glowing over her shoulders to her waist. Alkippe stood at watch far down the hall, to warn them when Menelaos approached.

Penelope and Helen sat in the silent bridal chamber, Helen in the bed with the sheet drawn up past her breasts, Penelope in a chair by the bed. They had eaten little, the quiet broken by soft, nervous laughter when their eyes met. A gentle breeze made the torches flicker. Penelope found she couldn't look at Helen, and concentrated on her weaving on the wall opposite the bed. She tried to find flaws in it, tried to discern a place where she should have put a different color, let the pattern go another direction. She found she couldn't think clearly enough to do even that. Her imagination kept drifting to the night when she would be the anointed bride, waiting in the bed.

Helen was hard to look at. She glowed, like she did when the glory of the slanting afternoon sun struck her from behind, creating a corona that could blind. Her eyes were a deeper, brighter blue, dancing with suppressed laughter and eagerness. Roses flushed her golden cheeks. Penelope envied her cousin's ivory neck and shoulders, adorned perfectly by the single strand of gold beads and pink pearls, a bridal gift from Menelaos.

"I envy you," she whispered.

"Why?" Helen laughed. It had a joyous, musical sound, but marred by nervousness. "You will marry Odysseus soon. Don't you want to marry him?"

Penelope shrugged and wrapped her arms around herself. She felt cold, and wished she had the energy to get up and go close all the bronze shutters to shut out the cool of the night. She had been strangely pleased when Helen had laughed for joy, hugging her, congratulating her, when it was announced Penelope would be given to Odysseus in three days. In the face of her cousin's happy anticipation, how could she explain her own worries?

They sat in silence and Penelope heard, far off and muted, the sounds of feasting in the great hall. She wondered what the failed suitors were saying to Menelaos. Wishing him well, blessing him, or giving mocking curses, envying his success?

King Nestor was among the celebrants. Penelope had greeted him and accepted the bridal gifts he brought for her and Helen—rings of silver and gold, hair pins with delicate designs of colored stones, and the ceremonial joining cups for their wedding nights. Nestor had complimented her on winning Odysseus as a husband, then laughed when she could only frown at him, puzzled by his phrasing.

Her thoughts turned to Odysseus. Did his thoughts move ahead to the night he would be the honored one, sitting at the high table with Tyndareos, accepting songs of blessing, eating the food blessed by the priestesses of Aphrodite and Hera?

"There is no reason to be afraid," Helen whispered. She leaned forward, reaching across the space between bed and chair to clasp her cousin's wrist. "Even if you don't know what to do, as long as you want to please your husband, and he wants to please you..." She trailed off, eyes dancing in delight.

Softly tapping, running footsteps approached. Alkippe pushed the wide doors open and stopped on the threshold. Her face was flushed, her eyes bright and she had to catch her breath before speaking. She didn't have to speak; her mere presence told them Menelaos approached.

Penelope stood, returned Helen's clasp, and hurried away after Alkippe. She glanced back once, as she tugged the heavy doors closed. Helen looked very small in the wide, high bed. Penelope followed the maid to the intersecting hall that led to her own room. She paused at the corner when she heard shuffling footsteps, the ring of metal against stone. Menelaos appeared, his face flushed, tunic rumpled, hair dark with perspiration. As he walked, he fumbled one-handed with the clasp for his cloak. The garment slipped off his shoulders and he caught it up with an unsteady arm. The movement brought his other hand up against the wall, making the silver cup he carried ring again as it hit and spilled a few drops of wine. Penelope hurried away before she could be seen or her mind could comprehend.

*   *   *

In the morning, Helen was too quiet when Penelope led the maids to the bridal chamber to attend her. She smiled at her cousin but offered no comment. Penelope looked for bruises, for some sign of Menelaos' drunken state the night before. The joy she had expected in her cousin's eyes was missing. Helen looked unharmed. The sheets were rumpled and stained with sweat.

CHAPTER 7

"Penelope." Eurynome shook her awake gently, a hand on her shoulder. "Child, we must talk."

"Is something wrong?" Penelope sat up and looked around her chamber. Then she remembered. Today, she began the procession of marriage prayers at the temples.

Her nurse sat on the edge of the bed. Her mouth settled into grim lines and she refused to meet Penelope's eyes as she began. "Your own mother should be giving you this advice. Perhaps if she were alive, you would not—"

"I am resolved to obey my uncle's choice for me."

"You are dutiful. May the gods bless you for that, at least." The woman sighed, nodding. "It is no use trying to match wits with Odysseus or arguing with him when his orders appear foolish to you. For the peace of your household, endure rather than resist. Be sweet and submissive. Agree with him and then find ways to do what is proper and sensible. Make him think you are his willing, docile bride and nothing he does will anger you. Then, you can train him to your leading."

"Eurynome, I—"

"Yes, it sounds devious and deceitful. You are marrying a deceitful, devious man. I will not let you go to his bed and his household unprepared." Eurynome sniffed, and Penelope was startled to realize the woman fought tears.

"He is not truly as bad as he seems. I think I could be happy with him."

"Give him no children."

"Eurynome!" She stared at the woman, startled more by the vehemence in her voice than the words.

And yet, hadn't she made the same vow moons ago, when she began her journey to her uncle's palace? Why was it that such a simple, sensible decision became muddled when it was Odysseus whom she would deny a son?

"You cannot refuse to share his bed or satisfy his needs. It is better, I think, to endure a man's hunger than to bear children from tainted seed."

"You will not talk of my husband that way." Penelope sat up straight, her voice hardening as she spoke. It startled her to see how Eurynome wilted in response. Her own response startled her.

The problem was that Odysseus was no nameless, faceless prince who took her as a peace offering. He had become her friend. She liked and admired him. He had argued and schemed and manipulated her uncle in order to win her.

He wanted *her*, not Helen.

"I love you, child. I want to protect you. There are potions to drink, to keep his seed from joining with yours. Oils and lotions to anoint yourself. I will make them for you. If you wish," she added, her voice dropping.

"You truly have been a loving mother to me." Penelope swallowed hard against the sudden thickness in her throat. "My aunt taught me, it is a woman's duty to decide if she will conceive or not. She taught me how to prevent conceiving. I had already planned... I will use what you give me, and thankfully. But don't tell me when it is right to deny my husband a child. That is between the Goddess and my own heart."

*   *   *

Likely, the priest wondered why a bride came to Athena's temple, rather than Aphrodite and Hera. Penelope didn't care. She was thankful the man agreed with her request to be alone. Alkippe attended her and stood now at the far end of the inner room, making sure no one approached.

"Please, great Athena," Penelope whispered, going to her knees. She kept her eyes fixed on the serene features of the statue, hoping for some response, some sign. "If you favor the one I must marry, take me under your protection as well. Give me the wisdom to please him. And please, touch his thoughts on our bridal night. I want to please him, but how can I if I fear him and he is tottering with wine? Please, let him come to me with gentleness and I will sacrifice to your altar first, on all feast days." She bowed her head, and waited.

Penelope heard a soft brushing sound near the doorway that led to an anteroom on one side. She looked and saw a shadow move. Her heart sank. Likely the priest waited for her to leave. The sound was probably his sandal brushing the stone pavements. She hoped the man had not heard her whispered prayer. What sort of request was that for a bride to make?

Alkippe met her at the doorway and handed Penelope her wooden doll. They would next go to Artemis' temple, to offer up her girlhood toys. Penelope stroked the carved features of the doll and remembered the day her father gave it to her. He told her of the day she would place the toy on Artemis' altar, and had told her she would be happy.

Penelope was not sure how she felt. Pride, that Odysseus wanted her so much. Anger, that Eurynome and the king both thought so little of Odysseus, to take his request as insult. Despair, that her escape had been thwarted. Curiosity, to know what made Melantho smile and slip away to numerous lovers. And anticipation of sailing the sea again, journeying to the island that Odysseus spoke of with such pride and affection.

Amid all the emotions churning in her heart, Penelope wondered if there was room for happiness. She hoped it would come, soon.

She nearly stopped when she thought she caught a glimpse of a man with dark red hair stepping into a doorway. Penelope hoped her face wasn't as red warm as it felt. Did Odysseus follow her? She didn't know whether to feel ashamed or flattered.

She remembered Odysseus' rage when Aias attacked her. Penelope realized there was so little she truly knew about the man she was to marry. When she knelt at Hera's altar, she prayed for help to always make Odysseus smile at her, and never give him cause for frowns or anger. She didn't want him ever to show such fury at her.

*   *   *

Penelope sat down slowly, trying not to listen to the music, laughing and singing that pulsed through the palace. She remembered how long the sounds had echoed through the palace on Helen's bridal night. She remembered the wave of laughter that likely signaled Menelaos' exit from the hall. Alkippe had come running soon after that, to warn them he approached. Penelope remembered how he staggered.

Now it was her turn to sit in the chair and be tended by the maids. To have the jewels and flowers taken from her hair. To have her hair brushed lustrous and smooth. To have her pearls and rings and rich robes removed, her body rubbed with scented oil. And then be led to the bridal bed. To wait, trying not to shiver in the cool night air, with Alkippe's silent company until Odysseus came to claim her.

Helen had not been afraid, Penelope remembered. She flinched as the last chain tangled in her hair. Melantho offered no apology and Penelope didn't rebuke her. The girl was still upset she hadn't been chosen as her companion.

Her thoughts returned to her cousin. Helen hadn't been afraid because she knew how to please a man in his bed. Yet, she had been too quiet when Penelope tended her the next morning. Menelaos had been clumsy from wine and claimed his bride as if she were a recalcitrant slave girl bought for breeding.

Odysseus had never grown drunk during the feasting, as far as Penelope knew. He had never winced at the morning brightness or complained of a sour belly or other pains from too much wine. She had watched for him often enough to guess his daily habits. She tried to comfort herself with that thought and drive away her fears. It didn't help. This was his bridal night and the other men would ply him with wine beyond even his endurance.

Alkippe brought over the vial of scented oil, which had sat warming by the fire. Penelope braced herself, ready for the maids to begin removing her clothes.

The door into the chamber swung open. The draft of air caught everyone's attention. She looked up to see Odysseus standing framed against the darkness in the hall, the silver cup in his hand. His tunic was still clean and smooth; no sweat gleamed on his face. He caught the clasp of his cloak and twisted it free. He never took his gaze off her.

For a moment she thought her heart had stopped. She saw all the maids looking to her for orders. Eurynome's instructions returned—please her husband in all things. Penelope glanced toward the door and nodded. The girls fled the room like frightened birds.

Odysseus closed the door, then dropped his cloak on a chair nearby. Penelope held still, watching him, waiting. He said nothing. His face was calm, pleasant but unreadable, and he watched her as he crossed the room. His beard glistened in the torchlight with scented oil.

"Sweet Penelope," he said, his voice a soft rumble, as he stopped before her. "I bring the cup of our joining. Will you honor me by drinking?" Odysseus knelt so their eyes were level as he held out the cup to her.

The spices in the ceremonial wine filled the air, thickening it so she couldn't breathe for a moment. Penelope gazed into the glistening depths, deep and dark as blood. She swallowed against the dryness in her throat.

"You honor me by giving it," she whispered. Her hands shook, but she raised the heavy cup to her lips for the required sip without spilling anything. It was warm from his hand.

She watched Odysseus as he took his sip, noting how his hand didn't tremble. There was a light like laughter in his eyes, but burning deeper and stronger. She hadn't been this close to him since he rescued her from Aias. The clean scent of him filled the air—leather and smoke, clean linen and wine.

"This cup holds more wine than I have tasted all day," he said as he put the cup on the table beside her. Odysseus stood and waited, watching her.

"You *were* at the temple." Penelope closed her eyes, feeling her face burning. She tried to recall the words of her prayer to Athena. Had she misspoken? Had she made Odysseus angry?

"Penelope." His fingers brushed her cheek, startling her so she opened her eyes. Odysseus smiled down at her. "Menelaos has never been able to hold his wine since we were boys." He chuckled, sending warmth through her that relaxed the tight cold filling her belly. "I want to remember every moment of this night. And not frighten you. You are frightened of me a little, aren't you?"

"I was not expecting you so soon, my husband." The word tasted strange on her tongue, but she smiled at him. "Startled, not frightened. They haven't finished preparing me for you."

"Shall I call them back?" He held out his hand for hers and helped her stand.

"No." Penelope's heart pounded harder, as if it would leap free of her flesh. A lightness filled her, a warmth that took away her trembling.

"Penelope, please...don't fear me." His hands rested warm and heavy on her shoulders. She couldn't meet his eyes, lost in the heat and trembling his touch sent through her.

"I'm not afraid." She knew she had spoken truthfully. Her one fear had been removed. She remembered Eurynome's instructions and vowed to be sweet and biddable in all things, to please him and keep him careful of her. "Except afraid that I might not please you," she added in a whisper.

"You please me more than I can express," he hurried to say, his voice thickening.

Her feet moved of their own volition, taking her to the bed. She heard him follow her as she removed her belt. As she reached up and loosened the clasp on one shoulder of her dress, she felt Odysseus work the other clasp. Penelope closed her eyes, feeling only warmth and a new vibrancy pouring through her body. The cloth whispered as her dress dropped to the floor. Odysseus' hands were warm and gentle on her skin as he slipped his arms around her and drew her back against him. She nearly flinched away, feeling his bare chest touch her naked back. His beard brushed the side of her face, his lips soft against her loosened hair. He held her close with one arm around her waist. His other hand brushed over her body, pausing to cup breast and hip. Penelope shivered, enjoying the heat that tore through her from the slow, soft caress.

Gently, he turned her around so she faced him. One hand cupped her cheek, tipping her head up as he bent his head down to her. Penelope closed her eyes, trembling without fear as he kissed her. A spark shot through her body, from her lips to deep in her belly. She trembled in his embrace, delighted to discover she enjoyed his touch. She thought for a moment about the oil to anoint her body, then realized that didn't matter.

"Do I please you, my lord?" she whispered, when he drew back.

"Very pleased. May I give you joy in return." He caressed her cheek, a stroke of his thumb as gentle as a bird's wing. "Is the rest of you as sweet, Penelope?"

"Sweet?" She opened her eyes, confused, wanting him to kiss her again.

"Your mouth tastes of honey wine." His smile trembled as he bent his head to kiss her again. His arms closed around her, drawing her tight up against him.

Penelope returned his kisses, daring to slip her arms around him. He laughed, a gentle sound that vibrated against her lips, all through her body. She clung to him, eyes closed, when he picked her up and walked the few steps to lay her down in the bed. His hands moved over her body with feather touches, gentle as the first morning breeze in spring.

*   *   *

Penelope lay still, feeling the thudding of her heart. She didn't move, for fear of halting the tender, gentle flow of Odysseus' hand over her body, strong contrast to the lightning sharp pleasure that held them a short while before. He held her close against him, one arm under her shoulders. Soft kisses, his beard tickling in places, rained down on her face and neck, moving to her shoulders and breasts. She caught her breath once, flinching against a sharp thrill of returning pleasure and opened her eyes. He smiled down at her and stroked a few strands of hair out of her face.

"Not as terrible as you feared?" he whispered.

"Helen said it could be wonderful. Why do the old women tell us to endure, to be afraid?" She felt her face heat as she realized how odd her words sounded. She was no longer Dyvis, free to ask any question in her head.

"Because lovemaking can be a sad thing, if the man thinks only of his own pleasure and not his wife's." Odysseus leaned over her, an arm on either side of her shoulders, studying her face in the light of the last burning torch. "My nurse taught me about the old ways. A king's most important duty then was to protect and serve and please the queen. She is the source of life and blessing for the land, as you shall be, dear Penelope. You will bring joy and new life to Ithaka, as you bring joy to me." He leaned down to kiss her. "Ithaka shall worship you as a priestess of the Goddess," he whispered, following with more kisses.

Penelope slipped her arms around him, holding him close, while new ideas spun through her mind. Athena, she decided, had indeed been watching over her, to give her to a man who would take her to a people with such beliefs. She welcomed the new life waiting for her, as she welcomed the warm weight of his body. When he moved off her to continue his caresses and she clung to him, he laughed.

"Slowly, my sweet lady. We have all the night before us." His smile grew deeper when a caress across her belly tickled and startled a laugh out of her. "I like your laughter," he said. "Like a harp."

"Grandfather said I had a foolish laugh," Penelope admitted, then wondered at how easily she confided in him.

"Your grandfather also thought you were a boy. Not everything he taught you can be taken seriously."

"How much do you know about me?" She felt a cooling of the warm pleasure that filled her belly.

"As much as your cousins could tell me, as much as I could learn questioning your servants and traders who had gone to Alybas. And as much as you told me." He turned onto his side, propped up on one arm, and looked down at her.

"You knew I was Dyvis." Penelope felt some pride that her voice didn't break and tears didn't fill her eyes. She wondered if the brightness in his eyes was mocking laughter.

"You are too beautiful to be a boy. I will take you anywhere you wish, tell you anything you want to know, but I will not risk someone else attacking you as Aias tried." He caressed another wisp of hair out of her eyes, the momentary hardness in his face softening. "You are most definitely the queen for Ithaka and I will risk no harm coming to you."

"I envied you, when you spoke of Ithaka," she whispered, trying to read his thoughts in his eyes.

Penelope remembered everything he had told her of his home. His voice soft, flowing with life, he had spoken of his parents. How his father, Laertes had brought peace to the island as well as prosperity. Of Antikleia, his mother, her golden red beauty and warring, cunning kinsmen. He told her about the house he had left half-finished, to come looking for a bride. Odysseus spoke of the hills of Ithaka where hunting was good. The shadows harbored mystery, where a god or goddess might step out at any moment, or a hidden crevice could cripple a man or dog. He had told her about his orchards and vineyards, the colors of sunrise off the shores of Ithaka, the joys of a misty morning, walking along the shore in the cool, damp sand.

"Penelope..." He sighed, shaking his head, and the soberness of his face turned into a smile. "I should steal you away, join King Nestor as he heads home to Pylos by moonlight. We should vanish this very night, before anyone realizes how blind they have been and tries to take you from me. Every man will envy me my bride, and Ithaka its queen."

"Don't." She felt laughter and tears choking her. "My lord, don't speak foolishness."

"Not foolishness," he murmured. His caresses changed, drawing waves of hot pleasure up through her body.

*   *   *

"Come, before the household wakes," Odysseus whispered, waking her with a kiss. He stroked her hair, then down her shoulder and arm.

Penelope trembled with the sweetness of his kiss and caress and hurried to follow his example. He had brought clothes to replace their wedding garments. She covered her tangled, unbound hair with a veil.

Odysseus wore a plain, dark tunic a farmer would wear. They went barefoot, silent in the dark stone hallways of the palace. Odysseus had obviously planned this, obtaining the plain clothes, the basket of food and skin of wine, and finding the path to escape the palace and their bridal chamber. He carried basket and wineskin and held her hand.

Penelope shivered with pleasure at a new thought. Any other man might hold her hand to keep her with him, to ensure she didn't try to run. Odysseus had no need to fear she would try to escape him after last night. He had been as gentle, as kind and giving as any girl could want on her bridal night. He held her hand for the simple pleasure of touching her as they walked.

In silence, they left the palace far behind, with trees between them and it, and the river sliding through the plains before them. They went to where the women spent the afternoons.

They bathed before eating. Penelope stayed near shore, kneeling on the pebbly bottom of the river, letting the cold, swift flowing waters tug at her body. She knew Odysseus watched her, and knowing drove away the chill.

"What a difference a single night brings," she whispered. The brushing of the wind against her body reminded her of Odysseus' first caress. Penelope hurried out of the water, looking for him and wondering if she had taken too long.

He was there before her, smiling down at her as he handed her a cloak to dry with. His eyes held the same joy and pleasure in morning light that she had seen in torchlight before they both fell asleep. Penelope felt her knees go weak and warmth spread through her belly. Odysseus caught her by the elbow when she swayed a little.

"I fear we are both faint with hunger," he said, his smile changing to fill with laughter.

She nodded, not trusting her voice, and watched him walk over to the basket of food. Quickly, she wrung out her hair and tugged her dress over her damp skin.

Odysseus set out a cloth on a flat rock that had often served the women as a table. He brought cheese, bread and honey, and figs out of the basket and set them on the cloth. Penelope knelt next to him and gently pushed his hands away.

"It is the wife's duty to serve her lord," she said, lips trembling as he turned his hands to catch hers. How long, she wondered, would his mere touch spread such warmth and weakness through her body?

"As you wish." His smiled was a caress.

She filled the single wooden cup he had brought and held it out to him. Odysseus caught her hand against the cup, raising it to his lips to sip and then guiding it to her mouth. She was glad he held the cup. She would have dropped it otherwise. When she held out a portion of the cheese to him, he ate it from her hand, kissing her fingers, tickling them with the soft curls of his beard. Memories of the night before made thinking hard.

"The first time I saw you, Penelope, I wanted you. I battered your cousins with questions about you because you fascinated me. Tell me, does it bother you to be called 'the little, dark one'?"

"Not as the words come from your lips." She found it easy to smile; his eyes sparkled so brightly as he spoke. "I don't feel like a half-grown child when you say it."

"No, you are definitely a woman. With the sweetest mouth a man could want." He laughed, catching up one of her hands to press to his lips. "And hands as quick as your mind. You hardly needed my help, that day by the river. You should have heard the others speaking of you later, and seen the bruises and cuts you gave our poor Aias. Menelaos said you were born an Amazon, switched in your cradle with the true-born daughter of Ikarios. The king and your cousins were rather pleased by that."

"And you?" Her hands trembled as she spread honey on the bread. Warmth spread through her body from the mischief and laughter in his voice. *Please, Aphrodite and Athena, let it be always like this for us.*

"I was terrified you would catch the heart of another prince or two. The timing wasn't right for me to speak to Tyndareos. I feared before I did, someone else would lose interest in Helen and begin speaking of you."

"Lose interest in Helen?" She nearly dropped the bread. A few birds by the shore rose up at the shock in her voice. Penelope laughed, surprised at the bitterness in the sound.

"You have still to grow fully into your beauty, Penelope, and despite your cunning mind you cannot see that. I thank Athena who guides me, I saw your promise before any other man." Odysseus caught her chin with two fingers, to make her look at him. "Your mind is as swift and beautiful as your body."

"You were hiding in the trees, watching our games and listening to us, weren't you?" Penelope laughed when he pretended to be ashamed and look away.

"Many nights, lying in my bed, I thanked Athena I was too proud to

85

leave when I knew I didn't want Helen. I nearly left for Ithaka before you arrived."

"I considered pretending to be a boy and traveling the world," she confessed. "Perhaps we might have met and joined forces?" Her words brought laughter from him. Odysseus wrapped his arms around her, drawing her close to kiss her. "Please, Fates, let me make you happy," she whispered against his lips.

"We will be happy, Penelope. Many long years together. I promise you."

"When do we leave for Ithaka?"

"Not soon enough." He sat back as he released her and glanced up at the sun, then back through the trees toward the palace. "The day progresses. They will be searching for us soon, I fear. More games and contests to celebrate our marriage."

"You need your strength, because you will win them all," she said, pressing a piece of bread into his hand. The honey had begun to dry, glistening in the morning warmth.

"Merely because I am the bridegroom?" he asked, laughing, before he took a bite.

"No. Because you are Odysseus."

A few droplets of honey caught in the curling hairs around his mouth. They glistened like polished gold in the sun. Daring and longing mixed in her. Penelope leaned forward and kissed him, tasting the honey where it smeared his lips.

*   *   *

Eurynome's voice rang across the plain from the gate where the palace opened out toward the river. Penelope paused, startled out of the warmth and pleasure of Odysseus' arm around her waist as they walked back to the palace. She was surprised to see her nurse come running to meet them.

"My—my lady, where have you been?" the woman gasped, her hand pressed over her heart. Eurynome's hair hung loose from a badly made braid. Penelope guessed the woman had dressed hurriedly, likely roused early from her bed.

"We went to the river to bathe." Penelope pressed closer against Odysseus. His arm tightened around her, then released her to hold her hand.

"My wife, I believe we have put the palace into an uproar." He smiled, with no humor in his eyes or his voice. "How many new brides and bridegrooms have vanished on their wedding mornings?"

"The king is in a fury," Eurynome whispered. Her gaze flicked away from Penelope, to rest on Odysseus with something like respect on her face.

Penelope nearly laughed to realize her nurse didn't particularly care for Tyndareos. Odysseus' hand tightened on hers as they walked to the gates of the palace. Glancing at him, Penelope remembered his argument with her uncle and knew the king's fury was only a continuation of that afternoon talk.

Someone else must have seen them coming, because Tyndareos came storming down the steps into the courtyard before they stepped through the gate. Her uncle's eyes blazed and his stride was stiff as he crossed the pavement to meet them. He glared at Odysseus, mouth pressed flat and tight.

"Penelope, go to your room. This is no place for you," Tyndareos said, his tone hard and brittle. His eyes burned even when they rested on her.

"My place is with my husband," she returned in as gentle a voice as she could manage. Odysseus squeezed her hand. She hoped it was approval of her tactics.

"I am your uncle—"

"And as such, you gave me to Odysseus. Now it is for my husband to tell me to stay or go."

"Penelope." Odysseus released her hand. "Will you go, or will you stay and hear what the king has to say to me?"

"I will stay." Her lips trembled a little as she forced a smile. Penelope slipped her hand back into his grasp. "Whatever makes you so angry, my king, we have done together this day."

"What sort of game—" Tyndareos' face went crimson. "What trick is this, Odysseus, to steal my niece—"

"Steal?" Odysseus' voice grew hard as a sword. "How can I steal my own wife? Or do you now take her back? Did you change your mind in the middle of the feast?"

"Be careful what accusations you make," the king said, his voice a barely controlled growl. Behind him, Helen and Menelaos came through the doorway and paused on the steps.

"Uncle." Penelope tried to make her voice soft and placating, when she felt fury beginning to boil. "We only went to the river to be alone. We wanted privacy."

"He needs no protection from you," Tyndareos snapped.

"He needs no help from anyone." She nearly laughed at how the king flinched at her snapped retort. "I was in the garden, Uncle. I heard you insult Ithaka and Odysseus when he asked for me. I know I am the payment to safeguard Sparta. Why are you angry with my husband?"

"I think the king repents his bargain," Odysseus said slowly, his eyes hooded, voice too soft. He raised her hand to his lips, pressing a kiss against her palm. "Your uncle wishes you to turn from me and beg him to take you back."

"Such insults—" Tyndareos began.

"Insults such as you threw at Ithaka and my bloodline? You were by the gate between the gardens, weren't you, Penelope? You didn't hear what he said when we walked further into the garden. If the king's words were true, you are the wife of a man less than a slave, the foulest coward, destined to live on a cursed piece of rock even the gods don't acknowledge."

"My husband, take me home to Ithaka." Penelope trembled with anger. "I won't stay here another day."

"Penelope, think what you say." Tyndareos paled, and this time not in anger. Penelope knew her uncle began to regret what he had said. "Think of the festivals, the games to celebrate your marriage."

"Celebrate what you regret?" Odysseus asked, his voice chill. "Yes, Penelope. We will leave. Today."

"You can't leave so quickly!"

"I won't stay in a household where my husband is insulted." She tugged her hand free and turned to Eurynome. "Call Dolios and tell him to report to my lord for his orders. Then join me in my room and help me pack." Penelope hurried to the door. She glimpsed Helen turning to follow her, but didn't slow for her cousin. By the time she reached her room, the trembling had left her legs, but a longing for tears wrapped around her instead.

CHAPTER 8

Odysseus had a chariot borrowed from King Nestor. Dolios harnessed the horses for the return trip before coming to Penelope's room for her belongings. He said little, except that he and his family and Eurynome would leave as soon as they were packed and rejoin her in Pylos. Dolios revealed little emotion when he told her the arrangements Odysseus had made, but Penelope guessed the man was bewildered and worried for her. She could not summon the words to reassure him, being unsure herself what she wanted or felt. She had chosen her husband's side of the argument, which was her duty. She couldn't decide if she had acted to spite her uncle or to support her husband. Or if Odysseus had touched her heart.

Menelaos and Helen came to see them off, waiting on the steps of the palace until Dolios loaded the chariot and left. The two cousins hugged, wordless. Penelope knew Menelaos and Odysseus exchanged words, but she couldn't make herself listen. She let Menelaos help her up into the chariot and his hands were gentle. Sorrow touched his eyes. She had thought badly of him after Helen's bridal night, but decided now that the man merely had weak places. He did care for Helen. The blush on Helen's cheeks when her husband wrapped his arm around her waist showed all was well between them, or would soon be.

"King Tyndareos says you leave too quickly to claim his bride-gift to Penelope," Menelaos said, his words halting.

"I have more treasure in my bride than her uncle will ever know," Odysseus returned. He guided Penelope's hands to the straps to brace herself. "As it is," he added, a smile in face and voice, "I won't have it said Tyndareos and Sparta made Ithaka rich."

Penelope choked, caught between wanting to laugh and cry. She felt the pride and humor that brought such words to her husband's lips. She smiled up at him. The brightness in his eyes overwhelmed her with longing to be far from Sparta.

"He will be over his anger soon, and then we can send messages," Helen said. "We can visit next spring."

"You could be fat with child by then," Penelope said. Odysseus' hand tightened on her shoulder. Was it in anticipation of their own child or because of Tyndareos' words about Ithaka? If the island kingdom wasn't fit for Penelope to be its queen, how could it be fit for Helen to visit?

"We could both be," Helen returned with a smile.

"As the gods will it," Odysseus said. "Menelaos, when the king is kinder toward us, tell him I would not have Sparta an enemy. If the oracles are to be believed, we will all need allies."

"I will tell him." Menelaos pressed his hand over his heart in oath.

"Ready?" he murmured, releasing Penelope to take up the reins. She nodded.

With a gentle lurch and a clatter of hooves on the paving stones, the chariot moved forward. It gained speed quickly on the smooth path from the palace, through the wide streets around the edge of the city. Penelope closed her eyes until the jouncing rattle of paving stones under the wheels turned into the smooth hissing of dirt road.

"Regrets, Penelope?" Odysseus said, as she opened her eyes and looked around. His mouth quirked up in a thin smile, but she saw no humor in his eyes.

"You are my husband. My place is with you." She bent her head and studied the straps, twisting her hands through them to brace herself more surely.

"You demean yourself, playing the submissive little bride." A spark of laughter touched his eyes when she met his gaze. "I heard you rebel against your uncle. You told me your dreams when you pretended to be Dyvis. I know you."

"I was angry with him," she admitted. Her face warmed under his scrutiny. "What you told me of Ithaka...it is beautiful, even if rocky and isolated and not as rich as Sparta. You love Ithaka and it is my home now. He had no right to mock you. He had no right to be angry that we wanted to be alone."

"And you were still angry with him, using you to buy peace for Sparta and Helen."

"That as well."

"I promise you, Penelope, you won't regret being my wife and queen of Ithaka." Odysseus turned away for a moment to correct the horses' path. He released one hand to slip his arm around her waist and draw her against him. "I wish I could show you the surprise on your face, enjoying our first lovemaking."

"There are benefits to marriage." She laughed with him and let go of the steadying straps so she could wrap both arms around his waist. Through Odysseus, she learned the swaying rhythm of the chariot better and grew more steady on her feet.

"Do you like to sail, Penelope?"

"Very much. I prayed Athena to let me be given to a prince who loved the sea."

"Shall I teach you to sail, then? I did promise to take you exploring and tell you all you wanted to learn."

"I would like that, very much."

"We have work waiting for us when we reach Ithaka, to prepare for winter. The last few years have been lean, rough ones—you and I will remedy that. But there will be time to explore. From the northern tip to the southern shore. You will know all the places precious to me."

Penelope nodded, unable to reply for the happiness that threatened to choke her. She tightened her arms around him as Odysseus whipped the horses into more speed. The chariot sang along the dusty road, leaving clouds in its wake that settled slowly in the warming morning air.

The journey passed swiftly. Penelope closed her eyes from time to time and pretended the swaying under her feet and the tugging of the wind against her hair came from waves and sea wind. Just when she attained the illusion, a horse would snort or whinny, or a cloud of dust would brush her face, making her choke. Odysseus spoke little, except to point out places along the road she might find interesting. Penelope decided he didn't quite trust the horses and gave all his concentration to controlling them.

She early gave up holding onto her veil. The wind tugged it off her head and tore strands of hair loose from her braids. She tucked the veil into her belt and leaned to face directly into the wind so it wouldn't whip her hair into her face. She smiled, remembering how Odysseus had played with her hair the night before—and what a struggle it had been to brush it straight in the morning.

"You like riding in chariots, then?" Odysseus said, when they reached a rocky stretch of road and had to slow. He shifted back to holding the reins in one hand, and brushed tangled, dusty strands of hair out of her face.

Penelope smiled, but her ready answer died on her lips when she saw the odd, intense light in his eyes. It made a lie of his light tone. Her answer was important to him, for some reason. She shook her head, then finger-combed her hair in a different direction.

"Men know nothing about women's hair," she said, wrinkling her nose at him. His snort of laughter reassured her, but not enough. "Yes, I suppose I like chariots," she said, choosing her words with care. "Comparing this trip to riding in that horrid cart, I adore chariots." Penelope watched his face carefully. Nothing changed in his eyes. "At Pylos, I didn't want to get off the ship. I wanted to keep sailing around the world."

"Did you?" Odysseus glanced up to check the horses for a moment, then looked back down at her.

Had she imagined it, or did a slight tension leave the muscles under the curve of her arm?

"I love the sea, sitting in the prow of a ship and feeling the wind against my face, listening to the singing of the waves. I wanted a husband who lived near the sea, who might be kind enough to take me out on ships with him. Ships are much easier to tend than horses, I think."

"You think so, do you?" He chuckled.

"If something is broken on a ship, you find wood or rope, and repair it. If a horse is broken, you have to kill it."

"There is that," he admitted. His arm tightened around her. Odysseus checked the horses again, then bent to brush a kiss across her forehead. She felt the slight grit of dust on her skin, under his lips. "Ithaka is too rocky and rough for horses. Everyone walks, and the ill, weak or old ride little donkeys my grandfather brought over."

"Then we have that advantage against raiders who might think to overrun us riding horses."

"Raiders?" He laughed. "Where did you hear about raiders?"

"It's a long journey by sea from Alybas. I listened to everything the sailors said, and the gossip at the ports."

"A wise woman, I have found." His tone grew gentle, soft, so she almost didn't hear his words over the thudding of the horses' feet.

*   *   *

They found a sheltered grove of trees at dusk and made camp around a shallow spring. Odysseus gathered long grass into a soft pile and spread their blankets over it. Their dinner was simple, bread and warm wine and olives. He asked her to sing for him, the songs she had sung with Helen and the maids by the river. Already it felt like a lifetime since those idle days.

They needed no fire in the warm night air, and went to bed soon after night fell. Penelope lay awake long after Odysseus fell asleep, studying the stars through the lacy canopy of leaves and branches. Her thoughts twisted and skittered like windblown leaves, sorting through the last few days.

Everything had happened so quickly. She felt some shame, but no real regret in standing against her uncle. Penelope knew she had matured in leaps. The reason lay beside her. What other man would see through her disguise and yet let her keep her illusion of freedom, answer all her questions and value her as highly as he had confessed to the king? Penelope liked to learn, to know what went on in the world beyond the walls of her home. Simply by listening, trying to understand, she thought she had a clearer picture of the world of the Achaians than most women.

Agamemnon, king of Mycenae, was the leader of the kings of Achaia. His rule was strong, his reach everywhere. Odysseus had gone to Mycenae to advise him several times. Times were treacherous, though. The sailors who brought her to Pylos carried knives in their belts and spears were always within reach. Tensions rose on the merchant vessel whenever a stranger ship approached. Ithaka, being an island, was a tempting prize for raiders, a place strangers would find hard to defend, but a good leaping point for those who wanted to raid the mainland.

She sat up. Odysseus murmured in his sleep and shifted the arm he had draped around her. Penelope smiled at his reaction. He was so careful of her, so eager to give her pleasure. Her breath shortened and her pulse quickened, remembering how he had guided her hands in their lovemaking that night, how he had taught her to guide his hands where his touch gave her pleasure.

"The old women don't know half," she whispered. Penelope remembered the talk she had heard growing up, about a woman's duty to pleasure her husband, to endure discomfort, to bear as many children as possible. They said carrying a child was the only time a woman had relief from her husband's demands.

The smile faded from her face. If she carried Odysseus' child, she would lose the pleasure of his bed for a time. She didn't want to become pregnant soon. Her aunt had taught her it was better to grow a while after becoming a woman, before bearing children.

Penelope slipped from the nest of blankets and crept to the smaller chest of her possessions. Among the healing powders, ointments and perfumes lay a tiny box, wrapped in cloth. The seeds, roots and leaves were whole, to preserve their strength. She brought out her tiny mortar and pestle and ground a pinch of the mixture, mixed it with water and drank the potion immediately. It was better when heated and mixed with wine, but still potent cold and would keep her from conceiving. She gagged on the bitter, chalky mixture but drank it down.

*   *   *

They reached Pylos early afternoon the next day. Slaves waited at the city gates to take messages and Odysseus sent one ahead to the palace. Penelope reluctantly loosed her comfortable hold around Odysseus' waist and set herself to fixing her hair and wiping away some of the grime of travel.

Nestor's son, Straltos met them at the gates of the palace. He was a few years older than Penelope. She remembered him as full of mischief, too tall for grace, always ready to pull her hair when no adults were around. She decided not to mention that memory to him, but if it would make Odysseus laugh, she would tell her husband later.

Straltos had gained grace and graciousness. He favored his father, with wide shoulders and long-fingered hands. His face like a falcon would have been fierce except for the brilliant light of joy in his eyes, the ready smile and laughter on his lips. Penelope smiled but said little in greeting. She felt Odysseus stiffen, his hand tightening around hers when Straltos kissed her forehead in greeting. It bothered, then flattered, then worried her when she considered his reaction.

No one had exaggerated, comparing Nestor's palace favorably against the palace in Sparta. Every wall was painted, murals in bright colors depicting scenes from legends, or pictures to give honor to a god or goddess, or simply beautiful patterns of squares and circles and vines running throughout. The colors glistened as if freshly painted—strong black, red brighter than blood, blue deeper than the sea. Even the tiles on the floors were in colors and patterns. Bold black and white squares. Soft yellow with varying shades of green, reminding her of the haze of young grain in the fields in the spring.

She nearly laughed aloud, partly in relief, when she saw the plain white ceiling and one bare wall in the chamber she entered. She could not, though. The housekeeper waited for a word of approval and two maids waited to help her bathe. All three looked enough alike to be mother and daughters, all pale gold hair, brown eyes, and round, somber faces. Penelope put on her mask of distant graciousness, thanking one, giving instructions to the others.

Her thoughts wandered to Odysseus as the maids bathed and oiled her tired body, plaited her hair and helped her dress. Her husband had likely hurried through his own bath and followed Straltos out to the beach. The king and the royal household were performing sacrifices there to bless the change of seasons. The men would eat dinner together and talk, most likely about war, piracy along the coasts and preparations for winter. Penelope would join Nestor's daughter, Polykaster for dinner, along with whatever brides had married his many sons since she had last visited.

Penelope looked forward to it. She was a married woman now. She could laugh with the others and understand the hidden meanings that had escaped her before. In the evening, Odysseus would come for her so she could talk with their host. Penelope felt torn in her desires. She wished Eurynome and the others would prolong their trip, to extend the stay in Pylos, and wished she and Odysseus could set sail without them.

*   *   *

King Nestor declared a celebration the next day. Penelope was awed and delighted to realize the man showed as much pride in Odysseus' marriage and choice of bride as he would have for his own sons. He ordered sacrifices to ensure blessings on the bridal couple, fertility, and safety on their voyage to Ithaka. The feasting and dancing and music started soon after dawn and lasted past sunset. Nestor ordered a special canopy erected for the women at the edge of the gaming field. Slaves with fans and jugs of wine, bowls of fruit and anything else necessary for their comfort waited at their pleasure.

Odysseus excelled at the games, as she had predicted he would in Sparta. Penelope knew her face was in continual blush from the attentions he paid her and the comments other men made in her hearing. She didn't mind, even when she heard men laugh at how cunning Odysseus was besotted with his bride.

Her husband joined her after every contest, often kissing her in full view of everyone. He sat at her feet and shared her wine cup, careful to place his lips where hers had touched. She grew drunk on more than the wine and the excitement of the games. The promises in his eyes made her eager for the night.

*   *   *

Shadows stretched long, thin and dark through the halls and chambers of the palace. Singing and laughter still rang in the open courtyards where some men and boys insisted on continuing the games. Penelope slowed her steps through the long hallway, listening for people moving about. She would be teased by those who knew her. Others would whisper, some elders smile indulgently if she were caught here, far from her chamber. A bride of three nights, she was supposed to wait for her husband to come to her, not wander the halls looking for him.

Penelope shook her head. She didn't wander. She knew exactly where Odysseus would be. After the long, hot, dusty day of competition, he would be in the baths. Perhaps by this time he would be lying still, with a servant rubbing warmed oil into his muscles. After such ministrations, she knew he would be tired and relaxed, eager for sleep. Penelope bit her lip against laughter at her thoughts and desires. She didn't want her husband to merely come to their bed, kiss her, and fall asleep.

As she thought he would be, Odysseus lay face down, naked on a padded bench, with a slave woman about to rub oil into his shoulders. His eyes were closed, hair dark and curling from his bath. The room was otherwise unoccupied, damp from water poured out, wet sheets hanging to dry, the air heavy with scented oil and torches slowly burning out.

Penelope signaled the servant to be quiet as she entered the room. A smile of understanding touched the older woman's face. She nodded and stepped back, snatching up a towel to dry her hands before she left. Penelope picked up the vial of oil and poured some into her hands. She rubbed it into Odysseus' back, working down to his waist.

Odysseus tensed for a moment. She watched him carefully, waiting, but he relaxed after a few seconds and lay silent, eyes still closed. She worked down his legs, remembering how the muscles had knotted during the contests of strength. Even coated with dust and sweat, he outshone all other men that day.

"Witch." Odysseus' voice came out low and rumbling. "Are you trying to put me to sleep?" Without a twitch of warning, he sat up, twisting around on the bench. He caught her by her waist and pulled her down onto his lap. "Are you?" he demanded, pretending fierce anger. Then he kissed her, as hungrily as if they had been parted for days.

"I didn't want to fall asleep waiting for you," she said, when he finally released her mouth. He laughed, shook her, and then held her close again.

"A witch indeed. An enchantress. Did you think I wouldn't recognize your touch?"

"I had hoped," she admitted. "Do you forgive me, shaming you like this by seeking you out?"

"Shame?" His chuckles vibrated through her body as he held her close. "Oh, my sweet Penelope." His laughter turned into a groan. "I should spirit you away this very night. I do fear others will realize what a treasure you are and try to kill me to make you their own."

"Whatever you decide, I will follow."

"Something bothers you. Your uncle's words?" he asked, releasing her enough to see her face in the torchlight.

"Not fully. Maybe it is just women's worries...or fears of losing you to another," she added, giving him an impish look.

Odysseus shouted in laughter and kissed her again. Many long moments later he released her enough to let her speak.

"I have a fear of my own, in truth," she continued in a whisper. "We will not be fully wed, our life together fully begun, until we are home in Ithaka. And though we are both young...my dreams shout to hoard our time together. We live an illusion of many years before us." It was hard to meet his gaze. Penelope rarely spoke about her dreams to anyone. Her dreams the night before, though woven with happy images of her life with Odysseus, had been troubling.

"I've already sent word to my men to prepare the ship," he said, releasing her and gently nudging her off his lap. He stood, reached for his tunic and pulled it over his head. "When your people join us, we'll sail." He twisted both hands into her hair as he drew her close again, and chuckled when she smiled. "That pleases you?"

"I heard King Nestor speak of keeping us here to celebrate for a week, at least."

"Nestor is a good friend and a generous host, but he understands that Ithaka calls. And he thinks I am merely an eager, jealous bridegroom. Which I am," he added. He twisted his grin into a frown when she laughed in pure delight. "Woman, don't mock your lord and husband."

"Odysseus—" Her words were lost in a gasp when he bent and slung her over his shoulder. She couldn't breathe for laughing. Her hair, loosed for bed, hung in her face, blinding her.

"You must learn not to awaken a man ready for his sleep, Penelope. And learn the consequences when you do." Odysseus strode out of the room, down the hall, up the stairs to their chamber. Penelope knew members of the household saw them, laughing together, her half-hearted struggles in his arms. She couldn't see them for her hair in her face or hear them for her heart thundering in her ears. She didn't care.

CHAPTER 9

Eurynome, Dolios and his family arrived in Pylos late afternoon the next day. A slave boy came to tell Penelope while she walked in the gardens with Polykaster. They rested from the heat and excitement of the games, though Penelope wished she could watch Odysseus continue winning. She thanked the messenger and hurried with Polykaster to the palace gates to greet the rest of her household.

They all looked tired, dusty, and hot from their journey. Penelope recalled too well the discomfort of riding in the carts and she pitied them. Polykaster called for servants to lead the newcomers away to baths and clean clothes. Penelope's heart soared. In the morning, they would leave for Ithaka.

When Eurynome came to attend her before bed that night, Penelope didn't notice the woman's somber mood at first. She chattered about the games and the richness of Nestor's palace while the woman brushed her hair. Only after a while did she notice her nurse's unusual quiet. Penelope doubted Eurynome was only tired from the trip. When asked, the woman shook her head.

"No, the trip was easy. Dolios sets a good pace. It's that girl." Eurynome put down Penelope's brush and gestured for her to lie down so she could rub her with scented oil.

"What did Melantho do?" Penelope smothered a sigh, wondering what new tricks her maid had discovered.

"She tried to run away. She said Lord Aias was going to ask for her."

"I can believe that." Images of Melantho lying under Aias' writhing body came back to Penelope. She felt some pity for her maid, wondering if she had ever found pleasure with the man.

"Be that as it may, you and Lord Odysseus were not there to listen to her screech and cry. Dolios had to tie her to the cart. That girl says you left to *prevent* Aias from asking for her. I would avoid her hands until her temper cools."

"Is that why she isn't helping you tonight?" She smiled, thinking of Melantho trying to hurt her with nails or barbed tongue.

Penelope was too happy to let such petty things bother her. She had heard Nestor telling Odysseus if he were younger or his youngest son were older, he would have requested her for his own family. Odysseus had laughed, but she saw the spark of concern in his eyes. It delighted her that her husband felt even a slight bit of jealousy.

*   *   *

"Your father was a good friend," King Nestor said, standing on the docks at Pylos. He rested his hand on Penelope's head in blessing. "He would approve very much of your husband. You are blessed, child. Odysseus will give you great happiness if you stay true to him."

"I know." Penelope fought the feeling of being very young and small and helpless.

"Even so young, he is known for his cunning and strength. The other princes and kings of Achaia look to him for advice. There are greater riches than a large house, fertile land and gold." Nestor nodded, emphasizing his words. "You hold his heart. Treat it gently."

"I would never willingly hurt him," she whispered. She held the edge of her veil, as the breeze off the water tried to pull it free.

"No...you would not." He smiled and offered her his hand. He helped her step up the sloping plank into the ship.

Odysseus' men worked to raise the sail, checking lines and stowing last-minute supplies. Penelope stood by the rail, unsure where to go.

Then Odysseus appeared, glowing with eagerness to set sail. He had left her sleeping hours before to prepare the ship. Penelope wondered that he had ever willingly left Ithaka to come so far to seek a bride. She murmured her farewells and thanks to Nestor, paying more attention to the last minute flurry of preparations, the way the final shreds of mist lifted from the water. Farewells always hurt, she decided. She wanted to be done with them and away.

Then the plank slid off the rail and the sailors hurried to their posts.

Odysseus led her to the stern, where he plied the rudder. Joy lit his face as the ship slowly pulled away from shore and out toward open water.

Penelope leaned against the railing at the stern and watched Pylos vanish in the early morning haze from the sea. She heard the thud of feet as sailors tended to the sail and re-adjusted the cargo in the hold, the creak of the rigging in the wind, the splashing of waves against the blue-banded belly of the ship. She laughed for pure delight and turned in her perch to face Odysseus, tending the rudder.

"Such a sad face, my wife." He shook his head. The laughter sparkling in his eyes ruined his disapproving expression. "Someone would think you were glad to leave such a gracious host as King Nestor."

"Perhaps you enjoy spending the day talking about ships and building them, fishing and sailing, the winds, and whether Ilion will increase its strangle hold on the Dardanelles. And then starting over again," she added quickly, when he opened his mouth to interrupt. "I would rather be on the sea than listen to talk of it, and mistress of your household rather than the most honored guest in the most beautiful palace in all Achaia."

"You should have been born a bard. You have a gift for words." Smiling, he gently took a handful of her loose blowing hair and drew her down onto his lap, to kiss. Penelope rested her head on his shoulder and closed her eyes.

They sat in silence. The gusting of the wind, the splashing of the waves, the creaking of the ropes and boards created music far different from that inside the palace. Penelope welcomed it and the changes it signaled.

During the last day of feasting and games, she had noticed a change in Odysseus. The richness and grandeur of Nestor's palace bothered him sometimes. Someone praised the fine drinking cups or the beauty of the wall paintings and Odysseus grew silent for a moment, studying the item praised. Penelope thought she saw uncertainty in his eyes then. Waiting for Odysseus to come to their bed that night, she considered the problem.

Tyndareos' insults to Ithaka *had* hurt her husband. His love for and pride in his home made him susceptible to insult and mockery. He compared Pylos with Ithaka, the household that waited for them, and found his home lacking. Penelope wondered if he feared her reaction when they reached Ithaka. She had a good idea what to expect, but how could she tell him that she welcomed the thought of a smaller house and a simpler life? Sparta and Pylos were pleasant, yes. The riches and countless servants made living easy. But she wouldn't welcome the task of being mistress of such a household.

Penelope knew she couldn't simply say those words. Instead, she asked questions about Ithaka that night until he laughed and pressed his hand over her mouth.

"I beg you," he had said, leaning over her, "wait until we are home and let me have my sleep now." He removed his hand and covered her mouth with kisses instead. When she was breathless, her heart pounding, he lay down again and gathered her into his arms. "We have enough for our needs on Ithaka. Food and clothing, solid homes, good hunting. Our shores are good for fishing and our shipmasters are the envy of other ports. Our men are born to the sea. We are strong because of our rough winters and the demands of the waves. Nothing beyond that, to claim fame or riches."

"It is the home of Odysseus," she had whispered into the darkness. "That is more than enough fame for any land." A last knot of worry had dissolved when he laughed.

Now, sitting beside him, Penelope hoped his worries had gone. She knew she would be happy in his home, no matter how simple. She promised herself, and him, she would manage his household well and make all other men envy him.

*   *   *

The second night out from Pylos, the ship made land between ports, on a wooded finger of land sticking out from shore. Penelope stayed on the ship while Odysseus, Dolios and his sons searched the woods. Sailing with the merchant ship before, she had always spent the nights ashore at ports, not making camp. She wavered between excitement at the roughness of their lodgings and worry over Odysseus' caution. When the men emerged from the woods, she cheered with the others. They carried a young boar strung on a pole between Dolios and his oldest son. Fresh meat for dinner.

The men had blankets in the grass far up from the pebbly shore, while Eurynome and Melantho shared one shelter of cloth and leafy branches, Aris and Dolios had the second, and Penelope and Odysseus shared the third.

When night came and the fires cast warmth in wide circles against the chill off the water, Penelope was glad they had stopped at this place. This simple life pleased her. One sailor played pipes and another had a lyre, making music the others could sing to. Melantho slipped off into the darkness, avoiding her mother's reproving frown. Soon giggles and stomping feet revealed the girl danced with one sailor or another.

Penelope smiled and leaned into the warmth of Odysseus' arm around her. She considered telling him she had dreamed they had nothing but their ship, and nothing to do but sail the world and see new lands. She knew he would laugh and kiss her, and if she looked closely she might see longing in his eyes.

She felt him tense and looked up to see him glancing around. Penelope listened and watched the other sailors. They had caught some clue from their master and came alert. The laughing and music around the fire faded away. Penelope caught a glimpse of one sailor, then another slipping into the darkness. Then she heard the crunch and slide of feet walking the pebbly shore. She looked to the left, down the shore toward the curve of the mainland, and saw a soft glow that grew brighter as a torch emerged from behind the trees.

"Greetings, strangers!" a man shouted. A pale speck in the darkness resolved into a man's face, lit by the torch, and several faces behind him.

"Greetings to you," Odysseus called, slowing rising to his feet. He shook his head, gesturing for her to stay put when Penelope made to stand with him.

She glanced at Eurynome. Her nurse had wrapped her cloak tighter around her shoulders. When she saw Penelope watching her, the woman lifted a portion of the cloth so it covered her hair. Penelope did the same. She gladly hunched into the warmth. The pleasant chill of the night air had grown clammy.

The newcomers were ten, all carrying knives or short swords. They smiled, but Penelope didn't trust them. The other nine men looked everywhere with appraising glances like traders on the docks, while their leader spoke with Odysseus. In the shadows and flickering firelight, they all looked alike; bronzed from the sun, shaggy hair, unkempt beards, some dressed in little more than loincloths. They had the distinct look of men who lived by their muscle.

"I am Aithon of Sikania," Odysseus said, in answer to the man's questions. "I serve a noble prince of that land."

"Why are you so far from home, then? And with so few companions?" The leader smiled wider, glancing around the group still sitting by the fires.

Penelope tried to hold still and ignore him when his gaze rested on her. She shivered. The man looked too pleased with their small numbers.

"My master sent me to find the fastest ship of all the Achaians and buy it for him. The sailors of Sikania are the best, so I only brought as many as I thought I would need." Odysseus shrugged. His face had become a mask to Penelope, a mixture of welcome to the strangers and embarrassment. She watched his back gradually stoop as he talked, and wondered if anyone else had noticed his tactic. In moments he was a stranger, a short, crooked man, somewhat simple in his thinking. No one of any threat.

"And the women?" The leader gestured with a negligent wave of his hand at Eurynome and Aris, then Penelope, and then out into the darkness beyond them.

Penelope studied the man more closely. He knew about Melantho, though she and her sailor were hidden in the darkness. She dared not look at Odysseus, but she knew he caught the implications. These men had spied on their company before letting themselves be seen.

"Servants for my master's house. They are not for sale at any price," Odysseus added after the slightest pause.

"We are too poor to buy, even at the smallest price," the man responded, laughing. The rocky sound of his laughter made her scalp prickle in warning. "If you like, we will stand guard to protect your precious cargo."

"I thank you." Odysseus bowed to the man, like an inferior. "But the men of Sikania are fierce warriors. We fear nothing."

"You are blessed with luck, then."

They exchanged a few more words, and the stranger offered protection again. Odysseus declined again, emphasizing how well his sailors could fight. They spoke of the weather signs for the next day and hazards to ships in the local waters. Then they parted.

Odysseus stayed on his feet, watching until the torch vanished in the distance and the sound of pebbles underfoot faded. Penelope said nothing as he settled down next to her. Speaking her worries would do little good and might distract Odysseus from precautions he likely planned. She welcomed the warmth and the strength of his arm around her and leaned against him. When he told her to go to bed, she obeyed in silence.

Penelope still lay awake when Odysseus joined her in the shelter. The moon hung straight overhead and the last hooting cries of night birds faded as they moved out to hunt. Penelope had gone to bed fully clothed and tucked her sandals under the blanket, within easy reach. Odysseus didn't take off his clothes before he slid under the blankets.

"You think they won't come back now?" she whispered. Her husband stiffened, then a low, gusting sigh escaped him. He turned onto his side and gathered her into his arms.

"Any other woman," he whispered into her hair, "would be asleep by now, thinking everything was fine. My sweet witch knows my thoughts, I can see."

"Other women were not trained by harmless madmen to consider numbers and strengths. We're in their territory. From their looks, they make a habit of greeting strangers."

"Too strong a habit," he agreed. They lay silent for a while. Penelope felt the tension running through his body, an alertness that made his pulse thud a little faster. She waited, listening to the darkness until he relaxed a bit.

"Who is Aithon of Sikania?" she whispered. A chuckle and a kiss rewarded her.

"No one, and anyone I wish him to be. Those men will try to rob us, I have no doubt. Whoever they think we are will affect the way they attack. If they knew we were from Ithaka, if I had given them my name, if they knew we were newly married...they might come back with more men and greater stealth. They see foolish merchants, foreigners, with a silly, boastful man for leader. They will come with too much confidence and not enough men. I hope."

"You frightened me." She pressed closer to him and felt the pulse in his neck against her cheek.

"Frightened you how?"

"I thought you had deceived my uncle, and you were not Odysseus at all."

For answer, Odysseus rolled her onto her back and kissed her thoroughly. It was hard to breathe with his mouth hard against hers and his hands finding every ticklish spot on her body, even through her clothes. The only way to resist was to press close to him, blocking his hands.

Then his touches changed, raising waves of desire. He mumbled a curse and tugged her skirt up to her hips. Penelope could only laugh, breathless and eager.

"Doubly a witch," Odysseus muttered, then kissed her again, lingering. "I should be grateful you didn't wear your cloak to bed as well."

Before she could think of a response, she felt him grow tense and alert again. She opened her eyes. In the pale glow of the waning moon, she saw him raise his head and look out over the camp. Bushes and tall grass stood between their shelter and the rest of the camp, for privacy. Penelope shivered, feeling isolated. She thought she heard footsteps through the soft, leaf-covered ground of the forest behind them. Or was that only her heartbeats? She felt Odysseus gather himself to get up and she released him. He crawled out of the shelter, then a moment later came back and pressed a length of wood into her hands. He kissed her fingers around the wood, and was gone.

Penelope tugged her skirt back down past her knees and rolled onto her side, to look out over the camp. She could see nothing but stars and the dark shadows of the high grass. She felt along the length of the wood, not surprised to find the bronze spearhead at one end. She reached for her cloak and wrapped it around herself.

She listened to the night until the only sound that filled her ears was the beating of her heart. Even the lapping of the waves had faded. She rested the spear on her lap and braided her hair, to get it out of her way.

Time dragged. She waited and listened until her eyes grew heavy and the soft shadows in the moonlight blurred. She could see nothing but bushes beyond the opening of the shelter. Shivering, she knew fighting her weariness would do no good. There had been no outcry, not even the rasping of voices in the night. Odysseus would walk a few times around their camp to ensure all was well, and then he would return to her. Penelope lay down facing the back of the shelter, one arm over the spear. She pulled the blankets up to her shoulders and tried to relax. Her heart slowed and she listed to the whispering of the waves on pebbles. The tension began to seep out of her muscles and she could close her eyes again.

Hushed footsteps came to her drowsy hearing. Penelope lay still, waiting. The footsteps paused at the front of the shelter, then the person knelt and crawled in, taking care to be quiet. She smiled, wondering what Odysseus would say when he found she had put the cloak on. He lifted the blankets and slid in next to her, pressing tightly against her back. His arms slid around her.

She smelled the metal tang and salt of old, dirty sweat, sour wine, and the stench of dirty, salt-crusted hair. Penelope gripped the spear as the man groped up her chest and dug his fingers into her breast. Fury bloomed, choking back the scream rising in her throat. She jerked the spear around, managing not to catch it on the poles of the shelter. She caught the man in the shoulder with the bronze point. He shouted in panic. Penelope smelled the warm salt of blood and twisted free of him. She left her cloak behind in his grasping hands as she thrashed her way through the leafy branches on that side of the shelter.

Somehow, she managed to keep hold of the spear through her struggles. Her hair tangled in the branches. She felt scratches on her face and her dress caught and tore. Penelope scrambled to her feet, gasping, listening through the pounding of her heart for sounds of struggle in the night. She ran from the shelter, holding the spear ready as Dymis had taught her.

Another man shrieked, and then stilled. From far off, she heard the thud of a body hitting wet sand. Men fought at the water's edge. She heard the crunching of feet on twigs and stones and backed further into the woods. In the haze of moonlight, she saw a man scramble out of the ruined shelter. She saw his features clearly—the leader of the raiders. He moved hunched over. His arm hung loose, useless, and he clasped his other hand over his shoulder. She thought she saw dark, glistening runnels moving down his arm, but couldn't be sure.

"Athena, thank you," she whispered, sure it was her husband's patroness who had guided her hand.

Penelope took two steps toward the woods to hide when Eurynome screamed. Her decision to stay hidden and give Odysseus free rein to fight vanished. Images of what the raiders could be doing to her nurse splashed across her mind. She ran toward the sound, trying to hold the spear level, ready to throw or thrust.

Dolios reached Eurynome before Penelope. He swung his sword around like Penelope had seen him use a scythe. The raider fell like wheat during harvest. Aris and Eurynome watched, standing before the ruined shelter. Their faces were identical pale moons, wide-eyed, lips pressed tight together. They turned, startled by Penelope's appearance and stared at her.

"My child—" The nurse's voice choked off in her throat. She hurried to Penelope, raising her arms to gather her close. Dolios followed, glancing in every direction to ward off attackers. Eurynome stopped short, a tiny gasp escaping her. "You bleed!"

Like in a dream, Penelope looked down. Drying spatters of blood darkened her bare arm. A crooked smile twisted her lips. The blood was not her own. Penelope shook her head. She had to think, to react like a man would in this battle. It was hard. She wondered that she had ever dreamed about pretending to be a boy and having adventures.

"We have to hide," she said, squeezing the words out. "The less people to defend, the better our men can fight."

Dolios nodded. A smile of approval cracked the dark mask of his face. He gestured for Penelope to lead. They barely took three steps toward the safety of the trees when Odysseus stepped out of the shadows. His tunic was torn clear off one shoulder. Blood streaked his sword arm and spattered his legs. In the shadows, his hair looked like dried blood, burning in the moonlight. A wild, furious fire gleamed in his eyes and his mouth was open as if caught in a shout. He stared at them, blinked, and the wildness fled like water flowing away.

"Penelope—"

"We're all right," she hurried to say. She wanted to fling herself into his arms and hide there. The blood and his fighting fury stopped her. This was a side of him she hadn't seen, even when he threw Aias off her. For a moment he had been a terrifying stranger and that moment frightened her more than the fear he had been hurt.

"Go to the ship," he said, nodding. "The battle is over. Leave us to clear the field."

She stared at him, meeting his eyes in his dirty, blood-spattered face. Slowly, she nodded and turned, gesturing for the others to follow.

"Penelope!" Odysseus caught her by her arm and turned her. "You're bleeding." His voice broke.

"Not my blood. One of them tried to—" She caught her breath and forced herself to smile at him. "One of them tried to climb into our bed. His blood, not mine."

"Which one?" His voice was a growl.

"Their leader, I think." Something in his voice warmed and thrilled her, even as another shiver of non-recognition passed over her body. Penelope hurried to the ship when he released her, glad she would not see what would happen next.

"Melantho," Eurynome gasped as she and Aris ran to catch up with her.

"What about her?" Penelope tried to remember if she had heard a woman scream besides Eurynome. Everything was a blur of fury and surprise. She studied Aris, quiet and expressionless in shock.

"She slipped out after I fell asleep. A sailor..." Eurynome's face looked gray in the moonlight.

"If Melantho is hurt, it's her own fault." Penelope bit her lip to keep back more angry words. How could she make them understand? "She chose to leave our camp. Even a fool would have known those men weren't going to leave us in peace. If she is hurt, Odysseus and Dolios will discipline the man she was with, not you." She lifted her skirts, tucking the torn end into her belt. She didn't wait to see if the women followed, but waded out to the ship.

*   *   *

The fire on the beach grew brighter, taller. In its light, Penelope watched the men moving about, cleaning up after the battle. She knelt in the prow of the ship and waited. The anxious tightness in her heart eased a little every time she glimpsed Odysseus in the firelight.

Dolios and a sailor, anonymous in the shadows, waded between shore and ship to bring their supplies back. Eurynome and Aris worked in silence to pack everything away, always hurrying back to the railing to look to the shore. Penelope reached for the spear from time to time, as if it would bring safety to the men.

The third trip back, Dolios led Melantho. The girl quietly wept. As she reached the ship and handed up her basket of tumbled food, her face showed bruises. Penelope said nothing until Melantho had climbed up the rope ladder into the ship and Dolios returned to shore.

"Were you able to hide?" she asked her maid, detaining her when Eurynome went into the hold with an armful of blankets. Melantho nodded, hurriedly wiping more tears off her face. "How did you get hurt, then?"

"He hit me." She looked up, her movement sharp and furtive when her mother stepped into view. The woman looked at her as if she had never seen her daughter before.

"Who did?" Penelope held her breath. She had seen Odysseus' anger now, in different phases. She would have been hurt but not surprised if he had hit the girl for acting so foolishly.

"Pherios. For taking him away when there was a fight." Melantho choked, wiping once more at her face. "Men can be such fools, sometimes."

"Sometimes," she agreed, then gestured for the girl to help Eurynome and her mother. Penelope silently scolded herself for expecting such things of her husband.

Dawn touched the sky with pink and gold when the fire on the beach suddenly caught and spread in a high, long pile. Penelope thought a moment, trying to see through the flickering, blinding flames of the funeral pyre. She knew of many men who would deny their conquered adversaries a decent funeral, and leave their dead, mutilated bodies to lie and rot under the sky like animals.

Against the glare of the fire, the men waded back to the ship. Some threw their weapons onto the deck and then ducked under the water of the rising tide, washing off the grime of their battle and labors. Penelope watched Odysseus return last. She leaned over the railing, holding her hands out to him. Weariness and the cold, ashy residue of anger made a cloak around him, bowing his shoulders. He looked at her unseeing for a moment, then reached up and took one of her hands.

"Wait a moment more." He squeezed her hand, then handed his sword and spear up to her.

Penelope took them gingerly, expecting them to both be spotted with blood. They were clean. Traces of sand from scrubbing stuck to the shaft of the spear. Odysseus dropped to his knees in the water, letting his head go under. He came back up sputtering softly, scrubbing his face and hair with his hands. As he climbed the ladder, she ran and fetched a sheet for him to dry with. He draped the sheet over one arm and led her to the stern.

"We sail now!" he shouted. The sailors let the sail fall. It caught the morning wind, streaked with pink and gold from the sunrise. Odysseus wrapped the sheet around his waist and took hold of the rudder.

In silence, the ship left anchor and headed out into deeper waters again. The flames of the funeral pyre grew smaller in the distance as Penelope watched. She shivered, wondering if the man who touched her was on the pyre.

"What are you thinking?" Odysseus asked, his voice a rough whisper, softened with weariness.

"How many died?" For a moment, she couldn't face him.

"Seven. Their leader among them. Dolios found him before I did," he added, one corner of his mouth rising for a second. "The ones who lived know who they were fighting. Maybe now they will not so easily attack travelers."

"They know...you told them, and released them?" Penelope shook her head, trying to understand. "What if they call their kinsmen together for vengeance?"

"Who would justify them? Who would help them?" He sighed, closed his eyes, and leaned hard into the rudder. "Penelope, they took their lives into their hands in a wager, and lost."

"I will never understand battle, or what drives a man to cut the life from another."

"Sweet Penelope, I hope you never do."

CHAPTER 10

The ship reached Ithaka in mid-afternoon, when the sun touched the top of the highest peak in the island's backbone. Penelope stood in the prow, leaning against the railing, trying to take in everything at once. Odysseus had described to her the greater and lesser bays. Their unfinished home sat in a narrow span of land, a wasp-waist bridge between the two islands that made Ithaka. She knew it was foolishness to try to see the house, the orchards and the high wall surrounding it, but she tried anyway.

She tried to see everything, how the water changed shades of blue as the depth changed, how the shading of green on the trees differed as they grew thicker and higher, the rippling white and gold of the sand along the shore. Penelope counted the seconds as the ship sailed past a cove on the southern side, going into the greater bay and then swung south and east for the lesser bay. The journey from the landing to their home would be a longer walk than from the greater bay, but the lesser bay provided good anchorage and protection.

As the sailors jumped over the side to ease the ship onto the sand for docking, Penelope caught glimpses of people running for the bay and others running away. She followed the path of a boy in a blue loincloth as he hurried up an incline. The ship had been recognized, and someone ran now to tell King Laertes Odysseus had finally come home.

Yes, she admitted now, Ithaka was a rough and rocky place. Penelope was glad of that. It made Ithaka hard to overthrow. Only those trained on the island, familiar with all the hidden places and the uneven landscape, could hold and defend it. She turned around, studying the wind-scoured crags, the slope of the beach. Even in the hottest summer, there would be cooling breezes from the shore. Penelope turned to look up to the ridge where Odysseus' home sat. Even from a distance, it looked rich and beautiful. Her husband had said the island had known lean years. Penelope wondered how Ithaka would be in lush times, because it was beautiful now.

"Home," Odysseus said, coming up behind her. His voice was thick with satisfaction.

She turned around and looked down at him from her perch. There was nothing she could think of to say, so she smiled and held out her arms. He reached up and helped her down, stealing a kiss and then tugging on her braid before releasing her.

"Tonight, we sleep in our own bed. Tomorrow..." A laugh of exuberance burst from him. "Tomorrow, we make plans."

"Plans for what?"

"Everything." He opened his mouth to say more, but a shout from the beach caught his attention. Odysseus waved in response. "Come." He strode to the railing and jumped down into the water, then reached up for her. Odysseus carried her until they reached the sand.

Penelope would have known his parents anywhere, just from Odysseus' descriptions. They were surrounded by people, some calling greetings, others watching. Penelope ignored them and concentrated on the couple advancing toward her.

Laertes stood tall despite the stooping weight of years on his shoulders. The flesh had begun to shrink from his face and arms, leaving a deceptive thinness. His hair showed streaks of silver among the warm, thick brown. His eyes were almost amber and sparkled with life and interest. He walked with a firm stride across the sand, guiding the woman with him by a touch on her elbow.

Antikleia, Odysseus' mother was a short, plump woman, her hair tending to gold with much red in it. Penelope saw tightness in the woman's mouth, wrinkles around her gray eyes. Sadness and worry hung on her like heavy ivy that sucked at her vitality. Shadows lined the pale, round face, where there should have been a rosy glow. Penelope felt pity for the woman, not the wariness she had expected.

Odysseus set her down on the sand and gripped her shoulder, gave her an encouraging smile and led her to meet his parents. Penelope heard comments now from the crowd. She nearly smiled when she heard a woman remark on her being "such a little, dark maid." Penelope found she didn't mind. Until she heard a man remark that he thought Helen was tall and golden. A tiny spark of anger turned quickly to laughter she could hardly repress. These people *expected* Odysseus to bring Helen as a bride.

A tightness in her chest vanished when Laertes smiled at her. Her face warmed and she felt the blush moving over her neck and face when Odysseus put his arm around her waist, drawing her close against him.

"Welcome, Penelope, daughter of Ikarios," Laertes said, resting his hand on the top of her head in blessing. "As my son has taken you to his heart, I welcome you to our home and family."

"I welcome a new daughter to our house," Antikleia said, her voice soft, almost breathless. For a moment, the worry at the back of her eyes faded and her smile was genuine. She glanced back and forth between Odysseus and his bride, hesitating. Then she leaned forward and kissed Penelope on both cheeks. "You make him happy," she whispered before drawing back. "For that alone, I welcome you gladly."

"I gave orders for a feast," Laertes said, his voice booming and hearty, cutting through the cloud of questions in Penelope's mind. "We were thinking we would have to endure the winter without you. The gossip from the ports said there was no man Tyndareos considered good enough for Helen."

"Menelaos is the chosen one," Odysseus said, looking around at the waiting crowd with a wide grin. "And that is all the news you'll get from me. Question my men to death, if you must know the market talk," he added with a laugh.

Some of the crowd laughed with him and began to scatter. Penelope was glad when Odysseus kept his arm around her as they left the beach. Antikleia walked at her side and Laertes walked next to his son. Penelope contented herself with taking in everything she could see, as they walked up the paths, across the narrow meadows. The men kept the conversation between themselves, Laertes asking questions and Odysseus answering, spinning everything into a tale.

Penelope stole glances at Antikleia from time to time. The woman watched the ground as she walked, as if she thought it would change suddenly under her feet. Occasionally she would look up, the sadness in her eyes fading as she looked at her returned son. She was oblivious to all else. Penelope doubted the woman would even hear her if she spoke to her.

Penelope felt some relief, touched with sadness. Odysseus had told her they would live in his parents' home until the house he built was finished. She had not looked forward to any conflict that might rise between his mother and her. As Odysseus' wife, it was her duty to take charge of his household, yet not insult or steal the authority of his mother. Penelope wondered how involved Antikleia was in the day-to-day affairs of the estate, and how much power the housekeeper had. She envied Helen, who had few changes to make in the household of the palace of Sparta.

*   *   *

"My son, you are the one who married her, not I." Laertes' laughter rang from the courtyard below, catching Penelope's attention. "Why do you try to convince me?"

She stepped to the window of the room she shared with Odysseus in his parents' house, her fingers fumbling with the clasp holding her dress up at her shoulders. Through the curtained doorway, Eurynome prepared her bath. Penelope had looked forward to the comfort of a warm bath after days of traveling and cold springs for washing. Until now. Her husband and his father had already bathed and changed and now talked in the courtyard alone. She knew it wrong to listen to a conversation that didn't include her; especially one *about* her. Penelope couldn't push away her curiosity. She hissed as the clasp finally opened and the pin pricked her finger. She held her dress up with one hand, sucked on the injured finger, and listened.

"You sounded skeptical. I merely want to convince you of the wisdom in my choice," Odysseus said. The two men stepped into her view now, walking from under the balcony below her feet. He smiled at his father, one hand on his shoulder.

"When have you ever made a decision that wasn't profitable?" Laertes' voice held teasing and laughter now.

"The reason for your doubts still escape me, Father. What more do I have to say? I asked everyone I could, to find out everything about her. She helped to manage her grandfather's household and farm. She can calculate like a scribe and keep records. I told you how she defended herself when we were attacked and when Aias—"

"Yes, yes." Laertes shook his head. "I never thought to see you lose your reason for a beautiful face."

"She is more than beautiful, Father." Exasperation touched Odysseus' voice. Penelope felt torn between amusement and embarrassment at the passion of his defense. "She is alive—alert—her mind is quick to grasp and remember what other women ignore. She has spirit and courage. She is more than just a decoration for my household and a body to warm my bed."

"Ah, and now we approach the problem." Laertes held up his hand, to forestall more protests. "She *is* beautiful and young. Perhaps too young and small. Can she give you healthy sons?"

"She is still gaining her growth. If all I wanted was a healthy son, I could have bought any wide-hipped slave girl for that. Father, why can't I make you understand?"

"I understand very well." He sighed and gestured toward a bench next to a pool at one end of the courtyard. Laertes sat down, moving slowly. "For the good of Ithaka, she must give you a son. Soon. If there is any power left in the old worship, it must be invoked now."

"Penelope understands the old ways. She understands more than she lets you guess." Odysseus laughed. "I learned everything about her that I could, then went to Pylos to see her when she arrived. She escaped her guards to go back to her ship to retrieve a toy, and when Aias accosted her, turned out a tale that later caused him great trouble. I knew then, she was the one for me."

Penelope's fingers dug into the stone of the windowsill as his words echoed in her mind. Odysseus had known who she was from the start? He had come to Pylos to inspect her? Would he have saved her from Aias if she hadn't impressed him?

She pushed aside that question and doubt as soon as it arose in her mind, yet couldn't do so completely. She wanted to believe Odysseus would have protected her because she was Helen's cousin, because she was Tyndareos' niece, and because she refused Aias' advances—not just because he had decided she would be his and he protected his property.

"Someday, your tricks and plans will be your destruction," Laertes said. "Do you trust your wife?"

"As much as I trust you, or Mentor. Father, if I couldn't have won her fairly, I would have stolen her. I spread tales to frighten any noble who showed interest in her. It took cunning to win her friendship when she disguised herself as a boy."

"As a boy!" He laughed. "I can see you've found a wife to match you."

Penelope felt something tighten inside, a sense of uneasiness. Was that a compliment? Should she be flattered Odysseus had worked so hard to keep her for himself? These confessions to his father confirmed what she had heard others say about him, and she wasn't sure she liked that.

"You are my only son." The abrupt return to seriousness in Laertes' tone took her from her musing. "You were born late to your mother. The day your son is born, you will be king in my place. I cannot wait forever. I want to rest."

"You make me sound like a selfish man," Odysseus said, settling down on the bench next to his father. He groaned, the sound turning into a ragged chuckle.

"Far be it for me to accuse you."

"The women of her family line were priestesses to the Goddess. She could have been a priestess."

"If she was, you never could have brought her here, away from her home and the altar she was born to serve."

"I know that. But the people who still hold to the old ways, who worship in secret, will follow Penelope because of her mother's line. She will bring the final unity to Ithaka that all your battles could never accomplish. War will not win the hearts of the women, and they influence their husbands."

"Does she follow the old ways? That is the important question. If so, how does she feel, being given away like a slave when her ancestors had the right to choose?" Laertes looked tired now. Penelope thought he disliked asking the questions he voiced to his son.

"She does. She understands already she will be more a queen than Helen could ever hope to be. She knows I need her, that I chose her because of her wisdom and strength."

"Do you hold her heart, to trust her so deeply? My son, I could believe you bewitched, to be so trusting."

"I am bewitched. And she is a witch." Odysseus chuckled, the sound warm, sending a warm pulse through Penelope in response. "Father, she is alive like no other woman. Alert. Cunning. Strong. She knows how to sway a man with her mind and virtues, not just with her beauty and her sweet body."

Tears touched her eyes and she blinked them away. Penelope berated herself for doubting Odysseus. Perhaps his ways were devious, but his motives were true. She had to believe that.

"I see more than you tell me." Laertes paused, looking his son up and down. "She is strong. A better queen than your mother, perhaps?"

"I honor and love my mother." He stood, towering over his father.

"But the day my sister died, Mother turned away from the land of the living. She made herself no fit queen for you. She abandoned the Goddess and the old ways. Ithaka needs strength. Dreams and oracles and Athena's priests have warned me of dangerous days ahead."

"Penelope." Eurynome's voice, though soft, shocked her as it broke through her concentration on the men below.

She turned and found another woman in the room with her nurse. This woman was dressed plainly, her hair braided close around her head. She stood tall and strong and straight, a woman of authority. Brown eyes weighed Penelope. Ruddy cheeks and smooth, firm muscles in her half-bared arms proclaimed this woman a hard worker, healthy, and active.

"I am the housekeeper, Eurykleia," the woman said, her words soft and slow.

A spark touched her eyes and her lips lifted a little at the corners. Penelope had the sense that she had just passed a test. She recalled what Odysseus had said about his parents' household. Eurykleia had been his nurse and a woman of influence in other areas.

"Is there anything you require?" the newcomer continued. She turned to include Eurynome in the question.

"For myself, I have what I need," Penelope said. "Have the rest of my people been settled?"

"And all insisting on taking their duties immediately. They train well in Sparta." The woman gave Eurynome a smile and a short nod of her head.

"My husband said you would be a friend to us," Penelope ventured, encouraged by the knowledge that her nurse and the housekeeper already respected each other. She had worried about that more than any difficulties with Antikleia.

"And so I shall, mistress." Eurykleia's expression warmed. "Come, your bath grows cold. You have had a long, wearying journey, but you are indeed home now."

Penelope nodded. She felt another cord of tension loosen inside her with this new acceptance. She wished that women's gossip told a girl how to find her place with her husband's family, rather than what to do on her bridal night. This was far more important.

While Eurynome tended to her, Penelope thought over the conversation she had overheard. She had assumed Odysseus believed the old ways, but now she suspected he only spoke the words to placate people. He needed her, yes. He had spoken the truth there.

117

She was proud Odysseus chose her for her skills and abilities, not just for a royal bride to give him a proper heir. Yet she wished he had dwelled more on how beautiful he found her. Penelope laughed at her foolish pride and when Eurynome gave her a questioning glance, shrugged it off as nothing important.

*   *   *

"The armory will be here." Odysseus paced out a square on the packed dirt. "The threshold, over there, will be raised so the doors shut tight against the winter winds. Hearths in the center of the large rooms. And see this."

He took Penelope by the hand and led her through the arch of an empty doorway. The sky was bright overhead, shining through into the roofless main hall of the half-built house.

They had awakened early, almost with the dawn, to walk the short distance to his unfinished house. Penelope welcomed the chill of mist that slowly burned away with the rising sun. She smiled at Odysseus, delighted with his eagerness and pride as he led her from one echoing room to another, telling her where stairs would be, hearths, partitions, and ceilings to make a second floor. Now he led her outside, past the servant quarters.

"I devised a way to bring the water of the springs closer to us, instead of the women carrying jars back and forth all day." He gestured for her to inspect the stone-lined ditch that fed water into a cistern in the courtyard. "When the winter storms blow, we'll be warm in our home and no one will need to leave it for anything."

"You're like a little boy with a new toy," she teased.

"Does a boy think only of guarding his treasure?" Odysseus returned, drawing her close to kiss.

"So many plans and schemes," she murmured. "You will drive yourself half mad someday, with your tricks and tales. How do you keep your stories from tangling in your head?"

"I do it because I must." He shrugged. "Here, I want to show you something, and then we must go back. Father has called an assembly of the elders this morning so I can answer all their questions at once." Odysseus sighed, putting on a mask of long-suffering.

Penelope shook her head, knowing he acted for her amusement. She knew he reveled in having an audience, drawing reactions with a twist of a phrase.

One section of the house had its roof already, next to the main hall.

Behind a door bound with bronze, a narrow, sheltered stairway led to the second floor. Odysseus took her up the stairs, to a series of three rooms overlooking the inner and outer courtyards. Bronze shutters were closed to protect the furnishings already placed inside. Odysseus flung open shutters in all three rooms and gestured for her to inspect them.

The walls were plain, clean white, awaiting decoration. A long table, a wide chest and a bed frame, all of the same dark wood, all carved with the same design of owls, waited in one room. Penelope stepped up to the table and inspected the fine carving.

"Your work?" she asked, already knowing the answer. She looked up and smiled at him. "Owls, to honor Athena."

"To ask protection for my bride." He beckoned, and they walked through the doorway to inspect the other two rooms. They had stools, chairs and tables, waiting for occupants, different designs but all made by Odysseus' hand. The rooms echoed, waiting. "These will be your chambers, if they please you."

"Very much," Penelope murmured. She looked to the shutters that could lock tight, keeping all inside warm and dry. She envisioned the rooms flooded with sunlight when the day grew older. She imagined she heard springtime birds singing, smelled fruit ripening on the branches and vines in the orchards beyond the house. The trees were abandoned now as fall approached and the gardens slept. She imagined what the estate would look like, once people lived there.

"When our home is finished, I will make you a loom. Many in Sparta spoke of your skill in weaving," he added, when she looked at him, questioning. "A new loom, for a new bride and a new life for us."

"What should I make first on it?" she asked, smiling acceptance of his promised gift.

"What would you like to make first?" he countered. Odysseus reached for her hand and when she gave it, led her back to the stairs and down again.

"It is bad luck, tempting the Furies, to make clothes for a child not yet conceived." Penelope smiled when his hand tightened around hers.

"Penelope—"

"Your father wants a grandson very much."

"You heard us." His voice went flat.

"I am flattered you see so much to value in me, so soon. Eurynome once told me a man values his wife for the pleasure he finds in her body, then for the children she gives him, and later learns to recognize her other qualities. You are a most contrary man, my husband." She kept her face and voice solemn.

"Be careful, Penelope." He gathered her close at the bottom of the staircase, a strange light in his eyes. Then mischief wiped that expression away. He laughed and bent to scoop her up into his arms. "Your sweet body makes me forget all other reasons for marrying you," he said, chuckling.

Odysseus carried her to the closed room next to the bottom of the stairs. He fumbled for a moment with a key he had tucked into his belt when they left the house, unlocked the door, then nudged the latch with his knee. The door swung open without a sound into a dark room.

The darkness surrounded them, blinding after the brightness of outside. She lay quietly in his arms, unwilling to upset his balance. Then Odysseus stopped, setting her down so she sat high off the floor. The surface was rough and gave slightly under her weight. He sat next to her, making the surface bounce a little. Penelope felt on either side of her and touched a tight, closely woven netting of ropes, then a wooden frame.

"Your bedroom?" she guessed.

"Our most secret and safe place in all the world. That door has been locked since I left for Sparta. In times of danger, the secrets of this room will be a password between us. Give me your hand." He took it before she could respond and guided her hand to the head of the bed.

Her eyes were adjusting now. Penelope could make out lighter shadows and a tall, thin blackness that was a bedpost. She let Odysseus guide her hand over the wood, feeling the designs carved into it. More owls. It frightened her a little, how much he trusted in Athena's favor and guidance.

"A living olive tree, its roots still solid in the ground under this floor. No one can move this bed without first cutting the trunk, and I can only think of one way to do that without ruining the whole." His voice softened, deepened. Penelope wondered what troubling thoughts went through his mind as he spoke. "This will be a sign for us if danger comes and we are separated. If there is treachery and you trust no one as messenger, send me word that my bed has been moved."

"Is danger approaching?"

"Not yet. Perhaps not ever." He sighed and wrapped his arms around her. Penelope leaned into the warmth and strength of his embrace. "Ilion and Troy cause trouble for those who would pass through the Dardanelles to trade or explore. Agamemnon would avoid war, but if the rumors are true, it could come. Ilion could retaliate by sending raiders of their own to our lands."

"We are half a world away from Ilion," she retorted. "What danger could Ithaka be in?"

"Perhaps none. I learned it is better to expect danger and treachery on every hand and get by on half a night's sleep, than to trust without reason and be murdered in your sleep. There are few men I trust wholeheartedly. Those I do trust have earned it and have my undying loyalty."

"Your father thought it strange that you trust me so much," she murmured. "I have done little to earn it."

"If I don't trust my wife, how can she trust me?" he returned, tightening his arms around her.

Penelope nodded and returned his lingering kisses. A tiny voice of doubt whispered that he trusted her because she had no choice but to be faithful, or he thought she had no power to hurt him with treachery. She clung to him, longing for the spark of passion to destroy such thoughts.

*   *   *

"Blood sacrifices will not make a strong foundation," Penelope said, as Odysseus closed the door of their bedroom for the night.

"Shall I take you to all the forts that have stood for generations, built on the blood and bodies of sacrificed warriors?" He smiled as if her words amused him and began undressing.

"Forts, yes. Built for war. We are talking about a home, a place to raise children and live in peace. The Goddess never asked for blood to be spilled, to please her." She sank down on the bench next to the door.

That evening, she had sat quietly with her sewing and listened to Odysseus and his father discuss the sacrifices and ceremonies to bless their new home in only a few days. She had looked forward to the final preparations and listened to their conversation eagerly. There was nothing else to do but sew. Antikleia accepted her, was kind to her, but was no company at all. Penelope had listened, wishing she dared to offer suggestions.

It didn't take long to realize there would be no anointing blessing for the house as her aunt had taught her to make. She had grown frightened, then angry, and bit her lip to keep from speaking in front of Laertes.

"Were we talking about our house?" Odysseus tugged back the blankets and sat down on the bed. "You never said anything while Father and I were talking."

121

"Because I am still a stranger here!"

"This is your home. All of Ithaka belongs to you."

"Only as your wife. The people don't accept me for myself yet, because I have hardly left this house since we arrived." She stopped and swallowed hard, feeling tightness growing in her throat, a burning in her eyes that foretold tears. Penelope refused to let her control fall apart so easily. "They don't know me. I hardly know your parents."

"We have all been so busy, preparing our home, tending to island matters," Odysseus said, his words slow. He stayed seated, when she wanted him to come to her, gather her up in his arms and hold her tight.

"I know that. Yet I can't help thinking of your promises that we would explore Ithaka together. You said you would teach me all about our home. I know nothing, the people don't know me. I am a stranger here."

"When we are in our home—"

"We will have more time to walk and explore and enjoy ourselves. I know." She tried to smile. "Odysseus, please—I'm not complaining. I understand. I can see how everyone demands your time. All I ask is that you change the blessing ceremony. Blood will not please the Goddess."

"The blessings of milk and wine will not please the other gods. Or the nobles of Ithaka. The Goddess is more understanding than our neighbors." He shook his head and held up his hand to forestall more argument. "I know what you want, and why. I'm glad you're careful of the old rituals. But in this matter my decision must stand. Come to bed."

Slowly, she stood and walked to the other side of the bed. Penelope blinked hard against the tears that still threatened. Eurynome had warned her times like this would come, she simply hadn't expected it so soon. She managed to smile for him as she took off her dress and hung it on a peg on the wall. Odysseus blew out the lamp flame and took her into his arms when she climbed into bed next to him. He kissed her and closed his eyes to sleep. She held still in his arms and stared up at the dark ceiling streaked with moonlight from the high, open window, and began to make plans.

* * *

The next night, Penelope waited until Odysseus slept before she followed her plan. She slipped out of their bed, dressed in the dark and hurried barefoot through the night to the empty, waiting house. She carried three small jugs, filled with wine, oil and milk, to bless the house as her aunt had taught her. Whispering prayers to the Goddess, naming her Athena, Penelope anointed the doors and the foundation from the three jugs.

The Goddess didn't demand spilled blood and death to call down her blessings. Laertes would perform sacrifices to bless his son's house in the morning. She wouldn't stand in the way of his duty. She simply knew that blood would not bring all the protection and blessing that their home needed.

Penelope lingered over the large, ornate bed in Odysseus' room, remembering the tale he told her of fashioning the bed frame. He loved puzzles and riddles and tricks. Every turn and twist that foiled an adversary was another victory in the struggle to protect everything precious to him. Penelope took special care in anointing his bed, to bring him protection.

When she finished, hurrying to keep from being discovered absent, Penelope returned to the wide, well-set door to anoint it a second time. She pushed it open to step out, clanking the nearly empty jugs against each other in her arms.

Seven silent, pale faces greeted her as she stepped out into the courtyard. Eurykleia stood at the head of the group. She held three pitchers cradled in her arms. Penelope regarded her husband's nurse in silence, returning the woman's silent scrutiny. What defense would she have if the woman denounced her, accused her of betraying her husband? Yet she dared hope those three pitchers were a good sign.

"Ithaka has a queen again." Eurykleia smiled. She gave a deep bow of respect to Penelope. The six older women behind her smiled as well. "Come, your blessing must be finished properly, as the Goddess instructs."

Penelope nodded and let the women lead her out of the courtyard, to the rocky cliffs three bow-shots away from the house. She didn't dare trust her voice. Relief made her knees weak, while exultation at discovering secret worshippers made her heart soar. It was more important, she knew, to have Eurykleia's approval than the support of Odysseus' mother.

The seven women led her down a narrow path along the cliff face to a cave overhung with creeping vines, damp with a spring that soaked through the cracks in the rock. The opening was narrow and long, like the opening of a womb. There had been no such place available in Alybas, the former sanctuary destroyed by warriors who attacked the area. The ruling elders, all men, had said it was useless to rebuild it, because no one needed such a place any longer.

Penelope trembled with excitement, seeing at last a proper sanctuary, attended by women as the Goddess instructed.

She heard a scratching sound behind her, then a hiss and sputter. A lamp flared into light and a woman put away the bit of flint used to strike the spark. Rough, rounded walls gleaming with paintings and damp surrounded Penelope. She stood still, gazing at everything until Eurynome raised her hand to gain her attention. The woman took a folded bundle of cloth from her outer wrap, put it on the low stone in the center of the cave and gestured for Penelope to unwrap it. Inside were honey cakes and pressed cakes of raisins, wet with wine and oil. Penelope understood what was to come next, though she had never before made an offering to the Goddess.

She walked around the stone until she found the hole in the floor of the cave, with cracks radiating out from it. As was proper and required, the hole led down to the bowels of the earth. Penelope knelt before the hole and held out her hands. While the other women chanted prayers for blessing and peace, fertile wombs and fertile fields, asking for warmth and shelter during the winter to come, Penelope took the pitchers from Eurykleia's hands and poured their contents into the hole. Milk, wine, and oil. Then one by one, she slipped the cakes into the hole, to follow the libations into the bowels of the earth.

"We have a queen again in Ithaka and all will be well," one woman whispered as the ritual finished.

The other six women filed out of the cave, leaving Eurykleia and Penelope alone with the flickering lamp. Eurykleia said nothing as she led the way out into the open air and the waning night. Penelope sensed approval and support from the housekeeper. It took the chill of the night away. She had come barefoot and without a cloak as was proper, letting little come between her and the Goddess' soil and sheltering night.

They walked back to Laertes' house together, quiet companionship drawing them closer. Penelope wished Eurykleia would be part of her household, to guide her in her duties as Odysseus' wife and queen.

As they stepped through the wide door into the front hall, where feasts and councils took place, Odysseus entered from the back of the house. He looked like he had awakened only moments before and dressed quickly. He stopped and stood still as a statue, watching Penelope and Eurykleia close and bar the door again. Penelope saw him and something tightened around her heart. She had been gone too long and he had awakened and missed her. She had no idea what to say to him, how to explain. Would he be angry? She *had* disobeyed. Eurynome's advice, to speak obedience but to do as she saw fit, was not as sound as it had seemed at the time. Then Odysseus' gaze shifted to Eurykleia and his guarded look relaxed.

"You must be cold. Get you back to bed." He nodded to his old nurse, his smile more in his eyes than his lips. Odysseus slipped his arm around Penelope's waist. "Your clothes are damp," he murmured as Eurykleia left them alone.

"Forgive me for worrying you?"

"I should have known better, but..." A muffled chuckle escaped him. "A dream woke me, and it was such that I reached for you before I woke."

"A dream?"

"A terrible dream." He led her back to their room. "I dreamed one hundred men pressed their suit to marry you and you looked at me and didn't know me."

"The day another man tries to claim me, I will be Dyvis again and run away." Her voice shook a little. She knew he wasn't angry.

"Penelope..." Odysseus caught her close against him to kiss her. She clung to him, feeling the warmth of desire begin to pulse. "You come from the Goddess," he whispered. "Penelope, bless me with your loving."

As he picked her up and carried her to their bed, Penelope felt a moment of regret for the bitter potion she had taken earlier. This night of all nights, a child so conceived would have been doubly blessed.

Later, as drowsiness wrapped around them, her thoughts returned to his reaction when she returned. Penelope pressed close against Odysseus and twined her limbs around him.

"Are you cold?" he whispered. He reached for the blankets they had pushed off the bed in their passion. All were out of his reach and he chuckled as he released her.

"You wanted me to go to the Goddess tonight, didn't you?" Penelope sat up, watching as he leaned over the side of the bed. It comforted her a little that Odysseus looked slightly shamed when he turned back to her.

"Would you have understood if I said, go and bless the house, but at night so no one sees you?"

"I think I understand a little, but...did you plan on my meeting Eurykleia and her companions?"

"That was a stroke of blessing." He settled down next to her and draped a blanket over them both. "Everyone knows the plans for the sacrifices. The servants of the Goddess will know what you did in the dark of the night, without your husband's approval. By showing you put higher value on protecting our people and serving the Goddess, rather than obeying your husband, you have made yourself priestess to the Goddess and proper queen of Ithaka."

"Eurykleia said that." Penelope sighed and closed her eyes and rested her head on his shoulder. The warmth of him felt good in the deepening chill of the night. "Must everything you do have a thousand reasons?"

"Not always." He kissed her, lingering, waking a spark of desire she had thought quenched for the night. "Trust me, even when you don't understand."

CHAPTER 11

There came a day when Odysseus didn't have visitors coming to their new home from every side of Ithaka, asking advice or judgment or help of some kind. It was a warm, early fall day, bright, with no clouds threatening on the horizon. Odysseus told Eurynome to pack some food in a cloth—grapes and bread, cheese and a skin of wine. He found Penelope in the courtyard, directing the planting of olive trees. When she turned to him, he caught her around the waist and led her to the outer gate of their house.

"They can work without your leading," he said, when she opened her mouth to protest. "Today is ours, to waste as we please." He laughed at the staring servants and gestured for them to go on with their work.

"But Odysseus—" Penelope stopped short to avoid running into a stack of firewood.

"I promised to show you Ithaka, moons ago. This may be our only chance before winter storms keep us housebound."

Penelope could think of no argument to his reasoning. She laughed and gave herself up to his leading. Whatever they did that day, she knew she would enjoy it. She missed the moonlit talks in the garden in Sparta, the hours of talk they had enjoyed on their journey to Ithaka. Lately, she only saw her husband in the evenings or when he came to her room to share her bed. Odysseus carried most of the duties of Ithaka's king for his father and it took large amounts of his time. All the more reason, she knew, to enjoy these few stolen hours with him.

They were barely out of sight of their home when they met a farmer and his grown son heading to the harbor with a load of grain on two donkeys. Both men saluted Odysseus and he returned their greeting cheerfully. Neither smiled; their bows of respect to their prince were stiff. They hesitated, studying Penelope a moment too long before greeting her and wishing her well. She smiled, nodded and stayed quiet.

"Is it because I'm a stranger here?" she asked Odysseus, once the men were out of earshot.

"Hmm?" He looked at her, then back over his shoulder. "You strike every man speechless with your beauty."

"Odysseus, don't mock me." Despite the prickle of warning raised by that introspective look in his eyes, she smiled.

"Who can guess the thoughts in a farmer's mind? Rumors travel this island faster than the wind. There's little anyone can do to stop the people from believing."

Penelope decided to give up. Either Odysseus didn't want her to know the reason, or he didn't know. She had expected all Ithaka to admire their prince. Whatever the farmers had heard, they had no affection for Odysseus at that moment.

A short time later, they came to a rise in the path. Trees lined the way and it curved so they couldn't see what came before or behind them. Shadows made a pleasant change from the warm brightness of the day. When Odysseus halted and turned to her, Penelope slipped her arms around his neck. Laughing, Odysseus wrapped both arms around her, lifting her so her toes dangled. They had barely begun kissing when she heard the distinct bleating of goats coming over the hill ahead.

"Did you bring me out here *only* to seduce me?" she whispered.

"Witch," Odysseus growled. His scowl became a grin. He set her down, releasing her with a caress. "I should pray for a storm to keep us prisoner for a week. Then I'd show you seduction."

"I am always willing to learn, my lord." She laughed when he snatched at her, and darted out of his way.

The goats poured around the shadowy bend, filling the path. Penelope pressed against a tree trunk as an aromatic flood of shaggy brown and white and speckled coats separated her from Odysseus. He stood on the other side of the path and laughed at the surprise on her face. In another moment, the herder came into sight. The man's mouth dropped open when he saw Odysseus. He ran up through his milling goats, using his staff to push the animals out of his way.

128

Penelope didn't like how the man looked her over and grinned before turning to speak to Odysseus. From the stiffening of her husband's shoulders, she guessed that he didn't either. The goats' bleating assaulted her ears, a piercing sound that kept her from hearing what the man said.

Then the goats were past and she could cross the path again. Odysseus didn't reach for her when she rejoined him. Neither did he introduce her to the herder.

"Despite the sparse rains, the meadow is filled with thick, sweet grass," the man said. He looked to Penelope and nodded to her. "You'd especially appreciate that, lady."

"I have no idea what my lord intends," she returned. She looked to Odysseus to avoid the herder's gaze, rather than find explanations in her husband's eyes.

"He should set his cunning to help Ithaka, not the lords of Mycenae." The herder's voice grew sharp.

"You should tend your goats before they are stolen," Odysseus returned. The bitter quiet of his voice sent more prickles of warning up Penelope's back. Though she never heard that tone before, she thought she knew him well enough to guess it was the quiet before the storm.

The other man paled and backed away. Mumbling about his goats, he turned and left without any farewell. He swung his staff, whistling for his creatures.

Odysseus took her by the hand and led her away. The pace was quicker than before and she stumbled once before she could adjust her stride to match his.

"Penelope." Odysseus stopped. He looked away, his jaw clenching moment. "Forgive me. You are the last person I should punish for an idiot's words."

"Can you tell me what he said?" She waited but he didn't answer. "It has to do with the meadow?"

"That cursed meadow should have been—" He released her hand and stepped away. He kicked at a branch in the path, then stopped and seemed to regain control. "Legends. Foolish legends, which people grasp at like dying men grasping bits of wood in a stormy sea. At one of the high places, there is a meadow sacred to the Goddess." He turned back to her, his mouth twisted in a tight smile. "Her priestess made the Sacred Marriage there to bring crops in the lean years. Once a child was planted in her belly, the seasonal king was strangled and buried there."

"He said—" A thrill of horror chilled her. Penelope envisioned Odysseus still and cold, his face purple from the rope. It echoed dimly one of her visions of disaster.

"No, he wouldn't dare." The sharpness of his smile made her shiver. "He did say I should take you there, to return prosperity to Ithaka. You are no proper queen until you give me a son, and I am no proper heir if I can't get you pregnant."

"If it would help—"

"Penelope!" His bark of laughter scraped at her ears. He held out his arms. She gave herself into his embrace. "Little witch, much as I welcome any excuse to enjoy you...I will not parade you, naked, in front of a leering audience."

"They would watch?" Horror made her stiffen in his arms. She would have pulled free if he hadn't held her so close.

"They may try, but we won't be there. You are mine, and I share you with no man. Not even in his dreams." For a moment, Odysseus' embrace squeezed the breath from her.

*   *   *

That night as Eurynome bathed her, Penelope told her nurse of the encounters. She wished she could have gone to Eurykleia as well. The few times the housekeeper had come to fetch Penelope for night rituals, she had given bits of advice or explained relationships and family standings on Ithaka that had escaped the young wife before.

"We were better off in Alybas," Eurynome said with a snort, when Penelope had finished her story. "I've heard similar tales and people dare to come to me and ask—" She huffed, and turned away to get a brush.

"Ask what?" Penelope thought she could guess.

"They want to know if you are with child yet. The harvests aren't good this year. They want you to give them assurance of fruitful crops next year. Savages! In Alybas, you might have been laughed at, but not treated like a breeding slave."

"My duties *do* include providing a son for my husband. Even more so, as a queen."

"That is between you and him. The rest of this benighted island has no right to watch for your moon flow and study the size of your waist." She brushed hard, making Penelope's head jerk twice before softening her strokes. "Your husband does not help matters."

"He handled it well this afternoon." Penelope regretted bringing up the subject.

"Yes, today. But I have been watching and listening, child. Ithakans follow Odysseus because they know he'll always come away with a profit. They know he's clever and strong and no one who follows him will suffer. But I see little love for him. They'll always need a *reason* to obey, something that benefits them, not because they trust him. That's not good."

"He's still young, and he's not yet king." She sat forward, tugging her hair free of her nurse's hands. "My husband will win their love. It takes time. He has plans to make Ithaka prosper. They will love him then."

"For your sake, I hope so." Eurynome snorted again. "I hope he doesn't expect you to produce a child every year."

"He has no say in that regard," Penelope whispered. She could still taste the bitter, chalky potion Eurynome had brought her tonight. Her resolve wavered a bit, weighing duty to the Goddess against freedom of choice.

Eurynome's words returned to her thoughts. It was true, the people of Ithaka didn't love their future king as they should. Penelope remembered the small criticisms spoken against Odysseus in Sparta, the unkind looks she had seen cast at him. She remembered her other moments of doubt. The moments he hid the truth from her, used her to get a reaction from someone else. All small situations, easily forgotten at the moment. She wondered if he used others to manipulate her in turn.

Is there a glamour in my eyes? she wondered. *Does he make me happy for other reasons than that he cares for me?*

*   *   *

The first bitter storms of early winter lashed Ithaka. Penelope liked listening to the soft brush of wind-driven rain against the sturdy shutters in her workroom. It spoke to her of the strength and sturdiness of the whole house. She spun the wool from the fall shearing and designed her first weaving project in her mind. When the day's work was done and there were no island matters to attend to, Odysseus came to her rooms to build the loom. Progress was slow, but she didn't complain. She watched the growth of the loom under her husband's hands and wondered how it would be to weave baby clothes and sheets.

Members of the household watched her for the first sign of a baby blooming in her belly. The days and weeks went by, the phases of the moon changed. Her body continued to fill out, slowly, but not the drastic changes of a baby in her womb. She still took Eurynome's potion. Part of her dreaded Odysseus' reaction if he ever learned the truth. His disappointment frightened her more than his anger. Penelope scolded herself not to care what the servants thought, and devoted herself to running the household.

Helping her aunt had been good practice. With Eurynome's help, Penelope established efficient routines for the new household. Melantho enjoyed her role as second to the mistress of the house. Penelope had worried about her maid's sullen moods the first few weeks after arriving in Ithaka. All seemed well now, and Melantho was a loyal, hard worker once more.

Penelope welcomed the storms. She was greedy for her husband's time and company. The storms kept the ships grounded and men caught indoors. Odysseus had more hours to spare for other duties beyond resolving problems and giving leadership, more time the two of them could spend talking, making plans for their future. Odysseus put half his vineyard and orchards and some of his sheep and cattle into her care, for her personal servants to tend. Aris and her sons were put over those possessions, while Dolios stayed in the house as steward, aiding Eurynome. Working with Odysseus, Penelope found, was as pleasant as the drowsy contentment that wrapped around them before they fell asleep in each other's arms.

*   *   *

"Exactly." Odysseus nodded and gestured for Penelope to stand back. He knelt, sighting down the line of bronze axes balanced against each other, twelve pairs in a straight, narrow dirt trench in the middle of the feasting hall. "It feels like years since I've done this," he muttered.

Outside, a storm howled and battered uselessly against the sturdy walls of the house. The evening meal was long over. The elders of Ithaka had come to Odysseus' house to discuss winter damage and how the ships fared. Laertes had come, but he listened more than he spoke, turning more leadership of Ithaka over to his son. Penelope had left her stairway and chamber doors open so she could catch snatches of conversation, whenever the howling of the wind lowered enough to let her hear.

She knew soon, Odysseus would be king of Ithaka in everything but name. That last waited on her. Sometimes, though she liked Laertes, she resented the man for resting the kingship on the birth of his son's heir.

Now, everyone had left for their homes before the worst of the storm hit, except Laertes. Penelope had come down to join father and son by the hearth, to tell stories and talk. She enjoyed these quiet evenings with her father-in-law and suspected Odysseus' tales of her disguised as a boy made it easier for the man to talk to her.

Their conversation had turned to the wooing of Helen and the suitors' contests of skill. Laertes mentioned Odysseus' bronze-bound bow and the test of skill he had devised.

"The idea is to set up a narrow channel between the angle of the axe heads," Laertes explained. Penelope stepped away from helping Odysseus and went back to the hearth. He wiped some ash off the edge of the hearth so she could sit next to him.

"And then shoot the arrow along that channel without touching anything," she guessed.

He nodded. Penelope studied the line of axes down the length of the feasting hall. A thick cushion hung from the wall to catch the arrow at the end of its flight. If it was not knocked off course, its energy spent by brushing against one or several axe heads.

"Perfect." Odysseus stood up and walked back to join them. "Penelope, you have a deft hand and a true eye. No one else I know of could have set them so straight and true." He bowed extravagantly to her, making her laugh.

"Excepting yourself," his father said, his tone dry, eyes dancing with laughter.

"True. Now, for my bow." He reached for the ox-hide case lying flat on the nearest table. He paused, a lopsided smile on his face. "Every time I come back to it after a long absence, I wonder if I will still be able to bend it." He slid the bow out of its case, firelight reflecting on the bronze wrapped around the tips and the grip. Wood and carved ivory gleamed with a warm, soft light as he ran his hands up and down its length, checking for rot or worms or dampness that might have harmed it.

Penelope knew little about bows beyond what she overheard her cousins say. Her grandfather had preferred the spear or slingshot. The bow had a different design from others she had seen, more curve coming away from the grip. She wondered if this was what Kastor had meant by a bow that was tight and stubborn, only yielding to a loving touch.

"Coward," Odysseus muttered, grinning. He tossed the ox-hide cover aside and balanced the end of the bow on the ground, braced against his sandal-clad foot. He pressed from the top, catching the bowstring up quickly and slipping the loop over. It caught, and the bow gave off a low, thrumming chord as Odysseus plucked the string. He snatched an arrow from the quiver lying on the table, strode over to the end of the dirt trench, knelt and swiftly loosed the arrow.

Penelope held her breath as the arrow skimmed down the narrow gap of the axe heads. She listened for the click or hum or the ring of bronze that meant the missile had gone awry. Silence, broken only by the subdued howling of the wind as the storm gathered its strength. Then a solid *thunk* as the arrow hit the cushion on the wall. She leapt from her seat and ran to Odysseus, to fling her arms around him. He hugged her one-armed, holding the bow aside. He kissed her and laughed and spun her around the open floor.

"Oh, Penelope, Penelope." Odysseus sighed, closing his eyes and resting his head against the top of hers. "You make me think I can do anything, that you never doubt me."

"You are my husband," she retorted, half teasing, half serious. "If I don't stand behind you, who will?"

"Indeed," Laertes said from his comfortable seat by the fire. "Son, guard her carefully. I see a hundred men coming to steal her from you, the moment you give her cause for complaint."

"Put no ideas in her head!" Odysseus said, mocking fear twisting his face into a comical mask. He led Penelope back to the hearth and sat down, with her between him and his father. "I admit, I did doubt my skill for a moment."

"A very brief moment," his father muttered, drawing a giggle from Penelope, a long-suffering sigh from Odysseus. "Have you told her the tale of the bow yet?"

"No, he has not." Penelope snatched up the ox-hide cover from the floor before Odysseus reached for it. "A thousand tales he has told me, but this is the first time I heard about bow or axes. Tell me now." For good measure, she sat on the cover.

"Father, I swear before all the gods, you're a bad influence on my wife. She only torments me like this when you're around." Odysseus braced the bow against his foot and loosed the bowstring, then balanced the weapon on his knee. He scowled at them, but Laertes and Penelope only waited. "Very well, if you both insist." He took a deep breath and the look in his eyes became distant.

"I was just seventeen and my sheep had been stolen by raiders," he began, looking at a spot on the floor, among the blue and green tiles. "Father gave me my own flock when I was twelve. The raiders took every one. I was furious."

"He was," Laertes muttered in Penelope's ear. "You should have seen the water jars he broke." She muffled a chuckle behind her hand, eyes sparkling.

"So," Odysseus continued, "I took a ship to the mainland to follow them. Only a few boys my own age accompanied me, to sail. On land, I went on by myself. The second morning after leaving the ship, I met Iphitos, son of Eurytos, the famous bowman. He carried this bow for luck while he searched for stolen horses. His horses were nearer to us than my sheep and we made an agreement to help each other." Odysseus paused, frowning.

"We were like boys anywhere, enjoying the adventure so much we didn't mind discomfort and hard work. Or danger. He taught me a few tricks with the sword I didn't know, and I taught him spear work where he was lacking. We were like brothers." He chuckled, glancing over at his wife and father a moment. "We found his horses, put them in the care of people he trusted, and then went after my sheep. Iphitos teased me unmercifully about my lack of skill in riding horses. We had a few friendly fights, then I challenged him to ride the rudder of a fifty-oared ship during high seas. That silenced him.

"We finally found the raiders who took my sheep. They had joined up with their kinsmen. Twenty men against two arrogant boys. We managed to rescue most of my sheep. The raiders paid dearly for the ewes they ate.

"Iphitos and I took wounds away. Our smaller numbers were the only advantage we had, chasing through the darkness in unfamiliar territory. I saved his life, stanching a wound that could have killed him, so he gave me this bow. It is said that only the true owner of this bow is able to bend it. No other man can bend it unless given to him as a gift...or until the owner has died," he added, his voice softening.

"Where is Iphitos now?" Penelope whispered, feeling the old memories that wrapped around her husband. She rested a hand on his knee and leaned against his shoulder.

"In the shadow lands. One of his precious horses threw him and broke his back."

Silence for a long moment, when even the wailing of the wind had softened as if in respect for the end of the tale. Penelope stood, picked up the ox-hide cover and gave it back to Odysseus. He caught her hand

and pressed a kiss against her palm. She wondered at the wistfulness in his eyes. Did he think about giving the bow to his son? She tried not to jerk her hand away from his grasp before he released it.

To move her thoughts to something else, Penelope stepped over to the table where the full quiver sat. Some arrows had a greenish-gray stain on the tips and were bound together into a bundle with black-stained leather thongs. She reached to pick it up and Odysseus caught her hand to stop her.

"Carefully. Those arrows are poisoned. I traveled two moons to find the plant and learn to make that potion." He reached beyond her hand and picked up the quiver.

Penelope kept her back to Odysseus and his father, waiting until they turned to another subject before she faced them again. She had learned many things about her husband that night, she realized. When he told a tale with no embellishments, he spoke simple truth about things that affected him deeply. The embellishments, the twisting of the truth, were for strangers, for people he didn't trust, people he manipulated with his story for the sake of protection or profit.

How many stories he told her, she wondered, were simple ones and how many to turn her thoughts and feelings where he wanted them?

She had been raised to believe the use of poison was a choice of cowards, yet she had never heard anyone speak disparagingly of Odysseus' bravery, skill or leadership. There had to be another reason for using such arrows. That they were bound meant he took precautions that they not be used lightly. But what use *were* they saved for?

Her husband took few chances, she realized, unless he had a better than average chance of winning. He manipulated the conditions. She remembered Aias accosting her, thinking she was a servant girl to be toyed with. He had acted out of ignorance. Odysseus wanted her from the moment they met and had taken steps to kill others' interest in her. She knew he had held back his plan for the suitors' oaths until Tyndareos was desperate, willing to pay any price for help. Penelope felt some pride in a husband so cunning and clever, yet it disturbed her.

How many people did Odysseus really trust? She had listened to snatches of conversations that came up the narrow stairs from the feasting hall when her husband led discussions. When he told her his plans and concerns beforehand, she could follow his trail of thought. Many times, he started in opposition to his true direction. Then, playing both sides of an argument or proposition against the other, he turned both sides to follow his lead. She admired his skill, his persuasiveness.

Now, she wondered how many of his friends, his followers, realized that he manipulated them as easily as he did his detractors.

There was only one man on Ithaka, besides Laertes, whom she knew Odysseus trusted with his deepest thoughts and secrets. Mentor, an elder of noble blood, a warrior crippled in a boar hunting accident. Odysseus had told her in simple words about the boar attack he suffered as a boy, earning the scar above his knee. Mentor had survived a similar attack, but nearly lost his leg. Penelope wondered if it was that shared experience, the pain and fears, which drew the two men together. Did it bridge the wall of stories and clever deceptions her husband used to protect everything dear to him? She only knew he never spoke a false word to Mentor in her hearing.

"You're too quiet." Odysseus came up behind her to rest a hand on her shoulder. "Something troubles you?"

"No trouble." She smiled at him, shivering a little at a sudden rise in the wind, the mumbling moan turning into a shriek. "I realize there is still so much I don't know about you. I feel myself a part of you, and a heartbeat later you are a stranger." Penelope shook her head. "This is foolishness. I'm just tired."

"I should go home before the storm grows worse," Laertes said in the silence when Odysseus looked into her eyes as if trying to see into her thoughts.

"It's bad enough already," she hurried to say. "Let me have Eurynome make up a bed for you."

"No. Antikleia will send servants after me." He chuckled. "She treats me like an old grandfather with brittle bones. I can reach home long before the cold touches me, and prove to her I'm not helpless yet." Laertes rested his hands on her shoulders and kissed her forehead. "Good-night, Daughter."

"Please be careful, Father." Penelope stepped to the far wall, where cloaks and boots hung from pegs. She heard Odysseus' voice, but couldn't make out his words as he spoke with his father. Whatever the two men discussed, they both smiled when they joined her and she handed Laertes his cloak.

The wind gusted in, tearing at the heavy doors like a wild animal when Odysseus pulled a bronze-bound panel open for his father to leave. The rain swirled in, heavy and stinging, with a core of ice in each drop. Penelope welcomed his arm around her shoulders, his warmth driving away the chill as the winter night tried to penetrate the hall. They watched until Laertes had turned into a shrinking black blot in the stormy night, before closing the door.

"What were you two discussing a moment ago?" she asked, as they went back to the hearth.

"Mother gave him detailed instructions to study you. She's concerned about your health." Odysseus picked up the bow and slid it back into its cover. He took special care to tie the cords that held the case closed.

"She could have questioned me herself. I did invite her. When Eurykleia came with the dye from the new merchant, I sent the invitation. When Eurynome went down to borrow the smaller millstones, she repeated it." Penelope sat next to him, leaning her head on his shoulder. "I try, but I don't think I'm a good daughter to her. Sometimes, I think she fears me. Other times she's so quiet, I fear her."

"She loves you. My mother believes a husband's mother is best loved when she doesn't darken the bride's doorstep too often." He wrapped his arm around her waist. "That does not, however, prevent her keeping careful watch over us both."

"I think she worries more than your father that I'm not fat with a baby yet."

"Why do you say that?" His hand moved lightly up her side, his fingertips just brushing her breast, then down to cup the curve of her hip. She knew he wanted to make love to her, but he would not ask, because she had said she was tired. Penelope chided herself for her earlier thoughts. He was a tender, considerate husband and she had no right to doubt him.

"You're not the only one who can see people's hearts and thoughts in their faces. I listen to what the servants say," she added with a laugh.

"My mother worries about everyone. It's one of the few pleasures left in her life." Odysseus tried to smile, but she felt the hurt in him. "Did you know I had an older sister? No, no one would speak of her yet. Not if they thought my mother would hear. Ktimene died in childbirth. Her death separated Mother from us, as if part of her had already gone down to the shadows with my sister. My mother worries because she doesn't see the strength and life in you that I do."

"Once we have a child, she will be more alive again?" Penelope didn't know if she resented this new pressure on her actions. She loved her mother-in-law protectively, as she had Helen. It hurt to take the duties of queen of Ithaka, because she knew Antikleia could have handled them if she had wanted.

She was proud to lead in the night ceremonies in the cave. She was glad to give bits of advice to the women who sent servants and children to ask. It was a proverb that Ithaka's women accomplished more in snatches of conversation, messages passed in gardens and on the shore, than the men did in a moon of meetings. She knew the people would ask her to intercede for them before Odysseus when they came to know her better. She was the queen, responsible for the peace and prosperity of Ithaka.

And Penelope knew the more pressure she felt to have children, the more she fought the idea. Antikleia's happiness was simply another gust in the wind pushing her. Another force she dug her heels in to resist.

"She would be happy to have someone new to worry over." Odysseus drew her closer and pressed a kiss against her temple. "She sees you as a daughter. It's not just words to her."

"She hardly speaks when we're together. I'm not sure how she feels about me. I know she worries for you, even when you're only gone for a day." A shiver wrapped around Penelope. "She started to tell me about a dream she had. You were in danger, living in rags, far from home. Gods prevented you from returning. Then she just stopped in the middle of the tale."

"She likely thought you wouldn't believe her."

"Sometimes I have dreams that…hint at the truth," she murmured.

"My mother has always worried overmuch for me. When I was a child, she worried I wouldn't grow to be a man. When I visited my grandparents, she worried I wouldn't return home alive. Then when she learned about the boar that caught me, she worried I would lose my leg—though it had already healed when she heard the tale. When I was old enough to look for a bride, she worried I would never find a girl who pleased me."

"And now that we are married," Penelope interrupted, pressing two fingers over his lips, "she worries you will not be a father before she dies." She jerked out of his embrace, swallowing a tiny scream when he bit at her fingers. "Odysseus, we are having a serious conversation."

"Must we?" He put a woebegone expression on his face. She smiled, relenting, and let him draw her onto his lap. "You feel badly because you don't carry a child yet?"

"My duty—"

"Your duty as a wife is between you and me alone. If I say I am pleased, that you are my treasure and delight, no one else's words matter."

"I hear and obey, my husband." Penelope rested her head on his shoulder, her arms tight around him.

"That's better."

"I hear the whispers, when I'm alone in my garden. Everyone expected the first cloth from my loom to be a child's blanket. Yet it would be a waste of an excellent loom, to make it sit idle and my belly still flat." She wondered if now was a good time to tell him about the potion, or even ask his advice and explain why she took it.

"I like your belly flat," he whispered, shifting his embrace so he caressed her hip and rested his hand on her belly. "Penelope, we will make a bargain. There is more than enough time for us to have children. You will use the loom, and I will start a new one just for children's clothing the day you tell me you are pregnant. Is that acceptable?"

"You are the kindest, most understanding husband any woman could hope for." She accented her words with kisses.

"See how understanding I am when you're too fat to share my bed," Odysseus grumbled.

"I am not fat now." Penelope slid off his lap. He let go of her reluctantly. His eyes gleamed when she took his hand and led him across the hall to the door of his chamber.

CHAPTER 12

"My daughter barely reached our home before the storm broke. She could have been lost, dead by morning!"

The angry, cracking male voice rang up the stairs to Penelope's workroom. She paused, a warp thread in one hand, a weight in the other. Melantho and the other maids grew still.

In the great hall below, several men of the island had come to Odysseus. To complain. Her husband had warned her when the ships were locked into the harbor by winter storms and hunting was impossible, the people of Ithaka grew short tempers. Quarrels and mediation were the main entertainments during the winter. Penelope had thought he teased until now.

It jolted her when her name came up the stairs several times, on different voices. No tones had been flattering. However, with the last clearly spoken remark, Penelope understood. More *young* women had begun to join the ceremonies in the Goddess' cave. Five days before, with a storm approaching, Eurykleia had summoned her to lead a ritual to ensure safety for the island. No one had been lost in the storm, no animals had wandered lost and died, no homes had fallen in the terrible gales. But now it seemed a daughter or two had taken too long coming home. Their fathers blamed Penelope.

"If you would speak with your wives, your mothers, you would know my wife has brought nothing new to Ithaka," Odysseus said. The reasonable tone of his voice reassured Penelope.

"Foolish old women with nothing to do," another angry voice

returned. His words echoed up the stairs. "They were the only ones who still held the old ways, until you brought that foreign woman among us."

"Traitos is still angry I didn't beg for his daughter," Odysseus observed.

His words earned a few chuckles from some men. Not enough, Penelope thought. It was hard to judge from such a distance.

"The girls find merit in the old ways with your wife's support," another said. "She acts as a priestess."

"My wife does not trouble me with such small things." A chair scraped on the floor tile. "You have brought me your grievance and your reasons. I understand your fears for your daughters and wives. Be assured I will act. My wife will mend her ways."

"How?" Traitos demanded. "What will you do? This woman is cousin to Helen. Does she consider herself a child of the gods as well, and above our laws?"

"What do you want of me?" Odysseus' voice grew deadly quiet, penetrating until Penelope thought the foundation stones rang in response. "Bring my wife out, strip her and beat her in front of you like a rebellious slave?"

The silence echoed in the hall. Outside the walls, Penelope heard the first moans of a new storm. She stayed still, though she knew movement would keep her maids from hearing the rest of the confrontation.

"A storm comes. Tend to the safety of your homes, and leave me to mine." His sandals made cracking taps on the floor as he moved off, away from the stairs. Penelope thought he led his unwanted guests to the doors himself, instead of waiting for a slave to take care of them.

"Go," she said, finally standing. She turned, daring any of her women to smile or disobey. Even Melantho paled slightly and hurried from the room.

Penelope sat down, still holding the thread and the warp weight. She tried not to listen to the sounds of feet leaving the hall, the thud of the door closing. By force of will, she returned to setting the new pattern on her loom. She had finished hanging the weights when Odysseus came to the door.

"You heard?" he said, and leaned against the frame. That he didn't waste time on small talk made her uneasy.

"How could I help it?" She didn't look up. Penelope ached at the wariness in his voice. She didn't want to see his face.

"You will have more supporters soon, Penelope. Those for the Goddess and against me will turn to you now." A broken chuckle escaped him when she glanced at him, startled. "Likely, gifts will come from nobles and their ladies who haven't dared to declare themselves before. If they think we are divided, we can control them."

"Aren't we divided? You said nothing in my defense. Those men have left thinking you are going to punish me. Punished for doing what you *encouraged*?"

"I only said you would mend your ways."

"How is that any different from—"

"Be more careful. That's all I ask. Take better care of your followers." Odysseus crossed the room to stand before her. "That is how you will mend your ways."

"My lord...some day, your scheming ways will be your destruction." Penelope closed her eyes. She sighed, bone weary though it was still morning. "Or perhaps your schemes shall be the destruction of my mind!"

"No, my lovely witch." He drew her to her feet, holding her close. Penelope welcomed his warmth, enveloping her, soaking into her chilled flesh. "You are stronger than anyone can guess. You will stand when all others fail."

*   *   *

She passed on the warning through Eurykleia to all the devotees of the Goddess. They held fewer ceremonies in the cave the rest of the winter. Penelope thought the Goddess understood. She was glad to spend more nights warm in bed, more often than not clasped in Odysseus' arms.

Spring came too soon, with the people watching for her to swell with child. Penelope tried to ignore the pointed looks, the conversations that broke off when she passed by. She buried herself in the spring work—directing planting, buying new breeding sheep for her flocks, purchasing geese. She had her own geese in Alybas, pets that produced sweet eggs and soft feathers for cushions. As a spring festival gift, Odysseus ordered a pen built for geese and gave her a few precious scraps of gold to buy them. Penelope looked forward to watching the eggs hatch, though she knew some would ask why she didn't hatch a child of her own.

With the softer weather, the ships rode the waves again. Odysseus began to make short, overnight trips to Kephallenia or other islands allied with Ithaka. She didn't like those absences.

Penelope was in her garden with Antikleia, discussing which plants to cultivate, the day the first ship arrived from far ports. She found it easier to work with her mother-in-law now. They didn't speak much, but she found the woman pleasant company. Especially when she sought advice.

Odysseus came to the garden to find her. He waited, listening, saying nothing, until his mother had gone home.

"Penelope, Agamemnon has sent for me. I must go to Mycenae," he said, leading her to a bench near the opening in the wall.

"Mycenae? Agamemnon wants something badly, to send for you so early in the year." She repressed a shiver of apprehension as she sat.

"Troy took nearly a fourth of the cargo in tribute from the first three ships through the Dardanelles. All Mycenaean traders. Agamemnon's man says he expects trouble this year, worse than the last five combined."

"And he wants your advice." The only alternative, she knew, was a call for Odysseus to prepare for war.

"He claims I *must* help him, now that we are kinsmen." He held her hand, toying with her fingers as he spoke, and didn't meet her eyes.

"Something more bothers you. After being land-bound all winter, you should leap at the chance to travel." She caught at his hands to still them.

"Sometimes, sweet witch, I wish you weren't so perceptive." Odysseus smiled and reached up to stroke her cheek. "I am most reluctant to leave you alone for as long as the journey and the council will take."

"I could go with you. Klytemaistra is not my favorite cousin, but I would like to see her daughters."

"Agamemnon already invited you, nearly made his request a demand." He shook his head, a short, sharp motion. "I won't chance taking you to Mycenae."

"I'm not with child. What risk can there be?"

"I know Agamemnon. I can believe he would kill a man to get a woman he wanted. Any woman. We are allies, but I don't trust him where women are concerned. I won't ruin the accords of the Achaians by tempting him with you."

"Odysseus!" She stared at him, caught between tears and laughing outright. Penelope decided laughter was the better course. "Agamemnon may care overmuch for his bed pleasures, but he's no fool. He wouldn't be High King if he were. He wouldn't risk the accords just to tumble *me* into his bed."

"I can believe he would kill me to have you."

"He *needs* you. Your advice and your loyalty as kinsman are more important to him. As it is…" She fought the breathless sensation tightening her body and struggled for words. "Has Helen been invited with Menelaos? There, you see?" she said, when he nodded reluctantly. "With Helen there, he wouldn't even see me. Do you think he would hurt his brother, to take *Helen*?"

"No." He smiled and embraced her. "Penelope, you are a hard woman to argue with. But do two things to please me, will you?"

"One is to agree to stay home in Ithaka?"

"And the other is, after I have sailed, look deeply and carefully into your mirror."

"Odysseus—"

"No more of this." He stood, holding her hand to pull her to her feet. "We have many arrangements to make before I sail with the dawn."

*   *   *

Laertes journeyed with his son, so Odysseus left Mentor in charge of both households. Penelope didn't mind. She respected the man and he was pleasant company. Mentor answered her questions in detail and told her anything she wanted about news from the rest of the world. He didn't talk down to her like to a child, as many elders were prone to do.

The day Odysseus sailed, Penelope stood on the beach with Mentor and Antikleia, watching the ship until it had vanished into the morning haze. Then she walked up to the house in silence and went directly to her chamber. She stood long in front of her mirror, as Odysseus had told her.

The polished sheet of bronze had been a wedding gift from Laertes, lighter in color than anything she had ever seen. Penelope knew it reflected her with more flattery than she liked. Even taking into account the golden tones it gave her skin, the softening of lines, she admitted she was fair to look on. More rounded in the hip, fuller in the breast, softer in her face. More pleasant than she had dared to hope even a year ago.

"But still no risk to your life or a temptation to Agamemnon," she whispered to her absent husband.

Penelope laughed, covered the mirror with its cloth, and went

145

downstairs. There was sheering to oversee and seeds to buy from the merchants. Too much to do to busy herself with worry and vanities.

Then a thought caught her, halfway down the staircase. Agamemnon *had* likely killed to have Klytemaistra. Few doubted it. And yet only a few years after marrying her, rumors said Agamemnon took other women to his bed. Not always when his wife was unavailable. Some rumors said Klytemaistra had tried to kill one or more of the women.

Penelope shivered, wondering if Odysseus had been more right to be cautious than either of them had known.

*   *   *

Odysseus returned to Ithaka in less than a moon, quietly fuming about the wasted time. When Agamemnon sent for him for advice, he had also sent envoys to King Priam of Ilion to complain. Odysseus had barely been at Mycenae two days when the envoys returned, with presents for Agamemnon and a thinly worded apology.

"Gossip was the only profit any of us had in the trip," he told Penelope as they walked up the path to their home.

She had been walking the beach with Mentor while the older man taught her about tides. Penelope recognized Odysseus' ship and ran into the water up to her knees to meet it. She didn't care that people had laughed and others had cheered. Odysseus leaped from the ship before it docked and caught her up in his arms. His first kisses made her dizzy, like strong wine. They had laughed together, walking from the beach, until she asked how the council had proceeded and what had happened.

"I wasn't aware men indulged in gossip. Certainly not the kings of the Achaians," she teased. Something had gone cold in her at the quiet anger she sensed in him and she longed to bring his laughing, teasing mood back.

"Continue like this and I will not tell you about your cousins," he said, arching an eyebrow at her. When she pouted, he squeezed her closer to his side. "Klytemaistra is with child. Again. Agamemnon claims all the oracles and priests say *this* child will be a boy."

"His reputation is in sore danger if they don't have a son this time."

"Indeed. More important, Helen is also expecting. She didn't come to Mycenae. Menelaos confided she is so sick she screams at him if he holds her hand." Odysseus chuckled. "He's in terror for her, but doesn't have the words to tell her so."

"Did you give him the words?" Penelope marveled at the image of

Helen sick and disagreeable. Her cousin had always enjoyed the best health.

"Wife, you have grown impudent in my absence." He frowned down at her. When she only laughed, he relented, gathering her close to him with a groan. "I missed you to the point of pain," Odysseus whispered in her ear.

"I have not missed the knots in my hair every morning," she retorted. It was a lie. She enjoyed Odysseus' touch when he played with her hair after they had made love.

"Witch, what should I do with you?" he growled, nearly squeezing the breath from her. She reveled in the strength of his arms around her, even as she knew, as her dreams had told her, Agamemnon would call him away again.

*   *   *

Their happiness in his homecoming didn't last long. The next morning, Odysseus went down to the bay to see to some repairs on his ship. When he returned a few hours later, Penelope heard his voice crack through the hall, scolding the servants, ordering his fawning hunting dogs away. She nearly dropped the tunic she had begun for Laertes, instantly worried.

Though she waited, Odysseus didn't come near her workroom. She didn't know whether to feel relieved or worried when he left the house a short time later. The tension left with him, but her worry only grew. Her own words grew sharp with her women, though she tried to control herself better.

As the afternoon wore on and still Odysseus had not come back, she retreated to her private garden. Sometimes the high walls made her feel a prisoner. Now, their thick solidity made her feel safe, able to hide. Odysseus found her there, her fingers muddy from tending a young olive tree with roots coming up from the soil.

"Someone would think you were hiding from me," he said as he came in.

"Do I have reason?" Penelope tried to take comfort from the smile he gave her. Then she saw the stiffness in his mouth, the forced brightness in his eyes. "Are more men complaining that I lead their daughters astray?"

"Do your dreams tell you this?" His smile faded. He came to her side and squatted next to her.

"Then I *am* the cause of your new anger."

"No, you could never make me angry." He took her hand, absently brushing the drying mud from her fingers. "Though there are some who would try to blame you for Ithaka's problems."

"Something happened at the harbor this morning. I guessed it had to do with me, when you didn't come near me all day." She smiled at him, feeling her lips tremble. Penelope wished he would take her into his arms and kiss her worries away.

"Too wise, my witch," he whispered. Odysseus shook his head. "The fishing is not good this spring, the rains are as bad as the year before. The planting is difficult and the early crops have not sprouted. All the same as the year before. Only this year, they blame it on us."

"No, they blame it on their prince's bride." She squeezed his hand. Penelope found it a strange relief to have that accusation out in the open at last.

"They blame it on *us.* Several 'friends' offered to make sacrifices to strengthen my manhood. Others say I should take you to Aphrodite's temple to have your womb opened."

"Why don't they blame Aphrodite, instead?" She would have laughed, but sparks of suppressed anger remained in his eyes.

"Now you understand."

"Odysseus—"

"I beat the man who said I should give you to another husband and take a new bride."

"My childlessness is none of your fault. I am simply not ready yet to conceive," she added, her voice trembling a bit. Penelope wished she had told him about Eurynome's potion. He might have handled the accusations more easily. Now, she knew it was the wrong time.

"Sweet Penelope." His expression gentled. "You are my delight, and not just in my bed," he added with a chuckle. "I would sooner sink Ithaka in the sea than give you away."

She flung her arms around him and made her kisses passionate and sweet. That night, lying in his arms, she resolved to stop taking the potion and to pray for a child.

*   *   *

The second call from Agamemnon came early in the summer. Again, Odysseus and his father both went, leaving Mentor in charge. No word came. Penelope sent the servants to the harbor every time a merchant ship arrived, to hear the latest rumors.

Her temper crumbled. She was not pregnant. She wished Odysseus had taken her with him to Mycenae, to consult with Klytemaistra. After all, her cousin had three children and a fourth coming. Penelope overheard talk blaming the bad year on her. She missed Odysseus and at the same time grew angry with him. She hated the island when he wasn't there.

One morning more than three weeks after Odysseus had left, she heard his name spoken from the other side of the wall in her private garden. Penelope habitually went there to think about him and wonder how the council concerning Ilion progressed. She heard his name spoken by a servant girl and was torn out of her longing thoughts.

"He kissed her ten times between the threshold and the harbor," the girl continued, her voice heavy with sighs. "I counted every one." A high-pitched giggle followed her words, helping Penelope identify the speaker as Autonoe, a girl bought that spring to help in the weaving.

"There's no good in counting kisses until you are the one receiving them," Nerilia retorted, her scratchy, deep voice unmistakable. A few other girls chimed in, agreeing.

"My father says only blessings can fall on a land where the king and queen adore each other," Melantho put in. "Men want me, but they never look at me like our master looks at her."

"He won't look at her like that for long." The speaker's voice held a sleek satisfaction that made Penelope writhe. What did the girl know?

A few girls asked what the speaker meant. She laughed, making them beg a few more times.

"When she's fat with his child, his gaze will wander," she explained. "It's the way of men. Then he'll start visiting your beds again."

"Again?" Laline snorted. She was a plump, golden girl, with a merry laugh and nimble hands for the weaving. As far as Penelope knew, she had no lack of sweethearts. "Our master has not even looked at us since he brought the mistress home. If his gaze hasn't wandered in nearly a year, what makes you think the rest of him will?"

"I wouldn't mind if Lord Odysseus visited me," Melantho admitted. "He must be deft. My lady always smiles after she shares his bed."

Penelope felt her face begin to warm. An ache of purely physical longing for Odysseus grew deep inside.

"What hope do I have?" the maid continued, discontent coloring her voice. "He'll take no other women because he loves her."

"Men love with their bodies, not their hearts. When she's too fat to be held and her temper cracks, he'll come looking for entertainment with the rest of you. And hopefully other island girls," the nameless speaker purred.

"Thoosa, you never had a chance before, and now you're—" Autonoe began, to be cut off by a cackling laugh.

"You're jealous because he won't look at the servant girls in his own house. What Lord Odysseus does on the rest of Ithaka, his wife can't control."

"You make him sound as if he fears her, not that he loves her," Nerilia accused.

"I've heard my mother and grandmother talking. They say the lady leads in midnight rites. Does she think she rules Ithaka and her husband only serves her, like in the old days?" Thoosa snorted, like a bull. "She has no power. Does she think she's a goddess because she's cousin to Helen?" She laughed and other girls joined her.

"She'll have no sway over him if she doesn't give him a child soon," another girl pointed out. "No matter what she does, she will lose him."

Penelope looked at her nails and wished she had not kept them trimmed to make weaving easier. She had seen two village girls scratching each other's faces in a fight once. She thought she could manage a creditable surprise attack.

Then she caught herself, physically and mentally. Reacting would only please Thoosa and give credence to her words. She dug her fingers into the ground and whispered a prayer to Athena for strength to endure. The laughter died, and Penelope strained her ears to catch every word, no matter how it hurt. Knowledge was her only defense.

"It would be nice for him to favor us," another girl said, her voice soft. Penelope imagined the girl blushed, she sounded so timid. "I wouldn't feel so guilty when he came to me, if she was pregnant."

Other voices broke in, a babble of agreement and contradiction. Penelope knew she should not feel hurt that Odysseus had slept with the girl slaves in his parents' household. She knew jealousy was foolish, and she had vowed not to give her heart. She concentrated on what she had heard; Odysseus had not touched another woman since bringing her back as his bride. There was reason for pride in that.

Penelope decided to tell Eurynome not to allow Thoosa into the household any longer. The girl was hired daily to help with weaving, carding, and kitchen work. A little extra work for the household girls would give them less time to gossip.

"I wish she was pregnant right now," one girl said, laughing. "By the time he returns, she'd be huge and hating his touch."

"Lord Odysseus would not have left with such bad grace if she was," Thoosa said, returning to her smug, oily tones.

"He wouldn't worry that another man would steal her while he was gone. Who would want a woman retching in his ship, the whole trip from Ithaka?" another put in, laughing.

"My lady would not leave," Autonoe insisted.

"She can't leave, even if she wanted to," Thoosa said. "Why do you think Lord Mentor watches the household?"

"To help her. To lead in defense if pirates raid us," another girl said. Penelope recognized the voice as Hypodamia, Autonoe's shadow. She felt some sympathy for the girl, as tiny, dark and easily overlooked as Penelope had been as a child.

"He fears another man would woo her. Simply being the cousin of Helen, many would want her. Even if she was as ugly as Cerberus," Thoosa added with a nasty chuckle. "Odysseus trusts Mentor because he fears him. My father says the two argued years ago and Odysseus *let* the boar through his defense to attack Mentor. And then he made sure the wounded leg heal crooked. Mentor lives in terror Odysseus will do far worse to him, so he is completely trustworthy. Likely the only man on Ithaka Odysseus trusts."

"He watches my lady to protect her," Autonoe insisted.

"He watches her because Odysseus distrusts her. He is always watching," Anglia said, her voice dropping. "Why should he trust her just because she shares his bed? He wouldn't trust any of us, would he? We're his property to sell or to kill as he pleases. We have more reason to be faithful. If she displeases him, he cannot punish her. Helen would bring Agamemnon and Menelaos against Ithaka. All Lord Odysseus could do is send her home to Sparta."

"He plays a game with her heart," Nerilia said, her voice mimicking Thoosa's for satisfaction. "While she is besotted with him, she will do nothing against him."

Penelope covered her ears with her fists, to block out the new, heated argument. Part of her screamed to cast dignity to the winds and rush out to scold the girls. Part of her shrank from doing anything except blocking her ears and trying to forget what she had heard.

Yet there was another part of her that struggled to keep silent as the tears gathered in her eyes. The part of her that had doubted and wondered about the small things her husband did. The tricks, the tiny lies and stories to get others to follow him. There was truth in the gossip.

Odysseus had told her Mentor protected her and the household. There were different kinds of protection, she knew. Sometimes protection imprisoned.

She had wondered before if Odysseus manipulated her emotions, her thoughts, for the sake of peace in their household and bed. She wondered now if he had merely resorted to sweet words and caresses instead of dominating her to get his way. An adoring, happy wife was certainly easier to live with than one who walked sullen and resentful or even cowered in fear.

"He works to please me," she whispered, her voice muted by the girls' voices on the other side of the wall. "He is either enchanted by me or plays a part to rule me with deception." The tears dried from her eyes. Penelope scrubbed her face with her sleeve and leaned against the olive tree.

She closed her eyes and examined her life with Odysseus. She had to evaluate, understand and see clearly. The doubts hurt like knives in her chest. She needed to deal with them honestly, even if it meant seeing her marriage as an empty charade.

Odysseus appeared devoted to her, as she was to him. What if that were all the truth of their marriage—appearances? She tried to conduct herself with honesty toward him. Yet if Odysseus trusted no one, how could he be sure she acted honestly?

If a man trusted no one, could he be trusted? Did Odysseus speak truth to her? Did his whispered words in the night mean anything? Or did he only speak and act to bring the desired reaction from her?

The shady, peaceful sanctuary of her garden became a prison. Was Mentor a jailor instead of a friend? She had thought the man's hesitancy was shyness. She had thought they were becoming friends. Did he relax in her presence because he knew his duty was easy and Odysseus would not grow angry with him?

Penelope thought until her head ached as badly as her heart, but came to no conclusion. Through the thudding in her ears, she heard the servant girls move on to another task elsewhere. She didn't move for a long time after that, and then only to the garden pool to wash her face.

Penelope smiled with trembling lips, remembering how often Eurynome had lectured her on guarding her expression, never revealing her heart, never giving her enemies anything to use against her. Now she would put that training to good use.

Mentor came to her that evening and said he would go to his own estates for a day or two, for family business. Penelope let him go, wishing him well. The man didn't even glance twice at her and she congratulated herself on how well she carried her part. Eurynome remarked on her thin appetite that day, but Penelope blamed a headache. Which was truth.

From that day, she didn't look toward the harbor every time she passed the gates of the courtyard. Her heart did not lift every time she saw an approaching sail. Penelope went to bed early that night and wondered how many days she would have to perfect her role before Odysseus returned. A man who played many roles, who wore deception like a garment would be adept at seeing through any mask. Until she decided what she believed, she had to pretend nothing had happened.

CHAPTER 13

A soft summer rain sprinkled Ithaka the day Odysseus returned. Penelope heard the clamor as the news echoed through the house. She set her jaw and continued weaving. Her hands trembled as she changed the color of thread. She didn't call her servants to return when they found excuses to leave the chamber and hurry down the stairs to hear news from returning sailors. Penelope vowed to finish three hand spans down the pattern before she moved. It was the most intricate part of the weaving, the most changes of colors, and could take her hours. Discipline and practice came to her aid, letting her lose all sense of time and the outside world while she worked.

"Penelope?" Odysseus' voice, quiet as it was, startled her. She swallowed a cry of shock but dropped the knife she had picked up to cut the deep purple thread. He hurried into the room to pick it up for her. Longing filled her when his hand brushed against hers.

"You startled me," she said, nodding her thanks without meeting his eyes.

"I didn't mean to. Your work has all your attention." He brushed a few loose strands of hair away from the side of her face and leaned forward to kiss her.

It took a massive effort of will not to flinch from the soft scratching of his beard, the warmth of his breath against her cheek. The next moment, it was all she could do not to fling her arms around him, burst out crying and spill the painful thoughts filling her heart and mind.

"It is an intricate portion." She congratulated herself on the steadiness of her voice.

"You were wise not to come meet me." He stepped back and sat on the bench against the wall. She knew he could see her face clearly from where he sat. She only cared that he no longer touched her. "The rain comes down harder every moment."

"It is good you are home, then. The seas would be rough." She forced herself to meet his eyes and smile as she spoke; it was the normal, expected thing for her to do. The way his face changed from a weary mask to brightness tore at her. How much was truth, how much show for her benefit?

"Was there trouble while I was gone?"

"Mentor hasn't spoken with you yet?" She was surprised by his question and ashamed at the picture in her mind, the two men in close conference the moment Odysseus landed.

"I sent him gathering the elders to meet. My reasons for staying so long in Mycenae—" He broke off as running footsteps came up the stairs.

Nisos, a thin, dark-haired boy scurried through the door. He stopped short, his wet feet catching on the smooth wooden floor.

"My lord, the elders gather," he blurted.

"Thank you." Odysseus dismissed him with a nod and waited until he was gone before turning back to Penelope. "I had hoped we could talk, but later?"

"As you wish." Penelope managed a gentle smile for him. She wondered if it would grow easier to dissemble as time went on. Was this the secret of the roles he played? Long practice? She held still, refusing to relax her vigilance until Odysseus kissed her and left.

The rain brought cool to the air, breaking the heavy summer heat and dryness. Penelope welcomed it, using the chill as an excuse to keep her chamber doors closed. She heard nothing of the meeting Odysseus held with the elders beyond a muted rumble of male voices, but threw all her concentration into her weaving. When Melantho brought supper to her, she was startled to realize the late hour.

"I'm not hungry. Thank you," she added quickly, smiling the same soft, all-encompassing smile she gave Odysseus.

Her maid frowned as she took the tray away. Penelope knew Melantho would conference with her friends soon. Would they guess trouble lay between the master and mistress?

She worked hard on her weaving, relieved to find her hands stayed steady. Penelope made herself go slowly to avoid bungling. Her maids whispered among themselves, the sound mingling with the patter of rain against the shutters. Penelope ignored them, throwing herself into her work so she thought of nothing else.

Downstairs, the scraping of benches against the stone paving, the sound of sandal-shod feet and the rising rumble of voices warned her the meeting had finished. By the ache in her back and arms and her empty stomach, she knew it was far into the evening. The lamp next to her guttered, low on oil. Penelope looked around the weaving room. Only Autonoe and Melantho remained.

"It is late," she said, standing. She nearly smiled at the startled looks the two gave her. "I have been a cruel mistress today, ignoring you for the sake of my design. Go to bed now and if you sleep late in the morning, do not worry."

It took her a few moments to assure them she needed nothing but water to wash before bed. She told them not to send Eurynome to her. To be alone was a relief. Penelope caught bits of words and voices. Odysseus and his father talked alone in the hall below. They likely waited for her to hurry down the stairs to join them and ask for the news.

"Like a silly girl waiting to catch all the gossip," she whispered.

Did they humor her? Did they enjoy sharing a man's world with her?

Penelope shook her head and closed her bedroom door, careful not to let it bang against the frame. Her fingers trembled on the latch. She still did not know what to think.

Was her husband honest with her? Did he play a game? Was she wrong to doubt him? Was she a fool for wanting to believe every sweet word and look and gesture?

"I wish I didn't care," she whispered to the quiet. "I have a fine home, everything I need. My husband does not mock the old ways. He needs me. He treats me kindly and listens to my questions and ideas. I find pleasure in his touch and his bed. I have more than many women could ever hope for. I should be satisfied." Penelope strode to the shuttered windows, stopping herself before she flung them open, to shout her question into the storm. "Goddess," she whispered, "why am I not satisfied?"

Penelope welcomed the shock of the chill water on her face as she washed. She nearly let her dress lay where it fell when she slipped it off. Old habit made her pick it up and hang it on a peg in the wall. Shivering, she snuffed the lamps and hurried to her bed to slip under the blankets.

Sleep had nearly caught her when she heard footsteps at her door. Penelope made herself lie still and relaxed, eyes closed, mouth slightly open, as she had done as a child when Eurynome threatened to spank her if she didn't go to sleep. The door creaked open. Torchlight flickered across her closed eyelids.

"Penelope?" Odysseus whispered.

He waited. The rain hissed, falling harder against the roof. The torch crackled in his hand. Then the door closed again. Penelope swallowed hard against the tears that threatened.

*   *   *

Antikleia came to see Penelope the next morning, wrinkled with worry beyond the usual. Penelope knew no matter how distracted, her mother-in-law cared. She wanted to turn to her for advice, but how could she say she doubted everything Antikleia's treasured son said or did?

"It's early to be visiting, Mother," Penelope said, fetching a cushioned chair. "The pattern goes well, does it not?" She gestured at her weaving.

Penelope found comfort in the deep absorption the intricate pattern demanded. Yet she worried at how quickly it progressed. Soon, she would have to find something equally difficult to absorb her.

"Are you well, Penelope?" Antikleia's soft voice held more whimper than usual. She reached out a faintly trembling hand and rested it on the younger woman's arm.

"As well as can be expected. The rain brought respite from the heat." She tried to laugh, surprised at how genuine it sounded. "Why?"

"You don't eat regularly. The servants say you are too quiet, that you retire to your bed sooner than usual."

"Ah, is that what they say about me?" Penelope smiled, feeling some measure of humor. When Antikleia referred to "the servants," she meant Eurykleia and Eurynome. Her mother-in-law rarely made conversation with any others. The two nurses could do no wrong, spoke nothing but truth in Antikleia's sight. "Did they give a reason?"

"Worrying for my son, we thought. Yet he is home now and you ate nothing last night and went to bed before my son finished speaking with the elders. If something worries you, please let me help. You are my dear daughter, after all." Antikleia's eyes shone with hope.

Penelope thought she understood what was in the woman's

thoughts. What had always been in her thoughts.

"Mother, thank you for your concern." She leaned forward and kissed her forehead. "It's just weariness. With the sudden rains, I likely caught a chill." Penelope sighed when the hopeful light grew stronger in the woman's eyes. "I am not with child. Perhaps that is part of it. Indeed, I think a belly full of child would be—" She bit her tongue against saying a comfort, and searched for a better word. "A child would be a welcome distraction. I wouldn't mind, even if I was as sick as my cousin is reputed to be."

It struck her as bitterly humorous that now, of all times, the idea of being pregnant appealed to her. Penelope knew if she told Odysseus, he would have found it humorous.

"Then it is merely a passing discomfort?" Antikleia's voice returned to a whimper. Shadows fluttered through her eyes and her shoulders slumped.

Penelope cringed at a wave of guilt. Of the family, she knew only Antikleia always showed her true feelings and concerns. The woman lived in a world bounded by her worries and dreams of ill omen, but she didn't dissemble.

Odysseus and his father had likely discussed her, then Laertes told his wife to talk with her. Penelope wondered what report she would make. She hoped it confused them.

When Antikleia left, Penelope sat before her loom, unseeing. Her hands moved of themselves, aching with sitting idle. She nearly put white thread in where she needed black, before she noticed.

"Now is not the time to wander," she muttered, glad for the covering chatter of her maids on the other side of the room. Penelope wondered what they would say of her actions. Already she was weary with the role she played, and the day had barely begun.

* * *

That night, Odysseus returned sooner than she expected. He had gone to Raven's Crag, at the tip of the island to inspect some new swine and the young man recently installed to care for the animals. Penelope had hoped he might stay the night.

She was on her way to her room after overseeing the drying of herbs for medicine, when he entered the house. She heard his footsteps and turned. Her heart leaped at the sight of his bright, smiling face, his hair shining from damp in the torchlight, arms wide open to embrace her. Hunger for his touch overwhelmed her. She wrapped her arms around him when he gathered her close and returned his kisses.

"That is the greeting I missed," he murmured, pressing more kisses against her mouth, then down her neck. Penelope shivered, feeling a throb of desire. He laughed and swept her up in his arms so he held her on his lap when he sat down. "Penelope, you are a torment to me."

"Torment?" She laughed at his words, torn between longing for the former times and fear this was just another trick. A role he assumed without thinking.

"I cannot hear your voice without wanting to see your face. When I see you, I need to touch you. When I touch you, I must hold you." He caressed her, a gentle touch that created shivers. "When I hold you—" He stopped, his mouth dropping open when she slid free of his arms.

"I am not well. My moon flow is early." Penelope turned so he wouldn't see her face. She couldn't be sure of the expression she wore.

"I worried when you slept so early last night and stayed in your rooms today."

"It will pass." She congratulated herself on keeping her voice even and steady.

"Were you ill while I was gone?"

"It was too hot." She turned back to face him and sat in the chair facing him. "I fear there is still much I must become accustomed to, living here."

"Sometimes I forget you have not been here with me always," Odysseus returned, smiling. He held out his hand and she gave hers to him, knowing he would wonder if she refused. "Penelope? What truly bothers you?"

"Why would anything bother me?" She silently cursed when her voice trembled.

"My words brought hurt to your face. Some still call you a foreigner?"

"Yes." She felt her face warm, glad for the excuse he offered. "Eurykleia and I went to the Goddess to pray for rain. One of the women—I can't remember her name—said I would never be queen of Ithaka because I wasn't born here. Eurykleia said not to listen, that her daughter had hoped to be your bride, but it didn't help."

"If Eurykleia says so, then that is the reason." He stood and pulled her to her feet. "You should rest if you aren't well." He looked around the hall, still deserted. "You were going to bed?"

Penelope nodded, unwilling to speak and betray her twisting emotions. She returned his kiss, relieved when he let her go up the stairs alone. She listened as he closed the stairway door behind her and heard his footsteps as he went to his own room. Odysseus had once told her he put his bedroom next to the stairs so he could defend her. He called her his treasure. Did he truly fear someone would steal her? Or was he a jailer?

When she reached her bedroom, Eurynome was hanging up a dress. It was newly made, washed that morning and left out to dry. The nurse looked long at Penelope in silence when she entered the room.

"He's hurt you, hasn't he?"

"My husband has done nothing." Penelope tugged on the combs decorated with shells that held her hair back from her face.

Her fingers trembled as she remembered in vivid detail the day Odysseus fashioned them for her. They had walked along the beach only a few days after they arrived in Ithaka. She had been delighted to find the tiny shells, glossy white and pink with frilled edges. Odysseus attached them to combs to help them remember the beauty of the day.

"Nothing more than his usual actions," Eurynome corrected. "You slept apart from each other last night, and will tonight. That's not your usual habit, and he newly returned. Only he is close enough to your heart to hurt you."

"You are still against my marriage," she shot back, nearly yanking the last comb from her hair. She tossed the combs onto the table holding her cosmetics and jewelry instead of throwing them at her nurse as she wanted.

"You would be happier if you were like other wives, resigned to serving your husband, only finding happiness in your duties and position." She startled Penelope, coming up behind her and resting both hands on her shoulders. "My child, why do you give him your heart? It is a life's work to keep your husband loyal. Every night you sleep alone, he can take another woman to his bed, and then you will hurt more."

"He has had no other woman since we married!"

"When he goes to Mycenae? Can you watch him there?"

"Eurynome, why do you say such things?" Penelope hated the hot feel of tears waiting to burst from her eyes. She preferred anger over crying.

"To protect you. Now, barely a year married, he treasures you, he will do anything to make you happy. But you must face the truth and turn from the illusion you live before his heart and body wander from you. It will not hurt so much then." Eurynome wrapped her arms around Penelope, gently swaying, rocking her like a child again.

"There is no need to protect me," she said, her voice cracking. "The illusion is gone. Let me find what happiness I can." Penelope pushed herself free of her nurse's arms. She couldn't be strong inside her childhood sanctuary. "Eurynome, I need to be alone."

Somehow, it was a comfort to see the beginning of tears in her nurse's eyes.

*   *   *

To her mixed consternation and relief, Penelope's moon flow started that night. She blamed the rainy weather for her pain and wondered if the Goddess helped and punished her. For the next two days, she could barely sit at her loom for the pains in her belly and back. Penelope had long hours of quiet to think. She had all the solitude she could have wanted. Her maids left her alone when she wouldn't tolerate their company and Odysseus went to settle a dispute at the northern tip of the island.

She could not go on this way, she decided the third afternoon, alone in her bedroom. She had been alone too much with her thoughts and found she didn't like the company. She would act as if Odysseus' actions were truth, and pray that if it was all an illusion, it would never shatter.

Penelope went down the stairs to find Dolios and see if he knew when Odysseus would return. She paused with her hand on the door latch, hearing voices in the main hall. She had to think and re-orient with the rhythm of the household.

The time for the harvest sacrifices approached. Penelope pressed the latch and stepped out into the hall, looking around with care to see how the work progressed.

Thoosa sat in a corner with Melantho, separating bundles of rushes to spread over the floor. Penelope felt heat spread across her face at first sight of the sharp-tongued girl. The two could have been sisters, both softly rounded, with curly golden hair, sparkling blue eyes and ripe red lips. Penelope watched them laugh and lean close to whisper to each other. Thoosa wanted Odysseus in her bed. Penelope speculated on the chance the girl had spoken those words in the garden knowing she would hear.

"Ridiculous," Penelope spat and strode across the hall. Neither girl looked up until she stood before them. Melantho blushed and looked away, giving Penelope an idea of their gossip. "Thoosa, you were told you were not welcome here."

"You need workers," she responded, staying seated.

"Who requested you come? What authority?" Penelope glanced at Melantho as she spoke, daring her slave to claim authority to override Eurynome's commands. She turned back to Thoosa and met her gaze, drawing on her training in silent command, which she had learned in Sparta.

Thoosa looked away first. She dumped the last rushes from her lap and stood, edging away as she did so. Her face went pink, but Penelope doubted the girl blushed for shame. She stayed silent, keeping Melantho still with her presence until Thoosa reached the door. Penelope went to the storerooms to look for Eurynome. She glanced back in time to see Thoosa and Melantho exchange glances. Both looked toward the door of Odysseus' room.

Penelope knew what they thought, what Thoosa hoped, and a new fury and resolve grew in her. When she found Eurynome, she gave instructions to drive Thoosa away next time she appeared, and to keep Melantho within the walls for the next moon. Her nurse said nothing, but Penelope thought she saw satisfaction in the woman's eyes. She wondered what other mischief her maid was finding.

*   *   *

When Odysseus returned the next evening, Penelope was ready to follow her plan. She felt well and whole and clean again, and had spent the last half of the afternoon bathing, perfuming and ornamenting herself. When she heard his voice in the hall, greeting the slaves preparing the house for the night, she hurried down the steps to meet him. He laughed and hugged her, holding her up so her feet dangled. She tried to be natural as she laughed and returned his kisses. Odysseus didn't pause, so she knew she had succeeded.

They ate together, alone in the echoing hall. She was grateful he did all the talking, telling her about the people he had visited the last three days, the problems discussed. The wife of one prominent man had sent a present for Penelope. From the way Odysseus rolled his eyes and refused to go into details, she guessed it was another fertility charm. She was glad he took it as a joke.

It was almost a relief when, after they finished eating, he stood and held out his arms for her. Penelope welcomed the soft pulse of desire that began when he caressed her. He led her up the stairs to her room, latching every door after they had passed through. She helped him remove her clothes, returning his caresses with all the skill he had taught her.

Desire didn't grow. She pressed herself tight against him, willing the passion to begin. The pulse of desire didn't die, but neither did it grow stronger.

"Penelope, what is it?" Odysseus shifted to his side, holding her close. His pulse still raced under her hands. "Am I too eager? Are you ill?"

"I am not ill." She hated the way her voice wobbled.

"Then what's wrong? You don't eat, you sleep too much, you give orders as if you don't care how this household is run. You move like a woman caught in a sorrowful dream."

"Did Mentor tell you this?" she snapped before she knew the words were on her tongue.

"What of Mentor? Why should he have to tell me what I can see with my own eyes?" He sat up and reached for the lamp left burning on the table by the bed. In the changed light, his face was creased with worry and frustrated passion. "Penelope, did something happen between you and Mentor while I was gone?"

"Nothing happened. He is a decent, gentle man who deserves far better than to be set as watchdog over any woman, no matter who her husband is." Penelope twisted out of his grasp and sat against the head of the bed. He stared, eyes wide and bright with confusion.

"He was glad to be of help. You enjoy his company and guidance. What has changed?"

"You set him as spy over me."

"Why should I make him spy—"

"Is it true you let the boar wound him? Is it true you could have killed the boar, but you let it past because you two argued?"

"Who told you that?" Odysseus sat very still, his face a stiff mask. Only his eyes showed anger, his voice dropping to a whisper. "Who tried to poison you against me?"

"I overheard some girls talking while they worked."

"Thoosa, Deiros' daughter." A disgusted sigh escaped him. "He would poison the whole island against me if he could."

"Does he have reason?"

"He thinks he does."

"Likely one of your schemes. Deiros was the victim and he didn't take well to it." She nearly laughed in triumph at the stricken look that dimmed his eyes. She had made a hit before his stern control took over.

"I remember good King Nestor, when you told him of the suitors' oaths. He warned your scheming ways would be your bane someday."

"Penelope, what is this madness?"

"Your scheme failed you, cunning Odysseus," she continued, ignoring his words. Her breath shortened and her heart thundered in her ears. His voice was too quiet, frightening her, but she had to continue. "All your pride in seeing what others couldn't see. The joke is on you this time. Joined to a wife too thin and small. The beauty you predicted hasn't come. Nor ever will. And barren into the bargain. A blessing, for how could you be sure my children are yours?"

"Barren?" His face twisted, as if he would laugh if not for the pain that burned his eyes, turning his mouth into a crooked, bitter smile. "In only a year, you think you're barren?"

"And I shall stay that way. Barren and ugly and thin as a stick. A very good bargain you made." Her throat hurt, her voice a hot rasp.

Penelope bit back a shriek as Odysseus snatched her out of the bed by her shoulders. He dragged her across the room to the bronze mirror. He held her tight, her back to him, his arm around her waist while he tore the cloth off the mirror.

"Ugly? Thin?" He caught her at her elbows and shook her. "See the woman I fought for." His voice cracked. "Penelope, I swear to you, I will find the man who poisoned you against me."

"If any man did," she retorted, refusing to struggle against the painful grip on her arms, "you did."

He straightened, shock widening his eyes. Odysseus released her, but she didn't try to move. She faced his expression in the mirror.

"You're like a bard, taking a multitude of faces and voices to tell your tale, to get the desired reaction from your audience. You played me like a harp and you played me well. But the music fades." She closed her eyes against the burning of new tears.

Silence. She felt his breath in her hair, the warmth of his body close behind her. Penelope wondered she didn't shiver in the chill of the room. She opened her eyes, caught by the sight of her naked body in the mirror. The light of the lamp cast shadows that accented every curve, making her hips wider, her breasts more full, darkening hair and eyes to midnight black. She was beautiful, even in her own eyes. She nearly laughed at the painful timing of that vision.

"Is that how you see me?" Odysseus whispered. His voice jerked her gaze up to face him in the mirror. Did the glimmer in the mirror come from his tears or her own?

"I no longer know what I see." She shivered, more tired than cold. The fury that had burned in her faded, leaving ice in her chest. "Cunning Odysseus," she whispered, letting the tears come now and not caring that he saw. "Admired by even your enemies. Tell me the truth, if only once. If you trust no one, who can trust you?"

"Is that what you think? That I trust no one?" He lifted his hand, as if to rest on her shoulder.

Penelope longed for his touch and dreaded it. She knew the feel of his hand on her skin would send fire sweeping through her body and what dregs of her control remained would crumble.

"I don't know what I think, what I feel. I want to believe you, in all things, yet how can I be sure you are honest with me if you are honest with no one else?"

"A dilemma," he whispered. "Your question is wise. And painful. I wish I had an answer we both could believe."

Odysseus looked away and when he turned back she saw his eyes shift as his gaze traveled over her shape in the mirror. She saw no desire in his eyes, only a new depth of sadness.

"I think you wish to be alone." Then, he left.

Penelope concentrated on her reflection in the mirror to try to push the memory of her burning words from her mind. A sob worked its way up her throat. She turned from the mirror and hurried back to her bed. She curled up under the blankets and listened to the slowing thunder of her heart.

"I hurt him," she whispered. "My words came too quickly. He had no time to prepare, to play a role. It was no game. And if I hurt him..." She closed her eyes, digging the heels of her hands into them to fight the tears. "If he deceived me, he would not have been hurt."

That night, her dreams were filled with visions of Odysseus lying torn and bloody before her. A knife covered in blood lay in her open hands.

CHAPTER 14

Penelope lived by rote most of the next morning. She came downstairs to inspect the spices and oil bought from the merchants the day before and stayed to give orders for baking and preparing ointment against winter sores. Not until noon had passed did she realize Odysseus was gone from the house. She reasoned he was at the harbor, seeing to his ship or off to Raven's Crag to inspect the pigs and decide which ones to kill at the first frost, for winter eating. When she thought of him, what she said the night before, she felt only relief that he was nowhere to be seen. There was only echoing numbness inside, where before she drowned in fury and sorrow. It made a welcome change.

When evening came, a servant from Laertes' house brought a message that Odysseus had gone to the island of Kephallenia to see about a shipment of bronze tools and weapons gone astray. Penelope took the news with more empty relief. She forced herself to eat, to assuage the worry of anyone who might be watching, and tried to stay up later than she had recently. Her eyes burned from straining at her loom and her back ached, but she couldn't sleep. She lay awake, staring at the black ceiling, listening for the sound of a particular tread and voice and knowing he would not return so late at night.

When she did sleep, she dreamed again of Odysseus, dead and bloody, and the knife that killed him lay in her bloody hands.

*   *   *

In the morning, the quiet that filled her began spreading through the house. Penelope remembered the words of the servant girls and wondered which ones rejoiced at the split between Odysseus and her. She knew it couldn't remain hidden for long. For all she knew, more than one set of ears had overheard the argument in her room. She struggled not to examine the servants' faces as she passed them during the morning, looking for signs of anticipation or satisfaction.

When she could take it no longer, Penelope retreated to her private garden. She hadn't visited it since the day she heard Thoosa speak her poison. Penelope didn't care if the place brought back memories, it was quiet and no one would intrude on her. She slipped between the crackling bushes guarding the entrance, checked to be sure she was alone and settled at the base of the olive tree. It was pure, cool relief to sit still with her eyes closed and hear nothing but the sighing of the breeze in the branches and the faint cackling of her geese in the outer courtyard.

"You have hurt your husband deeply, Ikarios' daughter," a smooth, deep, feminine voice said.

Penelope opened her eyes, swallowing down a gasp of shock. She had heard no one pass through the bushes. A rebuke hovered on her lips but she kept them pressed tightly together and her tongue silent.

A tall woman stood before her, gray-eyed, with long, thick hair blacker than night, simply braided and hanging past her waist. Her dress was of simple lines, dazzling white, girdled with a belt of precious stones and silver. Silver and precious stones decorated her sandals. She leaned on a staff with silver on the tip. An owl perched on her shoulder. Penelope stared at the owl.

"He treasures you as few men can cherish their wives, though there is truly much that is childish in him," the woman continued. "Your accusations were just, but such words should never have come from your lips. Tell me truly, has he ever given you cause to doubt him?"

"I don't know!" Penelope blurted. "If I was sure, it would not hurt so greatly."

"Then believe him and no other." The woman smiled, but with a bitterness that made Penelope feel she had been sorely rebuked. "Go to your husband. Plunge a knife into his heart and finish the killing of your words. Or, heal the wounds you made. Do not leave any job half finished, Ikarios' daughter. It is not worthy of you."

"You don't need to tell me that," she mumbled, wishing she could tear her gaze from the woman's face, the blazing of her gray eyes.

"Your words had truth in them, I admit. Odysseus must endure great trials yet before he is worthy of all entrusted to him. He trusts few, constantly guarding against traitors and thieves. Those few he trusts have the power to destroy him, far stronger than his most bitter enemies."

The sibilant of her last word stretched out, merging with the rasping hoot of the owl. It lifted from the woman's shoulder and flew over the wall. Penelope couldn't help but watch its flight. When she turned back, the woman was gone.

Terror made her tremble. She managed to scramble to her feet. Tottering legs took her to the kitchens. Mercifully, no one was there. Penelope snatched up a honey cake, still hot enough from the oven to burn her hand. She tucked it into her wide cloth belt, then went into the storage room for the sacks of grain. Penelope took a handful of the sweetest wheat and put it into the belt as well. The fine silver guest goblets sat on the table, freshly washed and polished. She snatched up the largest and filled it with wine from the skin Eurynome saved for the most honored guests. Penelope nearly spilled the whole of it before she returned to the garden.

She found the spot where the woman had stood. There were footprints in that one spot in the dust and nowhere else. She imagined the indentations were warm with unnatural heat. Penelope put the cake in the footprints, then the grain over it. She carefully trickled the wine over the pile.

"Athena, you have scolded me as I deserve. Now, I pray you, give me the words and the wisdom I need. My anger and sorrow have taken my wits from me. He is my beloved, but I fear I have lost him. Help me." Tears slipped from her eyes as she closed them. Penelope waited, wishing for a sign, a touch of divine fingers, the brushing of owl wings against her hair. Only silence reigned in the garden.

*   *   *

That evening, when she heard Odysseus' voice in the hall below her chambers, Penelope dropped her thread. She stared at it, unsure what to do. She felt Melantho's gaze on her and refused to give her maid any triumph. Penelope bent and retrieved the thread, but didn't continue weaving.

"We have done enough for the day," she said, without turning to look at anyone. "I have pushed all of you too much. Enjoy yourselves this night." Penelope sat still, studying the thread in her hands until all her women had gone. From the corner of her eye, she saw Melantho pause in the door to watch her, then shrug and follow the others.

Penelope waited, listening for the voices coming up the stairs, through the open doors. Odysseus stayed in the hall, talking. She caught the rumble of Dolios' voice, likely reporting on the fall plowing and other work done during Odysseus' absence. A fond, trembling smile touched her lips, grateful for the faithful man. Dolios was sometimes as oblivious as a wall, but his feelings were clear and true.

"Enough cowardice," she whispered to the still room. Penelope made her way to the stairs. She listened for the first sign of Odysseus leaving the hall, but his voice stayed steady. She wished she could catch the words, the tone of his voice, the inflections he used, to gauge his mood.

He sat at the hearth, examining a spear shaft with one of the hunters when Penelope reached the door at the bottom of the stairs. She paused in the doorway, watching him. Her husband smiled at some remark the slave made. Then he glanced up and met her gaze. His smile didn't leave his face, but faded from his eyes. With a jerk of his head, he bade the man leave.

"The journey went well?" she asked, voice trembling. Penelope forced her legs to take her across the hall to him. She was aware of the servants lingering, finishing various tasks for the day. She hated them. If she was going to confess, it had to be soon, but not with an audience.

"More than well." He stood and came to meet her. His hands on her shoulders, the kiss brushed across her forehead, were mere perfunctory gestures. Penelope swallowed hard against the sob that choked her. "I brought something for you." He dug into the pouch hanging from his belt and brought out a thin chain of polished bronze links. "Menthes, chief of the bronze workers of Kephallenia, sent this for you. He overflowed with apologies that he had not sent a marriage gift to us earlier."

"What did he gift you with?" she asked, letting him slip the chain around her neck. It hung light and delicate on her shoulders and down over her breasts. Penelope studied it to avoid his neutral, nearly empty gaze.

"A knife, some new heads for my arrows...and advice on how to treat a new wife." He paused. "He has three."

"Was his advice helpful?"

"Touching the woman concerned, no. Menthes likes to struggle with a new wife, usually obtained unwilling, and prove he is the master of his household."

"I came to you willingly," she said, lowering her voice so a man standing two paces away couldn't hear.

"Is that why you played Dyvis and tried to run away?" he whispered. When she looked up, he smiled sadly at her.

"Odysseus—"

"I laughed at Menthes," he said, brushing her cheek with his fingertips. "He said a new wife should be beaten regularly, whether she deserves it or not." He forced a crooked smile onto his lips. "I have messages I promised to take to my father tonight." He gave her a nodding bow and left.

Penelope waited, fingering her new necklace, gaze fastened on the floor until the sound of his footsteps faded. She went back to her room, controlling her steps and her face so no one would guess the storm inside her.

*   *   *

Penelope waited in her bed, two lamps lit, the door standing ajar. She heard Odysseus come back to the house and heard Eurynome greet him at the door.

Odysseus never came up the stairs, though she listened for the sound of his feet until the night rang with the pounding of her pulse in her ears. Penelope waited, counting the footsteps of the slaves as they closed up the house for the night. She heard the night insects singing without pause. Tears touched her eyes as she gave up and lay down.

The hoot of an owl outside her window brought her sitting upright. Heart pounding, Penelope waited for Athena to rebuke her.

Nothing. The owl didn't cry again.

Legs trembling, she got out of bed and reached for her dress. Penelope wiped the tears away with the hem, then pulled the garment over her head. She fussed with perfume and brushing her hair and debated whether to wear jewelry. Likely Odysseus already slept, but she had to go to him.

She carried one small lamp with her, going in her bare feet down the stairs. They felt cold in the damp of the night, smooth from constant sweeping. Every time she thought she heard a sound, Penelope paused and listened. She wanted no witnesses. Her heart had calmed to normal by the time she reached the bottom of the stairs and slipped through the open doorway.

A new fear touched her. What if Odysseus had locked the door of his room?

Penelope shook her head at this foolishness. There was no reason for Odysseus to worry in his own home. A moment later, her hand on the latch, she remembered her dreams and Athena's words about plunging a knife into her husband's heart. Penelope swallowed a sob and pushed the door open.

By the dim light of the lamp, she saw him lying on his side, the sheet pushed down to his waist, eyes closed, head pillowed on one bent arm. She waited, but he didn't stir.

She had an idea. Instead of speaking and waking Odysseus, she would slip into bed next to him and wait until he woke.

She put the lamp down on the table and turned her back on the bed as she slipped out of her dress. The room felt cold and Penelope wrapped her arms around herself as she turned. She stopped short, breathless.

Odysseus lay as she had first seen him, his eyes open, face unreadable in the shadows. For a long moment, they regarded each other in silence. Then, he lifted the sheet aside. Penelope slipped in next to him before she lost what little courage remained.

"I didn't mean to wake you," she whispered, her voice cracking with tears as he put his arms around her.

"I wasn't asleep." He caught her tears on his fingertips and after a moment, wiped them in her hair. "Penelope, I have wronged you. I could see the sorrow in your eyes, knew you wanted to speak with me, and I left. I wanted to hurt you."

"As I hurt you."

"But you didn't mean to."

"We have wronged each other." Penelope smiled through the tears burning her eyes. "Words wouldn't hurt so much, I think, if we did not love."

"Yes, you are my beloved." His voice rasped. "I swear on the scar the boar gave me, I have always and will always speak the truth to you here, in our bed."

"Please, tell me you forgive me for doubting you?"

"I would forgive you a thousand times over. What you did, coming through that door..." A ragged laugh escaped him. He pushed himself up on one elbow, so he leaned over her. "To have you near me now, after such a long wait—it is an agony not to touch you."

"A moment," she whispered against his lips when he leaned down to kiss her. She smiled through more tears as he moved away, wearing a puzzled frown. "You are greatly favored by Athena, my dear husband."

"So it is said. I have dreams sometimes, but—" He shook his head. "What other thoughts have filled your head since we argued?"

"Athena...scolded me, for how I had treated you. She told me to either kill you or heal the damage I had done, but not to leave you wounded. She said we few whom you trust have power to do more damage than your worst enemy."

"She *said*..." Odysseus stared, forehead wrinkling as he visibly struggled to understand.

"She appeared to me in my garden and scolded me, told me how much I had hurt you, and then vanished. I would rather die than hurt you."

"And yet?" he prompted, voice softening, when she hesitated.

"It was your hurt that cut through my doubts. That was the proof that you had been truthful and trusting with me, despite what I heard, what I had seen and knew about you." Penelope reached up, slipping her arms around him. "Tell me again you forgive me?"

"Again, I forgive you a thousand times." His eyes were still wide and dazed. "Athena intervened...for us...for our happiness."

"We must offer her a rich sacrifice in the morning," she whispered.

"In the morning." Odysseus' smile widened and he pushed aside the sheet to caress her. "Penelope, it has been agony without you..."

*   *   *

Later, with her head resting on his shoulder, Penelope whispered, "And what did happen in Mycenae?"

Odysseus laughed. A ragged, tired sound, it grew in strength. He tightened his arms around her, then rolled her onto her back. He held himself up on his elbows on either side of her shoulders and looked down on her.

"Sweet, sweet Penelope. *That* is what I waited to hear when I returned home. When you didn't come running, asking that question, that was the sure sign something was amiss." He kissed her long and lingering, bringing desire humming through her belly again. She laughed against his lips.

"Did good come of it?" she asked, when they had both caught their breaths again. "You were gone a long time."

"Too long," he agreed with a soft grunt. "The only good is that we will be prepared when the land of Troy, Ilion in particular, finally works mischief against us."

"They won't cease troubling the merchants?"

"Only the merchants who can afford to hire ships to escort them, bristling with spears and bows, through the Dardanelles."

"Will there be fighting, then?"

"Agamemnon might enjoy that, and likely some other chieftains and princes. As for me—and Menelaos—there are better things to occupy my time." He chuckled, a loud rumble in her ear. "Priam claims he is willing to talk peace with the Achaians. I don't trust him."

"There is a price for his peace?" Penelope waited. Odysseus held so still, she knew her guess had been painfully correct. "Is there danger in telling me what the Trojans wanted?"

"Not danger." He sighed. His embrace threatened her breath. "Priam wants brides for some of his many sons. Four very specific brides, reputed to be the most beautiful maidens of the Achaians. With them as visible reminders of the alliance, he would agree to a peace treaty with us."

"And who are these girls, to be sacrificed for the greater good?" A cold thread began to work through her chest, wrapping around her lungs. Penelope tried to make her voice light, her words mere humor, but she failed.

"Cousins. Two daughters of Tyndareos. Two daughters of Ikarios. Helen, Klytemaistra, Iphthine and Penelope."

"What did Agamemnon say?"

"He laughed."

Odysseus turned on his side. His hand slowly stroked up her side, hip to shoulder and back down. Penelope had seen him stroke his bow that way, when deep in thought. His feather-light touch brought no rising desire, but a feeling of mixed comfort and worry. She knew he needed to touch her for his own comfort.

"Agamemnon was quick to point out to the envoy," he continued after a moment, "none of the four were maidens and three had borne children or carried children now." He frowned. In the lamplight, his eyes vanished into dark shadows. "The response was that all the children were girls. With proper husbands, the women would all have sons. And she who had no children yet would quicken the first time she lay with her new husband."

"I'm not tired of my first husband," she snapped, trying to make him laugh. Odysseus appeared not to even hear. "What did Klytemaistra say to this? Did Agamemnon let her know what was said?"

"Klytemaistra heard. She insisted on listening to everything, to safeguard her son's future. She was flattered at the offer. Helen thought it was a joke."

"Helen? I thought she was deathly ill."

"She is, but she insists on being with her sister, for her help and advice." He shook his head, another heavy sigh showing what he thought of that. "No one thought to ask Iphthine what she thinks of the offer. What do you say?"

"I think it is dangerous and foolish. Even if they persuaded you to send me away, I wouldn't leave you."

"I will not be persuaded. Penelope, you are my treasure, more precious than my own life. I swear that to you." He kissed her again, reverence in his touch.

"What would you do if Agamemnon tried to take me from you?" Penelope reveled in the warmth of his body, the soft echo of his pulse just under the skin, vibrating against her slowly caressing fingers.

"He wouldn't be foolish enough to reveal his intentions. I would be dead, outnumbered or betrayed, before anyone realized he knew you existed. What would you do if he killed me to have you?" he returned.

"Raise your sons to honor—"

"Sons?" Odysseus laughed. "You claimed you were barren, and now you give me sons. How things change when a goddess speaks."

"I dreamed that I gave you two sons. I would raise your sons to honor you."

"Agamemnon would kill them, to prevent their vengeance." His tone was light, but there was pain and a choking sense of reality in his words.

"Then when he came to force me into his bed, I would kill him, and with justice in my hands, come to join you."

"I swear, Athena persuaded Aphrodite to cast magic on you, to make you love me. My sweet, beautiful Penelope," he whispered, beginning to kiss her again.

"Did she ever speak to you, like she did to me?"

"Once," he admitted, pausing, his face hidden in the curve of her neck, voice muffled by her hair. "On my way home after I met Iphitos, with the bow...she came to me in a waking dream and told me to treasure that bow, never let it leave my possession. It would give me vengeance someday. Protection against those who would kill me and steal what was most precious to me." He sat up so he looked down on her and cupped her face with his hand. "Should I kill every man who smiles at you, Penelope? Is that the only way I can protect you?"

"I cannot be stolen from you," she whispered.

CHAPTER 15

Fall came in gentle and mild after the hot, dry summer. The harvests were better than expected and some made so bold as to ask Penelope when her child was due. Their questions didn't hurt. She wanted a child now for love, not duty.

Odysseus drove hard bargains with the merchants who came to Ithaka, leading the way by example for his people. They were well-prepared when winter storms lashed the coast and cut them off from the other islands and the mainland.

The last ship before winter brought gifts and messages from Menelaos and Helen. They had a daughter, whom they named Hermione. Penelope grew quiet when she heard, frightened in a remote way by this proof that she had dreamed truth once again. Just a little over two moons ago, she had dreamed Helen held a tiny girl-baby, with wisps of hair as golden as her mother's. She hardly reacted when she heard of the birth of Agamemnon's long-awaited son, Orestes.

When the talk turned to Ilion, she slipped from the hall and hurried to the shrine to Athena, which Odysseus had built in the garden. Penelope knelt before the altar, listening to the whispering moan of the wind, ignoring the chill of the damp air that congealed on her arms.

"Wise Athena, Goddess," she whispered, lifting her gaze to the owl carving that sat on the roof beam. Dolios had made it as a gift for the dedication. "Help me understand. I have dreams that speak the truth and others that are only the fruit of my wishes. Show me which ones come through the gate of ivory, and which through the gate of horn. I fear for my beloved. I dream of darkness surrounding him, keeping him from me."

She stayed kneeling until the darkness closed in and Odysseus came looking for her. When she told him about the dream of Hermione, he was silent a long while. He gazed at the owl as well, eyes narrowed and dark with trouble.

"We cannot know the future. It is enough that Athena guides me. She speaks for me, I hope, before the gods I offend. I am sometimes not tactful or popular, my love."

"You are the epitome of tact," Penelope retorted, slipping her arms around him. "The trouble comes when you depart and people learn the truth in what you told them."

"Witch!" Mischief sparkled in his eyes. "Do you see this in your dreams, as well?"

"I need no dreams to tell me about my husband. My heart tells me." She lifted herself on her toes to kiss him. A soft sigh escaped her when he held her close, lifting her so her feet dangled. "This gift of dreaming frightens me."

"I can see."

"Not the dreams themselves, but that I cannot tell which are true and which false, until after the dream has come true. Helen warned me to tell no one, that it would cause trouble from the priests. That they would tear me from my home and force me to serve the temples. I thought she teased, but Helen sometimes speaks like an oracle herself."

"If Agamemnon can't take you from me, no priest will, either. I swear it." He forced a smile. "Do you have dreams of us growing old together?"

"Many."

"Then your gift gives us hope." Odysseus glanced at the sky as a stronger breeze reached them past the walls of the shrine. "Come inside. Another storm is coming. We must have a feast tonight, to honor Orestes and Hermione."

"I would rather the feast was for our own child," she said without thinking.

"There is time, Penelope." He held her hand as they walked through the courtyard.

She mumbled agreement, but a shiver took her that had nothing to do with the cool breeze. She had dreamed of them growing old and gray and stooped together. She had dreamed of sons, laughing together as they walked the hills of Ithaka. She had dreamed of long years without him, a single son growing up without a father, watching the harbor in vain for a familiar sail to return. Which of her dreams were true, and which mere shadows of fears and hopes?

*   *   *

Winter passed as gently as the fall had come upon them and the seas were open for sailing sooner that spring. An invitation came from Sparta. Helen longed to see her cousin, to show off her daughter, and Menelaos wanted to consult with Odysseus about the trouble in Ilion without Agamemnon leading the discussion. Nothing was said about the argument with Tyndareos and Penelope took that as a good sign. Even better, plentiful rains had come at the proper time that spring. She no longer earned dark looks when she left the house. Women returned to the worship of the Goddess and smiled at her. She carried no child yet, but she hoped.

Once the spring planting ended and the household settled into its routine, they set sail for Pylos and Sparta. Penelope didn't enjoy this voyage like the one that brought her to Ithaka. Odysseus was distracted, working the rudder against the high seas. Eurynome was ill, so Melantho went as Penelope's attendant, and the girl was sullen. Penelope blamed her low spirits on Melantho and her dreams.

She dreamed of dark clouds over Sparta, children crying unattended and betrayal filling hearts. When they reached Sparta she was relieved, yet curiously disappointed, to see the people happy and busy, the crops thick and green, the herds and flocks heavy with new calves and lambs.

Alkippe stood with Lystia and Menelaos to greet them when they reached the palace. Tyndareos had retired to a small holding in the hills, making Menelaos king in his place. And, Alkippe explained as she led Penelope and Melantho to Helen's rooms, the new mother was captive to her daughter's every whim.

"What she means," Helen said, as Penelope entered the women's chamber, "is that the whole palace dances attendance on the child. Especially her father."

She smiled, as golden and lovely as ever, but didn't leave her seat by the cradle. It sat next to the window seat Helen preferred, hung with curtains against the sunlight. Penelope went to her, leaving Melantho to greet her friends.

"We have a new goddess in this house, then?" Penelope murmured, taking the bench next to her cousin. Laughing, they embraced, then her attention went to the cradle.

177

Hermione was her mother in miniature. The child slept, but Penelope knew her eyes would be the same changeable blue. Golden curls like clouds graced the tiny head. Her skin was gold and ivory and roses. One tiny hand peeked from under the blanket, all delicate perfection.

"What do you think?" Helen said, when her cousin had gazed long enough.

"Again, I envy you. Helen, I think I will always envy you." She laughed, remembering to keep the sound soft.

"You have time for children. Or does Odysseus complain that you have none yet?"

"He laughs and says we have plenty of time. Yet my dreams contradict words, so what should I believe?"

"Dreams?" Helen's smile faded. She looked away, out the window. "Yes, I have dreams as well." She shook herself slightly. "He's a good husband to you, isn't he?"

"He is my beloved, and I am his." Penelope shrugged, unable to find any other words to explain.

"Then what is to worry about?"

"Every time I hear the men speak of Ilion, the troubles with the Dardanelles and the merchants and the tribute they exact...I shudder."

"As do I." Helen twisted her face into a mask of disgust, then a moment later laughed. "Leave such considerations to the men. That is their realm. Ours is to manage our households, be beautiful for our husbands and raise our children to be strong and happy and wise. And to give our men the sons they crave," Helen added, her smile fading, her voice softening. Penelope thought she detected a slight crack in her voice, like a threatened sob.

"Is that what Menelaos says?"

"Perhaps. I know our home is brighter when he doesn't tell me what the men discuss and I don't ask."

Penelope refrained from responding. She was glad Odysseus had placed the stairway to her rooms off the feasting hall. If she left her doors open, she could hear everything. He usually asked her what she thought of what she heard. She couldn't imagine what it would be like, not sharing their thoughts and day's work with each other.

"Is this your work?" she asked, going to the nearest loom. Helen's face brightened. With a glance for her sleeping daughter, she got up and followed her cousin.

"I've caught your trick, turning dreams into weaving." Her face took an expression that struck Penelope as strange. Part longing, part dreaming happiness, part despair.

The picture on the loom was one-third completed. It showed high walls, a city fortress and a flat, grassy plain leading to the sea beyond. A man stood in the foreground, finished from the waist up. He wore armor, dressed for battle, one hand holding a raised sword, the other grasping a spear. He wore no helmet and his head tilted back, mouth open in a battle shout. Golden brown threads made his sculptured face. Yellow curls descended from a noble brow.

"He is beautiful," Penelope murmured. The man wasn't Menelaos. This felt somehow dangerous.

"A hero from my dreams." Helen stroked the cloth with her fingertips, her eyes bright.

"Perhaps the son you will have someday?"

"Oh, he is too beautiful to be Menelaos' son," she said with an odd, uncomfortable laugh. "No, this is a dream from Aphrodite. The feelings in it are not fitting for a mother toward her son." She blushed, looking directly at her cousin. "Tell me honestly, Penelope. Do you have such dreams, even lying in your husband's arms?"

"No." A shiver passed over her. "My dreams warn me such joy cannot last. I heed the warnings and make sure not a day is wasted. I long to give Odysseus a son, but I will not let my desires poison the joy we have."

"Keep your dreams hidden." Helen gripped Penelope's shoulder. Her voice lowered, tight and intense. "Cousin, dreams are as often traps of the gods as warnings. Speak your dreams and you could lose all that is precious to you." With a guilty glance toward the man on the loom, Helen returned to the window seat and the cradle.

*   *   *

"I think Menelaos torments her for not giving him a son," Penelope whispered in the quiet of the night. She welcomed the warmth of Odysseus' arms around her, driving away unwelcome thoughts she had gathered during the day.

"Without knowing what he does," he agreed. "We spoke after the war chiefs left. He fears for Helen's life if she ever quickens again. She was ill while she carried Hermione and her labor nearly killed her. Menelaos thinks to take a slave girl to give him a son, to spare Helen."

"He won't spare Helen by doing that. What love she does have for him will turn to hate."

"I think Menelaos fears Helen, a little."

"He would be wiser to fear losing her loyalty. It would do them good to share their lives with each other. Helen has her daughter, her weaving and the household. Menelaos has the city to rule and the troubles with Ilion to worry him. They share nothing except their bed." She shivered as she sat up. "My love, all this frightens me. I see how happy we are. I remember the gods are jealous and don't leave well enough alone. My life was often affected by what happened to Helen, and now she grows discontent."

"I will speak to Menelaos, one new husband to another," Odysseus said, reaching up for her. She let him draw her down next to him. "I know that look, that tone, Penelope. You worry because we have no children, don't you?"

"A little. I would welcome being as ill as Helen was, I think." She wondered if she should confess her newest fear, that the potion had made her unable to bear children.

"I would not," he snapped in mock anger. "I would rather have you than twenty sons."

"Less work to keep me fed and clothed."

"Woman, your tongue is too sharp." Swiftly, he rolled her onto her back and tickled her, smothering her laughter with kisses, holding her still under him so she couldn't escape. Penelope welcomed the laughter and teasing. It was warm and alive, driving away her fears.

*   *   *

By the time they left Sparta to return home, Penelope had lost her worries. She had seen Menelaos with his wife and daughter. Despite the man's stumbling tongue, he adored his family and Helen knew it.

Odysseus told her how the councils concerning Ilion progressed. Many merchants found it more profitable to go overland around Troy. Despite the expense, they were better off risking bands of thieves than to go through the Dardanelles and lose their profit to tribute. Ilion learned its lesson slowly. Troy's merchants and wares were shunned or even evicted from some ports. Not all the kings and chieftains of the Achaians followed the accords set down by Agamemnon, but the pressure did work. Those merchants who risked passing by Ilion did not lose as much as the year before and the losses slowly dropped.

King Nestor shared the same news when they stopped overnight in Pylos. Penelope marveled that the man was still so healthy and strong, with all his years behind him. Polykaster had married and was hugely pregnant. Penelope would have been depressed, but Polykaster told her of a powdered root she had taken to make her fertile. She gave generously to Penelope.

They reached Ithaka in midsummer. Work waited for them, taking up their daytime hours. Spring storms had ravaged the coastline and fishermen had been lost. The plentiful spring rains had vanished with summer and now the fields were dry and cracking.

Penelope went twice as often with Eurykleia and the other faithful women to make offerings to the Goddess. Underneath the chanting and the sweet oil burned to bring help to their island, she sensed the unrest and worry, tasted and smelled the fear in the air. She heard the whispers. More than once, she turned to catch a woman gesturing at her flat belly, a look of frustration on the other's face. Penelope knew more people blamed the bad summer on her. If the queen wasn't fruitful, the land would be barren as well. She took Polykaster's powder and went every morning to Athena's shrine, pleading for help.

Eurynome watched her carefully, at Penelope's request. Antikleia and Eurykleia were included in the secret of Polykaster's gift. The four women spent hours together at a time discussing Penelope's health, the slightest change she felt in her body. When her moon flow came after returning from Sparta, Penelope cried. She knew her concern showed clearly because Odysseus often told her, for no reason at all, they had plenty of time for children. She loved him more for that, and loved Laertes that he never spoke of his longing for a grandson.

*   *   *

Fall approached, with signs that it would be a rough, stormy winter. Odysseus took regular trips to the other islands, braving the seas in a smaller ship. Reports came of raiders scouring the coastlines and smaller islands, and he went to help the people prepare their defenses. He always set a specific limit for how long he would be gone and made sure Penelope knew the route he and his men planned to take. It was common sense in such bad seas that searchers knew where to look for delayed voyagers. And, Odysseus told her when he was in a teasing mood, she was prone to jealousy. If she knew where he was, she would not suspect him of climbing into other beds. Penelope laughed every time he said it, comforted by his teasing.

Fall came in with rain that made the late crops flourish, and made the seas treacherous. Penelope barely heard when her husband and his father worried and complained about the dangers. She concentrated on the green fields, food for the winter, and the changes in her body.

Odysseus took a trip to Kephallenia, promising to be home in four days. Penelope waited until the ship was gone from the harbor, then sent Eurynome for Eurykleia and Antikleia. The four women talked and compared, and agreed.

Her child would be born with the return of spring.

Penelope spent the next four days in euphoria, planning and waiting, walking her rooms, trying not to give the rest of the household an inkling of what she knew. She had not thought of Antikleia being a weak link in the secret until Laertes came to visit her one dismal, blowy afternoon.

He came up to the door of her weaving room, refusing to let the maids announce him. Penelope worked several more passes of thread before she realized he was there. When she looked up at him, startled, Laertes laughed.

"Forgive me. I needed to really look at you." He stepped into the room. "Could we speak alone for a moment?" he asked, looking at Melantho and Autonoe, the only servants there at the moment. She nodded and the maids left. Laertes waited until they were gone, then brought a small ivory box from under his cloak. "Are you truly well, Penelope?"

"Very well, Father." She wondered at the brightness in his eyes. She knew how the cold and wet made his knees and elbows and fingers ache, yet he seemed unaffected today.

"Good, that is very good." He handed her the box. "A gift, given in joy, to my son's most precious wife."

"How did you find out?" she said, holding the box on her lap. Penelope smiled, despite her disappointment. Laertes looked joyously ready to burst, and twenty years younger. "Mother said she wouldn't tell anyone."

"She didn't. I read it in her face. She smiles continually. Her eyes shine. She sings. And she and Eurykleia reminisced about Odysseus as a baby, when they thought I couldn't hear." Laertes bent and kissed her forehead, his gesture like a blessing. "I will tell no one. Oh, but to be here and see my son's face when you tell him!"

Penelope decided she wasn't upset that he had guessed. She knew he could have made her miserable the last two years, pressing for a grandchild, making her feel inadequate as a wife. She loved the man as if he were her true father. When she opened the box, the jewelry inside took the breath from her.

Sapphires and emeralds, mounted on thin silver wires formed a necklet, thicker than her thumb, with a cunning latch to hold it closed. Thin bracelets of silver clashed and chimed, and at the bottom of the pile lay several rings, set with tiny chips of sapphires and emeralds. Penelope looked up from the sea-colored hoard at Laertes.

"I'm afraid of disappointing you," she whispered. "Father, such beauty—"

"Hush." He gently pressed a finger against her lips. "I bought these to give you at the winter festival. Now simply seemed a more appropriate time. They are for my son's wife, not the mother of his child. There is a vast difference."

Penelope nodded that she understood and kissed him in thanks. Only when Laertes had gone did the tears come.

*   *   *

On the fourth day, Penelope prepared herself for Odysseus' return. She chose a new dress, in celebration—white, embroidered with blue and green threads to match the jewelry Laertes had given her. She gave instructions for a special meal, to be started when Odysseus came through the door. Her thoughts wouldn't stay on anything but the news she had to give him. Penelope knew she would be useless to the rest of the household, so she settled herself in her weaving room to plan designs for blankets and clothes for the child.

Morning passed with no word of sails in the harbor. Noon came and she ate out of habit, not hunger. The afternoon dragged. Storm clouds gathered, slowly leaching gold from the light. She thought she measured every second with her heartbeats. When dusk fell, Penelope went to her room and had Eurynome bathe and perfume her. She put on the new jewelry, then removed it again. The thin chiming of the bracelets was over-loud in the waiting silence and she wanted to hear every footstep that approached the house.

Evening came. She ate only because Eurynome ordered her to. Penelope stayed in her room, sitting in the window that looked out over the garden. She concentrated on the coming child, trying to recall every dream to decipher what he would look like. She was determined her firstborn would be a son. Though a daughter would be a gift from the Goddess, to inherit her mother's duties, Odysseus and Ithaka needed a son. The world was a warrior's world and Ithaka needed a man to defend her.

At the back of her mind, she knew it was foolish to dwell on such things. She had little control over the issue of her womb. Penelope preferred a vain exercise to the alternative. Despite her concentration, visions of Odysseus' ship wrecked on the rocks or beset by raiders plagued her. When sleep finally caught her, she welcomed it.

Penelope sat sleeping in the window, her head tilted back against the thick frame so she faced into the room instead of out to the garden. Moonlight cast stark shadows across her garden, elongated streaks of black against white made it a place out of delirium dreams. Odysseus found her there. She didn't wake until he had carried her four steps away from the window.

"Go back to sleep," he murmured, his voice touched with laughter. "You're only having a dream."

"Good dream," she mumbled thickly. Her eyes flickered open. She managed to slide her arm around his neck.

Her mind and body stayed half-asleep while he carried her to her bed. Her senses felt strangely acute in this state. Every shadow and beam of moonlight stood out in stark relief. She could feel every individual hair on Odysseus' neck, under her arm. He smelled of the salt damp of the sea and of his ship—tar and wet wood, sweat and damp rope and fresh air.

Penelope buried her face in his shoulder and inhaled deeply of his scent. A ripple of desire went through her body, quelled by weariness, but waking her. She kissed his neck and managed to lift her head enough to find his mouth as Odysseus set her down. Her arm wouldn't tighten enough to keep her hold on him when he stepped back.

"You need your sleep."

"I waited for you."

"So I see." His smile went crooked and he sat on the edge of the bed. "The tides and winds were against us all the way."

"But you did come back in four days, as you promised." For the first time, Penelope didn't want another tiny lesson on the vagaries of sailing. Her hand strayed over her belly and now she didn't frown and silently scold herself for her unconscious reaction. "It hurts to see you go, but I know you always come back. You always keep your word."

"Penelope?" He frowned and gently cupped her cheek with his hand. "Beloved, why is it so important that we speak now, and not in the morning? Eurynome was adamant that I come up to you. Finding you in the window like I did, I was glad I listened."

"We wanted you to know before anyone else guessed." Penelope sat up, shifting to her knees and reached out for him. Odysseus frowned, his curiosity changing to worry and he drew her onto his lap. "The Goddess has heard my prayers." She laughed when his frown turned into a comical mask of dawning comprehension. "I carry your son," she whispered, the words trembling on her lips.

Penelope had thought long and hard on how she would tell him. The four words she chose satisfied her, speaking all her dreams and hopes.

Odysseus' arms tightened around her. He gasped her name, then hid his face in her hair. His body shook as soft laughter escaped him.

"Oh, my sweet Penelope." He leaned back and stroked the hair away from her face. His touch was gentle, slightly trembling. "The relief on your face. Were you that worried about having children?"

"We *have* been married more than two years." She let him lay her back down in the bed. This time, Odysseus stretched out next to her, keeping her close in his arms.

"There is time, more than enough time."

"No. This year was hard, and more of our people blame me. I blame myself."

"There's no need."

"Yes, there is." She nearly told him of the potion, but Odysseus kissed her, many soft kisses to cover her face. She laughed weakly when he kissed the tip of her nose.

"My love, the lean times were here before you arrived. A bad year does not make you a bad queen. Or a barren one, as you have proven." He tucked her head under his chin. "There is more than enough time, though I would not send this child back to the Goddess."

"No, neither would I. Yet still, we have so little time." Penelope tried not to let the slight chill wash over her again, as it had done every time she thought of her dreams. "Helen agrees with me. Many of my dreams hold the truth. My dreams tell me I shall give you a son. Dreams tell me our days of happiness together are limited. I see you sailing distant seas, walking distant shores. I see myself waiting, my hair gray with the frost of years."

"The gods shall send me on many journeys, then. But I will always come back to you. I promise you that. I swear on my life and my love for you." Odysseus gently laid his hand flat on her belly. "I swear on our child, I will always come back to you and not even death shall stop me."

She nodded, refusing to let the tears touch her eyes again. Penelope pressed herself close against him and said, "Tell me about your journey."

"I would rather talk about the child."

"There is more than enough time for that." A tiny laugh escaped her at the irony of her words. "Tell me about Kephallenia and what you brought back, and we shall decide what to set aside for him when he is grown."

"You are so sure you carry a son?" His voice had a sleepy rumble.

"I am sure. Now, tell me." She turned onto her side, pressed against him, her head resting on his shoulder.

Odysseus drifted off to sleep before he finished his tale. Penelope lay awake in his arms only a few breaths before she too fell asleep.

CHAPTER 16

"I think you've frightened them all away," Penelope said, voice low, as she looked up from her stitching.

On the floor at her feet, Odysseus fit a brace for the new loom. He frowned and scanned the weaving room. They were alone, no company but the muffled hiss of the coals in the brazier and the howl of the winter storm beating the walls.

"Why would they be frightened of me? Am I an unkind master? Do I beat the men and rape the women?" He tried for an aggrieved tone but failed, breaking out in chuckles.

"You did shout at Nerilia when she slipped and fell against me."

"The girl is dead from the knees down and blind into the bargain," he retorted, returning to his work. "Any fool could see the paving tile was crooked and slick."

"No damage was done and she was frightened enough for my sake before you shouted." Penelope leaned down, wrapped her arm around his neck and kissed his ear. "I should be flattered you're so careful of me."

"Yes, you should be." Odysseus caught at her hand when she released him and pressed a kiss against her palm. "Even if I were hard-hearted, I would still be careful of you. Eurynome is a harpy, watching and scolding and swooping down on the least offender. The woman frightens me."

"Poor Eurynome," she sighed and resumed her stitching.

"Poor Eurynome?" He turned, getting to his knees. "My love, she could frighten Ilion into peace with the Achaians. I thank Athena every day she finally approves of me."

"She was old to be a nurse when I was born. Now, she has to worry about our son. Anticipation makes her nervous. When the boy is born, then she will calm."

"She worries about her ability?" Odysseus got up onto the bench next to her.

"Possibly."

"Then let Melantho be nurse. The girl is steady enough, strong enough."

"She is, but Eurynome doesn't trust her." Penelope paused and considered for a moment. "I would rather Eurykleia be nurse to our son, if Eurynome cannot. Let Melantho be head housekeeper instead."

"Eurykleia would be pleased," he said slowly. "And that would take away half my mother's fears."

"She's found something new to worry her?" Penelope put down her sewing, to give all her attention to the problem.

"Your decision not to find a wet nurse."

"What could be better for a baby than his own mother's milk? I'm strong and healthy, and all the winter ills will be past by the time he's born."

"To please her, could you have a woman waiting, in case you aren't able to nurse?"

"And to please *you*, I wouldn't doubt." She laughed. "You put the blame on your mother, but I can see you worry for me just as much."

"As nervous as a boy on his first voyage, trusted with the rudder. And no instructions," Odysseus added, letting a grin brighten his face. "I agree it's better if you nurse our child, though not fashionable for royal ladies. Yet for the sake of caution—"

"I already spoke to Eurynome and she's watching for a likely new mother," Penelope said, pressing two fingers against his lips to silence him. She laughed, then squealed, jerking her hand away when he bit at her fingers.

"If this is any indication of your temper until the baby is born..." He shook his head, eyes sparkling with laughter.

A whimper broke the quiet between them. A brown hound pup sat in the open doorway, head cocked to one side, watching them. Odysseus stood and the pup lay down, head on its forelegs and whimpered again.

"This is the best of the litter," he said, bending down to scoop up the handful of damp fur.

The pup wiggled in his hands. His grin turned mischievous. Penelope barely had time to move her sewing before Odysseus dumped the pup into her lap.

"I admit, being able to climb all those stairs so young is a sign of strength." Her moment of indignation melted when the pup looked at her with pleading eyes and whimpered again. "What is so special about this one?"

"Every time I pass, he follows me. He tracked me all the way up here, didn't he?"

"You'd train him *now* to be a hunter?" She stroked the pup's fuzzy head. It closed its eyes and settled down, tongue hanging out, the image of contentment.

"Why not?" Odysseus sat at her feet again, his shoulder resting against her knee. He reached for the brace and went back to work. "There's precious little else to do, when the storms keep us locked indoors and the bard can't sing for sneezing. A hunting dog would make a good guard."

"Ah, now I understand." Penelope continued stroking the pup, feeling the thumping of its tiny heart. "I can see this one fully grown, sleeping under our son's cradle."

"One more guard I trust, to watch over both of you when Agamemnon calls me away. The peace with Ilion can't last."

"I know." Penelope shivered, glad he couldn't see her. She had dreamed of Helen's tapestry, where the man came to life, snatched up Helen and carried her away. "Have you thought of a name for him?"

"The pup? Perhaps Argus? A name from legend, for a dog that will perform legendary feats."

"You expect much from such a tiny one," she said, stroking the sleeping pup. "He wore himself out just climbing the stairs."

"He'll be stronger for it."

On fair days, Odysseus took the pup out with the grown hunting dogs, to exercise them and begin Argus' lessons. He trained the young dog so whenever they came in, Argus went directly to Penelope. When Odysseus built the cradle, he trained Argus to sleep under it. Penelope wondered what her husband feared, to take such precautions.

*   *   *

Penelope woke with a shriek choking her. She clutched at the blankets wrapped around her, trying to tear them away. They felt like hot hands tangled around her legs, catching at her dress. The room echoed with her scream, increasing her fear. The feel and sound of the place was unfamiliar; she was not in her own room.

Cold wet touched her hand, accompanied by a whine. She snatched her hand away, blinking in the darkness, and swallowed another shriek when something leaped up onto the bed next to her. Cold touched her arm, with a snuffling sound and a whimper.

"Argus?" she whispered. A thumping tail on the bed frame reassured her. Penelope choked and wrapped her arms around the dog, hiding her face in his short, scratchy fur.

The door slammed open, spilling light into the room, along with Odysseus, his father and Mentor. Odysseus jammed his torch into a wall bracket and gathered her into his arms.

"What is it?" His voice came out ragged, choking. His face was a pale mask in the shadows. She had never seen him afraid until that moment.

She stared at him, confused. Then reality and memory slid into place. She was in Odysseus' room. He had been out with Mentor and his father, inspecting a dock damaged in the last storm. Penelope had settled in his room to wait for him before the evening meal and had fallen asleep.

"I had an evil dream," she admitted, feeling foolish.

Laertes snorted, a sound of mixed relief and amusement. Penelope hid her face in Odysseus' shoulder, glad when he held her closer and pressed a kiss against her cheek.

"My lady, perhaps no one warned you," Mentor said, his voice gentle with humor. "Women with children in their bellies often have dreams of ill omen. It's best to ignore them. Queen Hecuba has learned that, to her joy and sorrow."

"Hecuba?" Penelope knew Mentor spoke to distract her and she was grateful. Yet mention of the people of Ilion irritated her, too. "What has Priam's queen to do with me? All her children are grown."

"When her second son, Paris was about to be born, she dreamed he would bring destruction to Ilion. The boy was exposed on a mountain three days after she birthed him."

"I had no such dream," she blurted.

"No one said you did," Odysseus assured her. He put her down on the blankets, keeping one arm around her. His free hand rested on her swollen belly. She often woke to find him touching her so. The protective gesture eased away the last tremors from her ill dream.

"Even if I did have such a dream, I wouldn't speak it. To kill an innocent child..." She snorted, despite the weak terror that fluttered through her. "What were you saying about Queen Hecuba and Paris?"

"Priam and his queen discovered the dream was nothing more than that. They obeyed it, of course, but the boy was found and rescued, raised in anonymity and only this last fall restored to his family. Paris is strong and handsome and his return has brought prosperity to Ilion, some say." Mentor shrugged. "Time will tell, will it not?"

"What of your dream, Penelope?" Laertes asked, his voice soft in contrast to the hearty comfort Odysseus and Mentor both put into their voices.

"No images remain," she admitted. "I only feel terror. Danger and threats." She swallowed hard, the words sticking in her throat. "Odysseus, be careful. Nothing remains of my dream but a sense of a cruel will, seeking vengeance against you. Someone strong, whom you have offended, will refuse to rest until you have paid."

"If everyone I offended made such a vow, many men would be dead now of exhaustion." Odysseus kept his tone light, a smile on his face. The expression *almost* touched his eyes. "Come, it is late and you went without supper to wait for me. Perhaps mere hunger gave you such a vision."

Penelope nodded and let him help her to her feet. Despite his words, she saw by his eyes he believed her dream. Penelope wished Mentor was right.

*   *   *

Winter held them close that year, strong winds blowing in from the sea every night, coating surfaces with ice, battering anything not fastened down or sturdily made. Penelope welcomed the constant moaning sound. Rough winds meant protective isolation. Messages and rumors of evil couldn't come to their island to trouble them. She lived an illusion that no land existed beyond Ithaka.

Odysseus only left the house for emergencies. His care for her sometimes grew heavy. She only had to remind him and he would laugh, apologize with a kiss, and let her have her way. Then a short time later, he would treat her as a fragile flower again. Some nights when she was too tired to walk, she let him carry her up and down the stairs. He joined her in her bed and held her close every night, holding her up when the baby's restless movements wouldn't let her sleep flat. In the mornings when she woke before him, she found Odysseus' hand resting protectively on the curve of her belly.

"It's true," she often told him and Eurynome, making husband and nurse laugh. "No matter how we began, my husband loves me now merely for the child I give him. I'm too fat for pleasure or to satisfy his eyes."

Penelope was delighted at the changes the baby brought to her body. She put on more flesh, smoothing over places she had thought would always be bony. She didn't mind the awkwardness of her body and dragging weariness, when before she had been lithe and quick and could stay up late and rise early. She endured cheerfully the aches in her back and legs. She wished winter wouldn't end, sometimes. There was a peace and security in their isolation she didn't want to lose.

*   *   *

"Penelope, I need your wisdom." Odysseus stood in the door of her weaving room, smiling in apology for startling her. He did that often lately, breaking her from daydreams. He wore his cloak and high boots from walking outside and she saw bits of sleet melting in his hair. "Will you come downstairs with me?"

"What could be so serious?" She stood, bracing against the side of the loom for her balance. Before she quite reached her feet he was there, one hand under her elbow, an arm around her waist. She thanked him with a smile, then smoothed her dress over the bulge at her waist. The child kicked once. "He doesn't want to move," she said, laughing.

"I am afraid we must." He brushed a kiss across her forehead and led her to the door.

He glanced back once at the maids at their tasks. Penelope saw his gaze rest on Melantho and suspected the cause of this meeting. Her servant had been too moody and quiet the last few days. Penelope had come upon Dolios and his daughter in the middle of arguments. She wondered what her maid had done to now involve Odysseus.

Downstairs in the deserted feasting hall, a village man waited. It took a moment of thought, but she recognized his black, curly hair, massive shoulders and lean, pointed face. Usually he laughed and sang when she saw him, his giant's body always in motion. Erymas was young to be a master shipbuilder, but his skill and strength gave him his position. Odysseus trusted him alone to repair his ships. Penelope had not recognized Erymas at first because the sparkle had left his eyes and his mouth curved down. As Odysseus helped her sit, she noted the shipmaster hunched over on his bench as if a great burden sat on his shoulders.

"Erymas wishes to marry Melantho and buy her freedom," Odysseus said, finally shedding his cloak. He flung it over an empty table and sat next to her.

"Dolios won't approve?" Penelope guessed.

"Her father approves and said he would speak with Lord Odysseus for permission," Erymas said. His words came in a voice deepened by confusion.

"I said we would free Melantho, as a wedding gift," Odysseus added. "He spoke to Melantho before we came to you. She *is* yours to free or keep."

"Melantho refused him?" She couldn't quite believe her ears. And yet, having grown up with Melantho, she *could*. Her maid was prone to pick up suitors like toys, giggle and kiss and share their beds, and then walk away. The only suitor she seemed to regret losing was Aias.

"Something is wrong?" Odysseus said when Penelope sat up straight, eyes widening.

"Erymas," she said, "did Melantho give you a reason?"

"She said I remind her too much of someone she loved. Every time I kiss her, I remind her of him." The shipmaster shrugged his massive shoulders. He looked so pathetic and sad, weak despite his bulk, Penelope would have laughed. She felt sorrow for him and anger for Melantho.

"Aias. Melantho still loves Aias."

Odysseus frowned, then looked at Erymas. He nodded.

"She shows wisdom," he admitted. "There would be no peace in a house where the husband's face makes his wife long for another."

Penelope barely heard as Odysseus explained to Erymas, trying to smooth over the problem. She remembered how Aias had snatched at her, how she had fought him. Did Melantho know how Penelope had shamed her sweetheart?

Erymas went home, his confusion resolved if not his disappointment. After Odysseus supported her back up the stairs to her weaving room, Penelope wondered if the solution was the right one. It might be better for all to force Melantho to marry and manage her own home. Her maid was over twenty, after all, and there was something not quite right in a woman of her age, and so lovely, unmarried and childless.

Penelope wondered if Melantho blamed her for that. If Odysseus had not argued with Tyndareos and left Sparta so quickly, Aias would have asked for Melantho. Now because of Aias, Melantho refused a suitor.

"She is a heart with many difficult layers," Penelope confided to Odysseus that night, when he joined her in bed and she told him what she had thought.

"You think this will lead to trouble? She looked relieved when her father told her our decision." He tugged the blanket up higher, covering her shoulders.

"I know, but I remember overhearing her saying things that made no sense then, but which disturb me now. She was proud Erymas resembled Aias so much. Many girls envied her that Erymas looked at her alone. Melantho may be true to her lover, but others will name her a fool for losing Erymas. Someday, she will blame us instead of being thankful."

"When that time comes and Erymas is still not married, we will fix the problem." Odysseus sounded sleepy, reminding her of all the hard work he had done that day in the sleet and cold.

"Yes, we will fix it," she agreed.

She slipped her arms around him. In moments he slept, curled around her. Penelope still worried, knowing how Melantho had carried grudges before, wreaking vengeance when time presented her with the chance.

CHAPTER 17

"Penelope? Child, where are you going?" Eurynome called from halfway down the stairs. She smiled, shaking her head, and held out her mistress' cloak.

"I wasn't going any further than the door." Penelope sighed and stopped. A wall was conveniently close, so she leaned against it to wait for her nurse.

"The breezes are chilly, despite the warm sun. A fine, worthy nurse I would be, to let you take a chill this close to—" She broke off with a gasp.

Penelope watched, frozen, as Eurynome's foot slipped on the step. The woman fell crooked against the wall, bounced off, fell two more steps, hit the other wall, then landed on her side on the floor. A shriek rose high and clear. When Penelope pressed her hands over her mouth, fighting her rising gorge, she found the sound came from her.

As quickly as she could, with her huge belly and awkward pace, she went to Eurynome. Two maids and a farm man reached the woman before her. Eurynome cried out as they rolled her onto her back. Her face had gone ashen and sweat beaded her forehead. Penelope gagged when she saw the extra angle in her nurse's upper arm.

*   *   *

Argus' claws clicked on the floor tiles, telling Penelope Odysseus had returned from hunting. She felt too tired and achy to even smile when the dog clambered up onto the bench next to her and nuzzled her hand, begging to be petted. She felt she had waited days while others tended Eurynome. No one had come to tell her anything. Her nurse, in the last of her strength, had forbidden her to come near. Penelope refused to go to her rooms. She sat in a shadowed corner in the hall, waiting, wishing Odysseus would return so she could let go her worries and cry.

She heard his voice, far off in the servants' quarters and she smiled, glad he would check there first. Argus' questing tongue let her know she ignored him. Murmuring an apology, she rubbed his head. There was comfort in the slight damp of his fur, the odor of wet dog and mud, the sense of normalcy and coming spring the animal brought with him.

Odysseus passed through the hall, heading for the stairs. She watched him walk past, too tired to open her mouth to call. Penelope wished she could sink into the shadows and negate all the events of that morning. If she hadn't decided to go to the door to feel the breeze and breathe the chill air, Eurynome never would have fallen.

Argus barked. Penelope imagined he sounded indignant. She let out a gasp that became a giggle and wondered if she was so tired she imagined things.

"Penelope?" Odysseus turned and hurried to her side. "What are you doing down here?" She welcomed the warmth of his arms around her, gladly resting her head on his shoulder. "Where are your women? How could they leave you alone? Your arms are cold." He snatched up the cloak she had dropped on the floor and wrapped it around her.

"Eurynome—" she began, and choked.

"She is fine, resting. Eurykleia came to help. She feels no pain." He adjusted his arms around her and lifted her onto his lap. "Have you been hiding here all this time, waiting for news?" A chuckle escaped him when she nodded, feeling like a naughty child. "Love, Eurynome would be grateful for your worry and scold you for not taking better care of yourself."

"I know. I would give anything to have her scold me."

"She's more concerned with her duties than her pain. She wants Eurykleia to take her place."

"Take her place?" Penelope winced when her voice echoed in the dark, deserted hall. "No one can take her place."

"Her arm will take too long to heal and always be weak. She and Eurykleia have decided she will remain head housekeeper. Eurykleia will come from my father's house to be nurse."

"What of Melantho?"

"My love, that woman is your property. She will do what you order her to do." Odysseus sighed, cutting the rising volume of his voice. "Forgive me. You're too soft-hearted."

"Melantho rightly expects to be head housekeeper when our son is born."

"Then we'll send her to my father's house, in Eurykleia's place." He tipped her head back so he could brush a kiss across her lips. "Will that soothe your too-soft heart and her pride?"

"Very much. Your mother gets along with her well enough, I think."

"Good. I am well pleased to have her out of my house."

"And have Eurykleia here instead?" she prodded, smiling now. She laughed when Odysseus had the grace to look ashamed, despite his smile.

*   *   *

Her labor pains began before Odysseus left for hunting that warm, bright spring morning. Penelope debated telling him and having him underfoot during the preparations, worrying and questioning. Eurykleia had warned her the first child would take long in coming. She knew she might still be in labor when Odysseus came home that night. So she kissed him, wished him luck, gave Argus one last scratch under his chin and sent them both off to enjoy their day hunting.

After she climbed the stairs to her rooms, where Eurykleia supervised sewing new clothes for the household, the gentle pangs stilled. Penelope congratulated herself on her common sense and silence, and sat down to continue her weaving. She had extra reason now to finish the work. It was a light, airy cloth to hang over the cradle against too-harsh sunlight.

The pangs came and went, sometimes making her clench both fists around the thread, then fading to the gentleness of the breeze in the open window. Penelope worked slowly and carefully when all her instincts shouted to hurry. She tried to make her work into a game, counting how many rows she could finish before another ripple of near-pain hit her.

"Penelope." Eurykleia's hand rested on hers, startling her. "Are you well?"

"Perfectly." She smiled at Eurykleia's frown. Penelope felt cool damp forming on her own face. She shrugged, giving up the small battle. "My son is impatient to join us."

"My lady." Surprise wiped away Eurykleia's habitual somber efficiency. She rested both hands on Penelope's belly, feeling the rippling of muscles. She smiled and shook her head. "You do not need to be so brave and strong."

"No." Penelope would have laughed, but another pang robbed her of breath. "I will not welcome my son with tears or screams. As it is, Odysseus would hear and come running. There's no need to worry or frighten him."

"That one is a danger to us all when he's frightened," Eurykleia agreed. She turned to face the other maids who had stopped their work. Comprehension took several forms on their faces—excitement, fear, worry. "This work is done for the day. You know your duties. See to them." She turned back to Penelope as the women scattered. "It's almost noon. You should eat for strength, while you still can."

Penelope nodded and let the woman help her off the bench and away from her loom. She looked at the pattern and smiled at the race she had lost.

*   *   *

Eurykleia made her walk back and forth through her rooms while the pangs were gentle. Small fires burned in the braziers. From time to time Eurykleia helped Penelope burn offerings of grain or pour out a few drops of wine in libation to the Goddess. Penelope welcomed the warmth of the fires one moment and the next scrambled for a window, to breathe clean, cool air to still the churning in her belly. She managed to keep down what she ate and was proud of that.

An incredible weight pressed on her body, making her legs feel like bruised reeds. "I need to sit down," she said, putting distance between each word so they wouldn't slur. Her tongue felt as heavy as her legs.

Hands helped her sit. Penelope closed her eyes, and for a moment even the spasming muscles in her belly stilled. With the weight off her legs, her feet no longer throbbed. She felt she could spread her arms into the breeze and fly. Then a stronger twisting, aching contraction squeezed her body and anchored her to the ground.

When she finished gasping, Penelope felt some release. She kept her eyes closed and dug her fingers into the wooden bottom of the seat. Odysseus' voice penetrated the momentary stillness, and Eurynome's answered. Penelope smiled, glad now she had made no outcry. She wanted to call him but knew that would not help. He would worry and get in the way of the women attending her.

She remembered teasing him that birthing was one place where he would be worse than a stumbling apprentice. He had countered that he had helped with many difficult births—cattle and sheep and dogs. Vaguely, Penelope remembered trying to slap him, pretending to be insulted. Odysseus had caught her hands and drawn her as close as her huge belly would allow and kissed her until she laughed.

Tears touched her eyes. Penelope released her hold on the seat with one hand to wipe them away, quickly, before anyone saw. She opened her eyes. Eurykleia stood before her, holding a damp cloth to wipe her face. Penelope looked away, feeling shamed that the woman had seen.

"Arrogant child," the nurse whispered, kneeling to wipe Penelope's face. The cloth was cool, the touch soothing. "Cry. Scream. It is how we release pain and find strength."

"I can't," she whispered, shocked at how tight and weak her voice sounded.

"He won't hear you. Eurynome sent him to bring his mother. That should keep him away." The satisfaction in the woman's voice brought a choking laugh from Penelope.

"Not long enough," she said, her voice breaking. Penelope clutched at Eurykleia's hands. "Is something wrong? Is that why you're sending for her?"

"First births are always long in coming." Eurykleia's face revealed nothing good or bad.

The afternoon passed into night. When Penelope gave in and opened her mouth, all that escaped were whimpers. She didn't think it helped, but Eurykleia and Eurynome both looked pleased.

Despite what they said, she knew something was wrong. Her belly twisted and squeezed and drove the breath from her, but she felt no shifting of the child inside her. When dawn touched the sky, Penelope thought she knew the reason. Her hips were still as slim as a boy's. There was no place for the baby to go in birthing. The bones weren't moving despite the painful, tearing contractions. She remembered Odysseus' words to his father, the day she arrived in Ithaka. Her husband would have to find a wide-hipped slave girl to give him a son, after all. She would have laughed at the irony of it if she had any breath.

Antikleia became her source of strength. The woman said nothing, but her hand was always there for Penelope to hold. She held a cup of water for Penelope, though all she could manage was a tiny sip at a time. Antikleia was the one who insisted Penelope try to eat, even if only a mouthful of bread. Penelope clung to the woman. For her sake, she held back the tears, the moans of fear that choked her.

There came a time when the pains abandoned her to exhaustion. Penelope managed to sleep for a handful of minutes. When she woke, the quiet frightened her until she heard men's voices in the hall below. Laertes, Mentor and other friends kept Odysseus company while he waited for their son to be born. She listened for her husband's voice, but didn't hear him.

It was unnatural for Odysseus to be so silent. He always had a story to tell, advice to offer, questions to ask. He was the one who spoke others to courage, drove away tears and anger.

She screamed as a pang tore through her body, sharper, stronger than any others that had shaken her all the long day. Penelope pressed her hands against her hips, pushing in to relieve the agony. It bit deeply at her, as if a giant hand slowly squeezed her bones to break them apart.

Tears filled her eyes when she opened them. Eurykleia smiled at her through the exhaustion that blotched her face. The woman wiped the sweat from Penelope's face and nodded.

"It is good," the woman whispered. "Your body opens to release the child. He will come now."

Penelope nodded, hearing words but not understanding. Her body was in control, not her mind or her will. She arched her back against another bone-breaking quake of agony and another scream escaped through clenched teeth.

Somewhere in the middle of the flurry of women's voices and hands that tried to soothe her and failed, Penelope heard Odysseus shout her name. She wanted to call him and opened her mouth to speak. Another spasm ripped the breath from her lungs. Knowing he was close gave her strength. She swallowed against the hurt and clutched at the bracing ropes Eurynome put into her hands until she thought she would break them. Penelope gritted her teeth, tasting blood as she bit her tongue. She pushed with her whole body, suddenly finding a way to work with the pangs instead of just enduring.

Heat tore through her body, driving away the creeping cold of exhaustion. She smelled blood, felt a tearing like knives deep in her belly. A cloud filled her mind, muting the sudden rise in women's voices.

Release. Penelope felt as if a cord deep inside had snapped, setting her free from her body like a ship loosed from its anchor and floating with the bobbing waves. She welcomed the soothing darkness, the fading ache. Darkness filled all her senses like a soft, warm, enveloping cloak.

At one point, she opened her eyes to see Eurykleia. Penelope smiled sleepily at the woman.

"You have a son," she said, her voice coming from far away, echoing inside Penelope's head.

"Knew," she mumbled. "Knew before everybody."

"Yes, you did," Eurykleia soothed. Her touch on Penelope's face, stroking a few strands of hair aside, came to her as if through several layers of cloth.

* * *

How long she drifted, Penelope didn't know. She welcomed the weightless, muffling warmth. From far off, she felt someone helping her to sit up. Opening her eyes beyond a slit took too much effort. A few rays of light penetrated the dark, enough to turn everything misty gray and streaked with rainbows. Penelope liked that.

Hands moved aside the blankets wrapping her. Some gray faded from her mind. From far off came a cry, like a lamb.

A tiny, insistent mouth fastened on her nipple. Awareness returned, spreading out from that contact like ripples from a stone thrown into water. Penelope opened her eyes. Her arms moved as if made of wet clay. She felt the blanket against her skin, and then the weight of a tiny body. A tingling warmth moved through her breast, fastening her returning attention to the shape in her arms.

At first all she knew were tiny wisps of dark brown hair on a head covered in pink, delicate skin. Her eyes moved slowly, like taking a long journey. Penelope watched the face take shape, delight moving through her as if arriving from a far distance. A tiny nose, no bigger than the tip of her smallest finger. Closed eyelids of translucent skin, like alabaster, with faint red and blue streaks in them. Amazing, thick lashes, glistening in the torchlight. Round, red cheeks that moved faintly with the insistence of feeding.

Full awareness returned with a sigh of contentment and tears welling up warm in her eyes. Penelope tightened her embrace under her son, and looked up. Antikleia sat at the end of her bed, watching. Eurynome stood by the open window, where dawn streaked the sky. Eurykleia was nowhere to be seen, but Penelope knew where the faithful woman had gone.

"He looks like his father, I think," she whispered. "Has Odysseus seen him?"

"Your son is not leaving this room until the day is warm enough." Antikleia had more strength in her voice than Penelope ever heard before. "His father is sacrificing the best this household owns, in thanks, as is proper."

Penelope thought to ask when they would go to the Goddess to make thank offerings, but the words died before they could reach her lips. All her attention returned to the baby. Pressure grew in her other breast and she tried to remove the hungry, sucking mouth to more nourishment. The boy let out an angry squall, startling her. Then his lips touched her other nipple and he resumed suckling. Penelope chuckled, amazed at how tired so little effort made her.

"He's so small," she said, daring to touch the delicate wisps of hair on his head.

"Now he seems small," Eurynome said, leaving her post at the window. She came to the bed and adjusted the blankets. "When you were birthing him, he looked as huge as a ten-year-old boy."

Weariness dragged at her as the boy finished nursing. Almost immediately he fell asleep again. Penelope would have laughed at that, but had no energy. Sleep took her, wrapping her in warmth and darkness again.

*   *   *

"Keep that filthy beast out of here!" The horror in Eurykleia's voice woke Penelope, rather than the volume.

She opened her eyes to see she lay on her side, her arm curled around the blanket wrapping her son. Penelope smiled, rubbing her eyes with a hand that felt not quite her own. Wriggling, whimpering dark brown fur entered her view.

"Argus," she said, her voice slightly cracking. The dog rested his forelegs on the edge of the bed.

"I can hardly control him, Eurykleia," Odysseus said. "Short of tying him outside, that is."

"Then do so." Some anger left the nurse's voice.

"He only wants to see the baby," Penelope said, trying to lift herself up on one arm.

Then Odysseus was there, helping her to sit, his hands gentle, slow and trembling slightly. Questions and worry clouded his eyes.

"I'm just tired," she said.

"Tired." His voice caught and broke on the word. With great care, he sat on the edge of the bed, shoving Argus away with his knee. The dog didn't resist but trotted over to the cradle and settled down underneath it.

"He's beautiful. And hungry." She laughed, feeling the pressure of milk in her breasts. Penelope tugged back the blankets with a heavy hand so their son's delicate, sleeping face could be seen. "Everyone knows now I'm a good wife and a good queen. I'm better than Helen or Klytemaistra. Your firstborn is a son. I made you king of Ithaka today."

"Penelope." Odysseus' eyes sparkled with mixed tears and laughter. He caught at her hand, kissing the palm and then pressing it against his cheek. "Beloved, you nearly killed me with worry." He tried to laugh, the sound broken but beautiful to her ears.

"The first is always the hardest."

The boy woke with a cry. Penelope's hands were still heavy and awkward. With whispered instructions, Odysseus helped her sit and lift their son to nurse. She saw awed delight touch his face.

"What name have you chosen?" she asked.

"Telemachos." Odysseus leaned forward, careful of the boy, and kissed her.

CHAPTER 18

Dragging, draining weariness held Penelope in her bed. For the first few days after birthing Telemachos, it was all she could do to nurse him, hold him until he slept and maybe work a few strands into the design on her lap loom. Then she slept. She refused to let anyone put her son in his cradle until she could get up and go to him when he cried. Odysseus moved the cradle next to her bed and raised it so she didn't bend or strain to move the boy. Eurynome tried to bring in a wet nurse but Penelope barred the woman from the room. After all, she argued, she wasn't ill, only tired. Her milk was wholesome. Odysseus and his mother made sure she had her way.

He slept in the room with her, loathe to leave wife and son alone. Penelope knew Odysseus slept next to her, but for the first week she never saw him in the bed. When she woke in the night, her breasts aching with milk, anticipating Telemachos' cry, Odysseus was awake before her. His touch was as deft as Eurykleia's, able to pick up their son without disturbing him.

Penelope enjoyed the quiet watches of the night. She leaned against Odysseus, his arm tight around her shoulders, Telemachos half asleep as he suckled. This happiness, she wanted to last forever.

*   *   *

The day Eurykleia permitted her to leave her room and spend part of the day outdoors, Penelope knew victory. She teased Odysseus for carrying her to her garden, even knowing she couldn't have walked.

The growth of her garden astonished her when she settled onto the cot. The herbs reached from their little plots as if they would spread across the paving stones. Flowers bloomed that she expected to be tight buds. The olive tree spread its boughs over her head, heavy with luxuriant dark leaves.

"The Goddess speaks her approval," Eurykleia said, breaking into Penelope's delighted reverie. She sat on the end of the cot and nodded toward the rest of the garden. "We will have more than we need this year, all over Ithaka. The rains come when we need them, in the right amount. The days are warm, the nights cool instead of cold. The people say you have brought this to Ithaka by giving Odysseus an heir."

"What would they say if I had borne a daughter?" Penelope countered, smiling. She shifted the warm burden of Telemachos in her arms, watching his face for the first sign of waking.

"She would belong to the Goddess, I think. They credit you with their blessings. That is all that matters."

"Must I bear a child every spring, to bless Ithaka?" she returned, chuckling.

"No." Odysseus knelt before the cot and clutched Penelope's shoulders. He would have shaken her, if not for the sleeping baby in her arms. "Penelope, I will not risk you!"

"Be sensible," Eurykleia snapped. A sparkle of humor mixed with exasperation lit her eyes. "Your son is a fine, healthy, strong boy. Penelope has narrow hips. The first is always the hardest birth. The next will not hurt her as much."

"Can you promise that?" he demanded. Odysseus waited, but neither woman spoke. "I thought not. Once, I would have sacrificed anything and anyone for Ithaka. Not now. Penelope, we will have no more children."

"Short of no longer lying with me, how can you prevent that?" she whispered. Penelope thought of Eurynome's bitter potion and shuddered. She refused to believe her life depended on taking it again.

"There are ways." He stood, glaring at both women. Penelope would have been angry but she saw the fear in his eyes. When he stalked out of the garden, she felt tempted to laugh. Odysseus rarely was at a lack for words.

"What shall we do about him?" she asked Eurykleia.

"Do you truly want more children?"

"Yes." Penelope gazed down at Telemachos. "When I give life, I am one with the Goddess. And I will bless Ithaka."

*   *   *

Three nights later, Penelope knew she had recovered from giving birth. She felt desire stir as Odysseus slipped into bed and put his arms around her. She turned his good-night kiss into many. He caressed her with a hesitation she never thought he would show. Impatience made her movements sharp as she guided his hands over her body.

"No," Odysseus whispered, catching her wrists to hold her still. "I don't want to hurt you. It's too soon."

"Beloved, please." Penelope tried not to let anger wipe away the sweet desire pulsing through her. It had been so long since she had felt it. "The pain will be small. Eurykleia said so." She smiled when he wavered. His nurse's word was among the highest authority.

"Even so…"

"Are you afraid of making me pregnant? Don't be. While I nurse Telemachos, I cannot conceive."

"You can't be sure of that."

"Who can be sure of anything?"

"I can." Odysseus looked at her for a few heartbeats more, then rolled out of bed and snatched up his discarded clothes. Penelope sat up, staring as he left the room.

He returned in only a short while, but it felt like half the night passed. Penelope bit her lips to keep silent when she saw the cup he carried. Odysseus sat on the edge of the bed and held the cup out to her. The familiar, bitter odor made her ill. She refused to meet his eyes, afraid of what she might see.

"What is it?" she whispered.

"You know very well, Penelope."

"How long have you known?"

"I guessed." He pressed the cup into her hands. "In my father's house, there are many places where a boy can hide to learn what adults would not tell him. I spied on my mother and Eurykleia, and learned women's secrets a man with twenty daughters would never learn. And some nights, your first kiss had a bitter taste."

"You never said anything, never reproached me." Her voice broke as wet warmth touched her eyes.

"I care for your happiness and the joy of our bed more than getting an heir on you. How happy would you have been, full of a child you hadn't chosen to conceive?"

"Beloved," she whispered. Penelope took the cup fully into her hands. She gazed down into the milky depths.

Once, the potion had been a way to rebel against destiny. Now, she felt a deep, aching sadness at the thought of denying another child to the world.

"Penelope, drink before it loses its strength." Odysseus lifted the cup to her lips. She thought she saw sorrow in his eyes, and worry.

"It will taint my milk."

"Eurynome and Eurykleia both say not."

"They—you spoke with them?" Penelope wavered between anger and amusement at the conspiracy.

"Eurynome feared the potion weakened you, when you carried Telemachos. She consulted Eurykleia, who came to me. They prepared this for when you needed it." Odysseus began to take the cup. "You don't need to drink this tonight."

"I need *you* tonight, beloved." She took the cup and emptied it in two swallows, nearly gagging on the last mouthful, and blinked back tears. Odysseus took the cup and put it on the floor. He drew her into his arms and kissed her, and she knew he shared the bitterness with her.

*   *   *

Penelope dreamed. Shadows on shadows, muted voices whispering words she could not understand. She remembered nothing when she woke, beyond an implied warning: guard happiness. She knew no one was ever happy for very long. Either contented carelessness led to a mistake that offended someone, or a jealous god or an enemy would attack. So she treasured and guarded each moment and let the days go by as they willed.

The people of Ithaka credited her with the bountiful spring and gentle summer. They loved and praised her, bringing gifts of early crops or young lambs and piglets. She dedicated her gifts of grain to the Goddess, to avoid punishment for taking undue praise. Penelope found comfort in serving the Goddess, one more step she could take to protect the ones she loved.

When rumors of trouble with Ilion began at midsummer, Penelope wasn't surprised. What surprised her was Odysseus' refusal of a summons to Mycenae.

"He can tell Agamemnon whatever he wishes. I will not leave Ithaka this summer," Odysseus said, recounting the conversation to her after the messenger returned to Mycenae. Outside, the afternoon darkened gently to evening. "He can tell Agamemnon I have gone mad, plowing the sand with dogs and using my best sword as a plow blade.

And sowing the seashore with rocks and coral, for good measure."

"You didn't actually use those words, did you?" she asked, looking up from Telemachos' cradle. It sat four steps further from her bed than it had the previous evening, a sign of her growing strength.

"I did." He stopped his slow pacing and met her eyes. A chuckle burst from him. "He'll likely tell Agamemnon I am my wife's slave. Which is near truth. What good will it do us to complain to Ilion? We have been patient, gave them time to mend their ways, offered them a place in our accords. Ilion and Troy stand apart and look down on the Achaians."

"Then only trouble will come from more waiting." She shivered and pulled the blanket closer around her son.

"Likely." Odysseus joined her at the cradle. His arm was warm, taking weight off her weary legs. Penelope closed her eyes and leaned into him. "If I am called away, it must be for profitable reasons, not to soothe Agamemnon's pride and let him preside over the Achaian kings like a priest with his acolytes."

"You should have sent that message back to Mycenae," she offered with a soft chuckle.

"Do you ever wonder what the royal wives in Troy say to their husbands about this problem?" Odysseus murmured.

"I think they say to forget about tribute and think more about improving their flocks and herds."

"We can only hope." He held her tighter, his hand moving slowly up and down her back.

Penelope pressed herself against him and remembered the dreams she had about two sons. How soon, she wondered, could she become pregnant again? When could she pour out the potion without Odysseus noticing? She had dreamed about two sons and Odysseus safely at home for the second one's birth. Could she protect him by carrying a second child?

*   *   *

"Helen is gone," Odysseus said before he stepped through the door into her bedroom one late fall day.

Penelope looked up, the words echoing in her ears but making no sense. Just a moment before she had been laughing, watching Telemachos crawl on the thick sheepskins spread on the floor, chasing Argus as fast as his chubby legs and arms would move. As if he understood his father's words, the boy stopped his game and went from all fours to sitting.

A cold howling wind outside presaged a storm. Telemachos flapped his hands for attention, but his parents didn't see. Argus came from behind the tall water jug and sat at Odysseus' feet. The dog whimpered.

"Gone?" Penelope finally said. "How?"

"Paris of Ilion came to Sparta on a peace mission. Or so he claimed." Odysseus dropped to his knees next to Penelope and put both arms around her. She felt the racing of his heart. He likely heard the news at the docks and ran all the way up the steep path to their home to tell her.

"Menelaos? Hermione?" She closed her eyes, imagining carnage in the beautiful, rich palace.

"Menelaos was called away to tend to a problem with his herds. It was a ruse. When he came back, Paris was gone and Helen with him. Half the servants say she went willingly, half say Paris carried her off. She left her daughter as if she forgot the child existed." Odysseus' face twisted, his mouth pursing as if he needed to spit out something foul.

Penelope reached to gather up Telemachos. The wide-eyed boy made no protest as she held him close. She wondered if he felt all the turmoil raging in her heart.

"Where did they go? The seas aren't passable. How did the messenger reach us?"

She thought of the storm that had beaten at the bronze shutters the day before. She envisioned her cousin riding the seas in a ship that could capsize at any moment. Helen didn't even like the sea.

"Menelaos sent to ask us to keep watch if Paris was foolish enough to sail," he admitted. "His men are searching all the land around Sparta. By now, Agamemnon's men should be joining the land search."

"I can guess what Agamemnon said when he heard."

"So can I. Probably hoping Paris is dead at the bottom of the sea, and Helen with him."

Penelope nodded. She wasn't surprised opinion already turned against her cousin. She remembered the visit with Helen more than a year before; the image of a handsome young man half-finished in the loom; Helen dreaming and discontented with her life and a husband who didn't share his life with her. Penelope wondered what Paris looked like. Even if he bore only a shadow of resemblance to the man in the weaving, Helen would have seen it and willingly gone with him.

Telemachos let out a whimper of protest. She realized she held her son too closely. Penelope apologized with kisses and tickled him to make him laugh. Looking at her son, she knew Helen didn't go lightly from her home, even if she went willingly. Half her heart stayed in Sparta with a golden-haired little girl.

*   *   *

Odysseus gathered more news after questioning the sailors who brought the messenger. Rumors were rife in Sparta and Pylos and half of Achaia. Some said a servant girl had met Paris at the palace gates and claimed to be Helen and he carried her off. Or Helen hadn't been in Sparta but was visiting her sister in Mycenae. Or Paris had sent out messengers with the tale of the kidnapping, to foul his trail while he remained in Sparta and killed Menelaos. Or Paris came with magic and put the household asleep, leaving him free to carry off the queen.

"Whatever has happened, the only surety is Menelaos is likely tearing himself to pieces," Odysseus said, when he finished sharing the tales with her.

"Should we hope they reached Ilion at all?" Penelope returned.

She nearly smiled at the gasp and frown her words earned from Odysseus' parents. Antikleia had come visiting with a new ball for Telemachos. Laertes had accompanied his son back to the house from the docks.

"It doesn't matter what really happened. We'll be feasting on rumors all winter," Odysseus added with a wry smile. "The truth will come with spring. Forgive me, love, but I truly hope their bones lie at the bottom of the sea. There will be no peace for Achaia or Ilion until this matter is settled."

Penelope saw the bleakness in his eyes and understood. Helen's suitors had sworn an oath to help Menelaos, should anyone carry off Helen. Odysseus had fashioned the oath, so it was binding in every imaginable aspect.

*   *   *

Winter passed too quickly for Penelope. She resented how the weather calmed and warmed, breaking their stormy isolation and letting merchants and messengers cross the water. Telemachos grew too quickly. In seeming days, he went from crawling to tottering around the room on his fat legs, holding onto stools and table legs, her hands or patient Argus' tail.

By common consent, she and Odysseus avoided the subject of Helen or Sparta or Ilion. They played with their son and planned for the spring planting and held each other in close silence during the long nights.

Tragedy struck them after the last storm of the winter. Laertes slipped on steps slicked with ice, breaking bow arm and hip. Penelope took Telemachos with her and lived in Laertes' house so she could help nurse her father-in-law. Too many nights the pain kept him awake, weakening him so he fell prey to fevers. While the ice melted and warmer days crept up on them, she watched him fight the fevers and weakness. She used all her aunt's teaching to brew healing potions for him.

Telemachos was his grandfather's delight, babbling and toddling around the sickroom. Penelope was grateful for the boy's distraction. Laughter was a better medicine, she learned, than the strongest physic or wine, but she worried about Laertes' spirits more than his body. The shattered side of his body lay stiff and still in splints and tight bandages while he fought fevers. She feared his reaction if, when the bandages came off, he couldn't move.

To her relief, Laertes could walk, but with a limp and on crutches for the first moon after getting up from his sickbed. The old man laughed and let Telemachos teach him how to walk again. Tears filled her eyes when Laertes spoke of taking his grandson on his first hunt.

*   *   *

When the weather warmed and they could spare the time away, Odysseus and Penelope took their son to the shore. Telemachos loved the water, would sit for long stretches at a time watching the waves come in. He would shriek and laugh, slapping at the froth, picking up whatever the tide dumped on the sand and exploring it to shreds.

One bright, warm day, Odysseus declared a day of rest for the household. No one was permitted to do any work unless they so chose and it was pleasing. Then he scooped up Telemachos, making the boy laugh, and led Penelope away at a near run. She saved her breath by asking no questions and struggled to keep up with him. Her hair was only half braided, her sandals not tied. She laughed at the picture she knew they made. They went down to a sheltered alcove where the greater bay met the lesser. Blankets, a skin of wine and a basket of food waited for them under a leaning shelter.

The day passed in laughter. In later years, threads of laughter wove together the shreds of memory. Odysseus bent double as Telemachos navigated the warm, soft sand, his little hands tightly gripping his father's fingers. Sitting at the tide's edge, her skirt pulled up past her knees to keep it dry, watching Telemachos explore bits of seaweed and driftwood that had washed up during the night. A moment of panic when the boy insisted on eating a piece of fruit covered with sand. Odysseus teased her about her caution and she responded with a handful of sand down his back when he didn't watch her. He pushed her down in the sand, tickling her until Telemachos intervened, crawling over them, laughing louder than both put together.

In mid-afternoon, Telemachos fell asleep. One moment he played tug-war over a piece of driftwood with his father. The next moment he yawned, scrubbed his eyes with his fists and toppled over. Penelope put him under the shelter, giving a cursory wipe to his sandy fists and legs.

Odysseus had straightened the blanket when she joined him on the slight rise overlooking the beach and the bay beyond. He smiled at her and gestured with a shake of his head out at the sea. Every ship lay at anchor. Waves of warm air bounced off the water. The only sound came from the gentle lapping of the waves and the occasional screech of a sea bird.

He caught her hand as she lowered herself next to him, tugging her off balance so she landed on his lap. Laughing, she wiped her hair out of her face and let him cradle her close against him. She rested her head on his shoulder and gloried in the strength of his arms around her.

"My father is talking of assigning some of his herds to Telemachos next spring," Odysseus said when the quiet had grown into a thick, drowsy blanket wrapped around them.

"What?" She laughed at the incongruity of the subject, brought up for no reason.

"He feels his years."

"Giving flocks to a baby won't make time speed or slow, if that's what worries him." She glanced toward the shelter where Telemachos slept. She already felt he grew too quickly; she didn't want him carrying adult responsibilities a day earlier than necessary.

"Not that, exactly." He shook his head, his gaze locked on some distant point over the water. "My father is tired. The battles he fought to bring peace to Ithaka when he was young...they stole his youth. He wants prosperity and peace for our island. He wants to assure the future for us and our son. He won't be able to rest until he's sure of that. Giving Telemachos his herds will make him feel better."

"Your father will outlive us all," she retorted. "A grandson is more reason than ever for him to live." She blushed as a yawn worked its way out of her, making her jaws creak.

"There is that," Odysseus admitted, grinning. "Just the other day, he was talking about which bow we should teach Telemachos to use first. I told him to wait until our son could *walk* the hunting trails."

"He will do everything well," she murmured as the warmth and quiet swept drowsiness over her. She closed her eyes. It was all she could do to listen to him and carry her half of the conversation, and becoming harder every moment.

When Odysseus put her down on the blanket and stretched out next to her, she couldn't remember. They slept, arms around each other.

The shadows hadn't lengthened by much when she woke. The certain feeling of something wrong drove the fog of sleep from her mind. As she disentangled herself from his arms, Odysseus woke. Penelope looked toward the shelter. Ice filled her belly when she saw Telemachos wasn't there.

Instinct guided her eyes to the water's edge. Relief touched her only for a moment when she saw her son toddling across the wet, packed smooth sand. The water came in with a hushed roar, foaming over his toes. The boy laughed, holding out his hands to the waves. He had lost his wrap somewhere between the shelter and the water.

"Te—"

Odysseus' hand over her mouth muffled her shout. She struggled as he lifted her to her feet.

"Don't frighten him," he murmured, then released her to hurry down the slope.

Her legs wouldn't move fast enough when she followed. Penelope watched her son step up to his knees into the water. The sucking waves immediately pulled him down, arms waving, without a sound. His head popped up. A thin, high cry escaped him. Then Odysseus scooped the boy from the water and lifted him high. Telemachos laughed.

Penelope walked on shaking legs to the water. Odysseus dropped to his knees in the water, making a game of plunging the boy in over his head, then raising him so quickly the water splattered in silver droplets. Telemachos kicked and splashed, laughing. He squealed when he saw her and held out his arms, begging her to join the fun. Penelope tucked her skirt up into her belt and waded out to join them.

Odysseus froze, staring out to sea. Penelope couldn't see what caught his attention through the haze of sun on water. She took their son and he didn't resist. Shading her eyes, she caught the shape of a long war ship coming around the curve into the lesser harbor.

"Mycenae," Odysseus said. His face hardened as he stared at the approaching ship. Then abruptly he turned and waded out of the water. "We have guests."

Penelope dried Telemachos while Odysseus gathered up their provisions. The boy squirmed and complained only a little. When his mother picked him up to leave, he quieted and slipped his arms around her neck.

Odysseus led the way as they followed the curve of the beach toward the docks in the lesser bay. Penelope didn't try to guess his thoughts from his face as they walked in silence. The choices of who came from Mycenae were limited.

The plank had been dropped from the ship—black keel, gold stripe, sixty oars—by the time they reached the docks. A man in a plumed helmet came to the railing of the ship and watched them approach. Odysseus raised his arm in greeting. The man waved and stepped down the plank to greet them.

For a moment, Penelope thought he was Menelaos. The same golden-brown hair and beard, square face, wide shoulders. Then she saw the hard jaw, the stiff, arrogant carriage. There was more brown to the man than gold, like rust or common soil had tainted his coloring.

"Agamemnon?" she murmured, glancing at Odysseus. Her husband spared a single nod. Penelope shifted Telemachos to her hip, wrapping both arms around him. She fought the urge to run all the way home and lock the doors behind her.

"We have confirmation," Agamemnon said as he followed Odysseus away from the water's edge. He spared her a single glance. "Helen is in Ilion, as Paris' wife. They admit her presence as if it were something to be proud of."

"How do they say she came to them? Willing or forced?" Odysseus' voice and face stayed neutral. Penelope didn't like how he hid his feelings. It boded trouble, either for Ithaka or Agamemnon.

"Most willing. Give them time, and they'll say Helen *sought* Paris and he came to Sparta to rescue her from my brother." He turned and spat, face twisted as if he tasted something poisonous. His gaze rested on Penelope and his scorn faded to a smile. "So, this is our youngest cousin," he said, his voice softening as he looked her over from head to foot.

"And our son," Odysseus said. "Telemachos is a year old."

"Congratulations are in order, my friend. And belated gifts. Hold." Agamemnon turned and shouted to someone on deck.

A sailor came running, a small chest of leather balanced on his shoulder. He set it in the sand at Agamemnon's feet and dashed back to the ship.

"Klytemaistra sent gifts, and Orestes sent a favorite toy for his new cousin. One prince to another," he added, his tone rich with pride. He bent and untied the intricate knot holding the chest closed. Opening it, he brought out a carved wooden dog, which he offered to Telemachos with a little bow.

Telemachos reached out one hand, then glanced at the tall stranger with the dancing plume in his helmet. He looked to his mother, eyes wide. Penelope smiled and nodded. She laughed as a wide smile covered her son's face and he reached out with both hands, tugging the dog from Agamemnon's hands.

"There, now the alliance between our houses is even stronger," he said with a laugh. "A fine, strong boy."

"You didn't come here to talk of our sons," Odysseus said, regret in his voice. He gestured toward the path away from the beach. Agamemnon nodded and they started walking. "So, Ilion and Paris have Helen. Does Menelaos know?"

"And insists they are lying. He says Helen didn't want Paris in their home when he first arrived. She was touched with magic, her mind and will taken from her."

"War," Penelope whispered, muffling her words with her lips pressed into Telemachos' hair. She dropped back, letting the men lead the way up the path. Neither man heard her and Telemachos was too busy with his new toy to listen.

CHAPTER 19

"Penelope." Odysseus stopped her with a touch on her shoulder when she turned to go up the stairs. He nodded to the hearth of the feasting hall, where Agamemnon sat. "Would you serve us? I would rather few hear about this for now."

"Eurykleia should be upstairs," she said. Telemachos blinked sleepily in her arms. "Give me a moment." Something tightened inside her when Odysseus brushed a kiss across her forehead before turning back to their guest.

The stairs had never stretched so high and steep under her feet before. Penelope was torn between hurrying back to catch every word or prolonging her safe ignorance. She handed over the boy when Eurykleia met her on the stairs.

"King Agamemnon has arrived. I will serve them, to keep listening ears away." She hurried down the steps, testing her hair with her fingers to be sure it was straight and neat. Penelope was glad she had no time to change her clothes or put on jewelry or perfume. She would serve, but she would not decorate herself to welcome a man who came to speak of war.

When she joined them in the hall with wine and cups, figs and bread, Odysseus and Agamemnon still discussed the story surrounding Helen's flight from Sparta. It sent a chill up her spine to realize the gods had to be blamed.

Alkippe claimed Helen had refused to go with Paris. She tried to run and slapped at his hands when he embraced her. Then she took on the expression of an oracle in ecstasy and obeyed his orders. When she picked up her daughter to follow him, he grew angry and ordered her to leave the child. Helen opened her mouth to speak, stopped and seemed to hear what was not there. Then she put down her daughter and let Paris lead her away, ignoring Hermione's cries.

"Magic or madness," Odysseus said when Agamemnon repeated other servants' tales of conflicting actions. He met Penelope's gaze, questioning. She nodded agreement.

"I would rather it were madness. The fewer to blame, the better for everyone," Agamemnon growled.

He looked at his cup and tossed it back in an abrupt, jerky motion, emptying it down his throat. Penelope hurried to refill it. Odysseus had told her once, Agamemnon could hold his wine like few men and his temper mellowed with drink. She made a gesture of refilling Odysseus' cup. Her husband had barely sipped his wine, compared to Agamemnon's two cups.

"You overreached us again," their guest said. His gaze searched Penelope and he smiled. "I must tell Klytemaistra she was right. The little, dark one has become a beauty."

"If I am beautiful," Penelope said, her voice soft despite the thudding of her heart, "it is because of my husband." She met Agamemnon's gaze, angry at his amusement. She sat next to Odysseus, who took hold of her hand. "If any harm should come to my husband, I will lose my charms and become a harpy, to seek vengeance. No one shall stop me, not even death." To her delight, Agamemnon looked away first.

"With such a mother," Odysseus said, his voice brittle and too bright, "Telemachos will be a warrior few will defeat." The shadows around the hearth darkened. "You came to speak of war."

"A war that has been long arriving. No matter the excuses, we all knew it was coming."

Agamemnon looked tired. Penelope wondered if his reputation for enjoying battle had become a burden. He was ten years older than Odysseus. She remembered the little boy waiting in Mycenae. Maybe Agamemnon understood now why Odysseus had refused to leave Ithaka last summer.

Telemachos' wailing filtered down to the hall, made louder by the silence after Agamemnon's words. Hurrying footsteps came down the stairs. Autonoe stepped from the shadows.

"Mistress, Eurykleia needs you." She paused, and the wails grew louder. "He won't be comforted. His teeth, she thinks."

Penelope believed otherwise. She looked to Odysseus, questioning. He nodded, a promise to tell all. She stood and gestured for Autonoe to precede her up the stairs.

"I think our son knows better than anyone what is to come of this day," she murmured.

Odysseus heard and his expression turned bleak before he resumed his neutral, polite mask. Agamemnon didn't hear her, gulping his wine as if it were his first cup. It amused her that a child's tears affected him so. Was the nursery so far from his quarters in Mycenae's palace that he was unused to the sound?

Penelope compared her home with the other Achaian kingdoms. True, it was small and rough, as her husband had warned. There was more than enough to eat. The people were healthy and strong, skilled, content with their simple pleasures and rich with their love of the sea. They either didn't know or didn't care about the luxuries they lacked. Penelope knew if Paris or one of his brothers had come to her offering all the riches of Ilion, she would have laughed in his face. Ithaka held all the riches she could ever want. She hurried up the stairs to her rooms, her arms aching to hold her son.

Telemachos leaped from Eurykleia's arms, reaching for his mother the moment she stepped into the room. Choking on sobs and tears, he clutched at her and hid his face in her hair. His wailing halted, leaving only a few whimpers like an echo. Penelope closed her eyes against tears. Slowly she rocked him, finding her own comfort in the warmth and weight of his body in her arms. Below her feet, the muffled sound of men's voices rose from the hall.

*   *   *

Odysseus paused in the doorway of Penelope's bedroom. He glanced at the nest of blankets next to the window where Telemachos slept, clutching his new wooden dog. He came to the window seat where she waited. He took her hand, holding it tightly.

"You're going with them." Penelope wondered at the dullness that had crept into her mind while she sat gazing out over the garden and let the tears come in silence.

"My oath." His hand tightened around hers, but she didn't hiss or draw back at the pain. "I confess, I considered playing the madman as I threatened once, to make Agamemnon leave without me. But I took the news too well. It wouldn't have made a good beginning. I should have known this news was coming and prepared to play madman."

"Madman?" A tiny smile touched her lips at the image.

"An ancestor of mine went mad once and plowed a field with ox and donkey yoked together, sowing the ground with salt." His smile was crooked. "Then I thought, will I make myself a fool my wife will flee and my son disown?"

"How long would you have to pretend your madness?"

"Ah, my insightful, sweet wife." He pressed her hand to his lips. "That is the problem. The moment I recovered, someone would send me to Troy. It's that damnable oath I created—"

"To win me."

"I refuse to demean myself because I could lose you, though I would take such action to stay with you. The world would blame Helen, not my longing to stay with you. I refuse to be a fool for that woman's glory." His hand tightened on hers again and his face stiffened into stubborn lines. Odysseus looked out into the garden, as she had done while he talked with Agamemnon.

"And there is the matter of your honor, and the oath," she said slowly.

"We come back to the oath. The oath I created, the sacrifices and ceremonies so binding. The oath I didn't need to swear because I was no threat to Menelaos. I swore it so no one would suspect or question before I could claim you. Even when you were promised to me, I feared another would win you."

"Or my uncle would break his oath?" she suggested. "He was too desperate to save Sparta and protect Helen. We both know he protested more for pride than any love of me."

"More fool he." Odysseus sighed, the sound turning into a ragged chuckle. "Nestor warned me. You scolded me. Mentor told me my cleverness and scheming would be my bane. Now, his prophecy has come true."

"How soon must you go?"

"We haven't talked that far. Agamemnon came to me first, because he needs me to help plan."

Now she gave in to her longing and the trembling she had fought so long. Penelope held out her arms and Odysseus drew her close. She pressed her face into his shoulder, wrapping her arms as tightly as she could around him.

"Promise me," she whispered. "Promise me you will come home in time to put Telemachos' first bow in his hands."

"Oh, my sweet Penelope." His words came on a gusting sigh. "If I have my way, the war against Ilion shall end before I set foot on the deck of my ship."

"Couldn't you send someone to kidnap Helen back?"

"They tried. There are too many guards. Her rooms are too deep inside Priam's palace." He sighed, tightening his embrace. "The attempt was bungled and their vigilance has increased."

"Agamemnon should have asked your advice *before* they tried." She was surprised when her words earned a chuckle.

"He won't admit it, but I know that's what he thinks. Maybe we should bring you along to advise us." Odysseus laughed again, bright and bitter when she stiffened in his arms. "No fear, my love. I would never ask you to leave Ithaka or our son."

"I would bring him, but I refuse to risk our son's life in a battlefield."

"And I refuse to risk you, even if you were Athena's oracle and the voice of twenty other gods as well. You put fear and respect into 'our cousin' Agamemnon."

"I?" She nearly laughed at that.

"If you meant to warn him to keep his eyes off you and leave me in peace, you succeeded. As it is, he needs my advice too much to harm me."

"But after the war?" Penelope couldn't help asking.

"After the war... He'll find some slave girl among the spoils and take her home to aggravate Klytemaistra."

"Agamemnon should pay more attention to his family. Klytemaistra never forgave anything when we were children."

*   *   *

Odysseus sailed with Agamemnon, to visit other princes who had sworn the oath and remind them of their vows. Mentor and Laertes gathered supplies, hired shipmasters to overhaul the war ships, and sought warriors willing to go against Ilion. Penelope had no heart to listen to long discussions of the preparations, so she worked hard to help them, to keep her hands busy so her mind would not wander into painful realms. She hoped every bit she did would shorten the time war kept Odysseus from Ithaka.

Two days after Odysseus left, she tore her work from her loom and began a new project. She had dreamed of fine clothes and determined to make them for him to wear. He would shine among the kings if her skill didn't fail her. Penelope dreamed of a tunic that shimmered in dull, pale purple, shading into rose and amber. She took out a cloak she had made for the next winter, thick, double-folded, rich purple, and set that aside for Odysseus to take. To close the cloak, she brought out the pin her father had made. She prayed the armies of the Achaians would strangle Ilion, as the hound strangled the hare.

A little more than a moon later, Odysseus returned home, grim in his satisfaction. Every prince had rallied to the call. He nodded his thanks for the accolades when Agamemnon and Menelaos claimed they could not have persuaded the others without him. Penelope knew he found the praise bitter.

There was feasting in the hall for three nights, as princes and war chiefs in western Achaia met in Ithaka and planned their next step in the campaign. Penelope kept busy with her weaving and Telemachos and tried not to listen to the raucous male voices raised in song and boasting. Of the damage they would do to Ilion. The pillaging and plunder and spoils they would bring home. Odysseus' voice rarely joined them, but that brought her no comfort. She remembered dreams of the hall filled with male voices and her husband not there among the unwanted guests. Danger waited in the hall of her dreams. Not even the heavy doors and locks between her chambers and the feasting hall could stand long against that onslaught.

The men of Ithaka came in groups to hear Odysseus speak of the battle against Ilion. He told them bluntly he wanted no one but volunteers. He would force no man to leave his family and home, his fields and flocks for a war more likely to be his death than profit. Enough men of Ithaka stepped forward to fill all twelve ships of fifty oars, with more besides to relieve them and tend the sails when the winds permitted.

Rumors said Odysseus foresaw large profit from the war and he tried to discourage men from coming so his share would be larger. Everyone knew of the riches of Ilion. Even if thousands took a share of the spoils, every man could hope to make himself rich and comfortable.

"You were too right," Odysseus said his last night at home, when he finally shared the story with her.

The sounds of feasting had vanished from the hall, their guests already beginning the trip along the coast to the ports near Mycenae. They had taken a quiet meal together in his room. Telemachos slept on a pallet on the floor at the end of the bed. Penelope wanted their son to spend as much time with his father as possible before Odysseus left.

She had given him the tunic, cloak and pin, explaining how she had designed the cloth in a dream. She told him how her father had made the pin and how she believed it brought good luck. Odysseus kissed her, held her close, then promised her, swearing on his scar and his love for her, he would not wear the clothing and pin until his return voyage. Then he told her about the useless struggle to keep Ithaka from following him to war.

"All my life I fought and schemed for the advantage," Odysseus said with a crooked smile. "Now, when I tell the truth to spare them, they see other motives in my words."

"All that matters is they have chosen to follow you. If they choose profit over loyalty, that's their fault and not yours." She sat on the edge of the bed, holding the cup they shared. It still held most of its first filling of wine.

"Is it?" He closed his eyes, letting a loud, gusting sigh escape him. "My love, I am weary already of this war. A moon would be too long for me and I cannot see it lasting less than four years. Ilion is rich and strong, the walls thick, the storehouses well provisioned. They boast they could survive a whole generation without planting or harvesting. If they decide to sit inside their walls and laugh at us, there is little we can do besides wait."

"Perhaps Athena will give you wisdom to find a way inside," she offered. Penelope stood and walked to his chair. She knelt next to him and pressed the cup into his hand. "I am weary of this war as well," she said as he opened his eyes. "Please, if only for this night, I want to pretend there is no world beyond the walls of this room." His answering, understanding smile had a sadness that squeezed the breath from her body.

Imminent parting gave them new energy in their lovemaking that night. A roughness, brought by desperation. Odysseus spoke little besides her name, like a magic spell to fulfill his wishes if spoken often enough, with enough passion and longing. When they finally slept, it was in a tangle of arms and legs, joined by sweat and the refusal to lose even a moment of their time remaining.

When Telemachos whimpered in his sleep, Penelope woke instantly. She lay still, afraid of waking Odysseus, and listened. She worked to release her breath slowly when she knew her son would not awaken.

The shutters in one window stood open, letting moonlight through. She watched Odysseus sleeping, one arm under her head, the other draped around her waist, his legs twined with hers. Tears filled her eyes. She would have moved away but she didn't want to wake him. She sniffed and rubbed her cheeks before a single drop could fall on him.

"I wondered when you would cry," he said, opening his eyes.

"Don't do that!" she blurted, a gasping laugh escaping her. Then the sobs started. She clung to him, shaking as weeping racked her body. Odysseus held her tighter than before, gently rubbing her back but saying nothing, doing nothing else. There was nothing either of them could do.

The storm passed as quickly as it came. When her body relaxed, he gently rolled her onto her back and leaned over her. His face was in shadows as he kissed away her tears. Penelope felt she had no strength in her body, could do nothing but lay still and wait and listen.

"You worried me," he said. When he sat up, moonlight touched his face. "So strong a spirit, I feared for you when you couldn't take the hurt any longer."

"I didn't want to send you away with tears in your memory," she whispered.

"You have a stronger, braver spirit than all the warriors of Achaia." Odysseus brushed damp strands of hair out of her face. His touch turned into a caress.

"I am not strong. I am not brave. I am a selfish woman who wants you beside me every night, to hear your voice every day. I would do anything to keep you here." A bitter laugh escaped her. "I should have listened to my dreams and strangled Helen when we were children."

"If not for Helen, I would not have found you."

"For Helen, I might lose you! Odysseus, love me again. So I always feel your touch, no matter how far you go." She slipped her arms around him and drew him down to her.

A single spark of joy lit the darkness in her heart. She hadn't tasted Eurynome's potion for two moons now and Odysseus hadn't noticed. If the Goddess heard her prayers, she would conceive. If her dreams were true, Odysseus would be home, safe, for the birth of their second son.

*   *   *

Penelope carried Telemachos, sleepy and quiet, down to the harbor the next morning and held him tightly during the farewells. The ships were bright with new paint, the sails boldly flapping in the freshening breeze. All the warriors wore their armor to present a bold, beautiful image in their farewells. One by one, men took last kisses and embraces from children, wives, mothers and sweethearts, and the ships moved away from the docks. Odysseus' ship sailed last. He stood on the plank, giving last minute instructions and requests to Mentor and Laertes. His gaze continually strayed to her.

Mentor was to lead Ithaka while Odysseus was away. Laertes could walk, but he couldn't draw a bow or cast a spear in defense of Ithaka. Mentor, though lamed, was the stronger man and the only other one Odysseus trusted. The two men would work together and Odysseus had instructed them to consult Penelope in all things. Since Telemachos' birth, abundance had flowed over Ithaka. The people saw Penelope as an extension of the Goddess and would obey her if no one else.

Penelope stood in a circle of silence, alone on the sands. None of the household had accompanied her to the bay and no women stopped to talk with her. Again, she felt like a stranger in her husband's home. She wondered if the women avoided her because Odysseus took their men away, or because they remembered she was Helen's cousin. Did they blame her because the power of the Goddess was not strong enough to keep their men from war?

None of that mattered whenever Odysseus' eyes met hers.

Odysseus finally sent away Mentor and his father and stepped off the plank to cross the sands to her. Wordless, he took Telemachos from her arms, holding the boy close. Their son wriggled, letting out a mumbled complaint. Odysseus lifted him high above his head, shaking him until the boy laughed, kicking his bare feet. He set Telemachos down on the sand and opened his arms to Penelope. Their embrace and kiss were long and bittersweet. She didn't care who saw or what comments they made.

Penelope engraved the memory deep into her heart. The hard bronze plates of his armor under her hands. The rustling plume in his helmet. The scratching of his beard against her face.

Then he released her and strode stiff-legged for the ship. Odysseus didn't look back and she was strangely glad of that. Penelope gathered up Telemachos and waited and watched as the ship sailed out of the lesser harbor. She walked along the shore, keeping the sail in her sight. Telemachos grew heavy in her arms as she stumbled across heating sand and rocks. She put him down, holding onto his hand, and followed the path of the ship with her gaze, across the water until it vanished from her sight.

*   *   *

Before the first merchant brought news of the ships and warriors, Penelope knew she did carry another child. She went alone to the Goddess in the dark, quiet watches of the night with offerings of thanks and made more petitions for the safety of all the men of Ithaka.

Summer turned into fall before anyone noticed the changes in her body. Penelope smiled and laughed when Eurykleia and Eurynome scolded her in delight for keeping the child a secret. She let Laertes hold a feast in her honor and saved the best portions to take to the Goddess' cave. That night, the women of Ithaka celebrated, dancing under the harvest moon.

Slowly, Penelope learned fear. When she carried Telemachos, she had blossomed overnight, her belly noticeable almost before the news had spread across the island. Now, she watched daily for signs of the child's growth and found little. This child was a talisman to protect Odysseus. Penelope refused to lose this child. She ate more than she needed, to try to force the baby to grow. She consulted the women elders and studied herbals.

The day she had to use a larger belt around her waist, Penelope cried tears of joy.

CHAPTER 20

Merchants brought news of the war, sometimes carrying home men injured too badly to continue fighting. Men hamstrung by slashing swords, crippled by spears. Men who lost hands, arms, legs—blinded and twisted and mad with pain.

The news was as disturbing, as mixed as the reception the returning warriors received. Some, no matter their injuries, were welcomed home with glad tears and feasting. Others were called fools who received their just reward. The only constant was praise of Odysseus as a cautious, valiant leader. Many told how their king risked his own life to rescue an injured warrior.

A merchant brought the first true gossip of the war, near the beginning of the fall storms. Laertes brought the man to the house to tell Penelope in private. He sat beside her as the merchant drank his wine and related his tale.

"It's said they were calmed five days, the oars sticking in their places, the men sick in their bowels, before anyone inquired of the gods." The man, dark of hair and eye, thin, with a pointed face, shook his head in disapproval. "It took nearly a day of casting lots, reading omens and making sacrifices to determine the cause and which god was angry. Artemis had been offended. By Agamemnon." His grin implied the news surprised no one. "The oracle said Artemis would only let the fleet proceed when Iphigenia, Agamemnon's daughter, was given over to her."

"Given over?" Penelope's mind raced. The wording of oracles was always vague and might have changed as the story passed from one person to another. "Given how?"

"There was almost a battle over that—my lady," he added quickly, giving her a nod. "Korestios, Agamemnon's man, wanted Iphigenia. She was promised him as reward when Ilion fell. He and Agamemnon and a few others said she was to be sacrificed. Can't understand that, if he was to marry the girl."

"If he couldn't have her, he wanted to be sure no one had her," she explained quickly. "But go on. You said a few others agreed. Who disagreed?"

"Menelaos, Palomides, Aias, Achilleus—and your Lord Odysseus. They said Iphigenia was to be a priestess to Artemis. They almost came to blows when Agamemnon sent a messenger in secret to Mycenae, to bring the girl."

"Surely Klytemaistra didn't willingly send her!" She looked at her father-in-law. Laertes shook his head. The sadness in his eyes didn't bode well for the tale.

"The lady queen thought Iphigenia was to be a bride. She and her daughter came dressed for a wedding. I was there when their ship reached the fleet." He paused, shadows in his eyes. Penelope pitied him. Despite his clear delight in gossip, what he had seen still disturbed him.

"Soldiers boarded the ship," he continued after a moment. "They separated mother from daughter at sword's point. The girl showed her royal blood, though. When she understood why she was there, she shook free of her guards and walked to the altar. Would have climbed onto it if she hadn't been shaking so badly. Her mother screamed loud enough to deafen every man there. She called down curses on all the warriors of Achaia."

"What did the men do, who opposed Agamemnon's plans?" Penelope's hand strayed over her belly, to protect the child. She refused to believe her dreams had been in vain. The life inside her was there to protect Odysseus.

"They kept protesting. But you see, the wait had grown so long, more men came over to Agamemnon's view. Some gave up and went to their ships to wait. Like they didn't care what was done, as long as they got on their way again."

"And Odysseus?"

"I never saw a man who could argue so fast and so long." A chuckle escaped him. He remembered his neglected cup and drained it in one slurping gulp. "He and Menelaos were still arguing until they put the girl on the altar and raised the knife."

"And when she was dead?" Penelope whispered.

"That's the hard part of the tale." He stood abruptly and stepped a few paces away, then turned back. "It all happened so fast, the wind and thunder. I feared for my ship, it was so bad. Agamemnon picked up the knife. Lightning struck. All the ground shook like a horse shakes flies off his back. Next thing we knew, the wind came back, heavy and cold with rain. We looked, and the altar was in a thousand pieces and the girl was gone. The knife with her. Did Artemis take her after she was sacrificed, or before?"

"We cannot know, can we?" Penelope murmured. She found she could no longer sit still. "Father?"

"I'll tend to our guest," Laertes said. He squeezed her shoulder and nodded for her to go.

Penelope hurried from hall, trembling. Whether in rage or pity or fear, she didn't know. She was glad, relieved Odysseus had stood against the plan to kill Iphigenia. Stronger, though, was the image of Klytemaistra's fury.

*   *   *

The news of the war, once the fleet finally reached Ilion, had little variety. Ilion's supply of warriors and arms appeared as limitless as their stores of food and water were reputed to be. The war slowed for winter, along with the dribbles of news that reached Ithaka.

Penelope wove new blankets for the child growing inside her. She halted her work at the first sign of weariness and listened to all the advice and cautions Eurykleia and Eurynome gave her. When the weather was harsh, she stayed home instead of going to the Goddess to make offerings. Penelope knew the Goddess understood why she could take no chances. The child finally began to move inside her the day an ice storm retreated from the island.

Penelope calculated when her child would be born. If she was right, the seas would be open nearly a moon before she came to labor. She knew Odysseus could reach Ithaka by then. Though the people around her discussed how many years the war would take, Penelope smiled and prepared new clothes for her husband to wear at his welcoming feast.

Spring approached. Penelope often took her son with her to walk to the cliff's edge and stand there for hours, watching the horizon for a familiar sail.

The first merchants to reach Ithaka's shores that year brought bits of war gossip, events that happened before winter had closed the ports. None of it was encouraging. Everyone agreed the Achaians would be years in siege of Ilion.

Her child would be born any day and Penelope tasted fear. Had her dreams lied? Would her child die before birth? Odysseus wasn't home, safe, where her dreams had placed him. She didn't know what to believe.

The smallness of her belly worried her. Then she began to hear gossip and rumors. The stories had grown faster than the size of her belly. Now they came to light. Her fear turned to anger—a welcome change.

Nerilia brought the first solid evidence of what the people believed. The woman had gone to the docks to fetch fish for a moon feast. She argued with another woman at the docks and the argument became a pushing, scratching fight accented with screeches worthy of a harpy. Mentor brought her to Penelope when it was over.

"Nerilia, if you have a charge to make against the woman who attacked you—" Penelope began, to be cut off by the woman's sharp laugh.

"I attacked her. Proudly. Everyone knows she was a fool to say such things." Nerilia bit her lip as if to hold back more words and looked away.

"What did she say?"

"Fools' gossip. Lies."

"If they are lies, you protect her by keeping the words from being known," Penelope reasoned.

"Protecting that—" She laughed. "Very well, Mistress. I'm likely a fool myself, reacting as I did, but she enjoyed her words too much." She looked around, as if noticing for the first time the workroom was empty of all others. "The word is that you are so small because the child is not our king's. You claim you conceived before the warriors left, to cover the truth that you have taken a lover and it is his child you carry. You will not birth in the tenth moon, but after the twelfth."

"Who is my lover, when all the best men of Ithaka are gone to war?" Penelope seethed, but refused to show her feelings. She could see her calmness impressed Nerilia.

"No one will say. But they do say no one is surprised. Rumors say Klytemaistra has already taken a lover, and Helen is the cause of the

229

war. You are their cousin."

"Indeed, I am their cousin. But my child is my husband's and no other man has or ever shall touch me. When my child is born before the end of this moon, *you* will be the herald of the news to Ithaka." Penelope dismissed her maid with a nod. She would have laughed at the new swagger in Nerilia's walk, but her heart was too sore and sick at what she had heard.

Penelope didn't worry long over the gossip. Her water broke three days later. Her pains came quickly as she climbed the stairs to her room. Penelope felt cold with fear for the child and cried out more in terror than pain as her bones moved to let the baby pass. She didn't believe her ears when the first thin cry penetrated the air.

"He lives?" she cried, nearly sitting up while Autonoe tended the afterbirth.

"*She* lives," Eurykleia said. "You have a daughter," she added, chuckling at Penelope's astonishment. The next moment, her delight faded into concern as Penelope burst into tears. "Child, what is wrong?"

"I dreamed—he would see our son—I thought the baby would die—Blessed Goddess, a daughter!" she ended on a gasp. Penelope held out her arms. "Give her to me!"

*   *   *

She named the girl Ktimene, for Odysseus' sister, to please Antikleia. Telemachos sat for hours on his mother's bed, watching his baby sister sleep, asking when she could play with him. Penelope felt torn between laughter and tears and tried to explain that a baby had to grow and learn to walk before she could play with her big, strong brother.

Ktimene rarely cried. Penelope held the tiny, quiet bundle in her arms whenever her duties didn't call her away, and wondered at the gift given to her. Besides killing rumors with her timely arrival, Ktimene brought another gift to her mother. She was clearly Odysseus' daughter, with soft red-brown curls and gray eyes.

That spring, crops sprang up where the farmers hadn't planted. Twins were born to the herds and flocks. The rains came when the farmers wished and the sun never scorched the ground. When Penelope took Ktimene to the cave to present her to the Goddess, five times more women came for the ceremony. Mentor and Laertes ruled Ithaka that year only in name; the people looked to Penelope as their ruler, and named their daughters for hers.

*   *   *

More news came from the battle, traveling with the ships that reached Ithaka to trade. Boys who had grown up over the winter set off to join their fathers and brothers on the plains of Troy. Along with the news came the injured. Penelope believed the tales brought by warriors over the gossip from the docks.

Spring brought forays against towns close to Ilion, to cut off any help the people might give. Penelope dreamed of battles, of Odysseus fighting, sometimes wounded. The tales the injured men brought did little to confirm her dreams or turn them into vain imaginings.

She comforted herself with imagining the surprise on her husband's face when he learned of their daughter's birth. Penelope knew he would rage that she had deceived him. Then he would laugh, proud of her.

Late in the summer, a merchant brought messages from Odysseus and a leather chest of presents, plunder he had sent away before it was stolen or lost. For Penelope, fine thread in colors she couldn't dye on Ithaka, a distaff of ivory tipped with gold, pearl necklaces and gold earrings. For Telemachos, soldiers carved of wood and ivory, all from his father's skilled hands. For Ktimene, jewelry and ivory combs and a silver mirror. Penelope laughed, knowing that when Odysseus returned he would be his daughter's adoring slave. She put the gifts away for Ktimene's bridal days.

*   *   *

Odysseus' prediction that the war with Ilion would not last less than three years was wrong. Telemachos and Ktimene grew quickly, though the years dragged by in Penelope's reckoning. When they were old enough to sit and listen and understand, she brought them in to listen to each merchant and warrior who had a tale to tell about the war and their father.

Telemachos had to be everywhere, touching and watching and learning about everything in their house. Penelope was glad Argus attached himself to her son, because the hound kept the boy out of trouble. She had thought to assign a slave boy to Telemachos so the two could grow up together and her son could have a confidant and playmate. By the time he was four, she knew Telemachos needed a grown man to keep up with him.

Ktimene stayed small and pale and quiet. She preferred to sit at her

231

mother's feet and play with bits of thread from weaving or scraps of cloth left over from sewing. Laertes showered the girl with dolls and balls and birds in cages. Antikleia held her granddaughter by the hour, silent and glowing with happiness. Neither grandparent could hold Telemachos for long or keep up with him. Penelope was satisfied that her daughter enjoyed the quiet closeness and her son felt no lack of attention.

For a while, Penelope feared Ktimene would never learn to walk and talk. Her daughter was willing to watch the world bustle around her, accepting attention or neglect with the same pleasant expression. Ktimene rarely cried, even when she was hungry or dirty. By the time her daughter was three, Penelope would deliberately keep toys and food from her, to prompt the child to ask, to cry, to crawl, to do something to change her situation. She learned, gladly, that when Ktimene did want something and her desires were thwarted, she had no patience. Penelope reminded herself of her earlier fears and tried to teach her daughter to act as a king's daughter should.

Training Telemachos was a comfort to Laertes and Penelope didn't object when he took the boy out on the ships or hunting in the hills years too early. There was something sadly humorous in watching her son struggle to carry a spear three times longer than himself. Argus was Telemachos' constant companion, sleeping by the boy's bedside, always in his shadow. Between his grandfather and the faithful hound, she knew her son was safe. She still felt an emptiness when he left her for the day, giving her only a careless kiss and hug. Her spirit brightened when he came running in, dirty and excited, babbling about his successes and failures, smelling of sweat and blood and forest.

Ktimene was her mother's delight despite her stubborn fits, and Penelope took care in everything she taught her daughter. The little girl napped on a pallet by her mother's loom and reached constantly for the loose threads. She tied knots and tried to make cloth of her own almost before she could wash and dress herself. She listened and watched everything with a deep, pondering expression in her gray eyes, much as Penelope imagined Odysseus had done as a child.

Mentor and Laertes had the duty of teaching Telemachos what his mother could not. How to hunt and sail. The history of Ithaka. His duties as prince. How to lead his people and be a wise ruler. Penelope kept for herself the harder task of teaching her children about their father. As the years went by and they grew, alert and intelligent, she found the stories and examples became threadbare. Three short years of happy marriage were not enough memories to fill the mind and heart of a boy going on eight years old, a girl nearly six, without a father physically present.

They took many long walks together in the hills and valleys, sharing the places she had explored with Odysseus before Telemachos had been born. She taught both children how to use a sling as her grandfather, Dymis had taught her. She reasoned Odysseus' son had more reason than most to know how to defend himself. And if such training had been good for her mother, then Ktimene would do well to learn. Telemachos excelled in hitting every target with a loud, hard slap of the stone. Ktimene mimicked him, but would only use the sling against trees. Penelope marked her daughter's soft heart and began teaching her the healing arts.

*   *   *

The spring Telemachos turned nine years old, she gave him a copy of the key to Odysseus' private storeroom and let him go inside for the first time. Penelope was the only one who had unlocked the door since Odysseus left. Inside were jewels of ancient make, family treasures, sacred items used for high festivals. The sapphire and silver jewelry Laertes had given her was there. Penelope had not worn it since Odysseus left. The bronze and horn bow of Iphitos waited there as well. Because of Athena's warning to guard the bow, Odysseus had left it in Penelope's keeping rather than risk taking it to war.

She let Telemachos slide the bow from its protective covering. As he held it, she told how his father set up the axes in a trench in the feasting hall and shot between their crossed handles to test his skill. She repeated to him, as many times as he asked, the tale of Iphitos and Odysseus meeting as boys, and their friendship. Telemachos was quiet, thoughtful, his eyes dark with deep thoughts the first time he heard the story.

"My father has good friends, even if they are few?" he asked, his words solemn and old despite his sweet voice. Despite the dark hair and eyes he inherited from her, Penelope saw his father looking back at her.

"Very good friends. Strong and true." She resisted the urge to lift him onto her lap and hold him. Telemachos had taken teasing from some village boys for spending so much time in his mother's company. "When you are older, you shall find friends who are worthy companions."

"Orestes?" he asked, his eyes brightening. Through messengers and trusted merchants, the boys had exchanged presents and were friends in a sense. Telemachos often made up stories for his mother, of adventures he and Orestes would have together when they were grown.

"Perhaps. Maybe next year, if your grandfather can spare us, we will journey to Mycenae to visit your cousin."

"He's older than me. He could come to us." Telemachos shook his head, lowering his gaze to the bow still resting securely in his hands. They were his father's hands, large for his age, the fingers slim and graceful, skilled at everything he tried. "I don't want to leave Ithaka until my father comes home. Then we can go to Mycenae together."

"Yes, we will go together." Fighting tears, Penelope turned away and busied herself with a pile of bronze cups that had grown green with age and tilted over.

"Mother, would my father be angry if I tried to string his bow?"

"Angry?" She choked on a laugh that was half a sob and turned back to him. "I doubt anyone, even his own son could bend Odysseus' bow. It is charmed to only bend to the hand of its owner. You could bend it if your father gave you permission. Or if he gave the bow to you as a gift. Until then, you might crack all your muscles trying." She smiled at the look of awe in her son's eyes. It took away the sting of the words she had not spoken: the death of its owner also would make the bow yield to another man's hand.

*   *   *

The news from the plains of Ilion was mystifying and tragic. The years of fruitless battle, of minor skirmishes and frustration, wore on the warrior kings and their men. Arguments broke friendships formed in their youth.

Penelope dreamed of fighting among the kings. The people of Ilion stood along the tops of the walls of the city and laughed at the Achaians in discord. She told her dreams to her children, despite the uneasiness such visions gave her. It had become habit over the years to share her dreams with them. First Telemachos, so he could listen to the gossip at the docks and compare her dreams with the news. When Ktimene began asking questions that showed deep thoughts, Penelope included her daughter in the discussions so they could unravel the images together.

Ktimene was seven that year, and she began to come to her mother with dreams that matched Penelope's. The child described Agamemnon, Menelaos, Aias and her own father. Comparing dreams every morning, deciding if they were true visions or merely hopes, became habit. Neither knew what to make of some images. There was little comfort in knowing Odysseus was not injured by in-fighting. His face was marked with weariness and anger in Penelope's dreams and she woke in tears many mornings.

Fall brought all the rumors together into a complete story. An argument over slave girls split Achilleus from the Achaians. Agamemnon's pride and his bed pleasures once more caused trouble. Penelope wondered how Klytemaistra reacted to the rumors that Agamemnon had planned to supplant her with the daughter of a priest of Apollo.

The trouble began when Apollo harassed the camp and the other kings forced Agamemnon to give the girl back. Penelope doubted anyone considered the feelings of Mycenae's queen.

The tragic tale fit her dreams. Achilleus refusing to fight. His friend Patroklos, wearing his armor, killed in a dreadful battle. The sorrow that filled and divided the camp of the Achaians. Then the reconciliation. Penelope watched her son's reactions when the tale turned to the death of Achilleus. The man was a hero to her son, second only to his father. Telemachos was as controlled and calm hearing the story as any prince should have been. She wondered if he would come creeping to her in the night like a much smaller boy, to be held while he cried his loss.

When she heard how Aias and Odysseus contended for Achilleus' armor, Penelope felt a chill of warning. Mentor and Laertes were there with her to hear the tale from a merchant, along with other elders of Ithaka. She dared not open her mouth to question the man who had brought the conclusion to the tale.

She and Ktimene sat in the shadows to help the men forget their presence. Telemachos looked to her once, smiling from his seat at Laertes' side. Penelope smiled back, hiding her worries. As the story grew, Ktimene climbed onto her lap but she never made a sound.

"No one really agrees on this part of the tale," the merchant said, giving a grin of apology. "They said Aias was a giant of a man, as fierce as thunderclouds. Odysseus had cunning and skill. Some say they wrestled and raced all day until they collapsed in exhaustion. Others say they competed in archery or riddles. No one is sure.

"One old woman said she heard from her son, who had returned from the war, they sent spies to listen to the people of Ilion at night. They said the gods would prompt the people to speak of the man favored to win." He shook his head, a grin showing what he thought of that last proposition. "Odysseus won the armor and Aias went mad from jealousy."

Penelope gripped the arms of her chair. Here it was, the reason for her worries, the dark cloud at the edges of her dreams. Aias and Odysseus had been friends, once. Did her husband still resent Aias for manhandling her? Did Aias hold something against Odysseus, for letting him make a fool of himself? In the years of war, what problems came between the two friends? Ktimene shifted on her lap to put her arms around her mother. Penelope realized the merchant still talked. She hugged her daughter and tried to listen.

"Early one morning, he ran wild, butchering all the rams of the flocks he could reach. The slaughter was so widespread to be awe-inspiring," the merchant added with a little chuckle. "They said Aias named each ram he killed. Calling this one Agamemnon, this one Palomides, that one Odysseus." He paused, sobering. A tiny shiver took him as he looked around the room. "It's said he killed Odysseus six times that day, before the madness left him. When he looked around at the slaughter, he let out a shout that rose to the throne of Zeus and fell on his own sword. He was dead before anyone could stop him."

Penelope closed her eyes against tears, closed her ears against hearing any more of the story. She gripped the arms of her chair tightly, struggling not to let out a sound, not to move. Ktimene's arms around her were a comfort.

Aias' laughing face touched her memory. He had not been an evil man, rather more foolish than stupid. He used his massive strength to make up for the cunning he lacked.

She knew Odysseus grieved for his former friend. And knew also that some would think his grief a pretense, a trick to smooth his way. Penelope knew her husband would blame himself for Aias' death. She shivered again, knowing others would do the same. She thought of Melantho and was glad the woman no longer served in her house.

*   *   *

The first fierce winter storm came in on the heels of the news that Ilion had fallen at last. The merchants passing through the Dardanelles only knew the city had fallen. No other details. The burning of the city, the last fighting, the division of spoils, was expected to take moons. Tales came of the gates fallen, sections of the thick wall torn to pieces and smoke rising up day and night.

Penelope took Telemachos and Ktimene to leave gifts in Athena's shrine. Five nights in a row, she and Eurykleia took Ktimene to the Goddess, to leave offerings and chant prayers. Her mind raced to the many tasks waiting for her that winter, to prepare for Odysseus' return with spring.

Despite the isolation that winter and the heavy seas that battered the shores of Ithaka, the entire island celebrated. Their men would not return until spring when the rough seas calmed, but now they *would* come home. The homes were warm and bright that year despite the icy weather.

Penelope remembered songs she hadn't sung for years while working at her loom. She taught them to Ktimene and the usually silent girl sang them often. In the feasting hall, Telemachos set up the trench and axes and practiced his archery, to earn praise from his father. During a period of clear weather, Penelope accompanied Telemachos and Laertes to Raven's Crag at the southern tip of the island to consult with Eumaios, the man in charge of Odysseus' swine. They chose the cattle to sacrifice and the swine for the feast when Odysseus arrived home.

The winter passed in happy, contented preparation. Penelope went to the storeroom and chose jewelry she had not worn in years, to decorate herself for the celebration. She sat in front of her bronze mirror for hours at a time, trying new ways to braid and decorate her hair, testing cosmetics to see which made her look best. She spent more time at her loom than ever, weaving cloth to make new clothes for her husband, new clothes for her children and Odysseus' parents, for the celebration.

The day sunshine broke the winter haze, dispelling it so spring could come, she unlocked Odysseus' bedroom. She had new ropes strung in the bed's frame. Guarding its secret, Penelope allowed only Eurykleia and Eurynome to help her. She brought new sheets and blankets, made by her hand all that winter. She spread herbs over the floor to freshen the air and opened the shuttered windows to let light into a room kept closed and dark for years. When all was in readiness, she sat at her loom to wait and weave, and dream of the second son her dreams had promised her.

*   *   *

A rough, wet spring let only a trickle of merchants approach the island at first. With them came stories of the fall of Ilion that matched

237

and resurrected dreams Penelope preferred to leave forgotten. She tried to ignore the stories brewed by people who had lost sons and husbands in the war, or men who returned from war without treasure.

As the days passed and more stories came in, along with them came messengers from other noble households and small kingdoms, asking for news of their kings, husbands and fathers. With Telemachos to act as her eyes and ears on the docks, and Ktimene's sharp mind to help remember details, Penelope put the stories together. They matched her dreams of curses and danger, becoming one complete pattern.

The victorious Achaians had offended the gods in their greedy pillaging of Ilion. They raped virgin priestesses on the altars where they served. They desecrated temple treasuries and smashed statues to pieces. For every leader who spoke caution and pious care, there were two who led their men in wholesale destruction and disregard for the sacred.

Penelope's heart ached when she heard how Odysseus helped find every male child of Priam's line, to kill them and purge the bloodline. She understood the reasoning, had heard Agamemnon talk of the need to destroy that family. Priam's own family had been slaughtered for their treachery when he was a child. The war with Ilion might never have come if he had not escaped. She still felt shame knowing her husband had helped. The children had committed no crime but to carry the blood of the enemy.

Penelope watched Telemachos' and Ktimene's faces as her son related the news to her. She wondered if the years of plotting and fighting had changed her husband that much, or if he had seen their son's face on each child he helped to kill. Telemachos didn't ask why his father had done such a thing. He spoke with no pride or shame, as if he felt nothing in telling of the deed. Penelope waited for him to ask for an explanation, but he never did. If he went to his grandfather or to Mentor with questions, she didn't know.

Ktimene, however, woke with nightmares three nights running after she heard the news. Each time, she cried out for her father to protect her from the dead children of Ilion. Penelope took to bringing Ktimene into bed with her, to keep the bad dreams away.

When the stories arrived of curses laid on the Achaian kings, Penelope felt no surprise. Every surviving priest or priestess spoke oracles of doom, destruction and betrayal against their conquerors. She dreaded every new thread added to the story, yet continued sending Telemachos to listen and bring travelers to the house to talk with her.

*   *   *

"Mother, I will be a priestess when I am grown." Ktimene didn't look up as she spoke. She sat at her mother's feet in Penelope's private garden. Mother taught daughter the finer points of using a lap loom. Telemachos had made a loom for his sister as a winter festival gift, but Ktimene had yet to use it.

Nine years old now, her face looked older, lacking the baby fat of most girls her age. Penelope looked at the shadows on her daughter's face and wondered if Ktimene's dreams harmed her health.

"I wanted to be a priestess when I was a child." Penelope smiled, remembering similar conversations with her aunt. She reached for a new skein of thread.

"The Goddess wants me to serve her." Ktimene brushed red hair out of her eyes and looked at her mother now.

"She said so, clearly?"

"No." She frowned, for a moment looking so much like her father it twisted Penelope's heart.

"Tell me your dreams and we can decipher them together." She put aside her loom. Ktimene immediately clambered onto her lap. Penelope chuckled at this contrast to her daughter's adult words and ambitions.

"I dreamed of the cave, full of light but no lamps." The child nodded, her brow furrowed in concentration. "I knelt all alone, praying to the Goddess. And she said...I heard words in my heart." Confusion dulled her eyes.

"That is how it often is with the gods. They never speak clearly, where hundreds can hear and understand."

"Oh. She said I would never leave my home. I would always be here, safe with her." Ktimene tugged on a half-unraveled braid, sticking the frayed tip in her mouth.

"A priestess doesn't chew on her hair," Penelope scolded, teasing. She hugged her daughter. "That is a very good interpretation. We will talk more of this when your father returns. I think he would be very proud of you, if you became a priestess."

"When is he coming? Grandmother is sick again. She thought Telemachos was Father when we visited yesterday."

"If I could, I would bring your father home tonight." She hugged her daughter again, then gave her a nudge to move her from her lap. "Come, we will find some offerings for Athena and make our prayers now. For your father and for your grandmother." When Ktimene slid off her lap, Penelope stood and took her hand.

They went through the gardens and courtyard to the kitchens. Eurynome sat in a corner with Eurykleia, both women deep in frowning conversation. Penelope watched them while Ktimene searched the shelves full of cakes and loaves of bread, deciding what to give as an offering.

Were they as worried about Antikleia as she? The winter had been wonderful for her mother-in-law. Penelope had never seen the woman so alive, so alert and full of laughter. At times, Antikleia had been like a young woman, showing what she had been in her youth. Penelope knew then why Laertes was still devoted to his usually sorrowful, gray wife.

Spring had brought even more happy anticipation to the woman. She took her grandchildren on long walks along the shore, watching for ships arriving in the harbor. She told incessant stories about their father as a boy and young man, filling all the gaps Penelope's tales couldn't cover.

But now, with spring turned to summer and tales of ships destroyed by a god's wrath, Antikleia faded. Penelope worried for the woman, listless one day, eager and hopeful the next, unable to even roll from her blankets the day after that. Ktimene had begun avoiding her. Penelope would have let her daughter stay away, but Ktimene's presence was one of the woman's few delights.

Ktimene's report that Antikleia had mistaken Telemachos for his father had shaken Penelope. How much further could the decline last?

*   *   *

Laertes came to Penelope in midsummer with the news that Nestor of Pylos had returned home safely. He offered to take Telemachos with him and sail to retrieve news of the other warriors. Penelope was glad Telemachos was out for the day, visiting with Eumaios, who had become a friend. Her pale face and moan of dread would have shamed her son.

"No. Please, Father, I can't explain why—"

"I understand." Laertes rested a hand on her shoulder and kissed her forehead. "Maybe for the same reason I want to take him when I sail. I will not argue with you. Who can tell? Odysseus may reach home ahead of me. I wouldn't steal Telemachos' chance to welcome his father home."

"I can welcome my father," Ktimene spoke up from the doorway. She leaned against the frame, listening, her red curls escaping her braids, her face a mask of hurt pride.

"Sweet one, how would your father know you?" Penelope said, holding her arms out for her daughter. She knew the hurt was momentary when Ktimene ran to her and climbed onto her lap. "If you meet him at the docks with Telemachos, the two of you close together, he will know you both. Your brother needs you to help your father recognize him, don't you see?" She hugged the girl, relieved when the child laughed and agreed.

"Then as soon as your father has kissed you," Laertes said, taking up the tale, "you must run as fast as you can to your grandmother, and let her know he is home."

"I run faster than everybody," Ktimene said, nodding for emphasis.

"Then run to Eurynome and have her bring your grandfather some wine. The day is hot and he has a long walk to make." Penelope nudged the girl off her lap, smiling when Ktimene darted from the room.

"She's like a little bird," Laertes said. "I still intend to voyage. Do you have messages for your friends in Pylos?"

Penelope smiled and thanked him and racked her brains for something to say to Polykaster and Straltos and other friends from her few journeys. She knew her father-in-law didn't quite believe her excuse, but she let him think as he would.

She refused to speak to anyone the certainty that filled her. If she let Telemachos leave Ithaka, with the gods so wroth against the Achaian kings, she would never see her son again.

CHAPTER 21

The last days of summer arrived on gentle breezes, perfect to carry the men of Ithaka home. Penelope left offerings at Athena's shrine and in the cave, begging for some vision to comfort her. Antikleia faded, in mind and body. She didn't recognize her husband. She took to wandering the villages of Ithaka, seeking her children. Mothers learned to picked up their toddlers and hide when Antikleia wandered by. More than once, they had to retrieve a child the woman claimed as hers. Penelope didn't force her children to visit their grandmother.

One night she went to bed with her window open to catch the breeze from the sea. She wearied herself with tasks that day so she wouldn't lie awake worrying and wondering. Her prayers for a vision barely left her lips before she slept.

Odysseus sat at the rudder of his ship, the wind filling his sails. A massive hide bag bound with silver sat between his feet. It glowed like rotting logs in a forest swamp and writhed. Penelope drank in the sight of her husband, safe in his ship. His eyes were puffy, red-rimmed from no sleep, his jaw set into stern lines. He sailed at night, his men asleep or keeping watch over the sea and sky, fear painting their faces green.

When Penelope woke, she ignored the fear for Odysseus' fate, choosing to take the dream as a good sign. She told Ktimene first the next morning and laughed when the girl asked what was in the bag that writhed between her father's feet. When she told Telemachos, her son hugged her and asked if his father would go hunting with him before winter came.

The next night, Penelope had the same dream. *Odysseus looked more weary—eyes more red and puffy. He nodded over the rudder, caught himself and sat up straight again. The bag churned on the deck between his feet, but he smiled when he looked at it.* Penelope reached out to him and woke when she called his name.

The next night, *Odysseus slept, clutching the rudder. The bag was gone. Terrified, Penelope tried to turn in her dream to search the ship. A twisted silver wire fell at her feet. Wind tore through her dream, whipping the waves white. Odysseus staggered to his feet. He fought the rudder in an unruly sea and shouted commands to his men.*

The storm screamed Penelope awake. The bronze shutters of her room banged against the wall. The wind raged with all the strength and cold of winter. She thought she heard the cries of men as they battled the furious sea. She staggered from her bed to close the shutters, then fell back into it, buried her head in her arms, and cried.

*   *   *

Winter came, with no word of Odysseus, though rumors told of other kings lost in their journeys home. Tyndareos sent word from Sparta that Menelaos and Helen had not returned. He asked Odysseus to spare some men to seek them.

The last tale of the year, before winter closed the ports, told of Agamemnon's fate and Klytemaistra's vengeance. Penelope listened to the tales brought by merchants and sailors, so similar she knew there was much truth in them. She felt nothing for her cousin or her husband, but worried for their children. She feared for Orestes, sent away by his sister to live in hiding. Elektra had been married to a slave as punishment for her loyalty to her father. Chrysothemis was the only child of Agamemnon's still in Mycenae's palace.

The intended sacrifice of Iphigenia had been the last blow for Klytemaistra. She took a lover before Agamemnon reached the shores of Troy. With him, she ruled Mycenae and planned to destroy Agamemnon on his return, and no one opposed her. Elektra sent Orestes into hiding, knowing the fate of sons of murdered kings, and tried to warn her father. Klytemaistra exiled her. When Agamemnon returned to Mycenae in victory, he walked into the arms of his wife and she killed him in his bath.

Penelope listened to the tales, wondering what people thought when they heard and repeated them. Perhaps the doings of noble houses were to them like tales of the gods, but it was the tragedy of her bloodline

243

bandied about the markets and docks.

She was glad when rough seas kept ships from visiting Ithaka. She locked Odysseus' bedroom and put away the clothes she had made for his welcoming feast. She set herself to wait out the winter and to pray spring would bring better news and happy stories.

*   *   *

Spring brought good rain, warm weather, an abundance of births to the flocks and herds, and more tales of heroes and warriors. Lost on their homecoming journeys. Killed by faithless wives or servants as they entered their homes.

Penelope wondered how many stories were wild speculation, created by jealous minds. It amused her a bit to speculate on her name being added to the list of faithless queens who took lovers and greeted their husbands with a poisoned cup or a knife. She hoped wherever his wandering took him, Odysseus heard and knew she waited in loyalty.

One day in late summer, Laertes and Telemachos spent the day together inspecting Odysseus' vineyards. Penelope gave her maids the afternoon to themselves. She took Ktimene to her garden and Athena's shrine, to think and pray and indulge in daydreams. Ktimene had grown too quiet and Penelope worried for her daughter as much as her mother-in-law. Both were lost in their dreams, one in the past, the other in the present. Penelope didn't know what to do for them. Life had stopped, caught like a cloak on a briar, waiting for Odysseus.

Antikleia forgot to eat for days at a time. She had given up her wandering search for her children, too weak from fasting and fevers to move from her hearth. Every boy was Odysseus, every girl her daughter. Penelope slept badly, expecting a summons in the night to tend her mother-in-law. She needed to rest, to hide from the demands of Ithaka a little, or she would be Eurynome's next patient.

Ktimene joined her mother in her prayers, laying out the handful of grain and pouring the wine over the small pile. When the girl climbed onto her lap and begged for a story of Alybas, Penelope obliged. She told one after another, trying to make her daughter laugh, hoping the sound would loosen the tight, waiting sensation that choked her.

The day grew hot. The bees droned and the plants sizzled in the warmth. Ktimene leaned against her shoulder and fell asleep. Penelope refused to disturb the child, who woke too often with bad dreams. She sat still, letting Ktimene sleep, and tried to find words to help her daughter. She heard a footstep in the garden beyond the walls and imagined it was a servant coming to tell her Odysseus had just sailed into the bay. She was able to believe for only a few heartbeats.

"Lady Penelope!" Melantho hurried through the rustling bushes that guarded the private garden. She trembled, nearly falling to her knees and her face had a new, unaccustomed pallor. "Oh, my lady, come quickly."

"What is it? Who is hurt?" Penelope stood, clutching Ktimene to keep from dropping her. By some miracle, the child didn't wake.

"My mistress, Antikleia—" A sob cut off the rest of Melantho's words.

Penelope got no more from the woman. Eurykleia heard and came running. Penelope put Ktimene in the nurse's arms and followed Melantho to Laertes' house.

Servants gathered in the dark, vaulted feasting hall. Penelope followed Melantho through the crowd. She stepped through in time to see Medon cut the rope and lower Antikleia to the waiting arms of her women.

Penelope shuddered, understanding. Antikleia's life was bound up in her son. Had she heard some terrible news about Odysseus and killed herself in response? Penelope shook off that feeling. She didn't dare indulge in morbid fantasies. Every eye in the hall watched her, forcing responsibility onto her shoulders. She was the mistress of the family and the queen. If anything was to be done, she had to decide.

"Medon, watch for Lord Laertes. Let no one tell him of this except yourself, and make it gentle. Let no word of this leave the house for now. We must take my mother to her chambers and prepare her as she deserves. It was a sickness that drove her to this. If she had been well, she wouldn't have taken her life." Penelope looked around the room to meet every eye, to impress her judgment on every mind. Deep inside she cried, wailing for Odysseus to comfort her.

She supervised as the servants washed Antikleia and dressed her in her best clothes. Penelope kept busy with details, bracing herself to face Laertes and Telemachos when they returned.

When there was nothing more to do, she dismissed the servants and sat with Antikleia's body. The woman looked peaceful, the ugly rope burns around her neck covered with garlands of flowers. Penelope had put the coin in her mouth, to pay the ferryman at Death's river.

"Mother, if your spirit still lingers, I beg of you, hear me," Penelope whispered. The shadows lengthened in the room, afternoon turning to evening. "I love you as my own mother. If ever I did anything to grieve you, I ask forgiveness. My son and my daughter love you. Your absence will be pain to us for many years to come. How shall I explain your death to Odysseus when he returns?" Her voice broke. "And if he is not to return, but already waits in the shadow lands, please, send me a sign."

She lifted one of the dead woman's hands, cold and woefully thin, and pressed it against her cheek. Penelope closed her eyes. She thought she heard the brushing of wings outside the open window, the soft coughing cry of a dove or the hoot of an early owl. Gently, she put Antikleia's hand back at her side, stood, and slipped from the room.

There were other details to attend to. Melantho, for all her years of experience, suddenly couldn't manage the household. Penelope sent another servant to tell Eurynome the news and stayed to put Laertes' house back into order. She welcomed the little details to distract her mind from dark thoughts. Penelope ordered more wood brought in, more grain ground for flour, wholesale scrubbing and cleansing of the house. She thought the servants welcomed the work, too.

"Mother!" Telemachos hurried through the open door, dodging the women with baskets of washing balanced in their arms. "Medon has news for Grandfather, but he won't let me listen." He flung his arms around her, his face bright. "Is it good news? Is my father home? Tell me!" Argus darted into the house, dodging feet, barking an echo of the boy's plea.

Penelope swallowed a sigh that was sure to turn into a sob. She wrapped her arms around her son. It startled her to realize how tall he had grown. His nose was even with her shoulder. "No, your father isn't home yet. That's the trouble." She sat, gesturing for him to join her.

"Is Grandmother sick again?"

"Again." She felt a hysterical laugh try to escape.

"Grandfather explained. She worries about my father so much she cannot eat or sleep, and that makes her sick. It hurts when she calls me by my father's name. She always begs me never to leave Ithaka." He shook his head, eleven-year-old wisdom peering from his eyes.

Penelope debated telling him the mistake was easily made. He was so clearly Odysseus' son, the shape of his head, hands and shoulders, the way he walked, even tricks of speech. She wondered if he would have Odysseus' mellow, persuasive voice when grown. There were times *she* had almost called him by his father's name, at night when she was sleepy, sitting by the fire and imagining a different silhouette across the hall.

"Yes, your Grandmother has been sick again." She breathed a prayer of thanks for this help in explaining to her son. "She loved your father so much, nothing else in life mattered. It hurts to wait for him, doesn't it?"

"Sometimes I hate the boys who have fathers. They tease me that my father can't take me hunting or teach me to sail." Telemachos smiled, a strange, grim expression on his young face. "When my father returns, I'll make him proud."

"You will. I know you will," she whispered. Penelope swallowed another sob filling her throat. "Your grandmother lost hope that your father would ever return. She went to look for him in the land of the dead." Penelope felt bile rising in her throat as the glib, stiff words passed over her lips. Simple to say once she found the courage, meaning much, explaining little.

"Dead?" Telemachos paled. He reached for his mother's hands. When she put her arms around him he didn't draw away, but pressed his face into her shoulder, as if he could hide.

Penelope saw movement in the doorway and turned to see Laertes enter the hall. He walked with Medon, silent, staring, pale. Stiffly, he followed the servant up the stairs to his wife's chambers. Penelope held still until Laertes vanished and she heard the click of a door closing.

"We must take care of Grandfather now," she whispered, releasing Telemachos. "We must be strong for him, so he doesn't leave us as well. Think how your father will feel, coming home to find both your grandparents gone?"

"He can come live with us," the boy offered, his voice husky from the tears he had shed. Awkwardly, he rubbed at his eyes with his fists.

"Yes, he can come live with us."

*   *   *

When Penelope returned home at sunset, she found the news had raced before her with ill results. Telemachos had gone home to take instructions to Eurykleia and Eurynome. He met her at the door, his arm around his sister's shoulders. Ktimene's face was a wreck of tears, wet and glistening, eyes swollen. She made no sound but held out her arms to her mother. Penelope gathered up her daughter and Telemachos followed her up the stairs. In a low voice, he informed her a woman had brought the news, shouting it so the whole house knew. Ktimene had awakened, alone and in the dark, and had screamed herself hoarse. She made no sound since then.

"Eurynome tried to hit her with a stool," Telemachos added, mystified and proud. They stepped into Penelope's room. He hopped up onto the bed as she sat in a chair, slowly rocking Ktimene. "She said she wasn't ever to come back to our house, or Dolios would kill her."

"Who?" Penelope muttered, distracted with wiping Ktimene's face with the edge of her sleeve.

"Eurynome called her Thoosa. She laughed and ran away."

Penelope thought of the sly looks Thoosa always gave her. She remembered Melantho and Thoosa watching her with delighted malice in their eyes. She knew, even though Melantho liked Antikleia, by now the two laughed together at this tragedy fallen on Odysseus' household.

*   *   *

The next morning, they lit Antikleia's funeral pyre. By evening, the ashes were cool enough to put into an urn she had made. Laertes brought it with him when he came to live in his son's house. Penelope helped him bury the urn in her private garden, where she and Antikleia had spent many contented hours, working together in silent, peaceful accord.

Laertes traded his house for land adjoining his son's fields and orchards in another part of the island. Before witnesses, he had a scribe make out a deed putting the new land into Telemachos' name. If grandfather and grandson spent more hours than necessary planting vines and seedling trees, Penelope didn't complain. It was good to have her husband's father in her home, to talk to in the evening, to teach Telemachos what father taught son. The boy's presence was all that kept Laertes from falling to the same depression that had devoured his wife.

Some of the household staff was sent away, either freed or given into the keeping of other noble households. The rest were divided between the new land, to tend it, or added to Penelope's household. Melantho returned to take her old place as Eurynome's assistant.

Penelope soon wondered if that had been wise, even if done out of common sense. Melantho *had* been with her from the beginning. Eurynome *was* growing older, slower, and needed help. Still, Penelope considered sending Melantho to the estate where Dolios had become overseer, his wife and sons joining him. It was no insult for the woman to care for her aging parents. In two days, Penelope glimpsed enough scornful looks, overheard enough bitter whispers, to know Melantho still nursed anger. Penelope remembered Odysseus saying it was better to keep an enemy in sight, and set herself to endure.

*   *   *

Penelope dreamed of Odysseus in a gray place of rocks and shadows. He stood gazing into the shadows, as she had seen him do in other dreams, bracing himself for battle at dawn. Things moved in the churning mist. Part of her did not want to know what her husband faced.

She watched as he marked out a square with the tip of his sword and then cut the dry ground and dug a pit. The chore could have taken mere moments or days. Then, when the pit was as deep as it was wide, he vanished, to return with three large jugs of fired clay. He filled the pit from the jugs, like offering a drink sacrifice—milk, wine and water. She watched him sprinkle white grains of barley over the liquid in the pit. Odysseus made an offering in this gray, muddled place, and the idea frightened her. Who did he propitiate? What kept him from returning home?

Then he vanished again. He returned with four sheep, killed them and spilled their blood into the pit. As he dragged the last carcass aside, the shapes at the edge of the dream grew solid. Pale faces, hollow eyes, bony limbs became visible, stepping from the mist. Penelope sensed the apparitions in the shadows could see her. If they could see her, then so could Odysseus, but she couldn't make a sound to get him to turn and look at her.

Odysseus crouched at the edge of the pit and waved his bright sword over the hole filled with blood, wine, milk and water. Light from an unseen source flashed off the blade. The light kept the shadow people away from the pit. Penelope watched her husband search the faces of the growing crowd.

She studied the faces, wondering who he sought. Faces took on character and color. Some people wore armor, others dressed like queens, with garlands of wilted flowers in their hair.

Penelope woke with a shriek choking her. Though she stared into the bright moonlight on her blankets, she couldn't wipe the scene away. Memory burned it bright and fast into her mind.

Agamemnon stepped from the faceless crowd. Elpenor, a young oarsman from Ithaka. Achilleus, the young hero who had visited Ithaka on his way to Ilion. Antikleia stepped from the shadows last of all.

Penelope didn't share this dream with Telemachos. How could she tell her son she had seen his father walk living into the land of the dead? Ktimene, however, came to her mother and said she had dreamed of her grandmother. After they compared dreams, the pain that had haunted the child's eyes faded a little. That night, they walked together under a full moon to the cave, to make offerings to the Goddess.

*   *   *

On a festival day, when the boys competed in wrestling and foot races, Penelope gave the household the afternoon to do as they wished. Laertes persuaded her to come to the beach to see the contests of speed, strength and skill. In the groves, young girls danced. This year, Ktimene asked to go without her mother's attendance, to dress her hair and arms with garlands of flowers. Penelope agreed, though she felt a pang at this rare sign of independence. It was good for her daughter to take up her heritage, to lead in the festivals praising the Goddess. Penelope contented herself with watching her son excel, joining her voice in the shouts of encouragement and praise.

Telemachos raced with the boys his age, meeting them shoulder to shoulder, giving as good as he took. She saw Odysseus in him, though the boy had her slenderness rather than his father's stocky build. Memories returned of that summer she and Odysseus met, when she waited in Tyndareos' palace for a prince to notice her, and he waited for his chance to win her. Odysseus had excelled in the games, hoarding his strength until his competitors wasted theirs. When his opponents thought him tired, weak, at a disadvantage, he knocked them off balance. Penelope fought tears when she saw Telemachos struggle to do the same. Did he act and move and think like his father because it was in his blood, or because she had told him so many stories of Odysseus that he tried to imitate his father?

"He is too much like his father," Laertes murmured, giving her a cup filled from a skin of wine he had brought. Penelope nodded her thanks and agreement. She sipped to keep from speaking, knowing her voice would break. "I am grateful to you, Penelope," he said, touching her arm.

"I?" Her voice did crack, the word startled out of her. Laertes watched the wrestlers in the sand several paces away. "You made my son happy. You raise his son so any man would be proud to claim him. You raise his daughter so that every young man of good blood will soon clamor to make her his bride. And you give me reason to remain in the land of the living." Now he met her gaze. "The gods blessed our household, the day my son saw and desired you."

"Father—" She looked away, the words sticking in her throat. "This is my home. What else would I have done?"

The roar of the crowd around them kept Laertes from replying. The wrestlers finished their tussle, a blond, thin boy somehow managing to throw down a black-haired boy nearly a head taller. Penelope shivered, thinking for a moment she saw a young Menelaos and young Aias getting up from the sand. The two wrestlers laughed, clasped hands and left the informal arena. Telemachos stepped forward to meet his next opponent. Penelope added her voice to the shouts of encouragement. Her son heard. He bowed to her, then turned to meet the larger boy, tanned and whipped thin by wind and sun, who came to meet him.

"A fisherman's son," Laertes said, gesturing at the other boy. "He grew up on his father's ship. That gives him a balance Telemachos will find hard to defeat." He chuckled. "Not that he will give up until he finds a way."

"Sometimes I wish Telemachos had never been born," Penelope said, under cover of the shouting people around them. She felt no surprise at the words that slipped between her teeth almost before the thought entered her mind.

"Nor Ktimene," she continued. "They remind me, growing and changing every day, how quickly time slips by. Telemachos was barely walking and talking when his father left. In a few years, he will be a grown man, ready to take his father's place. Ktimene will have suitors. I don't want her to marry without her father's consent, but how can I make her wait? I hate being reminded of the years we lost."

"Would you rather have been alone, with only memories?" he asked. From the softness of his voice, Penelope knew he understood and sympathized.

"My memories are alive because Telemachos and Ktimene keep them alive. They still ask me about their father, even though I have given the same answers a hundred times. In Telemachos, I can see his father as a boy. Without him or Ktimene, I might have followed their grandmother. They are a living source of hurt to me, and the fountain of my strength to live and endure."

CHAPTER 22

It happened late spring the next year. Penelope remembered the day well, every detail carved into her memory. She sat at her loom that morning to begin cloth for a new cloak for Telemachos. He had grown quickly that winter and all his clothes were too short. It took her most of the morning to set the threads, between answering questions about late planting and helping Ktimene with a new pattern. After a short noon meal with Eurynome and Eurykleia, discussing the state of the household stores, she returned to her weaving.

Laertes came to the door before she finished ten passes. Penelope saw his shadow before she heard his approach. She looked up to greet him and felt her heart miss a beat.

"Father? Are you ill?" She reached for him, alarmed. Laertes stared, eyes wide, skin pale.

"There is a man in our hall," he said, his voice strained and quiet. "Scarred from battles, abused by rough journeys."

"What does he want?" Something inside Penelope shrank from asking. A fragment of a dream gave her warning with no details.

"He says he is Odysseus."

"He says," she echoed. The two words put a cold hand on the hot leap of joy from the last three words. Penelope fought for another breath. "You doubt?"

She turned to see Ktimene watching, face unreadable and solemn. The girl came to her mother and stood by her chair, a hand on her shoulder. Penelope's mind raced, trying to remember where

Telemachos was that day.

She felt her heart ease a little, remembering he had taken Argus to go hunting. The aging dog couldn't keep up with the other hunting dogs. Telemachos treasured Argus as a last gift from his father and worked to keep him active.

"Father?" she prompted, when Laertes said nothing. "Why did no one tell us the ship had arrived?"

"They came in last night at the northern tip of the island. The man who accompanied him says they were not sure what island they had reached until this morning."

"Then he lost his companions after all." Penelope felt no reassurance in knowing another dream had spoken truth. No dream had warned her about the man sitting in the hall below, waiting to be greeted as her husband. "You doubt?"

"He has lived through horrible hardships. No man would be recognizable to his own. His companion says he has no memory of his past, his home and heritage." Laertes gestured toward the door. "Will you test him with me?"

Penelope nodded and stood. She clutched at the frame of her loom a moment when she nearly lost her balance.

"He's not my father," Ktimene said, her voice sharp and bright. "Father would play tricks on us and test us and make us laugh." She wrapped her arms around her mother's waist. "Make him go away."

"We must be sure, child," Laertes said. "Maybe you should stay here, and wait."

Penelope expected a protest, but her daughter only nodded and went back to her loom. She and Laertes supported each other, taking the stairs slowly. Her thoughts spun.

Why did Laertes doubt the man's claims? Because of his beaten and battered condition? Or did something not lie straight? She knew with a little questioning, her husband's father could have examined the stranger and his claims. He needed her help. Why? To prove he was right to doubt, or to prove him wrong?

Two men waited by the hearth in the feasting hall. Eurynome finished serving them bread, meat and wine as Penelope and Laertes arrived. One was tall, perhaps a few years older than Penelope. He had the tanned skin and windblown looks of a man who lived on the deck of a ship. His eyes were as black as his hair and sparkled when he saw her. She shuddered at the measuring look he gave her, as if she were a piece of property.

His companion hunched over on the hearth, holding his cup of wine with one gnarled hand and the stump of his other wrist. Penelope halted when she saw that loss. She had grown used to the sight of lost hands and limbs on the men who had come to tell her about the war. The thought of Odysseus so maimed sent cold weakness through her. She pushed that aside to study the man who claimed to be her husband.

His hair might have been red and thick once, but was bleached by wind and sun and the salt seas, thinned and graying from a hard life. His stooped shoulders might have been wide, strong, set on a stocky body. His tanned arms and legs were laced with scars. Burns scarred the flesh on his stump, where someone had crudely cauterized the wound. The left side of his face was a mass of scars and burns, the tissue still pink from healing. Gray eyes looked from the worn wreckage of his face, but they held no brightness she recognized.

Penelope stepped before the man, wondering at the lack of awareness in his eyes. They regarded each other until some spark came to his face and he smiled, revealing broken, yellowed teeth. He looked her up and down and licked his lips in a sloppy, animal gesture that revolted her.

She knew this man was not Odysseus. Despite all the justified ills spoken against him, her husband had never looked at a woman in that way. She backed up a step, her arm still caught in Laertes'.

"Daughter?" His voice held hope, despite his doubts. In desperation, she studied the man again. That was when her eye caught the lack.

"His scars. Father, look at his scars." She pointed at the man's legs.

"I've plenty of scars to prove my troubles, dear wife," the imposter said. His voice was harsh, as if someone had tried to strangle him. "Do you think I would have willingly stayed away from a woman as lovely as you, if enemies had not slowed me?"

"Yes, scars in plenty." She found strength in cold anger. Penelope gestured at the smooth skin around his knees. "Where is the scar the boar gave Odysseus when he was a boy?"

"That is a proof no one could create without risking losing his leg." Laertes' voice took on a strength that threatened to build into a shout to bring down the roof. "How do you explain gaining so many scars, and losing that one identifying mark?"

"Noble lord, gracious royal lady," the young man broke in. His voice was placating, with a touch of metal like a sword's edge. "As we told you when we entered your doors, my poor companion has long wandered without memory of birthplace or kindred. He said his name was Odysseus. There must be many other warriors with the same name."

"But only one who is king in Ithaka," Penelope said. "Only one who brought me here as his bride, father of my son and daughter, who killed the boar that nearly took his leg."

"It was a mistake! We meant no harm."

"Harm was done." She was glad for the momentary loss of control that made her voice wobble. She felt Laertes stiffen at her side. "Father, I will leave you to finish with our guests. I ask you, even for hospitality's sake, do not let them stay an hour longer in this house." She slipped her arm free of Laertes' grip and hurried to the stairs.

Penelope silently called down plagues and lightning on the two men. It was no mistake, she was sure, but an attempt to use misfortune to slip a thief into another man's long-empty place.

Honesty made her ask: what if her husband had returned to her, maimed by misfortune and accident and the capricious anger of the gods? Would she have willingly held him in her arms, kissed his lips, joined him in his bed when he called her?

Odysseus, she knew, might return home in disguise to test her. She wouldn't blame him after the betrayals that met other warriors. But he would not hide the signs and secrets they held between them.

Slow tears fell on the threads when she returned to her loom. Penelope listened for voices in the hall as Laertes handled their unwelcome guests. Perhaps it was cowardly to run away and leave him with them. At the moment, Penelope didn't care. She knew Laertes would forgive her.

"Mother?" Ktimene got up from her loom. She stood by her mother and touched her shoulder. "Didn't your dreams tell you?"

"No. Dreams are not always trustworthy." Penelope put her head in her hands and wept.

*   *   *

By evening, men from the household escorted the imposter and his companion back to their ship and forbade them to return. Penelope let Laertes tell Telemachos what had happened. She didn't have the strength for the task. Telemachos' anger comforted her. She lost that comfort to fear when the boy wanted to take his new spear and hunt out the man who tried to steal his father's place.

"No." She grasped his arm, stopping his words and his path to the door. For a moment mother and son fought a silent battle of wills. "If this is anyone's battle, it is your father's, to win by returning home. You will not help him by going against evil men and endangering yourself."

"But my friends—"

"I will not answer to their fathers if you lead them into danger," Laertes interrupted. A smile broke his stern expression. "You make me proud, you make your mother proud, that you want to defend us. But this is not the way. You're still a boy, despite your strength and skill. Take the time to grow up before you grasp a man's duty." He glanced to Penelope, apology in his eyes. "Think of your mother, boy. If any harm comes to you, she loses what little joy the gods have left in her life."

Penelope forgave his cruel tactic when Telemachos hugged her and promised he wouldn't sneak away to wreak vengeance on impostors.

*   *   *

"Why does Antinoos wish to speak to me?" Penelope murmured, expecting no answer.

Mentor ruled Ithaka with Laertes' tacit support. The womenfolk of the island appealed to Penelope to intervene on their families' behalf. Though many on the island considered her a power, her influence had faded in the years since Ktimene's birth, and others regarded Penelope as a foreigner, tolerated only as the mother of the heir. Antinoos was one. His request for an audience made her suspicious.

"He wouldn't say, but he has brought presents for us all," Telemachos said.

"What kind of presents?" Penelope glanced around to Ktimene in her window seat, waiting to learn a new style for her hair. She was blossoming and wanted to give up her childish braids.

"He brought me a hunting dog. Argus didn't like him," her son added with a grin. "He has gold bracelets for you and Ktimene."

"For me?" the girl squeaked. She started braiding her ember-colored hair with flying fingers.

"Gifts of jewelry from men not of the family are often dangerous," Penelope said. She hated to see the delight fade from her daughter's face, but warning was necessary. "If Antinoos comes bringing gifts when he has never been a friend, I can guess his reason quite well."

"Mother?" Telemachos frowned, puzzled.

"Your sister is lovely and becoming a woman. Antinoos is

unmarried."

"I don't want to marry anyone!" Ktimene backed away, as if her brother would drag her downstairs to her suitor.

Penelope swallowed a chuckle. She remembered her own protests when she had been Ktimene's age. She beckoned for her children and put her arms around them. "I will not give you in marriage unless I know you will be happy. No one will force my hand. Or your grandfather's. Now, let us go meet our guest."

Telemachos preceded them down the stairs, with stiff stride and straight back. Penelope saw his father's wariness and pride. She kept her arm around Ktimene's shoulders, to comfort the girl and keep her from running.

Antinoos had taken the liberty of spreading his gifts on a table while he waited. The hunting dog, a mere pup, curled up at his feet. Argus lay on the hearth by the coals of last night's fire and glared at the pup. Penelope couldn't help smiling at the picture the two dogs made. Then she saw Antinoos watching her and her smile faded.

He was handsome, she had to admit. Young like Odysseus when she first saw him. Vibrant and full of life and energy. He was golden and slim, where Odysseus had been like a banked fire, stocky and solid.

"Antinoos, you bring presents, my son says." She sat in the chair reserved for her at the foot of the stairs, Ktimene on her right hand, Telemachos on her left. "You rarely come to Odysseus' hall. Why do you grace us with your presence now?"

"It would have been unseemly before. Everyone knows the tales of other queens led astray. I would not have anyone say I tempted our lovely queen." He bowed, a practiced smile curving his graceful lips.

"Other lords of Ithaka visit without scandal. I know your intent. Don't waste our time with pretty speeches."

"I can see the elders spoke the truth—a woman who speaks and thinks like a man. A marvel." Antinoos looked directly at Ktimene. "Your daughter is a blossoming flower. You will soon be overwhelmed with suitors for her."

"Ktimene is still a child."

"My father said the same," he countered. "Then he admitted many saw *you* as a child when Odysseus brought you to Ithaka."

"I was nearly sixteen. I prefer my daughter not marry until that age, or older."

"And have her shamed, when all her year-mates are brides and mothers before her?" Antinoos laughed.

"No one shames my sister," Telemachos said, his face flushing. "My mother speaks from wisdom and experience. If you laugh at her, you must leave."

"Telemachos, Antinoos is a guest, however short a time he stays," Penelope chided softly. She met the suitor's gaze and he nodded he understood the warning. "Even if I were agreeable to a marriage bond between our families, Antinoos, I cannot give my daughter without her father's blessing." Under her hand, Ktimene's stiffness slowly melted.

"The old ways still linger on Ithaka. You could easily invoke them and no one would criticize you," Antinoos countered, his gracious smile turning sly. "In the old days, mothers took husbands for their daughters. Men went to live with their brides' families."

"If you follow the old ways, Antinoos, why have I never seen you at the planting and harvest festivals?" She waited but he gave no answer. She expected none. "Believe what you will, I *will not* give my daughter without her father's blessing."

"The war has been over for years now and he has not returned. Would you have your daughter die unwed?"

"In the old ways you invoke, Antinoos, many maidens *stayed* maidens, their virginity regarded as sacred gifts to the Goddess." Penelope stood, signaling the discussion was over. She felt a small measure of relief when he picked up his cloak. She glimpsed the movements of servants who had been listening. The story would cross the island soon. "Tell your friends I will not consider marriage for Ktimene until her sixteenth year. He who speaks of it before then will be turned away. Understood?"

"I understand very well, Lady Penelope." He bowed, and she thought she saw a touch of respect in his eyes. "Will you accept the gifts I brought?" Antinoos gestured at the jewelry laid out on the cloth and the pup still curled under the bench.

"They are wooing gifts, and as such I cannot permit them in my house. If I accept them, I must consider a marriage for my daughter. Blessings on you, Antinoos." Penelope nudged Ktimene, who turned and hurried up the stairs ahead of her. Telemachos stayed to see their guest to the door.

"I am to serve the Goddess. I won't marry anyone!" Ktimene burst out when she and Penelope reached her room.

"I said the same when I was your age," she told her daughter. Penelope sat in the window seat and beckoned for Ktimene to join her. She put her arms around her daughter. "You're too grown up to hold on my lap. That makes me feel very old." A tiny chuckle escaped the girl, showing Penelope she had spoken exactly right.

"You married Father."

"I tried to run away when I learned I was to marry your father." Penelope laughed when Ktimene stared at her. "I liked him, but I didn't want to marry anyone, ever."

"But he loved you—you loved him. Didn't you?"

"I was a rebellious little girl, and I would sometimes dress as a boy at night, to wander the palace in Sparta, trying to raise my courage to steal a horse and run away. I wanted to become an Amazon."

"Why didn't you?"

"Laziness, I think. And fear. It is fine to dream and to hate how your life is controlled by others. Yet if you do nothing about it...I wanted to rebel, but I couldn't. Your father met me in my nighttime rambles and befriended me even after he saw through my disguise. He taught me about the world. He understood my fear when he caught me trying to run away, and he never grew angry or hurt."

"You're not lazy, Mother. And you're not afraid of anything," Telemachos said from the doorway.

"Because your father taught me to take care of myself. Because I have no time to be afraid. I've grown up. And I promise you, Ktimene, on my honor as priestess to the Goddess, you will never be given to anyone unless I know you will be as happy with him as I was with your father. Telemachos, if anything happens to me before your father returns, you must keep my vow to your sister, do you hear me?"

"Yes, Mother." He nodded and reached for their hands. "I promise, before the Goddess, my sister will never be given to a man she doesn't want." He sighed. "If my father were here, Antinoos would never have dared come here."

"We will wait for your father to return. He promised he would always come back to me. Not even death could keep him away." Penelope closed her eyes, trying to remember the sound of Odysseus' voice, the feel of his arms around her, the touch of his hand when he made his vow. It was hard to remember anything but the words.

"I will never marry," Ktimene repeated. There was no anger in her voice, only that stubborn, patient certainty Penelope had fought since she was a baby. "The Goddess promised."

Penelope took Ktimene to the Goddess that night. The cool summer air had a chill foretelling an early fall. They went in silence, cloaked in dark colors to be hidden in the night.

Penelope had thought long and hard, and she sensed undercurrents to Antinoos' wooing.

The women of Ithaka wanted a new king. The blessings she had brought to the island with the births of her children were fading. The men left to lead in Odysseus' place were older now. Antinoos had spoken of the old ways. Did he plan to claim kingship by marrying Ktimene? Would enough people support him and wrest the inheritance from Telemachos?

Antinoos had spoken no threats, but she saw the warnings in his eyes. She knew he or his friends might watch her house from now on. More than the fear that someone might kidnap and forcibly marry her daughter, she feared they would follow her and desecrate the rituals for the Goddess. Penelope didn't relax until they neared the cave. She heard no footsteps behind them, no rattling of stones from unseen feet or voices.

In the cave, she made the offering in silence, then knelt with her arms stretched over the altar stone, waiting and listening. When even the sound of her heartbeat had faded into the enclosing silence, she spoke.

"Goddess, we ask your help. Men who scorn your teachings now use them against my family. They would use my daughter to steal my son's place as his father's heir. Protect us. Intercede with the gods and bring Odysseus home to us. We have need of him. Ithaka needs the true king. My son is not old enough to lead. He needs his father to bring him to manhood. I need my husband, my love, who brought me here to serve you. Please, help us." Penelope raised her head and looked into the darker recesses of the cave. "Help us."

She waited until the cold of the stone soaked through her body, chilling her. Ktimene had to help her stand. Her daughter stayed quiet through the long hours of waiting. Penelope saw Odysseus most strongly in his daughter in dark times. Ktimene held herself quiet, gray eyes hooded and distant while she thought deeply, and then acted decisively. Like her father.

When they returned home, Ktimene stayed with Penelope instead of going to her own room. She curled up on the foot of her mother's bed and spoke quietly, but with a strength that worried Penelope.

"Mother, I will never marry. I will serve the Goddess by staying untouched."

"I said the same when I was your age." Penelope knelt next to the girl and wrapped her arms around her. "In the old days, a girl had the right to stay virgin if she wished. Her father had no right to force her into marriage. Yet, I found great joy in serving the Goddess by bringing new life into this world."

"Mother, it isn't the same. You love my father. He loves you, though he hasn't come home. Why hasn't he?"

"I don't know."

"Melantho says he doesn't care about us."

"And who is Melantho, that you suddenly listen to the foolish words from her mouth?" Penelope forced her voice to stay teasing, to keep the anger out. She wished she dared send Melantho away, to get her poison out of the house. It was still safer to keep the woman under her supervision.

"She was talking to some others and I overheard..." Ktimene looked away, blushing a little.

"I was very fond of listening around corners and from the shadows when I was younger," Penelope admitted. "It helped me to learn, and gave me pain, too."

"Father has been gone longer than I have been alive. I hear others speak of him and he's different from the stories you tell. They say he is a liar and a schemer, tricking people into doing what he wants. He is a great warrior, but would rather fight with words than with weapons. He is strong, and skilled in all the games, but he would rather get others to work for him, and cheat to win. Which man is my father?"

"Both. I love your father. I always will." She hugged Ktimene, rocking her as if the girl was a baby again. "Yes, he tells stories and lies when he feels he must. He uses his mind more than his strength. People call him a liar and cheater because he defeats them and wounds their pride.

"He was a grown man when he took me as his wife. Yet there was something still very young and unfinished about him. I grew to love him despite his flaws, and I know he loved me as much as such a man can love anyone. He still needed to grow up in his spirit. I nearly died birthing your brother, and that frightened him. He changed the way he thought and the way he saw the world.

"He told me once he would have sacrificed anything and anyone for Ithaka. He changed when he thought he might have lost me. So I know he loves me, still, no matter where he is. He loves you, though he has never seen you."

"What if he is dead, like some say?"

"Does death stop love? I will always love your father, and I will never take another husband. Not even for Ithaka."

"Mother, I'm afraid," Ktimene whispered.

"I know."

"I don't know how to love like that. I can't."

"That's because you're still young." Penelope released her and kissed her forehead. "You still have time before you are grown. The world changes. You will change. Pray to the Goddess for help and wisdom. She will send a solution. There is always an answer, even if not the answer we prefer."

"Always?" Ktimene blinked away the tears threatening to fall from her eyes, and tried to smile.

*   *   *

Ktimene fell ill with the first of the fall storms. First a dragging weariness, a loss of her usual healthy color, then dying appetite. Penelope dosed her daughter with everything her aunt had taught her. A half-remembered dream prompted her to set Eurykleia to watch the girl at night. They caught Ktimene slipping from the house to the cave of the Goddess. She went every night to pray and make offerings. In the damp cave, she had taken a chill to her bones.

They kept Ktimene from going out at night. Her illness faded slowly, despite the medicines Penelope mixed with her own hands. Whenever Ktimene regained strength, she tried to escape her confinement to go to the cave. Penelope posted a servant outside Ktimene's door, to keep her in her room. Her daughter fashioned a ladder of ropes and climbed out her bedroom window. Laertes caught her.

"As stubborn and devious as your father," Penelope confided to Telemachos the next evening. Ktimene had retired to her room to sulk. "If I could send her away, where the men of Ithaka couldn't find her, I would."

"Ktimene will not be happy until no one wants to marry her," he retorted. "She told me yesterday, she wishes she had been born a boy, or could become one."

"If that were possible." Penelope shivered at the memory that came to her.

"Something is wrong?" Laertes joined them at the hearth.

"My aunt taught me many lessons I wish I could forget." She picked up her sewing and tried to push the words from her memory.

"How to make a maiden into a boy?" Telemachos guessed.

"Somewhat. Long ago, there was a sect that served the Goddess as virgins all their lives." She paused, thinking she heard a footstep in the shadows. But no one appeared. "They drank a potion which made them unable to bear children. For every five who drank it, three died." She shook her head. "I will not talk of it."

CHAPTER 23

"Mistress!" Dairee stumbled into Penelope's garden and nearly fell into the tiny pool. "Mistress, come quickly!"

Penelope didn't ask. She saw the terror that made the girl's face pale as ice. Dairee was Ktimene's personal maid. She followed the girl to Ktimene's room. Eurykleia hurried down the hall ahead of her. The tight frown and the fright in the old nurse's eyes terrified Penelope.

Ktimene knelt on the floor, arms around her middle, retching. A greenish pool of bile streaked with blood spread out before her. Penelope smelled the bitter, burned odors before she saw the tiny brazier, the mortar and pestle shoved under the table to hide. She knelt next to the girl, wrapping her arms around her. A quiet corner of her mind noted the bits of roots and leaves, the dried herbs and sand scattered on the floor.

"Mother!" Ktimene gasped, her voice broken. Her face streamed hot sweat, then turned bloodless white. "Help me?" She shivered, bending double as more retching shook her.

"Eurykleia, send them away." Penelope felt the presence of too many bodies in the doorway of her daughter's room. She tried to move Ktimene away from the puddle of her vomit. The girl cried out in pain and she gave up. "Ktimene, what did you do?"

"Tried—I heard—" Her voice broke into breathless, whistling whimpers.

"Mother, what's wrong?" Telemachos shouldered his way into the room, shoving aside the more stubborn onlookers.

264

"Help me carry Ktimene to my room. She drank something—it's killing her." Penelope's voice broke. She looked up, straight into Melantho's eyes. The woman's face was somber, but Penelope thought she saw a glint of delight in her servant's eyes. She opened her mouth to rebuke the woman, but Ktimene screamed and clutched at her. She held her daughter, tears blurring her eyes as the girl convulsed, then went still and limp in her arms.

They moved Ktimene to Penelope's room. Eurynome sent the other servants back to their work. Telemachos wanted to stay with his sister, but Penelope sent him to fetch Laertes. Eurykleia helped her undress Ktimene and clean the filth of her sickness. Penelope wracked her memories for a purgative, a general antidote of some kind to give to Ktimene. A specific antidote would have to wait until she could examine the scattered materials in her daughter's room. Penelope doubted she had the time.

"Where's that girl?" she muttered, kicking Ktimene's stinking, sweat-soaked dress to one side. "Her maid—she could tell me."

"Dairee is likely crying herself sick," Eurykleia said. "She often does that."

"Ktimene never complained." Penelope knelt at her daughter's side, holding her hand, feeling more helpless than she could remember.

"I've heard Ktimene was the one who made her cry, most times. Not to be cruel, but she could never stand fools or silly girls who frighten easily."

"What have the two of them been doing?" She shook her head, knowing Eurykleia couldn't answer. "Bring her here. I need—"

A choking gasp escaped Ktimene. She convulsed again, her back arching. Blood trickled from her ears and mouth. Sweat darkened her clean dress. Four times, the straining body spasmed, limbs stiffening, back arching, and then collapsed. On the fourth, Ktimene fell still like one of her forsaken dolls. The breath escaped her in a slow sigh and did not return.

Penelope moaned once, softly, as she gathered her child into her arms. She still sat there, eyes dry and staring, silent, clutching Ktimene's empty body, when Laertes returned.

*   *   *

Penelope insisted on washing Ktimene by herself for the funeral rites. She dressed her daughter in new clothes she had finished only the day before and wrapped her in the finest sheet she had, made years ago

265

for Odysseus' homecoming.

When Laertes touched the torch to the funeral pyre, Penelope stood at the head of the assembly. She refused to leave her child alone until only bones and ash remained. Then she walked back to her home between Telemachos and Laertes, still wordless and pale, and retired to her room. She curled into a ball of knife-edged misery and cried, finally, choked silent by her tears. She ached, in heart and body, feeling as empty and torn and weak as she had been at Telemachos' birth. She stayed alone, in the dark, long after she had cried herself voiceless and hollow.

Eurykleia was the first who dared to break her silence. Dairee, Ktimene's maid, hung herself after a night and a day of weeping. Those who had heard her reported the maid blamed herself for her mistress' death. Penelope tended to agree. The news also served to tear the numb cloud enfolding her.

"What were they brewing?" she whispered, after Eurykleia told her. "Ktimene's room—we must search it."

Someone had cleaned the dead girl's room. Even the tiny brazier, mortar and pestle were gone. Penelope stared and rage replaced the sorrow that threatened to eat her hollow.

"They killed my daughter," she said in the echoing room. She glanced at Eurykleia, who only looked back at her, waiting, anger like a slow fire in her eyes. "Two young girls couldn't know what to do, whatever it was they tried. Someone had to tell them what to do and how."

"And that someone cleaned the room, you think, to keep you from learning?" the old nurse guessed.

"I saw some ...I can guess what Ktimene wanted. She or her murdering friend heard me speak of a potion that rendered a woman infertile. Ktimene wanted to make herself unable to bear children, so no man would marry her." Penelope shook her head, wishing she could shake her whirling thoughts straight. "I must be like Odysseus. I must wait and watch, and catch my enemy sleeping."

"Enemy?"

"You said Dairee was weak and afraid. Perhaps she was too weak and afraid to kill herself." Penelope was glad for something to focus on at last. "My mind is not my own, such thoughts I have! The one who taught my daughter to make the brew killed Dairee and cleaned this room to hide the truth." She began to shake. Whether from new sorrow, new rage, lack of sleep or lack of food, she couldn't tell. "Speak to no

one of this, Eurykleia. We must be as cunning as Odysseus, and wait
for my enemy to reveal herself."

"You say our enemy is a woman. Because of the potion?"

"No *man* would permit such knowledge. Only women would keep it
alive. My aunt taught me each land has its own recipe for the potion. I
might have guessed the land by the ingredients. A woman *is* at fault
here. I will punish her, someday. I so vow, to the Goddess herself."

She left the room without a backward glance, and gave orders for it
to be sealed. "When your father returns," she promised her daughter,
"we will find vengeance."

Penelope assembled a network of faithful servants who haunted the
harbor for news, rumors, even the most far-fetched tale of Odysseus.
Some servants had friends who were sailors or merchants, and they
searched the harbors of other lands for news of Odysseus or any other
missing lord of Achaia. Penelope made it known that anyone who
brought her word of Odysseus would receive a reward, even if the tale
brought no help.

Rage and purpose helped Penelope regain her strength and put order
back into her days. Handsome young men of noble blood came to her
to express their sympathy and their sorrow. They claimed they had
hoped to court Ktimene when she was grown. Antinoos led them, and
Penelope wondered at the speculation in his eyes when he looked at her
face.

The young men mourned the loss of a bride they had not pursued.
She knew they mourned the loss of hope to rule Ithaka, rather than a
bride. And she knew they would not give up so easily. She vowed to
prepare against the next onslaught. Telemachos stood between the
young nobles and Ithaka. Penelope vowed to do everything in her
power to protect her son.

*   *   *

Less than a moon later, Agelaos came to speak with Laertes. He
brought gifts for Telemachos and asked for Penelope as his wife. The
boy was with his grandfather when the suitor came. He kept quiet and
ran immediately to his mother's rooms when Agelaos left, to report all
to her.

Penelope listened, wondering when Telemachos had picked up the
gift of mimicking voice and posture and face. She ignored the offer of
marriage to concentrate on her son's reaction. Telemachos didn't know
what to think.

"You think I'm rather old to be a bride, don't you?" she asked, when her son had finished his recitation and sat on the rug at her feet.

"No!" The force of his denial answered her clearly.

"I was your age when your father brought me here as his bride. It feels like a lifetime ago because it is. *Your* lifetime, do you see?" Penelope held out her arms, smiling as Telemachos came to her and wrapped his arms tight around her. "Are you worried I'll leave you?"

"But you can't marry anyone," he protested, his voice muffled against her shoulder. "You're married to my father."

"Of course I am. Though I assume Agelaos referred to me as Odysseus' widow, not his wife."

"He did," Telemachos growled.

"Until I see Odysseus' dead body, or hear his spirit call me from the shadow lands, I am his *wife,* not his widow." She squeezed her son close to her side for emphasis. "I won't leave you or your grandfather or our home, until you are a grown man and you *tell* me to marry another man. By then, I will not be at all desirable." To her satisfaction, Telemachos laughed. There had been little enough laughter since Ktimene's death.

"Mother, you will always be beautiful."

"Like your father, it is your love that makes me so." She kissed his forehead, hugged him once more and released him. She sat back in her chair, suddenly weary. Perhaps weary anticipation of the troubles to come? "Your grandfather will want to discuss this with you. Agelaos is only the first, I fear. You two are my protectors until your father returns."

"We have to plan, like warriors?" He brightened at her nod. Telemachos kissed her cheek before he hurried away.

How many men would it take, she wondered, telling her she was a widow and not a wife, before she believed them? Penelope knew she had been right when Antinoos first spoke to her. The young men of Ithaka had not desired *Ktimene* as bride, any more than they wanted her mother now. They wanted Ithaka. Their mothers and grandmothers longed for the old ways; many believed if the old ways were followed there would not have been a war. Penelope knew they would use such feelings to take Odysseus' place and rule Ithaka. If not through his daughter, then his wife.

She had to move carefully. She couldn't reveal she knew their scheme. Telemachos would pay for her mistakes. She had to tread the narrow line between giving her suitors baseless hope and promising herself to someone.

"Athena, help me. Give me wisdom. Give me the words," Penelope whispered, as she got up to stand by the window. "Even if I truly am a widow, I want no other husband. I will hold Ithaka for my son. Help me to hold it."

Penelope had to move carefully and let her suitors know she was amenable only while her son was safe and alive. She couldn't take the throne in her own right. Even if her suitors pledged to support the old ways, she knew it would be a lie. Her new husband would take the power from her hands. Mentor and Laertes would be cast aside, perhaps killed.

"Goddess, I must trust you to bring my beloved home to me. I must trust your solutions and your guidance." Penelope swallowed hard against a sob rising in her throat. "Even though you took my daughter, I must trust you."

*   *   *

More suitors came a week later, arriving in the evening after Laertes sailed for Kephallenia.

Penelope and Telemachos were spending a quiet evening by the hearth. She kept busy with her lap loom while the boy told her stories of hunting with his friends. Argus sat at Penelope's feet, dozing in the warmth from the hearth stones. The dog no longer went out hunting with Telemachos, but stayed in the house and slept at the foot of Penelope's bed. Eurynome answered the pounding on doors that had been closed for the night.

They were five, all rich young men, leaders and the sons of leaders in Ithaka. Antinoos, Eurymachos, Klesippos, Elatos and Leodes. All handsome, skilled, intelligent, and popular. They would all make capable kings.

She signaled Telemachos to remain quiet and listened to the five present their suit. She tried to think how to refuse them without bringing insult on their families or endanger herself and her son. She swore silently none of them would ever take over Odysseus' rule, home or bed.

"Good lords," she said when they finished, choosing her words carefully, "you honor me. I am not a young, tender girl. It is sixteen years since I bore my son. You flatter me that any man could want me for the pleasure of his bed or to adorn his house. But you forget, I am not a widow."

"Any man who would take so long in his homecoming is either a fool or dead," Antinoos said, proving himself leader of the suitors. "Odysseus was never a fool."

"Then bring me proof. I stay faithful to him until the day I join him in the shadow lands."

"Lovely queen, all of Ithaka honors your loyalty, but think of your son," Eurymachos said.

"I do think of my son," she returned, resting her hand on Telemachos' shoulder. Her son stayed by her side, his face carefully neutral as she had taught him. "I will not leave him alone in this house when he is not fully grown, to become a bride in another house."

Penelope hid her smile of triumph when her words brought guilty looks and twitches of surprise from the five. Her suspicions were right. They intended to take over this house, not take their bride to another house. She didn't know whether to be amused, insulted or relieved.

"That is our point," Antinoos said, taking up the thread his companion had dropped. "Your son needs a father."

"He has a father. Odysseus is merely absent."

"He needs a man to train him as a father would."

"Laertes, his grandfather fills that post admirably. He did, after all, raise my son's father to be a great man."

Inside, she seethed. She knew full well what happened to the sons of supplanted or murdered fathers. Even if the man who won her treasured her, he wouldn't hesitate to kill her son to protect the power gained through the marriage. Penelope raged at the foolishness of these men. They thought her a fool, not to suspect every word and gesture and offer.

Their other arguments were weak. It grew hard to be gracious as the conversation continued. Penelope regretted the dictates of hospitality that made her offer them food and drink. To her relief, the men thanked her and refused with cool, polite grace and left. Eurynome barely locked the door behind them when Telemachos turned to his mother, his face bursting with the anger he had held in check.

"You can't marry any of them! I won't let you!"

"You must learn, sometimes we have no control over our destinies. What we want or don't want rarely affects our actions." Penelope wondered why his anger amused her, when moments before she had been so coldly angry herself.

"I'll run away if you marry anyone," he announced, planting himself in front of her, hands on his hips. His fury melted into confusion when Penelope burst out laughing.

"No—oh, Telemachos—please, don't be angry with me," she begged and reached for her son, catching his arm when he would have stalked out of the room. "I'm not laughing at you, but at myself. Please, sit and listen." Penelope moved over on her wide chair so he could sit next to her. She put her arm around him, drawing him close so his head rested on her shoulder. He was so tall now, his shoulders wide with muscle. How much longer could she hold him like this and still feel he was her child, to be taught and protected?

"When I was only a little younger than you," she began, "I could have passed for a boy. A very thin boy. Because of the way my grandfather raised me, I thought I could pretend to be a boy and run away, making my way in the world by hunting, running errands, whatever it took to earn food and shelter."

"You're good with a sling," Telemachos admitted.

"Thank you." She kissed the top of his head. "I didn't want to marry. On the ship bringing me from Alybas to Pylos, to go to Sparta, I actually considered running away."

"But if you did, you never would have married my father," he broke in, dismay coloring his voice.

"Exactly. Though, when I admitted as much to your father, and suggested we might have met and been companions otherwise, he thought it funny." Penelope's voice broke for a moment, a pang running through her at the memory of those happy, tumultuous days after her marriage.

"Maybe we both could run away and look for my father?"

"I think he would want us to stay here and wait for him to come home to us," she said, tightening her arm around him. "After all, right now there is just one person lost, roaming the world. If we left, there would be three."

"If they try to make you marry anyone, Mother, I will run away—but I'll run to look for Father," Telemachos hurried to add.

"If anyone forces me to marry him, I will go with you."

"No, Mother." He laughed. "You're too beautiful to be a boy now."

She laughed and thanked him and then steered the talk elsewhere. Penelope didn't dare hope the subject had closed. As in other things, Telemachos would think long and hard on the problem of her unwanted suitors. Questions would slip from his mouth at the strangest times, months, even years later. She hoped Odysseus would be home by then, to deal with the problem. Eurymachos had been right, however.

Telemachos did need a father, no matter how close to manhood he stood. The guidance provided by Laertes and Mentor was no longer enough.

*   *   *

Only a few days later, Penelope learned neither Telemachos nor her suitors had dropped the subject. Mentor came to see her in her rooms, bringing Telemachos by a strong grip on the boy's arm. Her son's hands were dirty, gritty with sand and mud, his tunic spotted with damp. One look at the man's calm outrage and the boy's sullen anger told her something unusual had happened. Mentor treated Telemachos like one of his own sons, and the boy usually begged to accompany the man on estate business. For them to be angry at each other was unusual.

"Lord Mentor?" Penelope looked up from her weaving. Behind her, she heard the other women putting their work down to listen.

"Lady Penelope, perhaps Laertes would be better suited to handle this, but he is away." Mentor released Telemachos' arm and moved to block the boy's escape. Glaring at the man, Telemachos moved to stand next to his mother.

"What happened, Telemachos?"

"They said you *had to* marry one of them," he mumbled, ducking his head. "I called them liars. The arrogant one said he would thrash me for that, when he became my father."

"And what did you do?" Penelope didn't have to ask who *they* were; arrogant suited all the suitors. She studied his disheveled state. Had Telemachos attacked first, or had the suitors come at him en mass?

"He threw rocks and mud like a beggar's brat!" Mentor blurted. "Such weapons, and the words he used, aren't proper for Odysseus' son."

"You made him apologize to the young men he attacked?" Penelope found it hard not to laugh at the sudden mental image of Antinoos and friends running from a rain of mud and stones, flung by a skilled, accurate, angered boy.

"Those who remained after the first barrage." A half-smile touched the man's face. "His aim is wonderful."

"Unfortunately. Thank you for correcting my son. When his grandfather returns, we will finish the matter." She dismissed Mentor with a smile and nod. He looked relieved to be allowed to leave. When he was gone, she turned to her son, mindful of the listening servants. "Telemachos, we need to take a walk." She smiled at the boy when he hesitated.

They went to her private garden. The wind rustled the leaves of trees and vines sufficiently to cover the sound of their voices if they talked softly. Penelope wished she could rest her hand on her son's shoulder like she used to, but he stood taller than she did now and it felt awkward.

"You know you did wrong," she began. "Stones and mud are a beggar's weapons, or those of a child half your age. And yet, you are young enough to be excused for what you did. Another year and it won't be so."

"Mother, it wasn't what they said, but how they said it. Bragging. Swaggering. Calling you a widow and saying it like they were glad." Telemachos clutched at her sleeve, as if by touch he could make her understand.

"You had provocation, then." She gestured for him to sit on the bench under the olive tree. Penelope stayed standing, amused at the relief of being able to look down at him as she spoke. "I must admit, I am glad you did attack." A chuckle escaped her at the surprise and then relief on her son's face. "But that admission does not go beyond these walls, do you understand?"

"If they think you're angry at me—"

"Telemachos, consider our situation. Your grandfather is old and wants to rest. The death of your grandmother and then Ktimene took much of his strength. He would have followed them if you and I did not need him. He is a wall between us and the men who might take me away. Between you and the ones who would take your inheritance." She paused, waiting until the boy nodded that he understood. "For now, we do have protectors on Ithaka. Yet the longer your father is absent, the more people will expect me to marry again. You are Odysseus' son and Ithaka is yours someday. Until then, it is *my* duty to guard our home and land. We cannot afford to make enemies. Too many, and people might look the other way if anything should happen to you."

"I understand." A hard light touched his eyes. For a moment Odysseus looked out through his son's face, the cold, calculating look of anger that frightened Penelope more than uncontrolled rage in any other man.

"You are Odysseus' son. You must learn to wait and watch and plan like Odysseus. Stealth and guile, Telemachos, are strong weapons. Train your arm for sword, bow and spear, and train your mind to be sharper, faster and stronger. Your father could dissemble and take on faces and voices like a bard, to play people like a harp. You must train to do the same."

*   *   *

Three nights later, Penelope led the rites in the cave, in the dark of the moon. She stayed kneeling when the ceremony ended and the women filed out of the cave. She thought herself alone and it startled her when she stood and turned and found three women waiting, watching her.

"Ithaka needs a king," one said from the shadows of her veil. Penelope tried to place the voice, the posture, but she could not.

"Ithaka has a king," she returned. She tried not to panic, wondering where Eurykleia had vanished to.

"Our land needs a new king. A young, strong one," another woman said. She kept her face carefully hidden too, but Penelope knew her voice. Miriel, aunt of Eurymachos. "A king who is *here* to serve his queen and guard Ithaka."

"My son is heir to his father's place. Ithaka is well served by Mentor and Laertes and the elders, while my son is still a child."

"Ithaka needs a new king!" the first woman insisted. She reached out as if to grasp Penelope's arm.

"Why will you not wait for my son to become a man? How will you choose this new king you want?"

"You have suitors," Miriel said. "Young nobles. Worthy of the kingship. They are willing to follow the old ways, to serve the Goddess."

"They want to be kings, not bridegrooms?" Penelope widened her eyes, trying to mimic how Odysseus pretended innocent surprise and yet put his adversaries to shame for their words. If the trick worked or not, Penelope couldn't tell. Eurykleia came back into the cave and the three women fled before Penelope could say another word.

"Those three harpies mean trouble," the old nurse said, as she handed Penelope her cloak.

"They mean to become the three Fates and dictate the future of Ithaka."

*   *   *

Penelope grew to distrust her dreams. The dreams of Odysseus fell into two patterns. In one, he traveled the seas alone, always journeying but never any closer to home. In the second, he sat on the beach of a jewel-like island. He gazed out over the ocean, longing on his face. A woman's voice hovered in the air, sweeter than the songs of spring birds. From the sound alone, Penelope knew the woman was beautiful. When the song grew strong enough, Odysseus turned from the ocean. Penelope couldn't see his face, but she feared he smiled.

The dream always ended there. Penelope hated the unseen woman and preferred the dream of Odysseus forever sailing and never drawing closer. She didn't know which to believe.

Rumors continued about Odysseus. Some said he was in far distant lands, gathering great wealth. Some said his men had mutinied and killed him on their return to Ithaka and vengeful gods, led by Athena, destroyed the ships in punishment. Some said an exotic queen had made him stay as her king and he had already given her seven sons. Penelope managed to laugh at that rumor the second time she heard it, but not the third or fourth.

More offers of marriage came from the nobles of Ithaka and the surrounding islands which belonged to Ithaka. Penelope politely refused them.

The suitors' tactics changed from gifts and praises to invasion. They came in groups with gifts and provisions for a prolonged stay. With polite words that concealed traps, they asked her to give them time, to talk with them and consider them, and then make her decision. The years of Odysseus' absence were their best argument. Her fears for Telemachos' safety, their hidden weapon.

Though the suitors spoke well of her son and gave him gifts to win his support, Penelope knew one mistake on her part or his could lead to his death. So she played the game with them, struggling day and night for words to prepare against their renewed onslaught of mixed begging, cajolery and flattery. She adorned herself to be her most beautiful and hopefully stir them to jealousy and arguing. Penelope wished they would fight and kill each other. They never did, proving her suspicion that they didn't want a bride, but a throne, and many worked together rather than competing for a prize. She feared they had already divided Odysseus' property among themselves, and only waited for her to accept the man they had chosen as the next king.

How could she reject their praises without insulting them? How could she ignore their publicly repeated concerns for the welfare of Ithaka, without offending the elders?

If she were truly a widow, she should return to her father's house and let him choose another husband for her. Ikarios was dead, so who could she turn to? King Tyndareos had retreated from life since Helen vanished. Could Menelaos, as the king of Sparta, claim authority over her?

Penelope had heard Sparta still waited for its king and queen to return.

Her only other choice was to appeal to her brother, Ithios. He had traveled to Ilion in the war, been injured in the third year, and came home lame and bitter. Penelope wondered what he would say or do when he heard about her siege of suitors. Would he laugh or grow angry? Would he claim authority over her?

Penelope debated for days whether it would do harm or good, to tell the suitors to appeal to her brother to choose her new husband. If they insisted on her making the choice, she would have her proof they wanted Ithaka and not her. Yet there was the terrible chance several did want her more than Ithaka. If they went to Ithios, she would lose what little protection she did have. Penelope had no hope Ithios had softened to her in the past nineteen years. He might deliberately give her to the worst of the lot, or choose without thinking, simply because he was irritated. Or her brother might come to Ithaka as her guardian and claim Odysseus' estates and the throne. She wouldn't put it past her brother to kill her son, and her.

So she held her tongue and endured. Her days were full, trying to keep the routine of the household flowing smoothly while avoiding every man who tried to catch her alone. It made her angry. The constant invasion of the suitors interfered with her household duties. At night, she often cried herself to sleep with hopelessness and longing for Odysseus.

She wished she had let him teach her to use the bow. She would turn his poisoned arrows on her suitors and save the last for herself.

The visits of the suitors extended from days into weeks as summer turned to fall. Their numbers went from an easily handled eight or nine to twenty or so at a time. Eumaios the swineherd had become a friend and confidant of Telemachos over the years and Penelope trusted his opinions. When he complained to her of the damage the suitors' feasts did to the household resources, she knew something had to be done. This was not Sparta, with endless riches to spend on hospitality for moons at a time.

Her choices and resources were limited. She had visions of the suitors rising up and slaughtering Laertes and Telemachos if she ordered them to leave her home forever.

Penelope knew she could gain no help from Mycenae, where Klytemaistra still ruled with her murderous lover. Even if Menelaos and Helen had returned to Sparta, she couldn't ask the warriors to leave the homes they had so soon regained. Penelope toyed with the idea of sending to King Nestor of Pylos to ask his help. She risked angering her people, bringing foreign warriors to Ithaka. Her safety depended on retaining the favor of the people.

Sitting at her loom, weaving and losing herself in the pattern, Penelope thought about Laertes, ill and uncomfortable with a malady he could have ignored a few years before. Her father-in-law showed his years more as the seasons passed, mourning for Odysseus and quietly raging over his inability to cure her difficulties. Penelope looked at her loom and wondered how soon she would string it to weave Laertes' funeral sheet. Then the plan came to her.

She laughed quietly, half in fear, half in delight, when she hurried to Laertes' chamber to consult with him. The old man sat in a chair by the window, wrapped in blankets against the evening chill, gazing out over the orchards he had helped Odysseus plant. Penelope hurried to him and kissed his forehead.

"Father, I have a plan worthy of Odysseus. That is, I think it is one he would approve." She settled down on the floor at his feet, feeling like a girl again, giddy in her glee and relief. "Listen and tell me what you think."

She related to him the thoughts that had been going through her mind, then went on to propose her plan. She would tell the suitors— more than forty now within her walls, along with nearly fifty others who visited at regular intervals—that she had reconciled herself to remarry. However, she would tell them, before she could leave the house in the hands of her son, she had one more duty to perform.

"I will give them some long, involved history of tradition in my grandfather's country, where the funeral sheet must be made with prayers and ceremonies and the finest threads, the costliest dyes. I will tell them I cannot leave my home until I perform my duty to you in weaving that funeral sheet. The gods will torment me, and the man I marry, if you die with nothing proper to wrap you before you are given to the flames. I will warn them it will take years to complete the weaving. The phases of the moons and tides must be propitious. The dyes I use for my threads must come from strange and far-off lands, to be appropriate for so renowned and beloved a warrior as my husband's father. And, I cannot neglect my household duties for the sake of the sheet, or the gods will be angered and torment your soul and mine in the shadow lands. That will keep them away from our doorstep and our hall."

"Until you finish the sheet, Daughter," Laertes said. His eyes showed a spark of hope, despite the words.

"That sheet will never be finished. For every four threads I put in place during the day, I will pluck out one at night. The second I will declare worthless, badly placed. And as I remove it, to my dismay, I will damage threads that remain from previous days." She smiled at him, daring him to disagree, begging him to approve.

"Yes, that will keep the suitors from under our roof." He nodded, a smile starting to creep across his pale features. "Yet there is a problem. If you agreed to choose a new husband, how would I react to your announcement?"

"With anger, I hope." Penelope felt her bubbling relief begin to die. "Oh, I see."

"Yes, after all these years of waiting, I would grow angered at your lack of faith. I would leave this house, go to the house that guards Odysseus' orchards and vineyards, and continue mourning my son." Laertes rested his hand on her head. "My absence would remove what shallow protection you now enjoy."

"But the suitors wouldn't dare press their case. Not when I have promised to choose among them when my duty is done. They would lose honor in the sight of all the people if they overstepped themselves." She sighed and closed her eyes. "Overstepped themselves more than they have already."

"Nevertheless, it is a worthy plan. A deception Odysseus would approve with shouts of laughter. We will follow it." He struggled from his chair, his legs weak from the receding fever. Penelope hurried to stand and support him. "I have one small request in this, Daughter—no, two," he added quickly.

"And they are?" She supported him as he walked to the table. A cup of wine and healing herbs waited for him to take his evening dose.

"Wait until I am strong enough to play my anger to the hilt." His eyes twinkled for a moment in humor. "And do not tell Telemachos of this plan."

"He will be furious!"

"He is still untried and too honest to play the deception we need. His anger, his disappointment in you, will have to be genuine. Wait until he has calmed and cooled, then reveal the plan to him in secret."

"Yes, Father. I understand."

*   *   *

Telemachos kept quiet when she made the announcement three nights later, after the suitors had feasted. He made no attempt to disguise his relief as the men called for the servants to help them pack their belongings, to leave the palace for their own homes. But his eyes, when he looked up and met her gaze, held a glitter that promised a stormy scene in private.

Over the summer, her son had left the kicking and throwing stage behind, adopting his father's cold anger and dangerous patience. He kept his hands at his sides, his voice low and polite when he joined her in her rooms a short time later. The icy fury under his control made her wish he would break something. He surpassed his father's skill in giving his words two edges. Protecting himself from the flattery and disguised threats of the suitors had helped him sharpen that skill. He used it now as a weapon against her, praising her for finding a way to save their household stores from the suitors' stomachs.

"That is of high importance, is it not, my son?" She wished he would pace or move about and break the painful focus of his eyes on her.

She remembered the hurting look his father had given her during their one devastating argument, and how her heart had writhed in guilty agony. Penelope wanted to blurt the truth to him, to see the approval in his eyes, but they weren't alone. She had heard some of her women entertained the suitors in their beds. She didn't know who to trust within her own household.

"Mother, don't twist my words around," Telemachos snapped. He looked away, giving her a moment of relief.

"You are concerned with how their appetites deplete the herds and farms your father left in my care. I want them to remain as rich and prosperous as the day he left, until you are grown and able to take your inheritance."

"Is that all that matters to you? The wealth and prosperity of my father's house? Is that what it means to be a faithful wife? Assuring his goods aren't depleted? What of the promises you made to me, to stay faithful?" Angry tears glistened in his eyes but didn't fall. "You are no better than Klytemaistra. At least she had the courage to show her true feelings."

She slapped him, the sound echoing in the suddenly still room.

279

Telemachos barely flinched, as if he expected it. Penelope stared at the red mark on his face. Her hand stung. Anger boiled in her, at herself, more than her son.

He was justified in his rebuke, she knew. More than anything, she wanted to fling her arms around his neck and confess the truth with tears. Yet sixteen years of waiting and worrying, training her son to be worthy of his father, helped her stay in the role she had chosen.

"My son," she said, her voice soft to disguise the tears that threatened to make it crack. "You are still a child, despite your growth and strength. You are a dreamer. Open your eyes and see the truth." She sat down as her legs began to tremble. "Your father has been gone sixteen years now without a word, without even a message. Everything we know of him, we have heard from rumor. After so long, he is either dead or he has found a home he prefers to this one. Perhaps he has found a wife who pleases him better than I, and has many sons to make him forget the one I almost died to give him.

"Consider this, Telemachos. What man would want to come home to a son another man raised? It is like giving his estate to a stranger. Better for Odysseus to forget his home and make another, and raise the children who will inherit his riches."

"You are so right, Mother." His voice came out thin and harsh. "Hurry with your weaving. I look forward to a silent, empty house." He left before his words faded from the air.

Penelope glanced at her maids. Every one looked away. Some faces bore shock, sympathy, or a mixture of both. Melantho hid her face as if she were crying, but her shoulders didn't shake and she made no sound.

CHAPTER 24

Penelope overheard the discussion between Laertes and Telemachos the next morning, as the old man packed his few belongings to leave. She wondered how he felt, deceiving his grandson, agreeing to every unkind thing Telemachos said about her. Penelope made herself listen to the penetrating, furious voice of her son as it floated up the stairs. She left the doors open as she used to do before the suitors laid siege to her home. Penelope considered where her son's accusations had some grain of truth in them.

Had she lost faith? Was the wealth and prosperity of the household more important to her than keeping herself ready for her husband's return? Had she willingly ignored possibilities open to her?

The quiet that now filled her house made it hard to ignore the doubts and questions circling through her mind. Laertes was gone, taking a few aged servants with him. Penelope felt the censorious looks other servants gave her as the days passed. Telemachos avoided her, spending days at a time at the southern tip of Ithaka with Eumaios, hunting and, she imagined, spilling all his dismay and disgust to the loyal man. Argus was her only companion who didn't look on her with disapproval. Penelope wondered if she were losing her mind, to hope the old dog understood.

She vented her hurt in doubling her exacting standards for her weaving. The dyes the servants purchased from the merchant ships were not good enough. Or if they could be altered to match her tastes, Penelope insisted on handling the dying process herself, and then did what she could to bungle them without anyone suspecting. Those first weeks, she laughed at her stained hands, wondering what Odysseus would say if he saw her. The laughter turned to tears with painful speed.

She had warned the suitors she would not neglect her household duties for the sake of the funeral sheet. Penelope abandoned her weaving room for days at a time, supervising the smallest tasks in the household. When she did go to her loom, she concentrated on clothing and blankets for the household against the coming winter, ignoring the loom that waited, empty, for the sheet to begin. For luck, she had chosen to use the loom Odysseus made when she carried Telemachos. Part of her cried out in silence at the sight of the loom sitting empty.

Finally, she could not avoid stringing the loom and beginning the dreaded task. Penelope bore the disapproving silence from Eurykleia as long as she could. Eurynome, of all the servants, was the only one who didn't display a hint of judgment toward her. She waited nearly a moon's cycle, then called both women to her late at night, after the other servants had gone to bed.

"Eurykleia, Eurynome, if you would—examine the weaving I have done today." Penelope stepped back from the loom to give them room to observe the work closely.

The two women leaned close to examine it in the flickering torchlight. It had cost Penelope dearly to reach that point in her task. The border design was emerging, a bold slash of deep purple against a silver-white background. Change was easy to detect there, if someone had looked closely at it. She had made sure both women saw the pattern a few hours before.

Eurykleia realized the change first. She looked away from the loom, a sharp turn of her head. Tears touched her eyes, wiping away the hard disapproval in the old nurse's face.

"You're taking it apart," she whispered.

"Every night. As many strands as I can manage without anyone realizing the duplicity."

"Oh, my child. Forgive my unseeing heart." The old nurse opened her arms and enveloped Penelope in an embrace that wiped away all the silence and cold between them.

"I am relieved," Eurynome admitted. She kissed Penelope's forehead when Eurykleia had released her.

"Have you told anyone?" the other woman asked.

"Only Laertes knows, because I wanted his approval and help if I had overlooked any flaw." Penelope shivered, wrapping her arms tight around herself. "I am afraid until his anger cools sufficiently, I cannot tell Telemachos. The change in his temper would be too drastic. Someone would suspect and then we would all be lost."

"He is his father's son," Eurykleia said. "Trust him. He will not fail you."

"I do trust him," she countered. "Yet I asked myself, who of everyone here would Odysseus trust, if he advised me in this? His father and the two of you. His mother, if she were alive...I think he would keep the secret even from her. She was always too open with her feelings." Penelope shook her head. "Our son's role in this deception is crucial and he is untested. Odysseus would not take such a risk, no matter how much it hurt him. And neither will I."

*   *   *

Penelope woke, feeling her heart pounding with panic. She lay still, listening with every fiber of her being. In a moment, she recognized the sound. The rising howl of the winter storm woke her. She had thought for a moment she heard voices calling her name. Yet now that she was awake, a nagging sense of something wrong kept her from returning to sleep.

It was not her dream. Not this time. She couldn't remember a fragment of it. Penelope was relieved. When she woke from happy dreams of Odysseus' return or memories of their short years together, she cried for the loss all over again. It had been a long time since she took pains to hide her nightly tears from her servants.

When she had bad dreams, it was no relief to wake. They were warnings of sorrows waiting if she didn't walk carefully. Lately, she had begun another recurring dream. She slept in Odysseus' arms, yet when she turned in their bed to see his face, to smile and kiss him, another man pressed his naked body against hers. His hands were covered with blood, smearing her body, burning her. He had no face she knew. Penelope knew she *would* see that face someday if her weaving failed to keep the suitors from her house.

She nearly leaped from her bed, her heart pounding again. *The loom.* She had fallen asleep before taking apart some of that day's work. Penelope chided herself for that mistake. She had been nightly unraveling her web for nearly four moons now—how could she forget so easily?

The floor was bitterly cold against her bare feet. Penelope took the ache as punishment for her carelessness. She dressed quickly, throwing a blanket around her shoulders against the extra chill in the air. She put no sandals on, in case someone lay awake, listening. Bare feet were more easily kept silent. She lit a lamp from the glowing coals in the brazier by her bed, nearly burning her fingers when the wick caught too quickly. Then Penelope hurried to her weaving room, guarding the flame so it would attract no attention.

She lit more lamps after she shut the door. The cloth glowed softly in the dim light of the flickering flames. All that showed were silver, white and purple, a hand span of border on the very top. Penelope was proud that she remembered how to make the dye that turned threads silver. It took up large amounts of precious time and none of her women but Melantho had mastered the trick yet. It required a deft touch, both in timing the setting of the dye and picking the right threads to take the color. Penelope insisted on using large amounts of silver in the funeral sheet, to properly honor Laertes. Even if she truly did want to finish the cloth, it would take her a year to weave it if she ignored all her other household duties. Penelope made sure she attended to every other duty first. No one could fault her. She hoped.

Sighing, half in contentment at the success of her plan, half in dismay that she could fall off her routine so easily, Penelope set to work. She used the delicate tools Odysseus had made for her during their first winter of marriage to unravel her work. It was only appropriate.

The delicacy of her work required patience and time and concentration. It amused her, in a bitter way, that she used twice as much effort to take the thread from the pattern than to add to it. That was only appropriate, as well.

She had removed five threads before she felt the slight draft in the room. A chill touched her, unrelated to the storm blowing beyond the bronze shutters. Slowly, Penelope put down the tools, straightened and braced herself for whatever trouble would come. She turned to the door.

"Mother?" Telemachos stared at the loom, not at her. He carried no lamp, was barefoot like her, and the blanket he had wrapped around himself slid off his shoulders. The flickering shadows changed his shape, made him look like his father despite his slimness. The tears in his eyes hurt her.

"You should be sleeping," she said, unable to find any other words to say. It was hard to speak to him. They had fallen into the habit of quiet civility, speaking but saying nothing with their mouths or their eyes.

"I dreamed you called me." He finally looked up from the loom and the handful of broken threads on her lap, which she would burn in the brazier in her room. "I went to your room and you weren't there, so I looked for you."

"And what did you find?" she asked, her voice soft to avoid any inflection, any hint of her feelings.

"My mother still loves and still waits for my father. And she protects me against myself." The tears grew bright in his eyes. He came to her and knelt on the floor next to her seat. He wrapped his arms tight around her and pressed his face into her belly, like he had as a little boy who needed comforting. "Forgive me—all this time—I've hated you."

"If you forgive me for deceiving you," she murmured, reveling in the feel of his arms around her, the heat of his tears soaking into her dress. "Your grandfather and I didn't want to hurt you, but for the sake of the deception—" She broke off when Telemachos sat back, dismay on his face.

"He knew? The things he said against you—the things *I* said against you!"

"Hush!" She fought a chuckle of relief and pressed two fingers across his lips. "Would you wake the whole household and have them know?"

Telemachos grinned, shaking his head. He hugged her again, harder, whispering, "Mother, I love you. I am proud to be your son. Whatever you ask, I will do."

"Can you pretend to be angry with me for a little while longer?"

"How much longer?"

"A few more moons. Then say you are reconciled to losing me. You are almost grown and will take a bride someday. It will be easier if your mother is not here to challenge your wife's authority." She twisted her face into a mask of disapproval. Telemachos laughed, muffling the sound behind his hand. "Tell them you can see it will take years to finish the funeral sheet for your grandfather. You are satisfied with how things stand and even if you haven't forgiven me, you are no longer angry."

"More angry at myself, for doubting you. For not finding a way to free you of those suitors myself."

"You have always done more than any other son would. Now, go back to your bed before someone realizes you are gone. If they search for you, they will discover our secret. In the morning, if the storm has settled, go see your grandfather and tell him. He will be relieved."

Later, when she was back in bed, the betraying threads safely burned to unidentifiable ashes, Penelope let the tears of relief come. Telemachos' pride was precious to her. She imagined it an echo of Odysseus' approval.

*   *   *

The seasons flew by too quickly for Penelope's taste. Occasionally, a suitor came to the house and politely asked to see the progress of the burial sheet. While there was some progress visible since the last visit, no one questioned her or remarked on how slowly it grew. Yet the sheet did grow.

Penelope purposely planned it large, for a man twice Laertes' height and weight. Yet it still crept toward completion. Even when she considered that three years had gone by since she crafted her plan, she was not satisfied.

*   *   *

Penelope opened the shutters in the wall opposite her bed, welcoming the warm spring night. She dressed and pulled the lamp from its niche, where the flame couldn't be seen until she needed it. Her thoughts were more on her son this night than the weaving she went to unravel. Telemachos was twenty years old this spring. He carried many of a man's responsibilities. Maybe it was time to seek a bride of proper family for her son. He wouldn't want to marry for several more years—his father had claimed her after he was twenty-five—but it was good to start planning early.

She smiled as she entered her weaving room, and hummed a few notes to herself from a song Telemachos had taught her that evening. Penelope set down her lamp and retrieved the others to light them. She considered the sheet for a moment. It had progressed in three years to little more than half its intended length. She was proud of its intricate design. She had accomplished a particularly beautiful section that day, all in blue and red and green, and she felt a flicker of regret in having to remove most of it. Penelope shook her head at the cold comfort that she would recreate the design in the morning. She settled down at the loom and pulled the first thread free.

The door banged open, torchlight spilling into the room along with six men. For a moment she stared, unwilling to believe anyone would intrude, in the dead of night, into her private rooms.

They were suitors, not servants. Antinoos led them, his golden handsome face twisted in a sneer. He stepped toward her, his hand raised as if he would slap her. Penelope refused to cower. She snatched up the tiny knife Odysseus had made, determined to fight if the man touched her.

Antinoos paused, a flicker of uncertainty crossing his face. Her angry glare held him off like a wall of stone. He looked to the loom, with the thread half pulled from its place. A grin of triumph wiped away his hesitation.

"Proof!" he shouted. He reached for Penelope and she slashed at him with the tiny knife. He leaped out of her reach with an agility that made her shiver.

"You dare to touch me in my own home?" Her fury covered the terror at being discovered.

"As you dared to lie to the noble guests in your home," Eurymachos responded, the next intruder to step forward.

"I did not lie. I said when the sheet was finished, properly made for my husband's father, then I would choose a new husband." Penelope straightened on her bench, pressing her lips into a thin smile to hide their trembling. "I never promised the work would be finished."

Antinoos snorted in short, bitter laughter. He gave her a grudging bow of respect. "Well-spoken and well-planned. We will keep you to your promise. You *will* finish the sheet."

Shouts rose from the stairs, silencing her response. Penelope froze when she recognized Telemachos' voice. She knew her face went pale and hoped the shadows hid that. The struggle went on a few more heartbeats, then the men parted and let her son through to her.

"Do you try to kill my son in the night as well?" she asked, keeping her voice as cold as she could manage.

Telemachos had come running, barefoot, wearing only a hastily wrapped loincloth. His hair was tangled from sleep and he bore a few red patches on face and chest that would turn to bruises. He stood before her, blocking her from the view and reach of the angry men.

"Tell the boy not to interfere in the discussions of adults," Eurymachos said, his voice a lazy drawl. Penelope saw the stiffening in Telemachos' shoulders and prayed her son controlled his expression.

"Leave my mother be," he growled. Some men backed up, though they were fully dressed and carrying torches and knives, while Telemachos was practically naked before them.

"We will leave her be if she continues to weave. As long as the funeral sheet for Laertes continues to grow. And does not shrink," Antinoos added, snarling.

"Shrink?" Telemachos' voice held enough question Penelope could almost have believed him. He turned to her, his eyes asking if she were all right. She nodded slightly. "Mother, what are they saying?"

"Your lovely mother is not as eager to become a bride as we all thought," another man called from the back of the shadowy group at the door.

Amphinomos, Penelope thought his name was. Even after almost three years of partial peace, she could still remember their names and faces and voices. The short years of respite had not been long enough.

"She cuts apart at night what she puts onto her loom during the day," Antinoos continued. "For the peace and satisfaction of the guests in your house, royal Telemachos, move your mother's loom to a more open place. Where we all can see her working during the day, and where she cannot reach it at night to unravel it."

"And if I do not comply?" Telemachos stepped to the side to stand by his mother, one hand resting on her shoulder. "You will place a guard over her and her work, or invade my house once again? Do you intend to eat and drink us into emptiness?"

"The queen has given her word; when the funeral sheet for Laertes is finished, she will choose her husband," Eurymachos said. He smiled, bowing to Penelope, ignoring Telemachos. "It would be best if she chose a strong man, one who holds the hearts and approval of Ithaka. One who can lead them through danger. A man who would appreciate a cunning, beautiful wife."

"I have given my word," Penelope admitted, her words slow as she searched for the right thing to say. She bit back the impulse to plead with them not to take her from her home. The expected response would be a promise, and a veiled threat against her son's life. "Leave my rooms, leave my son's house. In the morning, you may return and witness that my loom is moved to the hall. Each evening, my suitors may come and watch me work. The web will not shrink while their eyes are turned away, I promise you. When it is finished and washed and sent to Laertes' household, then I will decide on a husband. And you all must abide by that decision," she added, her voice hard.

"We will. If you wish, we will make our oaths on sacrifices to all the gods," Antinoos added.

"No. That is foolishness." Penelope couldn't repress a shudder at the image his words called up. Memories of Helen, the oaths given before her marriage to Menelaos, and the tragedy that had come of those oaths.

When the men had left and the room was dark with shadows and the few flickering spots of light from her lamps, then she cried. Telemachos held her, his voice tight and sharp as he promised dire punishment on whoever had betrayed their secret and let intruders into their house.

"We can send to Sparta," he urged. "King Menelaos is home, the traders say. You are Helen's cousin. She would send help, wouldn't she?"

"Perhaps. But if I sent for help, our enemies would hear of it. Even if Menelaos came at the head of an invading fleet, would it be in time to save us?"

Telemachos smiled, though his lips trembled and angry tears touched his eyes. "Is it too late to pretend you are a boy, and run away?"

That night, Penelope dreamed of Odysseus sitting on the beach while beautiful singing filled the air. Yet there was a difference. He stared out over the ocean and wept.

*   *   *

In the morning, Penelope watched her servants. Some wore open relief at discovering the game she had played. Some dared praise her for the trick. She knew she had gained and regained the loyalty of many because of her actions. She heard Odysseus' name spoken in whispers on smiling lips. But it was the delight dancing in Melantho's eyes which caught her attention. The woman ran to greet Antinoos when he came to supervise the moving of the loom.

"Is it for revenge, then?" Penelope whispered when she escaped to her bed that evening. "For slighting you, when you thought you deserved a better position? For keeping you from marrying one of your sweethearts in Alybas? For Aias, because you blamed his death on Odysseus?" She shook her head, closed her eyes and let the angry tears slip from under her lids. "Were you the one who taught my daughter to make the potion that killed her? Melantho, I will not punish you now. I will not give you the satisfaction of seeing my anger. I swear, the day I must go to another man's bed, you will not follow me. I will leave you to Telemachos' cold mercy. Not even for the sake of your father will you be spared." More tears escaped. Penelope hid her face in her sheets, to muffle the sobs.

*   *   *

Three moons later, as summer began to relent its most oppressive warmth, Penelope neared the end of the weaving. She had used the press of her other duties in the household as an excuse not to touch the loom. Yet thread by thread, the sheet grew to completion.

On a hot night after she put the first purple thread into the bottom border, Penelope dreamed of Odysseus. Her first dream in many long moons differed from the two dreams of eternal journeying, or her husband sitting on the island beach.

Odysseus rode a raft of planed logs instead of his familiar, black-keeled ship. Joy lit his face despite the stormy seas around him. He knelt low on the raft, holding the rudder with an arm that bulged with straining muscle. The wind whipped rain into his face and he laughed into it.

Penelope cried in her sleep and the tears blended into a gentler rain in her dream. This was the Odysseus she remembered best, rejoicing in challenge, loving life. She longed to reach out to him, to brave the danger at his side.

The crashing, tossing waves threatened the raft but he held on and beat the growing storm. Thunder crashed, the sound seeming to lift the waves higher, sending the fragile raft flying. Penelope watched Odysseus look around, straining to see through the rain slashing in his face, and he struggled to guide his raft. The waves lifted it again, carrying it high, sending it crashing down so she thought she would see it hit the floor of the sea.

Odysseus lost his grip on the rudder, falling hard against the logs, sprawled flat for a moment. Then the rise of the waves flung him into the air. He grabbed at the ropes on the mast and they tore free in his fingers like charred threads. The raft spun as he tumbled into the sea. His head did not break the surface.

Penelope sat up, tears streaking her face, muffling her scream with her fist against her mouth. One last image remained from her dream. The raft spun in dizzy circles, sucked into a massive whirlpool. As it went down, it crumbled to pieces.

"He is dead," she blurted into the darkness, her voice thin, strained from the effort not to scream. The oppressive heat of the night felt chilly, like the land of the dead. There was no other interpretation for the dream. All her prayers for help, for guidance, had brought this answer.

Then anger touched her. Penelope refused to believe the dream. After all this time, how could she believe anything she dreamed? After all, she had once dreamed she bore Odysseus two sons. The second had never come.

"I need better proof than the dreams of a fool," she told the darkness. Anger gave her strength. "If I ask my suitors for proof, the brutes would find a red-haired man and bring me his battered head." She snorted in bitter laughter at the thought. "Proof no one can falsify. Then when I know he is dead, I will join him." She shivered again, despite the heat of the night. Far off, thunder rumbled, promising a storm and relief.

As she lay back down, the answer came to her, as if spoken in Odysseus' own voice. The bronze and horn bow of Iphitos, which no hand but its rightful owner could bend until given away in friendship. Or until the owner's death.

Penelope made her resolve and let the tears come, but she had no more left to cry that night. As she waited for sleep, she whispered prayers to Athena that the first arrow loosed from the bow would fly wild and strike her heart.

*   *   *

The day Penelope finished the sheet and took it off the loom, the suitors returned in full force to feast in her hall. She washed the sheet and hung it to dry in her private garden, then gave it into Eurykleia's and Eurynome's hands, to carry among the suitors to view as they ate. She kept to her rooms all that day, refusing to see anyone but faithful Autonoe. Telemachos didn't come to visit her in her rooms, and she understood. He needed to be strong to hold the unreadable mask he had learned from her, to face the suitors as they returned for their feasting and wooing. If he spoke with his mother that first day, he would lose his resolve.

Penelope heard the songs and shouts of the suitors in the hall below her, though every door between her and them was shut fast. She shuddered and worked at her loom, trying to block her thoughts from the present moment. She worked on her own funeral sheet, resolved to die the moment her unwanted bridegroom tried to claim her. She worked quickly, weaving her tears into it with dark shades to express her sorrow. Among the shadows, she wove scenes of remembered happiness with Odysseus. Only a keen eye, told what to look for, would

291

ever see the details.

Now, so sure of victory, the suitors indulged in rudeness to the household and neighbors. They openly told Penelope's women when to come sleep with them. They brought a burly, cruel beggar with them, named Irios, who let no other beggars near the house. Irios was a pet for them, to wrestle with pitiful wrecks for their amusement, run errands and hurl abuse at anyone who opposed the suitors' wishes. Penelope made no protests, though she knew Telemachos burned to do something. She didn't care. Soon, it would all be over.

Autonoe brought her the news that the suitors had ordered Odysseus' bedchamber opened and new ropes strung in the frame of the bed. Penelope froze, her breath nearly stolen by the horror and anger and renewed sorrow that combined in her heart. This was the final proof they wanted Ithaka, not a bride. They would take the king's wife, marry her off against her will, and the new bridegroom would claim her body in the king's bed.

"I know my path now," she whispered, after sending her maid away. "Yes, the bed will be readied. When I am dead, Eurykleia and Eurynome will wrap my body in the sheets spread on that bed, and use its wood for my funeral pyre."

*   *   *

"Telemachos is gone?" Penelope stared at Eurykleia. At the back of her mind, she congratulated herself on her control. Her face and voice showed little of the terror spilling through her body, like flames on a river of oil. She hoped she only showed surprise. Melantho was in the room. "How can he go without taking leave of me?" she asked.

The image of a band of suitors overtaking her son on some errand filled her mind. Penelope could well believe they would kill Telemachos, hide his body, refuse him funeral rites, then give out a story that he had gone on a journey. It would be easy to believe. Since childhood, Telemachos had spoken of taking a fast ship and searching for his father. Penelope wished now she had taken his suggestion, the two of them traveling the world to search for Odysseus.

"He said he didn't want you to worry for him or talk him out of leaving," the old nurse said, keeping her voice low. She chanced a sideways glance at Melantho. "As well, he hoped to stop his enemies from knowing his destination and keeping him from reaching it."

"Then he does go in search of his father." Penelope nodded. She managed a smile. "My son is nearly a grown man. What he does, he

292

need not answer to me any longer." She sighed. "Thank you, Eurykleia. Did he say when he hoped to return?"

"He only said his journey was long."

Penelope nodded, dismissing the woman. Her thoughts spun as she returned to her sewing. It felt useless to keep working on the embroidered sleeves of Telemachos' new tunic. She wanted to have it ready for him for the new moon festival, but he would be elsewhere, now.

Pylos? Her thoughts turned to the possible route her son took. It made sense. She had told him often what a good friend and staunch supporter good King Nestor was to his father. It was the sensible place for Telemachos to start his search.

If her son actually searched. Maybe he left to give her an excuse not to announce the contest of the bow. Until he returned, she couldn't leave the house for another man's home. Telemachos had to give his mother permission to leave his protection. The only other person able to do that was Laertes and the old man never left his estates now. He didn't have to pretend the sorrow that made him weak.

Her pride in her son's actions vanished when she deduced what he had done. Penelope knew more than her suitors suspected. Many wished Telemachos dead with his father. Telemachos' absence was the opportunity they wanted, to let them kill him.

Penelope hid her new fear. She hurried to Athena's shrine and spent long hours there in prayer and tears.

She had need of her prayers. Autonoe came to her in the evenings, repeating what she overheard from the suitors in their feasting and boasting. The men who had promised not to harm Telemachos now plotted to lay in wait for his return, to kill him. They had sent a ship and provisioned it, to await Telemachos and his daring friends.

Penelope could do nothing. Even if she knew where her son had gone, any messenger she sent would be waylaid. Perhaps killed.

*　　*　　*

Five nights later, Penelope dreamed she stood in the courtyard, watching her twelve white geese feeding on the corn she tossed to them in slow handfuls.

A shadow drifted by overhead, a small speck that grew larger as it passed back and forth over the courtyard. She looked up, blinded by the sun. Her geese did not notice or take fright. Then the shadow left the sky, transforming into an eagle that swooped down, breaking the neck of the goose standing nearest to Penelope.

She watched, transfixed with horror and a strange, compelling fascination, as the massive golden and black eagle killed all the geese. Before even one could make a sound or lift their wings to escape, they were dead.

The eagle landed in the courtyard, perching on the body of the first goose it had killed. Penelope watched, still caught in fascination, though a cold fear began to move through her when the eagle focused one large golden eye on her. She opened her mouth to cry aloud.

"Have no fear, Penelope, daughter of Ikarios, most virtuous among all women," a mellow, warm voice said. It penetrated to her heart, coming from everywhere around her. "Your geese are not truly killed, but are the suitors. This eagle of portent is Odysseus, come home in vengeance."

Penelope woke, hearing the honking of her geese as if something had frightened them out of their feeble wits. Dim dawn light peered through the bronze shutters. She hurried to fling them open. Down in her garden, the twelve geese scurried in frightened circles, honking at one another, flapping their wings as if they would fly away at any moment. Penelope thought she caught a shadow moving across the ground, but when she leaned far enough out the window to see up into the sky, nothing moved there as far as she could see.

CHAPTER 25

Eumaios brought Penelope the news when Telemachos returned weeks later. Someone warned him of the suitors waiting in ambush and he came home by a route they didn't expect. The man hinted a god had taken a hand in the escape. In the weeks between his disappearance and the swineherd's news, Penelope wondered sometimes if it were better her son never returned. She almost wished for a message from him, saying he had met old friends of his father's and had decided to go adventuring with them, or some war chieftain had adopted her son. Even living a life of battle, moving from place to place to fight off the seasonal raiders was a safer life than waiting in his father's home to be killed by his mother's suitors.

Or so she thought, until she knew her son had come home. She smiled and later told Eurykleia that Odysseus could not have done it better. Her delight grew when she noticed the suitors' disappointment, though she knew their anger at Telemachos would not let them miss the next opportunity.

Still, she wished her son had not returned. Now it was time to bring out the bow and begin the contest that would end her torment once and for all.

When the suitors left off their feasting for the night, whether to go to their homes in Ithaka or the beds they had appropriated in her house, Penelope ventured from her rooms with Autonoe. By the light of a single lamp, they went to the private storeroom, which Penelope had not unlocked in years.

In the dark room, Penelope examined the ox-hide cover on the bronze bow. Dust lay thick on it, showing no one had disturbed it since the last time she had touched it. She slid the cover off, listening to it crack and creak its stiffness. The bronze was dark from disuse. She polished it, rubbing hard with the sleeve of her robe. Soon it took on a dull glow, nothing like when Odysseus had played his game of skill for her entertainment.

She examined the arrows to be sure the shafts were still straight, the tips still secure. She contemplated the bundle of poisoned arrows, the black thong still tight around them. Penelope considered leaving the poisoned arrows for her suitors to use in the contest. Shaking her head, she took the bundle out and wrapped it in her veil. All the gods were against her nowadays. She would hide all the arrows, not just the one she intended for herself. If she left poisoned arrows with clean, someone would use them against Telemachos.

Her task finished, she nodded to Autonoe. The serving woman went to the door and looked out into the dark hall. When she signaled all was clear, Penelope followed her out and locked the door. In two days, she would bring the bow out for the contest. Penelope hoped the house would burn down before then.

*   *   *

When Telemachos returned late the next morning, Penelope greeted him with tears. Something had happened during his journey, she could tell from looking at him. For a moment the calm, stern mask he wore slipped aside and she saw jubilation in his eyes. He kissed her and promised to tell her all his story in a short while. First, he wanted to bathe and eat and make preparations for guests coming to the house. Penelope followed his directions and refrained from asking more questions. Her son had a plan and she counseled herself to be quiet and wait.

Mentor and some elders of Ithaka came to eat with Telemachos, to hear the news he had learned in his travels. Penelope sat in her chair in the shadow of a pillar at the foot of the stairs, to listen and spin thread while the men talked. She was proud of how her son spoke with the elders. Among the suitors, he maintained a neutral silence for safety. Here among men who honored him as his father's son, he spoke wisely.

He told them of Pylos, how King Nestor prospered. He spoke of the harvests waiting on the mainland, the condition of the roads between Pylos and Sparta. When he spoke of meeting Menelaos and Helen, staying in their home during Hermione's wedding feast, Telemachos met his mother's eyes for the first time. His gaze promised messages and news for her ears alone.

Penelope was content to wait. She had sometimes wished evil on the woman whose actions had robbed her of so much. Now, too much time had gone by. Penelope told herself to forget the past. It was unchangeable and her bitterness would never affect Helen.

After the elders left, Telemachos came to her rooms. He told her about the presents Helen had sent, for him to give his own bride when he found her. He told her the curse Menelaos spoke against the suitors, and the prophecy he had been given of Odysseus' return.

"If a god says my father is still alive, struggling for his homecoming, then it must be so," Telemachos concluded. There was a strange glint in his eye, as if there was more he wished to say. Penelope waited for him to continue but he said nothing.

"You said Menelaos learned this news long ago, before he rescued Helen a second time." She rested her hands on the arms of her chair, studying the carved owls as if she had never seen them before. The words hurt, but she had to speak them. "Things change. Even Zeus has uttered prophecies through his oracles that did not come to pass."

"Mother, believe me, please. Wait a little longer. Just another day or two. Please?" Telemachos knelt before her chair, taking both her hands in his. He pleaded with mischievous joy in his eyes, like when he was a small boy asking for treats he knew would make him ill.

"One more day. Tomorrow, I announce the test of the bow. Then we will know if your father is alive or dead. Then it won't matter." A bitter laugh escaped her. She felt tired, longing for her bed and the momentary, sweet deception of her dreams.

"One day is all I need." He laughed at her frown and leaped to his feet. He kissed her forehead and cheeks and hurried from the room. Before he left, he called back, "I have a guest coming, a beggar Eumaios befriended. He has news of my Father you should hear."

Penelope nodded and closed her eyes. Was that the cause of his high spirits? More gossip, more false hopes? She wished she hadn't filled his head with tales of his father when he was little. Her son had more faith in Odysseus' tenacity and cunning than she did.

For a moment, Penelope thought she heard an owl calling outside her window. A shadow moved across her room. She thought someone entered but before she could turn to look, she leaned her head back in her chair and slept.

When she woke, the suitors had arrived for their feast. As had become her habit since the sheet was finished, Penelope prepared herself to face them for a short time. She took pains to make herself beautiful, desirable, on the slim hope that even now she might sow seeds of discord among them.

She put a veil as light as mist over her hair and face after her maids adorned her with jewels. Penelope knew it hid little, but the veil tantalized the men with a sense of more to see. It gave her a feeling of security from their bold, probing gazes. With Autonoe and Hippodameia as attendants, she sat in her chair at the foot of the stairs and let the suitors begin their usual round of praises, flattery and cajolery.

While she gave half her attention to the words, Penelope surveyed the hall. Every suitor sat in his accustomed place, organized by the rank they had established among themselves. Telemachos sat near the back of the hall, by the smaller hearth. He had chosen the spot before the suitors could relegate him to the anonymous place. At the time, Penelope had applauded his tactics. Now she wished her son sat at the front of the hall by the larger hearth, to be near her.

Movement by the doors caught her eye. She saw Eumaios lead a man in, the beggar Telemachos had mentioned. Penelope smiled, seeing how one faithful household woman hurried to meet the two men. Eumaios followed the woman out of the hall but the beggar came further into the room, hands outstretched in the customary manner. Penelope frowned, wondering what happened to the beggar Irios, who usually sat by the doors. He was a big man with a twisted foot and she had heard many complaints that Irios beat other beggars who approached her door. She wondered how this beggar had escaped Irios' rough hands.

She studied him, ignoring more cajolery heaped on her. They were the same words used the day before, and the days before that. As if the suitors could not find any new words to speak to her, any other thoughts in their heads.

The beggar had wide shoulders under his rags and dirt. They were stooped now with age and harsh living, but she thought they once might have been powerful. He shuffled when he walked, like he had damaged his leg in the past. There were many men in Ithaka who shuffled like that, the few warriors lucky enough to come home early, injured in the battle against Ilion. The beggar's hair was so thin, faded from age and rough living, Penelope couldn't guess what color it might have been. The same for his beard.

His head, when it was not bent in a placating way, had a noble bearing. She could imagine a plumed helmet sitting on that head. Many men had tumbled from glory through wounds, wars lost and lands fallen into someone else's hands. She felt pity for the man, whoever he might be. That Telemachos and Eumaios both wanted to help him spoke well for his character. She resolved to send for him later and speak to him. If only to delude herself for a little while that Odysseus might be coming home.

Then the beggar looked up and met her gaze. His eyes were large, gray, piercing. They didn't belong in that haggard, abused face. Penelope felt herself being tested and probed by those eyes, as if the man knew the thoughts in her deepest heart. She looked away, frightened yet drawn to the man. When she looked back, he had moved on, standing with his back to her. The feelings that ran through her were hard to understand. She couldn't sit still any longer.

"I am wearied of this pretense we play," she said, standing and interrupting Leodes' speech. Penelope doubted anyone minded. He said the same words every night. "Why should I sit here night after night and listen to words that mean nothing? How can you speak praises to me, woo me, when it does not come from your heart? You claim you despoil my son's house for love of me. Your actions do not speak love, or else you would listen when I say I will not marry another man."

"You have given your promise, queen of Ithaka," Antinoos called from the center of the gathering.

"Yes, given my promise. Brought to it by desperation. I will set the contest among you soon, so the will of the gods will choose my new husband. On that very day, I will leave this house where I was such a happy bride. Until then, I wish to see none of you or hear your voices boast of deeds you never accomplished and love you don't feel. Some of you, I know, take pleasure in knowing I fill my bed with tears every night, mourning my husband who stood above all men on Ithaka who live now and who were ever born."

In the silence created by her words, Penelope left. She struggled to keep her feet steady, her back straight, her poise intact. Before she had gone halfway up the steps, the suitors erupted in talk. She caught fragments of their words, admiring her spirit. A few expressed, loudly, their longing to take her as bride. Penelope wondered if they were drunk already or if she had finally created some wedge in their accords.

Aktoris, her newest maid met her at the top of the stairs with the news that Argus had been found dead outside the doors of the feasting hall. Penelope stopped short, unable to feel anything for a moment. She closed her eyes against tears.

"My husband's house slowly falls to pieces around me," she murmured. "Is it a sign from the gods that it is time to move on?" she said, turning to Autonoe.

"Mistress, should I tell Telemachos?" the girl asked.

"No. He would be hurt and the suitors would mock him for caring. Find Eumaios the swineherd. Tell him to take Argus away and give him the funeral rites of a hero." Penelope lifted her veil and used the edge to wipe away the stubborn tears. She didn't care that her maids saw. "That dog was more faithful than many people I have known. Perhaps he will find his master in the shadow lands." She went to her room, closed the door and laid herself down on her bed to cry. Her sobs were quiet because she had no strength to be loud.

When her maids brought up the renewed flood of presents from the suitors, Penelope quieted to listen to them talk. She thought about the herds of swine and cattle slaughtered to feed the suitors and knew no matter how rich the presents they heaped on her, they could never repay the damage done to her home. She lay still and refused to answer when one maid after another knocked on her door to bring her out to see the gifts. After a time, she managed to sleep, her eyes wet with tears.

After the suitors had left for the night, Penelope returned to the feasting hall. Eurynome had done as she asked and made sure Telemachos' beggar guest had food and drink to satisfy him and offered him a bed for the night.

Something inside her shivered in fearful anticipation of talking with the man and she couldn't understand herself. Likely, he would repeat some story she had heard before. If she was lucky, he would use his imagination and add new details to prove his story true. She would give him sandals and a cloak if his story deceived her for a few seconds. A few moments of wishing belief were worth the price.

The man sat by the dying fire when she reached the bottom of the stairs. For a moment, she thought her eyes had deceived her in the hall that afternoon. The shadows gave him dark, thick hair and beard, touched with red. The dirt of travel and harsh living that stained him didn't appear in the flickering firelight. For a moment he was a man twenty years younger, bronzed from the sun, strong with good living and hard work. Then the beggar shifted in his seat by the fire and looked at her. The illusion faded, leaving him stooped and gray.

Penelope was glad the shadows hid his piercing eyes.

Eurynome brought her chair from the pillar by the stairs and Penelope greeted the beggar graciously, asking if her household had treated him as a guest deserved. The man spoke well, proving he had indeed fallen from noble station.

"My name is Aithon of Sikania," he said, when she asked his name and birthplace. A spark of humor touched those gray eyes, meeting hers for a fleeting moment before he turned his face back into the shadows.

Penelope shivered, thinking she saw anticipation in those eyes. Was his name significant? She thought she had heard that name before. But where?

The man described Odysseus as he had seen him several years before, when his own fortunes were much better and he feasted with kings and lords as an honored guest. Aithon claimed Odysseus had been long delayed in his return home, all his companions killed by treachery, his treasures destroyed by the perils of the sea. Odysseus was coming home, but taking his time to collect new treasures so that his welcome would be sweeter.

Penelope smiled at the story. This was something new, as if the man had actually met Odysseus instead of repeating what others had fabricated in hope of a gift. She could believe her husband, deprived of his spoils from Ilion, would pause in his homeward journey to gather more treasure.

The beggar went on to describe the clothes Odysseus had worn at the feast where they met. The deep purple cloak in two layers that she had given him when he left for Ilion. The tunic of muted gold, rose and purple, of thread so fine it was almost sheer, the dyes she had mixed with her own hands. She felt the tears coming into her eyes, sorrowing that she had never seen Odysseus wearing those clothes.

The tears stopped when Aithon described the pin that held the cloak.

"A master craftsman made the pin," Aithon said. "Many who saw it wanted it, and offered your lord husband the bounty of entire ships. An amazing piece, made so that when it closed, it looked like a hound strangling a hare. Odysseus would not part with it. He said his beloved wife's father had made it. His wife had given it to him for luck and he was determined to give it into her keeping again when he returned home."

"That is proof no man has ever offered me," Penelope whispered, her voice choked as she fought sobs. "My love swore he would never wear those clothes, never let any other see that pin, until he was on his homeward journey. So many spoke false words, hoping to comfort me or for their own profit." She fought the tightening of her throat. "Noble sir, that is proof undeniable you have seen my dear husband. Please, tell me if you have heard any word of him since."

"Only rumors, carried from one ship to another." Aithon shook his head, settling further into the shadows. His voice had a scratchy rumble, as if he twisted his throat to change the sound. Penelope wondered she had not heard it before. She sensed if he spoke just a little louder, she would know his voice.

"You have brought me comfort, knowing that even a few years ago, my husband was alive and happy and honored. Ask of me, and I will give you a sword and sandals, clothes and gold, and passage on a ship to anywhere you wish. This on top of the guest gifts my son gives you." She smiled at the man and was startled to see a momentary gleam of tears in his eyes before he turned his face to the shadows once more.

"Thank you, gracious queen. Your kindness and gratitude are food, drink and shelter enough for me. Your son has been too generous with this old, worn out wreck. You have an overbearing burden of guests in this house, I can see, and I would not take what you cannot spare."

"Then let me order a bath and clean clothes for your comfort this night, at least."

"Again, my thanks." Aithon shook his head. She thought his voice mellowed for a moment, growing richer, touched with humor. "It is no wonder every man wishes to claim you as bride, if you are so kind to the meanest beggar. I must refuse. The gods have seen fit to put me in this condition and until they raise me from it, I will not permit myself the comforts of more noble men. If you will, let an old servant of this house bathe the road's dust from my feet and I will be more than happy."

"As you please. My husband's own nurse will tend you." Penelope signaled for Eurykleia. She knew the woman had been listening, though pretending to tend to work on the other side of the hall. The old nurse nodded approval when Penelope explained what she wanted.

Penelope turned her head when the beggar hunched over, visibly uncomfortable when another torch was brought. She thought she understood. If he had once been a noble, rich man who had guested with kings, he would not want his hostess to see the full extent of his fallen condition revealed by torchlight. She tended to other work, giving instructions for the morning to the servants while Eurykleia bathed the man's feet in an old bronze basin.

The clatter of the basin and Eurykleia's gasp startled Penelope. She looked back, catching a glimpse of the beggar drawing his foot back under his rags. Feeling shame for the woman's clumsiness, Penelope turned her back on the proceedings. She heard the hissing of urgent whispers and imagined Eurykleia apologizing, Aithon assuring her he was not angered.

There was a graciousness about the man, Penelope decided, a turn of phrase in his speech that proved he had indeed once spoken with kings. She pitied him his fall and his humble condition. Despite his refusal, she determined that he would indeed have new clothes and everything else she had promised him. Even if it was the last command she gave before she joined Odysseus in death.

CHAPTER 26

The next morning, Penelope woke to chanting. She lay still, listening as priests walked through Ithaka, calling blessings on every household. It was a feast day, sacred to three different gods and their consorts. She took it as a good omen for the day.

With Autonoe, Penelope went to the storeroom in full view of the household, unlocked the door and brought out the bow and quiver of arrows. Again, she debated whether to return the poisoned bundle to the quiver and let the Fates dictate the day's outcome. If she had finally roused division among the suitors, maybe she had hope. Especially if the contest of the bow didn't prove easy for them. She smiled despite the grisly scenes in her imagination as she returned to her rooms with the bow. Penelope retrieved the poisoned arrows from their hiding place and kept back one to hide in the sheets of her bed. She shook the quiver, to mix clean arrows with tainted.

When the suitors arrived in mid-afternoon, she gave them time to enjoy their games of skill, to listen to Phemios play his harp and to begin feasting. Then, carrying Odysseus' bow, she went to face the suitors.

Several stood when she came into sight. Penelope refused the chair that waited for her. She would meet her destiny on her feet. She set the bow across the arms of the chair, took the quiver from Autonoe and leaned it against the chair. Then she looked around the feasting hall, taking time to gather her thoughts before speaking. She saw the beggar sitting on the steps leading to the doors with a basket of food by his side. She allowed a bitter smile. The suitors were generous enough with food that didn't belong to them.

"Noble men of Ithaka," she began. "For many long, weary years you have pressed me to choose a new husband. I refused often and you still did not listen. In fear for my son, my husband's father, for the sanctity of the house where I was so happy as a bride, I agreed to choose among you. No man ever reached the excellence of Odysseus, who brought me here in such happiness, too many years ago. Yet many of you claim you are more than able to surpass him."

Penelope looked around the hall again. Every eye watched her. No one spoke. She caught triumphant grins on many faces. A few men, ones she sometimes suspected not as hard and arrogant as the others, looked touched with guilt at her words.

"By your words, you have helped me choose the test that shall choose my next husband," she continued. She raised her voice, bracing against the pain. "You have made me a prize to be awarded among you, with no regard to my wishes. Therefore, I make myself the prize in a contest. Often for entertainment, to keep his hands and eyes in their skill, Odysseus would set up a row of twelve axes, like logs forming a cradle for a ship. With this bow he would shoot a bronze-tipped arrow between the handles, never hitting a one, never going astray in its course. You claim you are equals if not better than my excellent husband. Now you may prove your words and your worth."

She paused, smiling slightly as a murmuring like the waves moved through the hall. Penelope looked to Telemachos. He nodded, his smile grave and terrible, full of promises she couldn't read. He reminded her of his father, just before leaving to face an enemy.

"The man who strings the bow—*if* any man can string the bow—must then shoot an arrow as Odysseus once did. He must set up the axes, send the arrow between them without touching a single one, and hit the cushion set against the wall." Penelope stepped back, gesturing at the bow so it became the focus of all eyes. "Who will begin the contest?"

"I will." Telemachos laughed lightly as he stepped forward. "You have often told me how much I am my father's son. Now I will prove it, though my full growth is not on me. And if I string the bow of my father, my mother is free of her vow to marry. She will stay safe in my house and no man will force her from it."

As he spoke, he caught up the bow and turned to the suitors. Penelope's lips trembled and tears burned at the corners of her eyes.

Her pride in him mixed with terror that some angered suitor would strike him down.

A few called taunts, but they soon fell silent as Telemachos scraped out the trench and set up the axes. Penelope saw her son as a young boy, eager for his father's return, practicing through one long winter in the hall. She knew Telemachos could shoot nearly as straight as his father. She prayed that though it hurt, her son *would* bend his father's bow.

Silence filled the hall when Telemachos finished his task. Penelope couldn't take her eyes from her son as he sat, braced the tip of the bow against his foot and caught the loop of the string in his hand. He glanced toward the door before bending himself to the task. Penelope held her breath, memory showing Odysseus in the same posture.

Where the bronze and horn bow bent easily, almost like wax in Odysseus' hands, for Telemachos it moved slowly, stubborn and stiff. Yet it did move. Sweat beaded on his hands and the metal suddenly slid from his grip. Her son looked up, baring his teeth in a fierce grin of delight. He wiped his hands on his tunic and bent to the task again. This time he had the loop of the bowstring to within two fingers of the tip of the bow when he gasped and gave up. Again, he glanced toward the doorway.

Curious, unwilling to watch him fail a third time, Penelope looked toward the doorway. The beggar, Aithon now stood and watched Telemachos with an intensity that frightened Penelope. She could well believe the man wished all his strength and support to her son. A gasp took her attention back to Telemachos. He had failed again. He looked toward the beggar, and Penelope saw the man shake his head.

"Let no man say I didn't try to keep my mother in her own home," Telemachos announced. With reverent movements, he wiped the bow clean on the edge of his cloak and set it back into place on the arms of the chair. "I dare any man of you to try to do better."

For the next two hours, the suitors stood for the test of the bow. Penelope listened to them criticize the bow, call down curses on its maker, and claim the bow would not yield because it had sat idle for so long. Toward the end, some called for wax and flame, to warm and soften the bow and to let everyone who had gone before try again. She smiled behind the safety of her veil and rejoiced to see her vain suitors sweating and working, cracking their muscles and cutting their soft, idle hands on the tough bowstring.

When everyone had tried and failed, Antinoos stepped forward, sneering. He bowed to Penelope and then to the bow.

"I understand your schemes now, beautiful queen. Your plans and tricks are worthy of your dead husband in all his cunning. This is a feast day, holy to the gods. No man can string a bow or use any weapon of war on a day like this. She thought that in our eagerness to win her," Antinoos continued, turning to the others, "we would forget the day and so try, fail and accept our defeat. No, we will return tomorrow and take the test again, unhindered by the gods. And tomorrow, there will be a bride for the man who wins the contest of the bow."

A roaring wave of agreement rose from the suitors. Penelope held still, refusing to even breathe or she would speak her distress. In a single night, many things could happen. The bow could vanish, stolen, and her scheming suitors would declare the test invalid.

"Mother, have no fear," Telemachos said, stepping forward to take her hand. He smiled, the same secret delight in his eyes, touched with dreadful anticipation. "All will be well. I swear on my life."

"Indeed all will be well," Eurymachos said, stepping up to join them with a sardonic grin. "Tomorrow will be a wedding feast and then this house will be your own again, noble Telemachos. Unless your mother decides now, without the bow, which worthy man among us shares her bed?"

"The bow speaks for me," Penelope said, finding her voice again in cold anger. "Very well, let it be as Antinoos proposes. The contest of the bow is ended for this day. Leave it to be decided tomorrow."

"If the contest is ended," Aithon said, his voice suddenly smooth, strong and clear enough to penetrate the subsiding din in the hall. "May a guest try his hand for the memory of his youthful strength and kinder times?"

Laughter, angry and mocking, rose at the beggar's words. Penelope shivered, touched in long-buried memory by that voice. She thought of the eagle from her dream, yet when she turned to Aithon he was still the faded, stooped old man who had aroused her pity the night before.

Pity turned to anger as her suitors mocked him, throwing scraps of food, calling for the servants to throw him out.

"Noble Achaians, do not degrade yourselves!" she called, pitching her voice above their laughter, letting out all the bitterness in her soul. "Do you fear this man will succeed where noble blood has failed? Do you think he would dare carry me away as his bride? He has stated the contest is ended. If he does string the bow where you have failed, I will give him sandals and sword, two sets of clothes, gold in his purse and passage on a ship to take him anywhere he wishes to go. That is all the prize such a man would want."

The suitors calmed and quieted at her words. Whether in shame or because they realized the truth of what she said, she could not tell. Penelope turned to her son. Telemachos watched her with a new light in his eyes. Was it pity she saw? Or something else? A mocking smile twisted his lips.

"Mother, you have too long ruled this house. Bows and contests are not your concern. Go up to your rooms and let me handle these men and this bow, as is proper. I am a man grown, and this is my house."

Stunned at his words, Penelope nodded agreement and moved to the stairs. Autonoe followed her in silence. Despite the trembling in her legs, Penelope hurried up the stairs to her room. She had the strangest feeling Telemachos laughed at her and yet begged understanding.

At the door of her room, Penelope dismissed Autonoe. Even through the closed doors, she heard the last rumblings of outrage from the suitors. Then silence. She imagined Aithon preparing to string the bow. She wished him success. A shadow of strength and mighty days still rested on him, despite his rags.

"I have used my last trick, beloved," she whispered, sitting on the bed. "Tomorrow, I will use the arrow. The suitors will find a way to bend your bow. Then I will pierce my arm and let the green dust fill my blood." A bitter laugh escaped her tight throat. "You never thought when you learned to make that poison, it would reunite us in the shadow lands."

An owl hooted outside her window, loud and clear though the sun had only begun to fall toward the horizon. Penelope started up from her bed but heavy weariness pulled at her limbs. Her heart should have pounded in fear but her body was too tired to react.

Black-haired, gray-eyed Athena stepped into her sight, unchanged in so long a time. She shook her head as she looked down on Penelope, pity in her penetrating gaze.

"Be not so hasty, Ikarios' daughter. Endure and sorrow but a little longer." She raised her hand, reaching toward Penelope's forehead.

Penelope blinked and found herself lying on her bed, still fully clothed. The room was filled with shadows from sunset. Down in the hall, she heard a sound like weeping, the thuds of heavy objects being moved. For a moment, she thought her dream of discord among the suitors had come true and they had unwittingly used the poisoned arrows to kill each other.

"Foolish child," she whispered, sitting up. Her head felt heavy with sleep. The fragments of a dream, a vision of Athena, flickered through her thoughts. As she tried to grasp it and remember, it vanished.

Eurykleia pushed the bedroom door open. The old nurse's face glowed with delight. Seeing Penelope sitting on the bed, blinking and rubbing her eyes, she laughed. The sound rolled out like a sweet, bubbling river of wine.

"My dear child, come down and see! All our prayers are answered. The years of suffering and hoping are over. Even now, your husband is below in the hall, cleansing it from the evil that plagued us. He has killed the suitors and directs as the servants carry away the dead."

"Eurykleia, have you drowned your wits in wine?" Penelope stared.

"I know, it is unbelievable, but it is the truth!" She laughed again, her voice a cry of triumph and kissed Penelope. "Come see. He is like a great lion, spattered in blood, the fierce light of battle still in his eyes."

"If only it were true." Penelope considered the strange sounds she heard. True, the sounds of feasting and riotous laughter were gone. She dared to let herself believe the news. "If the suitors are truly dead, then it must have been the gods who acted. Even Odysseus could not have killed them all by himself."

"He did not. His son stood by his side. Oh, to have witnessed the sight!" Eurykleia tugged on Penelope's arms to pull her to her feet. "Eumaios the swineherd and that new man, the ox-herd, they helped. And surely one or several of the gods lent their aid."

"Indeed, the gods lent their aid this day. I will thank their emissary gladly." Penelope stood. She paused by her bronze mirror to straighten her clothes and found her face pale even in the shadows.

Penelope listened as she went down the stairs. She heard the echoes of tables and chairs being dragged across the tiles. The splashing of water. She smelled brimstone and sulfur burning for purification. Something great and terrible had happened in her hall while she slept. The sounds faded, making it easier to move. Her legs carried her down the stairs when her heart wished to retreat. After so long, she knew her dreams could not possibly come true.

At the foot of the stairs she stopped, her knees weak. For a moment, she stood on the beach two days out from Pylos on her bridal journey to Ithaka. The man standing across the hall from her was the image of Odysseus, half-naked, garbed in rags, spattered with blood, a fierce light burning in his eyes. He stood tall and straight, leisurely wiping his sword clean of blood on an abandoned cloak. Of the suitors, she saw no sign except a few overturned tables and chairs, the last trampled remains of their feast, and abandoned articles of clothing. And blood. Streaks and spots and blackened, congealed pools of spilled blood where the hall had not been cleaned yet. It made a dark, somber contrast against the glistening tiles where water had washed the hall clean.

The man didn't see her yet, intent on cleaning his sword. His muscles moved smoothly under his skin, bronzed in the torchlight, streaked with white scars that gave definition to every curve and line. Strength filled out his body, narrow hips and wide shoulders, thick beard neatly trimmed and full curls of dark red hair. Like dried blood. The rags around his loins concealed little of his body. Penelope saw the scar above his knee, glowing white like ice amid the dirt and gore of battle.

Her knees betrayed her and she would have fallen if she had not clutched at the chair sitting by the stairs. The sound she made caught the man's attention. He turned to her, silent and watchful. He studied her with hooded, unreadable gray eyes. Her gaze was drawn to the sword, still raised in his hand. Penelope thought of Klytemaistra and other wives who had been unfaithful to their husbands all the long years of the war. Did this man clean the sword to cover it with her blood next? She knew how her household might appear, full of suitors waiting to win the wife of a man only assumed dead.

A tiny whimper escaped her lips. Pain touched the man's eyes. He shook his head, a bitter smile twisting one side of his mouth, just like Odysseus. He put the sword down on a table and crossed the hall to her. Penelope sat and held herself straight. Her whole body trembled. She was sure this was another dream, sent by a vindictive god to torment her. One moment she knew Odysseus walked across the damp tiles to meet her. The next moment it was a stranger, holding out bloody hands to strangle her. She remembered her dream of the stranger who burned her with blood when she thought to embrace Odysseus in their bed.

"Mother!" Telemachos entered the hall. His wrist was bandaged, clean white against the dirt and blood that spattered his clothes. His face shone with triumphant glee, making him a little boy again.

He ran to her, leaping an overturned table in one spot, a trampled basket of bread in another. Behind him, the serving women returned, carrying buckets of water and sponges, brooms and shovels, to continue cleaning the hall. The man stopped advancing on her then, leaving a space of ten paces between them. Telemachos reached them, joy fading from his face.

"Mother, don't you know him? Look, the scar on his leg that you described to me so many times. He bent the bow. He killed the suitors. Athena herself came down to help us." Telemachos came to her, gentling his voice and knelt in front of her. "Mother, my hard-hearted mother, how can you sit there so silent and not greet my father?"

"Telemachos, leave her be for now." The man spoke and even his voice belonged to Odysseus. "I am filthy from battle and that makes me distasteful to her. She never liked the rage that touched me when I fought." Laughter echoed in his voice, teasing, mocking. Challenging her.

"My son, the gods are skilled in disguises, so even the most chaste wife has been deceived into betraying her love." Penelope met the man's gaze, finding new strength in the sting of his words. "Much as I long for your father's return, I have given up hope of ever seeing him this side of the shadow lands. If this man says he is Odysseus, then he must prove it to me by signs and secrets only we two know. We must speak privately."

"Indeed. And you will not hear a word I speak until I am more presentable. Good nurse," the man called, beckoning to Eurykleia, "a bath and decent clothing. Then maybe my dear wife's heart will soften toward me." He chuckled, the sound warm and familiar, sending new trembling through Penelope's body.

He turned to Telemachos. "We must keep the people from suspecting what has happened for now. When the women have finished cleaning the hall, deal with them as we agreed. Then you and the faithful among the household must go into the courtyard and garden. Kindle torches and bonfires, make music and dance and sing. Let the people outside our walls think it is a wedding celebration, and calm suspicions until morning."

"Yes, Father." Telemachos released Penelope's hands and stood. He kissed her cheek, then hurried to obey. Joy gave him speed and agility, made his whole body glow with life.

"Will you wait for me to return, Penelope?" His voice held teasing laughter, but his eyes betrayed his humor for pain.

"I have waited many years for my beloved. It is the one thing I do well. Whether you dare to come back here matters not to me." She turned quickly, hiding the tears that sprang to her eyes. The shock on Eurykleia's face hurt more than the man's chuckle. Penelope couldn't quite breathe until she heard his retreating footsteps fade.

311

While the maids finished cleaning the other end of the hall, whispering and crying among themselves, Penelope huddled in her chair. Her thoughts raced in a multitude of directions. She trembled, first in cold, then in burning anticipation. First fear, then delight.

Just when she had made up her mind that yes, she was not deceived, Odysseus had come home and avenged the injustice against them, she despaired. Another had come, empowered by the gods, coming from darkness and returning to darkness. That was the stuff of legends, after all. She shivered and the next moment felt her whole body burn. Whether desire or terror, she couldn't be sure. When the maids finished their work and left the hall, she nearly cried out in relief at being alone.

She was startled when the man came back from his bath. She expected to be told he had vanished. He wore a cloak against the night cool, sandals, and Eurykleia had given him the tunic Penelope had made so long ago for Odysseus' homecoming. The sight brought burning tears to her eyes. It was hard not to bite out bitter rebuke to the old nurse for taking such a liberty. She waited in the doorway, delight and anticipation on her face.

Then Penelope realized it was not a liberty. The old woman truly believed the man sitting before her was Odysseus. The tunic was his, made for a homecoming celebration. Who had better right to wear it? Telemachos believed this man was his father. The suitors, though all dead now, believed Odysseus had returned with vengeance. The servants believed, or they would have raised the alarm. Penelope suspected she was the only person in the house who doubted.

"You are a strange one, Penelope," he said, after gazing at her long in silence. "Of so many wives of noble Achaians, you alone waited without taking a lover, without abandoning your husband's home and bed. Yet when he comes to you, bringing revenge for the wrongs you have suffered, you sit and stare as if he were a stranger."

"You are the strange one," she returned. "If you are Odysseus, you know what a short, happy time we had together. To the tenth year of the war, and now the tenth year since it ended, I have waited. Men change in face and form in that much time. I am to recognize him, recognize you? I look at you and you are Odysseus. I look at you again, and you are a different man entirely."

"Stubborn woman. You will make a curse out of your faithfulness, instead of a virtue." Grudging respect tinged his voice. He smiled. "Witch," he whispered, making her heart leap into her throat. "Eurykleia." He gestured for the old nurse to join them. "The night grows old and I'm tired from this day's heavy work. Make up my old bed for me, though it is cold and likely covered in dust and spider webs. It will be a sweeter, warmer place than my lady wife's bed this night." He turned back to Penelope as Eurykleia and Autonoe hurried to obey. He met her eyes, challenge in his face and voice.

"Yes, make up his bed," she said, trembling deep inside. "Bring it out here into the hall, since he objects to the dust of years of neglect."

"Penelope, you wound me more than you can know!" He stood up, towering over her. Angry dismay filled his voice, but she saw clearly the delight in his eyes. It was all a game to him, one last, precious move to play before they both could rest.

"What man has moved my bed? You and I alone know the secret of the frame," he continued, lowering his voice. They were alone in the hall. "It is impossible to move that bed without destroying the frame, unless the secret is known. I built my bedchamber around a living olive tree, leaving the root in the ground, trimming the branches, boring holes in the trunk so it became the living head of our bed. Only a god could move that bed without your help."

"Odysseus." Her voice cracked. Penelope leaped from her chair, throwing her arms around him. Tears racked her body as she clung to him. "Forgive me! I had to be sure. The years have been so long, and others have come, claiming to be you, trying to steal your place. I wanted to believe—"

Her words broke off in sobs, muffled as he kissed her, hard, a torrent of kisses that robbed her of what little breath she had left. Penelope's legs lost all their strength, but his arms were tight around her, holding her upright. She felt the heaving of his breath in his chest, heard the rumbling of his sobs, felt the damp of his tears mixing with her own. When he kissed her, searching her face, then capturing her lips again, she tasted the salt of their tears.

He sat down, cradling her on his lap. Penelope shivered at the pleasure of his embrace that sent new life through her body. She wrapped her arms around his neck and kissed his forehead, his eyelids, and caressed the damp hair back from his face as she returned to the sweet wine of his lips.

CHAPTER 27

"Beloved," Odysseus whispered. He drew her head down to rest on his shoulder. Penelope felt the thunder of his heart, he held her so close against him.

"You do forgive me, then?"

"Penelope, what is there to forgive?" He laughed, the sound ragged, shaking his whole body. Penelope suspected tears waited to return. "I beg your forgiveness, for taking so long in returning, for leaving you at all."

"You couldn't refuse what you had promised," she said, drawing away so she could see his face. Penelope drank in the sight of him. So close, she saw the marks of years of fighting and travel, but he was still strong and vibrantly alive, young and handsome. "I think you were prevented from returning."

"Your dreams?" A heavy sigh escaped him when she nodded. "My love, the story I have to tell you could fill our hours until the moon rises and sets again."

"All that matters is that you are home now, safe, to stay." Penelope caught the tension in the deep quiet that settled over him. "You *are* home to stay?"

"Penelope...that is part of the story I have to tell you. Later, I would prefer." He caressed her and fire trailed across her body. "As I remember, you always demand the tale of my journey *after* we enjoy our bed."

"You told Eurykleia you were weary," she whispered against his lips as he bent his head to kiss her again.

"Weary of fighting, of struggling," he corrected a few breaths later. "Not weary of joy."

"Then you shall have your bed whenever you wish." She slipped free of his arms and off his lap. She flinched at how easily she escaped his grasp. He had always been able before to read her body and predict every move she made. Penelope knelt by the chair, taking hold of his hand and pressing it against her cheek. "But please, my dear husband, tell me first. You are not home to stay. What journey must you take now?"

"Oh, my sweet, sweet...stubborn Penelope." A weak chuckle shook his shoulders and Odysseus nodded. "As you wish, though you will get no joy of hearing it."

The sound of a door creaking on stiff leather hinges interrupted him. Penelope looked up, startled. She had forgotten they were not alone. She saw Eurykleia and Autonoe going into Odysseus' bedroom, their arms piled high with blankets to make the bed. She looked back to Odysseus and he smiled.

"Yes, there is time for a story after all. On my journey home, I met an enchantress. A witch, but with different magic from yours," he added, giving her a mocking scowl. Penelope laughed, marveling at the sound so soon after tears. She leaned against his knee, looking up at his face, drinking in the sight of him as she listened.

"She said I needed to consult the prophet Teiresias." Odysseus nodded, a short, sharp movement. "I know—Teiresias has been dead many years. She sent me to the shores of the land of the dead. She told me what rituals to use to propitiate the shadows so I could pass safely among them and gain the knowledge I needed."

Penelope bit her tongue to keep silent. Another dream had been truth. She wondered now about her other visions of her husband through the years and consoled herself with knowing that in a while, he would indeed answer all her questions.

"Teiresias told me I had offended Poseidon," Odysseus said. "He told me if ever I reached my homeland, I had one more journey to make after that, or I would never live in peace or grow old in the land of my birth. I must journey by land, with the oar of my ship over my shoulder, until I reach a place where the people don't know the sea. I will know I have reached it when a man tells me my oar is a winnowing fan. There, I am to offer sacrifices to Poseidon. After that, I may come home and live out my years. Death will come from the sea when I have reached sleek old age."

He smiled with a distant sadness in his eyes. Penelope wondered what other memories her question had stirred. She stood, slipped her arms around his neck and kissed his forehead, both cheeks, and then his lips.

"There, my love, I didn't intend to give you sorrow. You want your bed and you shall have it and all the joy I can give you this night." Penelope held out her hands to him, waiting, letting her longing shine in her eyes. The response in his eyes made her pulse sing.

The sounds of music, singing and dancing penetrated the quiet of the hall. Odysseus stood and took her hand and smiled.

"All the people passing by will hear the music and say their stubborn, beautiful queen has at last given up waiting for her wedded lord. I hear wedding festivities," he said as they walked to the wide, heavy doors of his room.

"In a sense, it is our bridal night once more," she said, her smile growing wider.

"Are you a nervous bride again, Penelope?" he teased.

"I was never nervous, my lord. Worried about a man's drunken, clumsy strength, but never nervous. I was well instructed in what to expect on my bridal night."

"And were you disappointed, or pleased?"

"Very pleased." She let him stop them several paces from the door. In a moment, she knew, he would take her into his arms. Penelope wanted to prolong the deliciously painful anticipation. "Do I still please you, my lord?"

"Yes. Your mouth still tastes of honey wine." Odysseus slid the cloak from his shoulders, catching it in the crook of his arm. "I planned my strategy well that night, you must admit. I made you love me from the beginning."

"In a manner of speaking." She laughed when Odysseus blinked in confusion. "At the beginning of our marriage, I loved your strong, sweet body that gave me pleasure with the slightest touch. Then I loved you for the children I wanted you to give me. And now, I am learning to love you for your other qualities." She paused, delighted at the laughter in his eyes, barred from his face. "Such few there are."

"Witch," Odysseus growled. He lunged at her, arms outstretched to capture her, but she dodged him.

Penelope slipped through the gap between the doors into the bedchamber. The bronze shutters hung open to let in new air and herbs were sprinkled on the floor to freshen it. Eurykleia and Autonoe finished spreading blankets on the bed. Penelope was glad now the suitors had ordered new rope in the bed frame. She had a vision of the bed collapsing under their weight, and that would never do. Not tonight.

She tugged the pins from her hair and wrapped them in her veil. She stepped away from the doors as Odysseus pulled them open, and removed the rest of her jewelry. His face showed no trace of the game a moment before. He nodded thanks to the two serving women and stood aside for them to leave. Penelope walked to the bedside, ignoring everything but the rising clamor of her heart in her ears. Dimly, she heard the doors close and the scratching sound as Odysseus locked the heavy panels.

"Our bridal night," she said, voice trembling. Eyes closed, she fumbled with the belt of her dress. Then Odysseus helped her, his hands shaking ever so slightly. Penelope turned her mind to memories as he lifted the dress off over her head. She turned to face him as he put his arms around her.

*   *   *

Later, they lay with their limbs intertwined and talked, as they had years before, often interrupted with kisses as they caressed each other with gentle, slow touches. Not from desire, but the need to reassure themselves they were indeed together, at last.

Penelope demanded he tell the tale of his journeys first and completely. She spoke not a word until Odysseus had finished telling her all he had experienced since leaving Ilion for Ithaka. She smiled whenever he related a piece of story that fit her dreams. She had vague memories of dreaming the Cyclops, Polyphemos. And the cattle of Apollo, which his men slaughtered against all warnings. And the island of the king of the winds. She had been there when he visited the land of the dead and saw his recently dead mother. She had seen him on the island of Kalypso, the nymph who had kept him prisoner seven years.

Then when he finished, narrating up to the battle with the suitors, she began her side of the tale. Ktimene's birth, raising their children, comforting Laertes when Antikleia died. Her dreams and how they intertwined with his adventures. Ktimene's rebellion, the man who pretended to be Odysseus, and the onslaught of the suitors. He stayed quiet in his turn until she had finished.

"A wise, resourceful wife I won in my youth. A wise, faithful wife I have regained. My love, you awe me." Odysseus drew her closer, making her ribs ache with the embrace. She smiled, welcoming his strength. His hand tangled in her hair, he tipped her head back so he could kiss her lips. "It was jealousy of our happiness that prompted the gods to keep us apart."

"Jealousy," she whispered in agreement. "We thought we would grow old together, have years of safety and contentment and joy. If ever we unwittingly offended the gods, surely we have paid now."

"We have paid now," he whispered back, his voice thickened with a yawn. Penelope listened for the sound of his breathing to change into sleep. Before she heard it, sleep enfolded her.

*   *   *

Penelope felt Odysseus slip from her embrace before she woke fully. She moaned a protest, sure this was another dream turned to nightmare. She struggled to stay asleep, to prolong the sweet dream, but warm lips spread kisses over her face. She felt the soft scratching of a beard, the gentle touch of breath against her skin. She opened her eyes to the first dim glow before dawn in the open windows, and Odysseus drawing away to sit on the edge of the bed.

"Don't leave yet," she murmured, sitting up and holding out a hand to him.

"I would give all my treasures of Ilion to stay here and hold you." Odysseus shrugged, his endearing, crooked grin lighting his face. "However, the treasure I won is in Poseidon's realm and you are my only treasure. And the matter of yesterday is not fully settled. Soon the hue and cry will go around that the suitors are dead and someone will shout for vengeance. I am taking Telemachos and going to my father. It would be a crime if everyone knew I had returned but he did not."

"And the three of you will plan war strategy." Penelope nodded. She had tried to forget the outcome of yesterday's slaughter. It had been easy in her joy.

She pushed aside the blankets and slipped out of the bed. As she picked up their clothes, sorting them out, she felt Odysseus' gaze on her. It was like their first morning together at the river in Sparta, all over again. Would drastic changes come on them this morning as well? She slipped her dress on and sat waiting until he had dressed.

"Telemachos did well?" Something tight inside loosened when a bright smile touched his face and he laughed.

"Penelope, what a glorious son you raised!" Odysseus knelt before her. He held both her hands, kissing the palms. "Your mark is deeply stamped in him. I would have known him for your son, even if no one had told me. I fear he would not be as resourceful, as thoughtful, if I had raised him."

"I weaned him on stories of you. Always, his questions ended with 'what would my father think?' or 'what would my father do?' And your father and Mentor taught him everything I could not." The memory of bitter words came to her. In the last dregs of sleep, with happiness still so fresh, she couldn't keep the hurt from her face.

"Penelope?" He stood, pulling her to her feet and took her into his arms. "What is it?"

"I spoke harshly to him, to aid in the deception of the loom. I told him no man would welcome coming home to a grown son he had not raised. Does it rankle you, that he is grown and you had no part in his teaching?"

"It grieves me, yes. Shames me. Makes me rage in my heart against the powers that kept me from my home." Odysseus kissed the top of her head and rested his cheek against her forehead. "Yet I dare any man to say he is a son not to be proud of." He chuckled. "I did have a hand in his training, you know. I chose his mother most wisely."

Penelope laughed, though the sound took on a bitter note when he released her and gently pushed her back down to sit on the edge of the bed. She watched him scoop up his cloak, hang it over one arm and go to the door. He unlocked it and looked out in the hall. She heard no movement, no sign anyone was awake and at work in the household. It hurt her that he had to practice caution in his own home.

"Dear, sweet wife." Odysseus made as if to cross the room back to her side, then thought better of it. "There will be fighting, I know. And calling and crying in the streets. Have your women lock the doors and let no one into the house. Stay in your rooms and speak of yesterday to no one. Wait, and pray to Athena who guides me. If she is still with me, we will have peace by nightfall." He waited until she nodded that she understood, and then opened the doors. In a moment he was gone.

Penelope found her veil and wrapped it around her hair. It was a tangle she couldn't straighten with her fingers. Odysseus had always loved playing with her hair as they lay talking after their pleasure.

It was a strange feeling but welcome, to slip out into the quiet, empty hall. The faint odor of sulfur from purifying the room lingered in the air. No blood, no spilled wine or the smoke of the suitors' incessant feasting remained. She hoped the hall would stay quiet and empty for many days. Empty but for her husband and son. Penelope welcomed the thought of those two male voices filling her ears.

"Oh, what wonderful evenings we would have had," she whispered, pausing at the hearth.

Her imagination conjured images of Ktimene sitting at her father's feet, begging for stories, trading riddles with him. Her daughter would have been eighteen if she had lived, her hair a dark flame like Odysseus', her body slim and beautiful. He would have been enchanted with her, unwilling to let any man take her from her home. Penelope had not missed the stirring of questions and regrets in Odysseus' eyes when she spoke of Ktimene. When greater burdens and dangers were dealt with, Penelope knew long hours sharing stories and tears awaited them.

She met no servants on her way up the stairs to her rooms. Eurykleia, Eurynome, and a third of her personal serving women waited in the weaving room, their work in their hands. A second look revealed no one worked. Their faces were pale, their backs stiff as they listened to the morning quiet.

"You are all early risers today. Where is Melantho?" Penelope smiled at her women.

"Melantho is dead." Eurykleia's voice was quiet and sleek with satisfaction. "She and all the women who betrayed you with the suitors are dead."

"At whose hand?" Penelope slowly sat on the bench of her loom.

"Your son's." The old nurse laughed, a sharp sound near a cackle. "He forced them to clean up after the dead bodies of their lovers, then denied them a clean death because of their treachery toward you. He hung them in the courtyard. They were like birds with their necks caught in snares."

"Birds that will nest no more in my house." She nodded, unable to smile, though she was glad at the vengeance. A touch of alarm made her look around the room, to be sure none of her innocent women had been taken. A glance showed them all accounted for. "Autonoe, help me bathe and dress my hair for the day." She stood again and stepped toward the door. "My lord husband instructs us to stay here today and let no one in the house, nor speak of yesterday's events until he returns."

"So he instructed me," Eurynome said, nodding. "The doors are locked and the loyal men are stationed with spears and swords to safeguard us."

"Good." Penelope paused at the door. The dark weaving of her funeral sheet on the loom caught her eye. She was both sickened and amused by the sight of it. "Rip that out. I will weave something pleasing. In celebration."

*   *   *

Gradually, as the day went past, Penelope felt her women relax their mute, stiff terror. No one came knocking on the doors of the house. No voices were raised beyond the walls, demanding entrance or explanation or vengeance. She worked at her new pattern on the loom, using the colors at hand, letting the design come as her fingers willed. She felt she moved in a dream. Nothing else existed beyond the walls of the room. When her women tried to open the windows and look out, she stopped them. Whether to prolong the illusion or from some wordless compulsion, she did not know.

Eurynome and Eurykleia fetched food for them when they grew hungry. The other women, she kept with her. The two nurses returned, reporting the men still kept silent watch at the doors. No one had approached the house since Odysseus, his son and allies left.

"We are already in the shadow lands," Aktoris whimpered. "That is why no one comes to this house. We are swallowed whole into Hades' kingdom."

"Nonsense," Penelope snapped, then surprised herself by laughing. "Why would Athena guide my husband home after all these years, strengthen his hand for vengeance, and then let us all be destroyed? Rather, she protects us. We are all sheltered in the favor she bestows on him."

She saw hope brighten a few eyes that had been dark with worry. Penelope returned to her weaving. She wasn't sure what she would make of the cloth yet, but it was bright and beautiful in its haphazard clash of colors. Soft and fine, like the netting over a baby's cradle to protect from wind and cold and too bright a sun.

Penelope caught her breath. The one dream she had abandoned now filled her heart. She was still young enough, strong, and if her mirror spoke the truth, looked far younger than her years. Judging by last night, her husband still found her utterly desirable. She could yet have another child. Ktimene's loss could be soothed, at last.

Then all the tearing and hurt of Odysseus' absence would heal. New life would bring blessings on Ithaka and protect the land. She let herself think again of the journey which the blind, dead prophet had ordered for her husband. The idea didn't rankle or give her fear. No matter how soon he went away, Odysseus would return to her. She believed her dreams. She would carry another child.

*   *   *

Odysseus returned home at dusk, Telemachos and Laertes with him. The change in the old man astonished Penelope when she hurried down the stairs to meet them. Her husband's father glowed with life and strength, as if he had regained the flesh and height lost with his declining years and sorrow. When Odysseus embraced her, he smelled of sacrifice fires and roasted meat. His mouth tasted of wine when he kissed her.

"All is well?" she whispered before he released her.

"Reconciliation. Judgment passed. The families of our dead enemies agree they have no cause for vengeance. Reparations are to be made for the despoiling of our property. We will have peace in Ithaka." He turned to Telemachos with a mocking scowl. "Son, have you no greeting for your mother? You spoke harshly to her yesterday."

"And with just cause. My love, you have just said there is to be peace in Ithaka. Let it start in our house." Penelope laughed and held out her arms for Telemachos. She smelled sweat and wood smoke in his hair and his arms around her had a new strength and assurance. "To see you and your father together, working in union—" She broke off, fighting the tears burning her eyes. "This is a happy time, not one for tears."

"In deference to the losses in the noble houses of Ithaka," Laertes said, "we should keep our own celebration quiet."

"Indeed. Are you hungry? Do you want to bathe first?" She looked around for her women, to give instructions.

"Our beds would be more welcome than anything," Telemachos said. "We rose with the dawn and crept through Ithaka to my grandfather's home like invaders." He laughed, sharing a companionable glance with his father that warmed Penelope. The battles they shared had closed many gaps she had feared would stand between them. "Then we began a battle, to be stopped by Athena herself. Then came judgments, vows, sacrifices and a feast to seal the peace. It has been a long day, Mother."

"Then your beds you shall have," Eurykleia said as she and the other women joined the small group. She gave orders, bringing the household out of its waiting and back into its ordinary routine.

Penelope felt the last tension and worry leave the air, like birds that had perched in the rafters.

*   *   *

"Does it hurt you to speak of Ktimene?" Odysseus whispered, when Penelope thought he had fallen asleep.

"A dulled pain." She stirred in the crook of his arm and sat up. "Did Telemachos tell you—"

"He said you suspected Melantho of teaching her to make the potion that killed her."

"He did?" Penelope shook her head. "I trained him to observe and to think deeply, to be like you, and he still surprises me. I never told him what I suspected."

"Telemachos knew Melantho hated you, and she did what she could to cause discord without being caught. He told me he would have killed her himself the day after Ktimene died, but your actions made him wait."

"I have made many errors, in handling Melantho and her selfish, disobedient ways. Our daughter might be alive right now. The suitors might be alive. We would—"

"Hush, my love." Odysseus stopped her words with a kiss. "There is only pain in considering what might have been. Tell me about our daughter. I want to know her well, before we rejoin her in the shadow lands."

"Yes, she will wait for us." Penelope choked on a soft laugh. "Perhaps now, she has learned the patience she lacked. She was a gift from the Goddess. Perhaps the Goddess took her back, by whatever painful means, when her safety and happiness were threatened."

"If she had been here, the suitors might not have set their greedy sights on you." Hardness touched his voice.

"A fine mother I would have been, hiding behind my child, sacrificing her for my own safety." Penelope lightly slapped his shoulder, turning her words into teasing.

"You know what I mean, beloved."

"They didn't want me, or our daughter. They wanted the rule of Ithaka. They thought to use the old ways without following them. The Goddess tripped them in their schemes. After a painfully long wait," she admitted.

"Too long. The gods play with our hearts and lives. Even the ones who support and help us."

Penelope heard a new note in his voice, partly old frustration, partly renewed pain. She reached for the lamp on the narrow table by the bed and held it over him. Odysseus' face wore hurting lines that wiped away the pleasure they had shared, the victory behind them.

His words took on new meaning. She remembered what he had said of Kalypso, the nymph who had held him captive on her island. There was nothing he could have done to escape. Her magic made every attempt futile, until she gave him permission to leave. Until Zeus, at Athena's prodding, ordered Kalypso to let Odysseus go free.

"You are a most desirable man, my love," Penelope whispered. She put the lamp back on its stand and leaned over him, twining her legs around his. She chuckled when he startled, looking up at her in confusion. "The nymph held you captive, hoping to make you love her."

"That is not how to grow love in a heart," he grumbled.

"You must admit, most men take brides that way. No regard for the girl's wishes. They expect their brides to love them for no reason but that they are married. Did we learn that from the gods, or did they learn that from us?"

"Witch." The last hurting anger fled his face with laughter. He held her tight as he rolled them onto their sides. "You have changed, grown too wise for me. You see into my heart and thoughts, and discern my troubles before I understand them."

"What else is there to do in years of waiting, my love, but to raise your children, tend your house and think deep thoughts?" Penelope smiled to take the unintended rebuke from her words.

"Indeed, what else?" He kissed her, a gentle brushing of his lips over her face. "I am coming to know our son. Tell me of our daughter?"

"She was yours, completely." She let out a small sigh, glad the hurting moment had come so quickly and would be over soon. "Her hair was yours, and her eyes. The quickness of her wit. She understood riddles you taught me as quickly as Telemachos, and she two years younger."

"And who was your favorite child?" Odysseus chided, tightening his arms around her.

"They were *both* my treasures. It was good she looked so much like you. Before her birth, rumors said I leaped into another man's bed the day you sailed away."

"Who spread such tales?" He pushed away from her, supporting

324

himself on his arms. Anger creased his face, so recently relaxed in teasing.

"Foolish people who had nothing better to think about. Women jealous of my good fortune, men who knew they had no chance to win my heart. All silenced by your daughter's most timely arrival and the color of her hair." Penelope glared up at him, teasing, until he relaxed and lay down again. "You would have been her slave, or fought with her at every turn."

"You think so?" He pressed a light chain of kisses slowly down her neck.

"She was too much like you. Always thinking. Always asking questions. She wanted to know the why of everything. She asked about you, every story I could tell her. She had your stubborn nature. Ktimene wouldn't give up what she wanted. Even if it cost——" Her voice caught and broke.

"There is pain again," he whispered, leaning over her to kiss her eyelids, then the tip of her nose.

"Beloved." She nearly laughed at the old teasing. "I think perhaps it was better the Goddess took her from us. She couldn't have withstood the lies men tell to win a maiden's heart. She had an innocence, despite being all the rebel I never had the strength to be. She would have been miserable as a toy wife. She wanted to serve the Goddess. Very young, she told me the Goddess had called her to be a priestess. Only as a priestess-queen could she have been content. Our world is not made for her kind any longer."

"Our world is made for warriors and battles, and blood spilled for the sake of petty riches and moving boundaries." A choked sound escaped him. Odysseus pressed her close against him. She felt the damp of his new tears.

*   *   *

They agreed Odysseus couldn't leave on his final journey until spring. Fall approached with much work to do to prepare for winter. And there were affairs to settle in Ithaka, troubles and alliances allowed to sit idle too long.

Penelope welcomed the storms of winter, the quiet evenings around the hearth. She stayed silent during the long talks, letting father and son grow acquainted and busied herself with spinning and sewing. She told no one of her hope, and whenever the winter storms permitted, went to the Goddess' cave to make prayers and offerings for the child she dreamed of.

Laertes died in his sleep, the first morning of true spring. This was after a long evening of talk and feasting, when the elders of Ithaka gathered in Odysseus' hall and remembered long-gone days of glory. Laertes had sat in the seat of honor between his son and his grandson while the elders spoke his praises. Penelope saw the gentle smile on her father-in-law's face when she came to wash and prepare his body for the funeral rites. She knew his spirit had gone in joy to the shadow lands, with no regrets, no longings, all his dreams fulfilled. She spoke peace to him in the silence of the room after she had sent the other women away.

The funeral pyre was tall and many came from all over Ithaka to put gifts on the wood. Laertes' body lay wrapped in the cloth Penelope had made and many remarked on its beauty. For herself, she was glad to see the bright sheet destroyed, with the memories of suffering it kept alive.

That night, when Odysseus lay sleeping, his arms still tightly clasped around her, Penelope whispered to him that she carried another child. She refused to tell him when he could hear. His new ship lay ready at the shore and she would not delay his final journey any longer. She kept her precious news secret, going daily to Athena's shrine to lay small offerings of thanks, and counted the days until Odysseus' departure.

When he did leave two weeks later, she kissed him farewell, flung a newly-woven cloak around his shoulders and let him walk down to the harbor in his son's company. She stood in the narrow doorway that looked out over the cliffs and the sea, watching for his ship to sail, and her hand rested on her still-flat belly.

"You will return safely, my love. I have dreamed it. The child inside me is the promise," she whispered to the wind.

And when the sail had vanished against the glare of the rising sun on the sea, Penelope turned and went back into the house, to weave more dreams into her loom.

MICHELLE L. LEVIGNE

Michelle Levigne got her first taste of fantasy fiction with the *Cat in the Hat* books, and graduated to "harder stuff" with a graphic novel version of *The Lion, The Witch and The Wardrobe* in a Sunday School paper in elementary school. She has a BA in theater/English and an MA in Communications, focusing on film and writing, along with the 2-year correspondence course from the Institute for Children's Literature. She was heavily involved in fandom for several years and has more than 40 short stories to her credit in various fan magazines and universes, including *Star Trek*, *The Phoenix*, *Stingray*, *Highlander*, *Starman*, *V*, and *Beauty & the Beast* (live action TV show). Her first professional sale was in conjunction with winning first place in the quarterly Writers of the Future Contest. "Relay" was published in Volume VII. Since then, she has published ten SF/Fantasy and Contemporary romance novels through various electronic publishers, with several books pending future publication. Most of these books are in the SF universe called The Commonwealth. *The Bainevah Series* is her second foray into historical/fantasy/romantic fiction.